A Most
Inconvenient Wish

A Lady's Wish Series by Eileen Richards

An Unexpected Wish

An Honorable Wish

A Most Inconvenient Wish

A Most Inconvenient Wish

A Lady's Wish

Eileen Richards

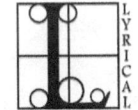

LYRICAL PRESS
Kensington Publishing Corp.
www.kensingtonbooks.com

LYRICAL PRESS BOOKS are published by

Kensington Publishing Corp.
119 West 40th Street
New York, NY 10018

All Kensington titles, imprints, and distributed lines are available at special quantity discounts for bulk purchases for sales promotion, premiums, fund-raising, educational, or institutional use.

Special book excerpts or customized printings can also be created to fit specific needs. For details, write or phone the office of the Kensington Sales Manager: Kensington Publishing Corp., 119 West 40th Street, New York, NY 10018. Attn. Sales Department. Phone: 1-800-221-2647.

Lyrical Press and Lyrical Press logo Reg. U.S. Pat. & TM Off.

First Electronic Edition: July 2016
eISBN-13: 978-1-60183-447-8
eISBN-10: 1-60183-447-0

First Print Edition: July 2016
ISBN-13: 978-1-60183-448-5
ISBN-10: 1-60183-448-9

Printed in the United States of America

For Susan and Pam

And for Rick

ACKNOWLEDGMENTS

Being the last book, this one was tough to write. Thank you to Erica Monroe, Morgan Eden, Darla Kraft, and Christy Carlyle for the critiques and for talking me off the ledge time and time again.

Thank you to Martin for not losing it with a rookie. For Jessica for being there for me when I needed you.

Thank you to Rick for keeping my world together when the words flowed and taking me out on the lake for a break when they didn't.

Finally, thank you to my readers. I was terrified to send my stories about three sisters into the world. Your enjoyment of my little fairy stories makes it all worthwhile. Thank you for your kindness and acceptance.

Chapter 1

At no time in her life did Sophia Townsend ever picture herself standing at the bottom of the blasted Fairy Steps with the need to make a wish. She put her hands on her hips and examined the uneven stone formations that towered before her. The steps were much steeper than she remembered. It was a good thing she'd worn her sturdiest boots for the task. She swatted at the stupid feathers on her new bonnet. The breeze kept blowing them into her face. Sophia pondered removing it for a moment but changed her mind. If she encountered someone from the village, it wouldn't do to look like a total ragamuffin. She was already at risk of looking like a total fool for attempting to climb the Fairy Steps.

Situated off the lane to the Lodge, the home of her married sister Anne, these stupid steps had been the bane of Sophia's existence for four years. Both of her sisters swore that the magic of a fairy wish had helped them find their husbands. They were both happily married. And Sophia was *not*.

Sophia was no believer in love and happily ever after. She was not so nonsensical as to believe that a wish could have that much power, despite the happy marriages of her sisters. Marrying was what young ladies did. Young men pursued the church or the military if they were poor. A young lady married. It would allow her to improve her status. She could have children, pin money for shopping, and her own servants. She could have a life in London Society, with parties and balls.

It was too bad marriage had to come with a husband.

Her looks had allowed her four Seasons in London, her favorite place. It had granted her a popularity she'd never have in Beetham. Sophia had enjoyed her popularity in Town. She'd danced most dances and been well received in Society. She had gentlemen callers equipped with gifts of flowers and sweets. She'd been on drives in Hyde Park. However, none of the calls ever ended in a proposal that she could agree to.

Society had labeled her cold, aloof, haughty. Why couldn't they find another word for it? Unfortunately, being labeled such was like waving a red flag in front of the male population of London. Why did men have to try to kiss her in dark, close spaces? Those places terrified her.

It wasn't their fault. Most of them were very nice gentlemen. She couldn't help it that she was beautiful. Nor did she want to. Men seemed to think that if a woman was pretty, she gladly accepted the pawing, the groping, and the inappropriate comments. It was the price of being desired. Just like with the footman all those years ago, she knew exactly what they desired. She wasn't going to allow it. Not ever again.

Until she'd been introduced to the Earl of Bateman.

To her delight, the earl had shown so much interest in Sophia while they were in Town. He'd danced every waltz with her and always took the supper dance. He sent flowers. He took her for strolls in the park, where they could be seen by everyone. But Bateman never pressed her for a kiss. He never pressed her for anything. He'd been the perfect gentleman. The gossips were full of tittle-tattle about his impending proposal, but no proposal materialized and the gossips eventually turned on Sophia, much to her dismay.

Sophia had not suffered the disdain of Society in the four years she'd been in London. She'd taken great pains to make sure that she was all that was proper. No whisper of scandal, nothing that would give anyone a moment's concern, until Lord Bateman didn't propose. She didn't like the snickers of laughter behind the fans of the other ladies at the balls. She hated the cuts by the very same people who had hung on her every word just a week earlier because she was on Bateman's arm. Their cuts were like barbs in her skin.

She wanted to marry Lord Bateman. He treated her gently. He didn't try to paw her or kiss her in the dark. He liked to sit and talk. He didn't even seem to mind those long silences that were usually uncomfortable with other men. And so she found herself at the Fairy Steps. She would wish for Lord Bateman to propose to her. She would marry and have everything she wanted: pin money, several houses, and a life in London society on the arm of an earl. She would endure him until they had several children, and then he could happily find himself a mistress. She could tolerate the act at least enough times to get with child.

It was the perfect plan for the perfect life, the life Sophia dreamed of.

The alternative was not to be borne: to be left on the shelf, an old maid to be ridiculed. At twenty-six, Sophia felt as if she'd come to an impasse in her life. She either had to marry or be stuck in spinsterhood forever. Her popularity would shift as she aged. Already there were beautiful young ladies vying for the attentions of the gentlemen who formerly had sought her out. Sophia had no intention of allowing Society to force her to the wallflower wall with the rest of the spinsters. She looked horrible in caps.

Desperate times called for daring measures. Sophia eyed the gray steps as they towered before her. Moss and leaves covered the uneven stones. The wind blew across the steps with a low whine. She almost laughed at the theatrics of it all: the gusting wind, the darkening sky heavy with rain, the distant rumble of thunder. The stage was set for something dramatic, like a scene from the Minerva novels her sisters were always reading.

The steps were wider at the bottom, growing narrow as they wound toward the top of the stones. Sophia chewed her bottom lip, wondering if her hips would fit through the opening at the top. She wasn't nearly as thin as she used to be. Nor was she as thin as her sisters. She probably should have avoided eating so many of Cook's delicious apple tarts in the few weeks since returning to Beetham.

A gust of wind pushed at her, urging her forward. Nothing ventured, nothing gained. Sophia placed her foot on the first step, then the next. The stones were dry, but the moss made them more slippery. She crept up the steps slowly, making sure her feet were steady before continuing. Her hands clutched the peach muslin of her dress to hold it out of the way and to keep from grabbing the sides. The urge to do so was so strong.

The gray walls closed in around her as she went up the stairs and she felt a pang of panic in the pit of her stomach. She fought for control as her skirts dislodged bits of moss and leaves. Pebbles made a pinging sound as they fell down behind her. Sophia closed her eyes and tightened her hands as she clutched her dress to keep from reaching out to steady herself. She could not quit now. She would not quit.

One step was a bit higher than the last and her foot missed the edge. She wobbled and squealed.

"Woman, what are you doing?" A deep voice, tinged with a Scottish burr, broke through the fear that was threatening to take hold of her.

Sophia cringed. It was the one man she could not manage to avoid, the man who had become her severest critic when watching her make a cake of herself. Ian McDonald had a talent for finding her at the most inopportune times. There was no going back now. She was over halfway there. She took another step and tipped backward. She stiffened her legs to steady herself. "I'm climbing the steps. What does it look like I'm doing?"

"Trying to get yourself injured or worse is more like it."

She glanced behind her and found him standing at the bottom, his dark hair wild from the wind, his arms crossed in front of his massive chest. His jaw was set. His blue eyes glared at her from beneath strong brows and above his crooked nose. As if a glare was enough to stop her. She smiled sweetly at him and turned back to her task.

In the three years she'd known him, Mr. McDonald had taken great pleasure in teasing her. He drove her mad. She had no choice but to tolerate him. He was a good friend of the Matthewses and a frequent visitor in London and in Beetham. The son of a steward, he'd made a tidy fortune and was now accepted in Society, for the most part. Money seemed to fix everything.

Unfortunately, Mr. McDonald made her feel things she had no business feeling. She'd learned the painful lesson of falling in love with someone beneath her years ago. It was certainly not going to happen now.

"People have been climbing these steps for centuries. I'm sure it is perfectly safe." She took another step and wobbled again. The stones were definitely getting more uneven. Sophia fought the urge to reach out and grasp the towering gray walls on either side of her for balance.

"Stay there. I'm coming to you," he shouted.

Sophia took another step. There was no way she'd make a wish if

Mr. McDonald caught up with her. She took another step, this time a bit faster in order to stay ahead of him.

"Sophia Townsend, stop now!"

"I'm fine, Mr. McDonald. I'm nearly there." She placed her foot on another step, and then another, but her foot slipped. She swallowed a scream as stones slipped down the steps behind her.

"Damn it, woman, you're determined to get us both killed."

Better dead than stuck on a path that led to being alone for the rest of her life. Sophia put her foot firmly on the next step. Excitement quickened her pace. Just two more steps. She could do this. She could make her wish. She nimbly took the last two steps, finally reaching the top. "There! I did it."

Mr. McDonald was breathing heavily as he raced up the steps to her. "I could shake you." He bent over his hands on his thighs. "You could have broken your pretty neck."

"I told you I could do it. Did you doubt me? Of course you did, you always do." She was sick of being underestimated by him—by everyone.

He glared at her. "That is not what I meant."

A cool wind rattled the limbs of the trees. It swirled around the skirts of her peach gown. Sophia shivered at the sudden change of temperature. "Do you feel that?"

Ian straightened. "In case you haven't noticed, there's a blasted storm approaching. Or are storm clouds necessary to encourage the fairies to come out?" His blue eyes were filled with humor, making it impossible for Sophia to stay angry with him. His teasing smile crinkled around those eyes. He really was quite handsome. He was also a nonbeliever.

Sophia wasn't so sure. "The temperature of the air changed. You did not feel it?"

"Sophia, there are no fairies. No wishes. Just you and me on this stone rock." Ian glanced up at the sky. "About to get drenched if we do not start walking back to the Lodge."

Sophia looked at the sky and the dark clouds gathering on the horizon. "We have time. Do you have a wish?"

"I'll not waste my time encouraging this silliness," Ian said. "I'm a businessman. I don't believe in fairy tales."

"Why am I not surprised by your attitude? You spend too much time with your ledgers and numbers."

"Don't tell me you believe in this nonsense. I know you better than that."

Sophia fought the urge to huff. He thought he knew her so very well. How wrong he was. She had wishes, dreams. Maybe they weren't the same as her sisters', but they were hers. She closed her eyes, trying to put what she wanted into words. She had to get them just right.

"Please tell me you are not making a wish at this very moment."

The disbelief in his voice pricked her temper. "I should wish that you be stuck with me forever. Think of the amount of torment I could rain down on you for a lifetime." Sophia's eyes flew open and she slapped her hand over her mouth.

The cold wind whirled around them both, pushing her into Ian. She reached out her hands and grasped his arms, trying to keep their bodies from touching.

"What is going on?" Ian demanded.

"No! Please no. I didn't mean it."

"That was the wish?" Ian threw his head back and laughed. "Be careful what you wish for, Sophia."

"No! It's not the wish. It cannot be the wish." She tried to step away from him, but he grabbed her arm.

"Only you, Sophia Townsend, would make the wrong wish."

Winds swirled around her skirts, causing them to brush against Ian's buckskins, pushing her harder into his arms. She slipped on the uneven rocks. Ian grasped her arms to hold her steady. Sophia looked up into his blue eyes and felt the strangest sensation. She didn't like it at all.

Ian clasped Sophia's arms, steadying her, even as the wind picked up and shoved them closer together. "The rain is coming faster. We have to leave—now."

Sophia lifted her head to the sky, stretching her neck. Even with the ridiculous frilly bonnet she was wearing, the soft pale skin of her neck tempted him. She always tempted him. For the years he'd known her, Sophia Townsend had danced into and out of his reach, teasing him like a cat with a piece of string.

"I've wished for the wrong thing. I've ruined everything."

Sophia hung her head down, crestfallen, the feathers of her silly hat tickling his nose.

"Then it's a good thing fairies and magic aren't real."

Sophia glanced up at him, her eyes doleful. "Do you not believe in anything?"

She bit her bottom lip. Every time she did that, he felt something tighten inside. He forced his gaze to glance at the darkening sky. "I'm sure even fairies believe in second chances. Restate your wish quickly. I'm not in the mood to be drenched in a cold rain."

"I don't think it works that way, but it can't hurt." Sophia's thick lashes fell, covering her dark eyes. Her full lips moved with the words, but he couldn't make them out. What could she be wishing for?

"There. Done," she said. "For all the good it will do."

Ian added another thing to the list of things Sophia blamed him for. The list seemed to grow longer every day. Thunder rumbled in the distance. They needed to get indoors. He held his hand out to Sophia. "Come, I'll help you down the steps."

Sophia jumped as another clap of thunder rumbled in the distance. "There is a faster way to the Lodge through the woods. I can show you."

Ian followed her into the woods as they raced for the house, the wind at their heels. The ribbons of her bonnet whipped behind her, catching the breeze. Feathers bounced as she moved. He caught a glimpse of slim ankles as she lifted her dress to quicken her pace.

Sophia was different from her sisters in every way. She was curvy where Juliet was slight. She was petulant where Anne was calm. Ian didn't know why he was attracted to her except that she was like a bright light on a cloudy day. He'd had more than his share of cloudy days in his life.

They stumbled upon the ruins of an old cottage on their rush to the Lodge. "Hurry. It's starting to rain. You don't want to ruin your bonnet," he teased.

"Especially because I just purchased it." She looked back at him, then up at the sky. Her eyes widened with alarm. She lifted the edge of her skirts a bit higher and took off running.

Ian looked back behind him. The sky was eerie shades of black, gray, and brown. He cursed beneath his breath. The temperature dropped as a gust of cold air threatened to remove his hat. He sprinted to catch Sophia, seizing her hand as he caught up to her.

Huge droplets of rain started to splatter his coat and hat as well as her thin dress. He turned toward the stables in the distance, dragging Sophia behind him. Thunder crashed and lightning flashed, filling the air with a chemical smell. The storm was close, almost overhead. They needed shelter—now.

She pulled on his hand. "The Lodge is that way, Mr. McDonald."

"We won't make the house in time." Thunder roared, drowning out his words. He glanced back at Sophia, who looked terrified. He pulled her along as he raced toward an outbuilding.

Sophia stumbled and he grasped her waist as lightning crackled around them. She trembled against him, her face beneath that frilly bonnet white.

"Are you all right?" he asked.

"I'm fine." She tried to pull away from him, but he kept her close and rushed her toward the nearest outbuilding. Rain started coming down in sheets, soaking her dangling bonnet. Her dark hair hung in damp clumps around her face.

"We'll take shelter here," he shouted over the storm.

He yanked the door of the small building open and hauled her inside as lightning hit a tree just beyond where they had been standing. Sophia shrieked, covering her face. He tugged her deeper into the darkness of what appeared to be a shed and closed the door behind them. The air was stale and smelled of earth and damp. Gardening tools hung along one side of the wall. A workbench lined another wall. Bits of broken pottery were scattered on the earthen floor. One small window, so dirty he could barely see outside, offered a bit of light. The roof seemed sound and that was all that mattered.

Rain beat hard against the roof. The wind howled, shaking the small building with its force. "We should be safe here," Ian whispered as he rubbed Sophia's arms. Her skin was cold and she was shivering. He needed to get her warm. Ian pulled her into his arms, against his warmth, but she stiffened against him.

Sophia shoved out of his arms as if the thought of his touch sickened her. She crossed the door and tried to open it.

Damn stubborn woman. Ian moved to the door, ready to catch her if she ran out. "You cannot leave until the storm has passed."

"I cannot stay here." Her face was pale, her eyes wide. "You cannot make me stay."

Thunder shook the walls and rattled the glass in the window. Lightning flashed within seconds of the crash. The storm was overhead and strengthening. He could hear limbs snapping in the wind and banging up against the walls. "Sophia, it's not safe."

Ian gently took her arm and pulled her away from the opening as a limb of the nearby tree crashed in front of the door on the other side of which she was standing.

Chapter 2

Sophia screamed as the branch crashed right where she had been standing a moment earlier. The small building groaned under the force of the wind. Thunder rattled the windows. The flashes of lightning lit up the dark corners of the building in eerie white light. But the storm was secondary to her fear as Ian dragged her deeper into the small structure. The darkness wrapped around her like bands of thick rope, choking her. She could feel the damp warmth of his body as he drew her closer. She dug in her heels, fighting against his pull.

"Sophia?" Ian McDonald's voice was soft, calm. "It's all right. It's just a late summer storm."

She yanked her hands from his and edged closer to the door. Distance; she needed distance. "I'm fine."

"You're freezing. I can hear your teeth chattering." He reached for her and rubbed her bare arms to try to warm her. She couldn't stop the flinch at his touch. He stopped immediately.

She wrapped her arms around herself as if she could hold in the panic, the fear. Walls seemed to close around her, boxing her in, stirring memories of another time, another man who had made her feel safe, then had made her feel anything but safe.

"You're shivering too. We must get you warm," Ian said gently

His jaw was set as he stepped forward and pulled her against the warmth of his body. His arms wrapped around her, trapping her against his hard body. He held her there, perfectly still. Panic rolled over her like a cold wave of seawater. Terror fueled her fight as she shoved at him, punched him, shoved at him to free herself from his grasp. "No."

He released her immediately.

She hated the look on his face. She'd seen that look countless times, the pain, confusion, even anger. She stepped back from him, her chest heaving from terror, and moved toward the safety of the door. "Stay away from me."

He held up his hands. "I'm not going to hurt you. I promise."

She looked out at the rain. The storm raged outside as her fear raged inside her. She had thought she was beyond being afraid of such situations.

"Sophia, sweetheart, move away from the door. You might get hurt if you stay there."

His voice was soft, gentle, sad. Sophia's mind knew not to be afraid of Ian. In the three years she'd known him, he had never been anything but a gentleman. She stepped back into the center of the small shed but still kept some distance between them.

"Do you want to talk about it?"

"No." Angry tears burned her eyes. She thought she was beyond this. She thought she had control over her reactions.

"You're still freezing. At least take my coat." Ian removed his damp wool coat. "May I put it around your shoulders?"

She nodded. He stepped close to her slowly and draped the coat around her shoulders.

"Thank you."

Slowly, her fears started to calm. Her teeth stopped chattering and she started to feel warmer. "I'm sorry."

"There is nothing to be sorry about. I'm sorry I frightened you." Ian was leaning against the wall of the outside of the building. "I would not have hurt you."

She pulled in a deep breath. "I know that, Mr. McDonald."

The questions were there on his face. He wanted to know why she had reacted this way. She didn't want to discuss it, especially with him. She turned to continue watching the storm, focusing on the time between the lightning flashes and the thunder, anything to avoid that expectant look on his face. Sophia opened the door just a bit to peer out. "I think the storm is finally passing. We should be able to leave in just a few more minutes."

"Matthews tells me you are expecting guests from Town. When do they arrive?"

A safe topic. She almost sagged with relief. She felt humiliated enough without having to explain it all to him. And he would eventually demand an explanation. He wouldn't be able to let it go until he knew all her secrets. "Tomorrow, I believe."

"How many in the party?"

"It shall be Lord Bateman and his sister, Lady Catherine, and two others.

"A small party, then. Good."

Sophia was looking forward to seeing Lord Bateman, but Catherine Grayson was the most unpleasant person. Sophia knew she herself could be unpleasant occasionally, but not mean like Catherine. There were many young ladies who were terrified of Catherine. She could make or break their Season with just one cutting remark. Lady Catherine disapproved of Lord Bateman's attentions to her.

"Do all dark, closed spaces affect you like that?" Ian's voice cut through her thoughts.

Drat; he wasn't going to let it go. Sophia had no intention of discussing such a personal memory with him. "That is part of it."

"Is the other part me?"

She could hear the distress in his voice. "It's not personal."

"You fought to get out of my arms. How can it not be personal?"

"It is an old wound—do I have to open it up here and now?"

He winced at the sharpness of her tone, but perhaps he would get the point that she had no intention of discussing this with him further.

"I would not have hurt you."

He moved closer to her and she tensed but did not run away. With the door partially open and cool air circulating, she could control the fear better.

"I know you won't hurt me."

"Are you still cold?"

She shook her head, clutching the edges of his coat to her chest. "Do you wish to have your coat back?"

"No."

He moved closer, slowly, not in a threatening way but with purpose. Sophia could feel her pulse speed up, but she fought the urge to run. He wasn't an angry man. And she wasn't fifteen. "What are you doing?"

"Testing a theory." His voice was soft, gentle.

"I'm not some insect for you to dissect and examine."

Ian halted in front of her, scrutinizing her. The panic she had felt earlier didn't rise up as much this time. She had the open door beside her. She could see the outside. Still, she wanted Ian McDonald at a distance. There was something about him that pulled at emotions within her that she'd not felt in a very long time. Emotions that drove her to make hasty decisions; change the course of her life. More space was needed here. She stepped away from him.

Ian McDonald must never know how much she was attracted to him. She had no intention of becoming emotionally involved with the son of a steward, no matter how rich and handsome he was.

He brushed a strand of hair from her face, then another, almost as he would a child. She waited for the panic but none came. Instead was this quivery feeling of anticipation.

His touch was so gentle, so caring, Sophia closed her eyes to keep him from seeing the longing welling inside her. Her heart longed for more of this cherishing touch, but she couldn't let herself be ruled by it. She made as if to step back again, put some distance between them, before Ian's touch, his scent, his very maleness, reeled her in like a fish on a hook.

"Don't," he whispered.

Sophia's eyes flew to his face and widened at the emotion she saw there. His eyes darkened to the color of the storm clouds outside the doorway. He gazed at her face, her mouth. What did he want from her? Her heart thumped in her chest, but she didn't fear him. It was a novel feeling.

Ian stepped closer, and instinctively, Sophia stepped back until she could go no farther, the door frame against her back. Cool, fresh air from the passing rain washed over her face, calming her. He moved closer to her, his hands at his sides, nonthreatening. His eyes focused on her mouth.

He was going to kiss her. Sophia was torn between wanting to know what his mouth on hers would feel like and worrying that she'd give away how drawn she was to him. His eyes burned a deep, stormy blue. She felt her breathing quicken, her pulse race.

Ian bent his head to hers, allowing his mouth to brush oh so softly against hers. He lifted his head to see if she was panicking. He dipped his head again, his tongue worrying the spot where she'd bitten her lip.

The only place where he touched her was her mouth. His stance, his arms remained steady, nonthreatening. But oh, his mouth!

Sophia's eyes drifted closed as Ian's lips fit between hers in a perfect kiss. One kiss followed another. Sophia's hands itched to touch him, pull him closer. Never had anyone made her feel like this. Never had her blood felt like syrup running through her body.

He lifted away, ending the kiss. Her eyes opened as she watched him, waiting to see what would happen next. He nodded to himself, as if she'd been some problem he'd worked out in his head.

"Did you discover what you wanted, Mr. McDonald?" she asked.

"Not quite. I think it will require more study."

Ian watched as Sophia's jaw tightened in anger, even as her cheeks flushed. She pushed past him and stepped into the rain.

"Where are you going?" He couldn't keep the tinge of laugher from his voice. He had finally had his answer. Sophia wasn't as immune to him as he'd thought.

"Away from you." She stomped through the grass with wide strides.

"You'll catch your death."

"A little rain never hurt anyone. I find it cools the passions rather well."

Ian caught up with her easily. Lightning still flashed dangerously in the sky. "At least stay away from the trees." He took her arm and guided her into the garden, toward the house.

She had every reason to be angry. He'd pushed her, tested her to see what had triggered the panicked response in the shed. Something had frightened her and he needed to know the cause. Sophia Townsend was vain, aloof, and had the tendency to lash out with words. Fear was not something he'd ever seen in her before.

This was a woman who cut a swath through Society that he envied. She had no fear of new situations. She could hold her own even in the most pompous of crowds and look down her pretty nose at them.

Not once had he seen her as afraid as she'd been in the potter's shed. Afraid of him.

That was the rub. She'd winced at his touch. She'd fought his arms as if he were the very devil himself. He had to understand why because if it was his touch, his presence, he might as well give up the game now.

The game to win Sophia Townsend as his wife.

She would make a fine wife. She could handle just about any situation. She wasn't cowed by the prejudices of the Ton. She could hold her own in any type of society. He needed that if he was going to further his business dealings. Sophia Townsend could be a great asset for his future.

It didn't hurt that she was breathtakingly beautiful. Having her on his arm would garner attention. Not to mention that he wanted her.

Hence the experimental kiss. He had eliminated the closed-in spaces, allowing her the ability to escape easily. He'd pressed his mouth to hers and had been lost.

It had taken all his resolve not to pull her into his body as her mouth accepted his. The fear had been gone. Experiment successful, and in the process, he'd found that the rumors of her coldness were unfounded. There was a great deal of passion in Sophia Townsend. She'd responded to him. Not so very cold after all.

"We should decide how we want to consider this further study, Miss Townsend."

"There will be no study."

"Admit that you enjoyed it."

She stopped, heedless of the rain and the fact that it made her look like a wet kitten. He rather liked this undone version of Miss Townsend. He smiled.

"Hear me well, Mr. McDonald: There will be no repeat performance of what just happened. I am not interested."

"Funny but you felt very interested. In fact, I think I could kindle your interest very quickly."

She moved away from him. "That kiss changed nothing."

"It changes a great deal, Sophia."

She smirked. "Really, Mr. McDonald, it was just a kiss."

"Do you allow men to kiss you like that on a regular basis?" The thought of any other man touching what he considered his was abhorrent. He'd never thought of himself as a possessive man, but Sophia had changed that when he met her.

"That would make me fast," Sophia said primly.

"It's still a valid question."

She glared at him. "I am not fast and you are no gentleman for suggesting it."

"I'm no gentleman at all, according to you."

"True." She turned away from him with that cold reply and started back toward the house again.

He stopped her by grasping her arm. Irritation, his normal emotion where she was concerned, reared its ugly head. "If I'm no gentleman, why did I stop, Sophia? We both know I could have taken the kiss a great deal farther than I did."

"You were testing me."

"Yes."

"It won't happen again."

He almost smiled at the lack of conviction in her voice. She wasn't going to be able to hide from him any longer. Her reaction to him was of equal strength to his reaction to her. Yes, she would make a very passionate wife. "Yes, I think it will. I think it will happen a great deal from now on."

"Don't be coarse." She turned away and stared at the rain. "A gentleman wouldn't say such a thing."

"You claimed I wasn't a gentleman, remember?"

"And you've made my case for me."

Ian was quiet for a long moment before saying, "Don't forget what you wished for at the Fairy Steps."

She did not respond, her eyes flashing her anger.

He pulled her closer. The rain was easing now. Her hair fell in wet clumps around her face. "You wished to be stuck with me for life."

"You don't believe in magic."

"But you obviously do. I really didn't think you were the type."

"I don't think I take your meaning, sir."

"Neither of us are the type to leave important decisions up to fate or fairy magic, Sophia. But in this instance I think I'll make an exception. What are you going to do to prevent the wish from coming true?"

She said nothing, her jaw tight, her lips pressed together. He could see her trying to come up with some sort of tart reply to his question. She turned and stomped toward the house.

He laughed. He easily caught up with her again.

"Did your inopportune wish foil some grand plan to marry a certain earl who is arriving tomorrow?"

The stiffening of her body was his answer. She had planned to wish for a proposal from Bateman.

"This should be entertaining to watch."

"You will not be here to see it."

But he'd been invited by Bateman himself. The man probably needed money. Funny that he should come to the son of his old steward to fix his problems. "Mrs. Matthews has invited me to stay to even out the numbers of the party. Looks like the wish is working already, doesn't it?"

Sophia barely contained the urge to turn around and knock Ian McDonald on his bum. She wanted to hit him so badly she could hardly control herself. Hateful man! She turned and threw his coat at him. It hit him in the face. Good.

He ruined everything.

What had possessed her sister to invite this scoundrel to the party? Evening numbers? Seriously? She'd have a chat with Anne about not consulting her before changing the guest list that she'd very carefully put together.

"You didn't answer my question," he called out after her.

"I have no intention of discussing this further with you, Mr. Mc-Donald."

Oh, how she wished she could give into the urge to rescind the invitation, but it would only lend credence to his remarks and that she would not do. Sophia was determined that things would be done in a proper manner and no one would change that.

McDonald caught up with her near the rose bushes. They were in sight of the house. She could see Anne watching them through a window.

"Have you let Bateman kiss you?" Ian's voice was low and harsh.

"Of course not. He wouldn't take such liberties," she spat as she lifted her gown from the higher grass.

"Then he's not in love with you."

Sophia smiled up at him. "A man doesn't have to be in love to take advantage of a lady. Look at you—you hardly tolerate me, but you had no problem pawing me a few moments ago."

There was the old, familiar tick of his jaw as her jab hit home.

"You don't deny it?"

"You were a willing participant, Miss Townsend." He ground out the words.

"Perhaps, but let me ask you another question: Did you kiss me because you have feelings for me or was it simple lust?"

Ian said nothing, attempting an air of boredom, as he usually did when he couldn't win an argument. Sophia let the smugness wash away the bit of lingering desire she'd felt for him. It was so much better to keep him at arm's length. "I'll take your silence as an affirmation." She turned with a flounce toward the house.

"You have no idea what you're talking about."

She looked back at him and raised one eyebrow. "I've been groped at enough functions over the last four years to know exactly what I'm talking about. Lust is common. Very common."

Sophia left him standing in the drizzle. The man drove her to insanity. Why had her heart decided that he was the one who would get her blood moving? Why was he the only one who could push back the panic she felt when a man got near her? What was it about him that instinctively told her he would not hurt her? Why couldn't it be anyone else?

Chapter 3

Ian sat across from Sophia during dinner. She was patently avoiding him, but he'd expected that. In any confrontation with the lady in question, she ran away rather than facing her feelings, especially feelings that were contradictory to her current goal: marrying a man with a title.

He wouldn't continue this tortuous pursuit of her had she not responded to his kiss during the storm. He was every bit the cur for taking advantage of the situation, but he didn't regret it. He'd sensed for years there was a fierce passion buried deep within Sophia Townsend. His hunch had proven right. Now there was the more pleasurable task of convincing the lady that she belonged with him and not the high and mighty Lord Geoffrey Bateman.

He was not looking forward to seeing the man again. In Bateman's eyes, Ian was the worst of the nouveau riche for having earned his own way into society. Money had a way of paving the way into even the highest circles. Ian wasn't above taking advantage of it. Bateman and his snobbery could go to the devil.

"Sophia, do you actually expect a proposal from this earl?" Nathaniel asked rudely. The man took his job as brother-in-law quite seriously. Ian didn't approve. He kept his eye on Sophia as she pushed around the food on her plate.

She set her fork down and folded her hands in her lap. Ian knew this meant she was strategically planning her attack.

Let the war of words begin.

"I have reason to hope for a proposal, Nathaniel, given his attention to me in Town." She picked up her glass and sipped. Ian watched as her face grew calmer, sweeter. In his experience, this was the face she made before she went in for the proverbial kill. Ian set his fork down and sipped his wine, waiting for the rest of her statement.

"Of course, had we not had to leave before the Season's end, I would know for sure, wouldn't I?"

Anne quickly moved to diffuse the situation as color darkened Nathaniel's cheeks. "Sophia, we had no choice, dear. You can't blame Nathaniel."

"I would never hold him responsible, Anne." Sophia picked up her fork and moved the peas from one side of her plate to the other.

Ian smiled inwardly. Sophia Townsend was a master of the art of dramatic pauses. This trait had cost him an argument with the lady on more than one occasion.

"I do, however, feel we should have had more notice before leaving Town," Sophia continued. "Luckily, I was able to issue the invitation to Bateman and his sister before we actually left."

"For which you did not ask permission," Nathaniel said.

"I didn't think I needed permission to invite friends to call on me in the country. Bateman has an estate in Carlisle. Beetham is the perfect stopping point." Sophia smiled at Nathaniel. "Surely even you see the benefit in such a connection."

"Sophia—" Anne tried to interrupt.

Sophia ignored her. "Aren't you the one who wished me to marry a man with the proper connections?" She looked at Anne. "Didn't I hear that correctly?"

Anne looked to the heavens, picked up her glass of wine, and drank deeply.

Lady Danford laughed. "She has you there, Nathaniel."

"I didn't mean for her to take four years to find a husband. Lord, Juliet only took two Seasons."

"Juliet married your brother, Nathaniel. Hardly the same thing," Lady Danford said. She turned to Sophia. "I have to say, though, that at your age, you had better hope Bateman proposes. There won't be many more opportunities for you."

"She might as well start wearing those stupid caps spinsters wear," Nathaniel threw in.

Ian watched the color rise in Sophia's cheeks. It was clear she was sensitive about her age.

"You make me sound decrepit," she grumbled.

"You aim too high," Nathaniel said. "And because of it, you shall end up a spinster."

"A man can be ambitious and he's praised for it. Look at Mr. Mc-Donald, here. He is a successful attorney and sheep farmer and we all praise him."

"Don't draw me into your argument, Miss Townsend." She had the bit between her teeth now. Ian really felt sorry for Nathaniel. An angry, righteous Sophia Townsend was a sight to behold. Her cheeks turned a delicate rose color. Her dark eyes flashed.

"Yet a woman who is ambitious is looked at as a social climber or worse, aiming too high for pushing to improve her station in life. Why should I not marry an earl or a duke? I am within my own sphere. I am the daughter of a baronet."

"It's not the same thing, dear," Lady Danford said. "Your brother is not a peer of the realm. Dukes and earls marry within their own social set."

Sophia threw down her napkin. "I've seen it done."

"Yes, but those women were much younger and much wealthier than you, Sophia," Nathaniel said. "Given how much older you are than the other young ladies, you don't stand much of a chance. Bateman could do much better."

"I would have thought you'd be happy to marry me off at the earliest convenience."

"I would have been, had you accepted one of the many offers you had that first Season in London. No, you had to wait for a better offer and now there are none."

"There are offers." She bit out the words so quietly that Ian had to doubt the truth of her statement. Had she had any offers this Season?

Nathaniel glanced at his wife, who shook her head. Nathaniel had been lucky to marry for love. Ian was in a different position. He was in love with a woman who wanted something completely different. She wanted a fashionable marriage and a fashionable life.

"I'm not going to ask you to name them, Sophia," Nathaniel said quietly.

Sophia looked relieved. The conversation as a whole was making Ian uncomfortable. While Ian enjoyed the banter, he didn't want to witness what was turning into a very personal fight between Sophia and Nathaniel.

Nathaniel picked up his fork again. "If things get desperate, I'm sure Ian, here, would have you."

Ian watched as Sophia went pale as the words sputtered out of her mouth, making no sense. Nathaniel had no idea of his and Sophia's very passionate kiss in the shed, but it was clear Sophia was remembering it—and not in a good way.

"I have no plans at present to marry, Miss Townsend, so you are safe from me." Ian worded his sentence with care. He wanted her to feel more comfortable, but he didn't want to give up yet. Her face relaxed and the color returned.

"You're even too old for him," Nathaniel crowed.

Sophia glared at him. "Wasn't my sister my age when she married you?"

"I believe I was," Anne added. "And I wasn't wearing caps yet."

"Nor shall I."

"Personally, I prefer a lady to be a bit older. Those debutantes in town are witless, always chatting about gossip or fashion. A man can't even hold a decent conversation with one of them," Ian said.

"I believe he has you there, Nathaniel," Sophia said with a smile.

"Can we all quit this arguing and eat?" Lady Danford added. "This topic grows as cold as my food."

Sophia resumed eating her own food, her lips forming a small smile. Ian wanted her to raise her eyes to his, acknowledge that he'd stepped in and defended her, but she didn't. Disappointment took the edge off the triumph he'd seen in her face for a brief second after he'd made his comment. He should have known she wouldn't give him the satisfaction.

"What activities do you have planned for our guests, Sophia?" Anne said.

"The gentlemen will want to do some shooting," Sophia replied. "We'll go horseback riding with the ladies. And there's always shuttlecock."

"How long will they be staying?" Nathaniel asked.

"Perhaps a week, maybe a fortnight."

"I'm sure it will depend on the seriousness of Lord Bateman's suit," Ian mumbled.

"Ladies, shall we leave the gentlemen to their brandy?" Anne said, standing.

Ian got to his feet as Sophia rose from the table to follow Lady Danford and her sister. Nathaniel chuckled as the door closed behind the ladies. "You have it bad."

Ian glared at him. "What are you talking about?"

"Why don't you just marry the girl and take her off my hands?"

"She won't have me. She wants the title and the prestige that goes with it." There were times when he questioned his attraction to this one woman above all others. What made her different? "She wants Bateman."

Nathaniel said, "Sophia doesn't know you are the son of Bateman's steward, does she?"

Ian shook his head. "It's common knowledge in the Ton. I'm sure she's heard the gossip." He'd be a fool to remind her of his lower status in society.

"You are going to have to remind her."

"To what purpose?"

"Sophia does not deal well with surprises and Bateman will bring up the connection."

Ian only nodded. Bateman would surely bring up the connection to reinforce his own superiority. How could he counter the truth?

"Lord Bateman isn't coming here because he's planning to propose to Sophia, is he?"

"I received a letter from him recently insisting he wanted to meet me here."

"You had little contact with him in London?"

Ian shook his head. "I was well beneath his notice in Town."

"It is odd that he contact you to meet him here of all places."

"Bateman owns land adjacent to my estate in Dumfries. I've offered to buy it."

"Do you think Bateman will sell?"

Ian shrugged. "The earldom is in dun territory. My offer is fair, so I suspect he's suggested meeting me here to finish the sale." Ian hoped that was the case. The estate in Dumfries had stood almost empty for a long time.

"He's that desperate? I had no idea. I suspect Sophia doesn't know either."

Ian nodded. "Lord Bateman takes great pains to hide how bad his finances are. I know because of my connection to the estate." Money was the only reason Bateman would acknowledge his presence. Of course, it helped that the meeting was so far out of London that no one would hear of it.

"There are many other peers in the same circumstances."

"The world is changing and we must change with it. Those who choose not to change with the times are going to find themselves sinking deeper."

"I doubt very seriously the aristocracy will be going anywhere," Nathaniel said. "They are too firmly entrenched in society. If it were going to change there would have been a revolution by now."

Ian laughed. "Aren't we in a revolution of sorts?"

"You have a point, sir. How do you plan to explain to Sophia your connection with Bateman? She is bound to notice the familiarity. He won't hide the connection, especially this far out of London."

Ian didn't want to tell her he was the son of old Bateman's steward. She already saw herself as being above him; he didn't want to add any more fuel to that fire. "I'll tell her tonight. It's not going to help my cause, but I'll do it."

"Do you honestly think there is cause to hope?"

Ian shrugged again, not wanting to answer Nathaniel's question. Sophia felt something for him. Her responses to him were too passionate for her not to have some strong emotion toward him. He just wasn't sure if she wanted to acknowledge the emotion.

Sophia settled a wrap around Lady Danford's shoulders. "That should keep the chill away."

"Thank you, child," Lady Danford said.

"Sophia, I wish you would not argue with Nathaniel in front of guests. What must Mr. McDonald think?"

Sophia took a seat beside Anne and picked up her embroidery. "I really don't care what Mr. McDonald thinks." The man got under her skin worse than a rash.

"He likes you," Lady Danford said. "He's always liked you."

"I can't see why," Anne inserted. "You've treated him horribly."

"I'm polite."

"Barely."

"A man likes a woman with spirit. Lord Danford was always riling me up," Lady Danford said, her eyes closed. "Said it made me prettier."

Sophia looked at Anne. "I don't care whether Mr. McDonald likes me or not. He's not my type."

"Evidently, there is no one who is your type," Anne said. "I've always thought you were too picky for your own good. You've turned down quite a few perfectly good marriage proposals. What are you waiting for?"

"What happens to a girl who isn't settling?"

"There is not settling and there is trying to grasp for something you know you can't have. A smart woman knows the difference," Lady Danford said.

"I am not grasping. Is it wrong to want to live my life a certain way?"

"It is time to face reality, Sophia. You are firmly on the shelf now, and you've let perfectly good opportunities pass you by. There won't be many more chances after this," said Anne.

"No thanks to your husband," Sophia grumbled. "What's wrong with going to London for the Season?"

"It's a terrible inconvenience, especially with two young children."

Sophia had to agree with that. Anne's two boys and the long carriage ride had her ready for Bedlam before they even reached the halfway point. "Perhaps Lady Danford and I could go?"

"I'm done with Town," Lady Danford said. "I'm too old."

"Lady Danford, you say that every year, then you change your mind."

"I won't be changing my mind this time, Sophia. The trip is too laborious. It takes me at least two days to recover from the carriage ride."

Sophia stabbed her needle into the fabric. This was not to be borne. How was she going to survive living the rest of her life in this small village?

Going to the Fairy Steps had been a desperate measure, but she hadn't really thought she'd need a wish to capture Lord Bateman. It was a good thing too, because she'd botched the wish and good, thanks to Mr. McDonald.

The door to the parlor opened and Nathaniel and Ian entered the room. Ian's eyes met hers and she quickly looked down at her work.

Ian took the seat next to Sophia. She stabbed again at the fabric, pulling the thread too tight, causing it to pucker.

"Angry embroidery tonight?"

His voice was low, with a hint of a Scottish burr that rumbled across her senses in ways she'd never experienced before. Damn the man. What was his hold over her? Sophia took her needle and loosened the stitch to remove the pucker. "I'm not angry."

He chuckled. "Miss Townsend, may I have the pleasure of your company while taking the air? The moon is out and it's quite lovely."

Sophia felt a nearly uncontrollable urge to say yes, as the thought of what could happen while they were alone sent tingles under her skin. She could not allow herself to be distracted by him. "It is too cool after the rain."

"We need to talk, Sophia."

Talking was the last thing she wanted. A vision of their kiss flashed through her mind. Good heavens, where had that come from?

"I'm not going to stop asking until you say yes."

She set down her embroidery. "I suppose if I'm ever to have peace tonight, I'd better comply. Are you always this persistent, Mr. McDonald?"

"You have no idea, Miss Townsend."

Sophia stood and accepted his arm, refusing to give either Anne or Nathaniel a glance. She didn't need to see their questioning looks. They exited the room through the French doors into the garden. A full moon tinted everything with silvery gray light, catching on the drops of water left behind by the earlier storm. It was a beautiful night, she had to concede.

He led her away from the house and deeper into the garden.

"Is this wise, Mr. McDonald?"

"I don't want to be overheard."

Sophia pulled her arm away. "What could you possibly say that I wouldn't want overheard?"

"Are you serious about Lord Bateman?"

The change of topic startled her. "Of course I am. He's a handsome lord— why wouldn't I be serious?"

"So you are expecting a proposal?"

"He wrote to me, accepting my invitation. What else am I to think?"

Ian took her hand and led her a bit farther into the darkness.

"Should we stray so far from the house?" she asked.

"Would you accept his proposal even after the kiss we shared this afternoon?" Ian persisted.

Sophia was now thankful for the darkness. It covered her blush and a multitude of other emotions that filled her at the question. "I've already told you, the kiss changes nothing, Mr. McDonald."

Ian grabbed her arm and jerked her backward into his arms. "Has he kissed you?"

"What?"

"Have you allowed Lord Bateman to kiss you?"

"My relationship with Lord Bateman is not your affair. You overstep, sir." She pulled out of his arms. She turned to leave, anxious to put as much distance between them as possible.

"Sophia, wait, please."

She turned back toward him.

"I apologize. I should not have asked that."

She stood as he approached, his hands held out in supplication.

"You drive me mad sometimes," he said.

"The feeling is quite mutual. It is late and we've been out here alone for too long." She stepped carefully through the wet grass.

He touched her arm. "Please, don't go yet."

There was something in Ian's voice that tugged on emotions Sophia didn't think she was capable of feeling. "I think I must. I accept your apology sir, but I don't think it would do for us to be alone together. Someone might get the wrong idea."

"Or the right one."

She shook her head. "It would be wrong for me. Good night."

Sophia turned and made her way to the parlor without a backward glance, leaving Ian behind. It was for the best, though she was more tempted by these strange, racing emotions than she wanted to be.

It was better to discourage his attachment now rather than lead him on. Better for both of them. She couldn't allow herself to weaken. She wasn't capable of giving her heart and would only end up hurting Ian.

Chapter 4

The day the Earl of Bateman and his party arrived was hot and humid. Summer was refusing to give in to fall. There wasn't even a wisp of a breeze to offer any relief. The humidity frizzed Sophia's hair. Her muslin dress hung limply on her frame. There was no saving the dress or her hair in this heat. She should have known this wouldn't bode well for her guests.

Worse yet, Anne's children were cranky. The whines of the two boys echoed through the house, setting Sophia's teeth on edge. The household was in an uproar. There was no way she would make a good impression with the pandemonium around her. Lord Bateman was going to step out of the carriage and into chaos. He'd take one look and get back into the carriage headed for the nearest inn. This whole idea was brewing into a first-rate calamity.

Anne placed a hand over Sophia's. "Be calm, Sophia; your guests will be so tired of being in the carriage that it won't matter how the children behave."

"I sincerely hope so." Because she couldn't take any more whining. How did Anne stay so calm?

"It's so unlike you to be nervous about guests."

"Please tell me you spoke with Nathaniel. He won't embarrass me, will he?"

"How foolish you are. Nathaniel would never do such a thing."

"He'll embarrass me, tease me in front of our guests, or worse, provoke me." Nathaniel couldn't resist teasing her in front of company.

"You have as much control over that as he does, Sophia."

"I just want everything to be perfect." Sophia stared out the window, watching the lane just beyond the Lodge. She glanced back at the mantel clock, then back to the road.

"Watching the clock or the park will not hasten their arrival," Anne said.

Sophia didn't care. She felt an excitement she'd not experienced in a while. Lord Bateman would come, propose, and her life could begin. She'd finally have the life she most wanted. She knew Anne thought her shallow for wanting to marry a titled gentleman and live in London, but she couldn't explain how badly she hated being so far away from good society. Their neighbors, Mrs. Dellwood and her husband, the vicar, were not good company. Lord, she could hardly sit and listen to Mr. Dellwood's sermons without wanting to drift into a doze.

She heard the wheels of the carriage before it came into view. "Anne, they are here!" Sophia raced out to the park.

Anne followed behind her. "Slowly, Sophia. Calm and graceful."

"Where are Nathaniel and Mr. McDonald?" Sophia said. "They should be here to welcome our guests."

"Honestly, Sophia, it is better that they aren't."

"But we have guests arriving. Nathaniel should be here at least." What kind of impression would they send if Nathaniel wasn't here to greet them? Sophia wanted everything to be perfect. What would Lord Bateman think?

"All will be well, Sophia, you'll see. Besides, our guests have traveled days in that carriage. I'm sure they'll want time to rest and refresh themselves before dinner tonight," Anne said.

Sophia said nothing as the carriage and two riders approached the house. Lord Bateman and another man sat upon the horses. She'd forgotten how handsome Bateman was, with his dark brown eyes and dark hair. He dismounted and handed the reins to a groomsman.

Sophia dipped a curtsy. "My lord, welcome to the Lodge. You remember my sister, Mrs. Nathaniel Matthews?"

Bateman took her hand and pressed his lips to it. "Miss Townsend, so delightful to see you again." He nodded to her sister. "Madam, thank you so much for your hospitality."

"Our pleasure, my lord."

"May I present Captain Crispin Smith-Williams?"

Sophia smiled up at the captain. He was tall and slender, with hawkish features and dark blond hair. "Captain Smith-Williams, welcome."

"Thank you for your hospitality, Miss Townsend, ma'am."

Lord Bateman moved to assist the ladies in the carriage. Lady Catherine stepped out of the carriage as if she'd just stepped out of a shop in London. Her dark blue carriage dress and matching bonnet were the latest style. Even the feather in her bonnet bounced as she moved, defying the high humidity. Her face held no shine from the heat. Not one hair was out of place. The blond ringlets that framed her perfect complexion were still perfect.

Sophia felt like a wilted piece of lettuce next to her—the poor relation version of lettuce. She should have changed her dress or done something else with her hair.

It was so much easier in London, when they could meet at assemblies or musicales. There they were on equal ground. Here at the Lodge, Sophia would be subjected to the judgment of Lord Bateman and his sister. She had a feeling there was nothing she could do to measure up.

"Heavens! I thought we'd never arrive," Catherine Grayson said as she looked around. "How very quaint! Dare I hope it will grant us a relief from this heat?"

"Catherine, I believe you remember Miss Townsend," Lord Bateman said.

"Lady Catherine," Sophia said with a small curtsy. "May I present my sister, Mrs. Nathaniel Matthews?"

"Welcome to the Lodge, my lady," Anne said.

"It is a pleasure to see you again, Lady Catherine," Sophia said, though her eyes darted to the other woman in the carriage. She looked vaguely familiar, but Sophia could not remember her name. Lord Bateman assisted the lady out of the carriage. Sophia's heart sank at the infatuation etched on his face.

"Mrs. Matthews, Miss Townsend, this is Miss Theodora Hamilton," Lady Catherine said. She whispered to Sophia, "I hope to soon call her sister."

Theodora Hamilton was petite and very pretty, with large brown eyes and a sweet smile. She wore a simple carriage dress of dark plum. Judging by the fabric and design, it was very expensive.

"Welcome, Miss Hamilton," Sophia said with a forced smile.

Anne shot her a questioning glance. "I'm sure you'd like to freshen up after your journey."

"Thank you, Mrs. Matthews, but are you sure you have enough room for us all? This place looks very small. The park is quite small indeed."

"I'm sure you'll be quite cozy, Lady Catherine. You must be very tired from your journey. Our housekeeper will see you all to your rooms," Anne said with an edge in her voice.

Sophia said nothing as Lady Catherine breezed by her, followed by a quiet Miss Hamilton. She'd met Theodora Hamilton only a few times in London. The daughter of a wealthy merchant with a very large dowry, Miss Hamilton had been pursued by many gentlemen.

Miss Hamilton curtsied. "I hope we aren't an inconvenience, Mrs. Matthews."

Anne smiled. "We have plenty of room, my dear. Please make yourself at home."

"You are very kind," Miss Hamilton said.

Anne followed Miss Hamilton into the house. Sophia trailed behind to accompany the gentlemen into the house.

Lord Bateman walked at Sophia's side. "Miss Townsend, is this all there is to the party?"

"No, my lord. We have another guest, Mr. Ian McDonald. He is a business associate of my brother-in-law."

Lord Bateman smiled easily. "Good. Then we shall have even numbers for entertainments."

"Are you acquainted with Mr. McDonald?"

There was a long pause before Lord Bateman spoke. "We have not been introduced. I have been wanting to meet him."

"Mr. McDonald is out with my husband but will be here for dinner tonight, my lord." Anne said. "I'll let him know you've arrived."

"Thank you, ma'am."

Sophia studied Lord Bateman for a long moment. There was something in his tone that did not ring true. Why would he want to be introduced to Ian McDonald? The man was a sheep farmer.

"What time should we be down for dinner, ma'am?" Captain Smith-Williams asked.

"We sound the gong at six, sir," Anne said.

Sophia watched them walk up the stairs. "Why would Lord Bateman be interested in meeting Mr. McDonald?"

"What a snob you are! Mr. McDonald is a successful businessman. He is well known in Town for advising various members of the Ton with their investments. Perhaps Lord Bateman would like his advice."

So he wasn't just a sheep farmer. Sophia kept that comment to herself. The man still irritated her on a daily basis. Still, there was something in Lord Bateman's manner as he spoke of Ian McDonald that warranted further study.

A walk to Horneswood, her sister's home, would give her time to think as well as recover from the disappointment of the appearance of Miss Hamilton. Sophia wanted to wallow in her defeat for a few minutes alone. She wasn't ready to give up, but even she had to admit that her chances of being on the receiving end of a proposal were looking rather bleak. Sophia could kick herself for wasting a perfectly good wish on Mr. McDonald.

"Do you need me, Anne?"

"I think the housekeeper can handle things. Sophia, are you all right? I know you thought Lord Bateman was here to propose—"

Sophia pasted a smile on her face. "I'm fine, Anne. Really. I thought I'd walk through the woods. It would be a relief from this heat, if you could do without me."

"Certainly. I doubt our guests will be down for tea after such a long journey."

"I'm sorry for Lady Catherine's comments. She can be—"

"Challenging?"

"Indeed," Sophia said. "Challenging is the perfect word."

Ian McDonald leaned against the fence, watching as sheep were rounded up by Tony Matthews's staff. He had transported several rams from his own flock in Scotland to breed with Tony's sheep. The goal was to breed a better quality of wool. This was the second year of their experiment and it was showing promise. So much promise, he was ready to invest in more land and settle on his estate in Dumfries to raise more sheep. It meant he would no longer need to travel to London regularly for business.

He hated Town. The smell, the thick air, the noise had no appeal to him. The theater was nice, as were other amusements, but he still preferred the green, rolling hills of his home in Scotland.

There would still have to be trips to Town, but not every single Season. He'd have to make a few trips to negotiate future investments in the factories he wanted to build, but most of those would be of short duration. Having Sophia on his arm would be a definite plus. She knew her way around Society. She could be a real asset when he was ready to expand his business.

Of course, that was assuming she didn't marry Lord Bateman and condescended to marry him. She wasn't the only one who had set her sights high. The heart didn't seem to care what Society thought.

Ian half hoped the stupid wish Sophia had mistakenly made would come true. If she were stuck with him forever, he'd have ample time to convince her to care for him. Unfortunately, in his experience, there was no magic, just hard work.

"How's it going? Has the ram picked his prize yet?" Tony asked, coming up beside him to lean on the fence.

Ian glanced at Matthews. Marriage had changed him in a good way. Ian was almost envious of Tony's life. The man was happy, at peace. "He's being picky. Maybe we should have limited his choices."

Tony shook his head. "Let him pick more than one. We can split the lambs next season."

"The wool from the last batch is of exceptional quality. I think we should broaden the plan. Include Nathaniel, and others if they are interested."

Tony looked at him. "Do you think we have a new breed?"

"We will," Ian said. He squinted at a movement in the distance. A woman marched toward them from the Lodge. Her arms swung with purpose, pushing her forward. This was a woman on a mission. "Are you expecting anyone?"

"No."

As the woman drew closer, Ian recognized her. Sophia Townsend marched toward the stream that ran between the two properties. Since Tony's purchase of the Horneswood estate, a foot bridge had been built. He could almost hear the stomping of her feet on the wood as she crossed. "Does Miss Townsend know not to come through the pasture?" It was mating season; the rams would be dangerous.

Tony laughed. "Sophia? You're bamming me, right? I'm not sure she could tell which were the ewes and which the rams."

Ian's heartbeat picked up as she opened the gate, stepped inside the enclosed pasture, and closed the gate with a snap. She swung her arms and walked quickly across the pasture, right past the ram with his latest conquest, who didn't look too pleased.

A fear he'd not known he possessed picked up his pulse. "She's going to get hurt." He jumped the fence and took off running. "Sophia! Stop!"

"Ian, you'll never get to her in time," Tony shouted after him.

Ian ignored him. An angry ram could not just knock Sophia Townsend on her pretty bottom but seriously hurt her. Visions of those horns and what they could do to her raged through his head as he ran full out toward her.

The space between Sophia and him seemed a mile wide but was, in fact, only a brief distance. He reached her, gasping for breath so badly that he couldn't speak. His eyes were on the ram, who was lowering his head.

"Mr. McDonald, I demand to know what your connection is to Lord Bateman." She spat out the words. "Imagine my surprise when he asked for you specifically."

The ram had taken his stance. The damn animal was going to charge right at Sophia Townsend.

He grabbed Sophia's arm and jerked her behind him.

"Ow! That was uncalled for." She moved back beside him again, her hands on her hips.

"Stay behind me."

"I will not stay behind you. How dare you speak to me that way?"

Ian had no choice; the ram was coming for them both. He shoved Sophia hard. His heart pounded in his chest as the ram moved forward, his head down. He'd only seen this maneuver performed by others. He'd never had to be the one to do it. God give him the strength.

Sophia's complaining faded into the background as he put all his focus on the animal. If he failed, they would both be at risk of injury. His heart bounded in his chest and his body tensed, ready for action.

"Mr. McDonald . . ."

"Quiet!" Amazingly, Sophia shut up.

As the ram approached, Ian bent down and grabbed his horns and twisted to send him in a different direction. Confused, the ram ran past, then turned and lowered his head again in a defensive stance.

"Did you just grab that sheep by its horns?" There was awe in her voice. "I have never seen anyone do that."

"Get out of the pasture." He couldn't spare her a glance, but he also didn't hear her moving toward the fence. "Now!"

The ram turned, even angrier than before. Ian could hear Sophia struggling behind him. "Sometime today, Miss Townsend."

"How dare you bark orders at me as if I were—were one of those stupid sheep!"

"Sophia, get the hell out of here!" He bent to meet the ram once more.

As the ram charged, his hands went for the horns. The rough texture chafed, keeping him from getting a good grip. The sheep was large, heavy, and moving at charging speed. Ian dug his heels deeper into the soft ground for purchase as he pushed the ram away once more.

"Matthews! Get her the hell out of here." Ian dare not look away from the ram watching him just feet away. He could hear Tony's feet pound against the ground as he ran toward them.

"I will not allow you to treat me thus," Sophia said from behind him. Her voice trembled despite her bravado.

The ram snorted and pawed at the ground, eying the weaker target, Sophia. She gasped behind him.

"Come, Sophia," Tony said. "Now."

He could hear the rustling of her gown as she stood. "I'm covered in mud!"

Better mud than gored. His mind could picture what those sharp horns could do to her tender flesh. The urge to glance behind him and verify that Sophia was safe pulled at him, but the angry ram and its posturing kept his focus.

"But what about you?" Sophia asked in a worried tone.

Now was a fine time to show concern for him, he thought. Still, he clung to those four small words, letting them feed the kernel of hope he'd felt when she'd returned his kiss. The ram snorted again, pulling his focus back. "Let me know when you're safely through the gate, Matthews."

Ian stood perfectly still, holding eye contact with the beast. He dare not blink. The ram glanced at the ewe nearby.

"She's safe!" Tony yelled from the fence.

Ian took several steps backward, watching every move the beast made, ready to move in case of another charge. The ram lowered his head, his eyes back on Ian.

Ian moved deliberately backward toward the gate, not relaxing his stance until he saw the sheep lose interest in him and go back to the ewe. Finally, Ian stood upright, the muscles in his back protesting from being held so tensely for so long.

With the danger past, anger coursed through him like lava from a volcano. He wanted to shake her until her teeth rattled. He sprinted the rest of the way to the gate, closing it behind him with more force than necessary.

Sophia jumped at the loud clang. Her face was pale and there was a smudge of mud on her cheek. She clenched her hands in her skirts.

"What in the bloody hell were you thinking?"

Sophia's eyes widened at his roar and she took a step back. "You have no right to be angry with me, sir. How was I supposed to know that the stupid sheep would charge after me? Usually they just stand there and eat grass."

Ian stepped closer to her, crowding her, trying to intimidate some sense into her. "Never cross a pasture like that, especially during mating season. You could have been seriously hurt."

Her lips parted with a gasp as the gravity of the situation finally settled in. He waited for an apology, but she said nothing, just stared up at him and trembled.

It was the trembling that got him. Ian fought the uncontrollable urge to take her into his arms and hold her. His hands tightened into fists.

"You didn't have to push me into the mud," she grumbled. "I'm a filthy mess."

Tony sniffed. "I don't think that was mud."

Sophia looked at her hands and twisted to look at the back of her dress, her nose wrinkling at the smell.

Ian couldn't help it; his lips twitched with humor at the disgust on her face.

"Do not laugh at me, Mr. McDonald. This is all your fault. I wouldn't be in this condition had you not shoved me to the ground."

"No, you'd be bleeding all over the blasted pasture," Ian barked.

Tony stepped between them. "Sophia, go up to the house. Juliet will see that you have something to change into."

"We are not done with this conversation, Mr. McDonald." She practically growled the words before turning and marching up the hill to the house.

The back of her dress was covered in grass and muck. He really had shoved her into a dung pile. He unclenched his fist and winced. He looked at his hands, scratched and bloody from the horns of the ram.

"I'd never seen anyone do that with a charging ram, McDonald."

"One of the workers had to stop a ram from charging him once. It looks easier than it is."

"You need a brandy and someone to look after those hands."

"Brandy sounds good." Now that his anger had faded, he felt as weak as a baby.

"Thank you for saving her. I couldn't have gotten to her fast enough. Come up to the house. We'll see to your hands."

Ian followed Tony into the house, hiding his still trembling hands in his pockets.

Sophia walked awkwardly toward the house, the muck on her skirts causing them to stick together. The smell was even worse. She couldn't decide if she was going to gag or cry or both. Never had she been so humiliated. She pulled at the back of her dress, trying to move it away from her body.

Juliet and a maid were waiting in the doorway, watching her approach.

"You are covered in mud. What happened?" asked Juliet.

"It's not mud and don't ask." She wasn't in the mood to talk about it yet. Her emotions bounced between fear and admiration for Mr. McDonald, something she didn't want to feel. She wanted to hold on to her anger. It was the only thing keeping her from throwing herself at the man.

He'd rescued her. He had put himself between that stupid sheep and her. He'd taken that creature by the horns and kept her safe. No one had ever done anything so heroic for her. She'd had no idea he was so strong.

Men had fawned over her. Sophia knew it, and had manipulated those men over the years. She liked being the center of their attentions. She liked their flattery. It fed her vanity. Vanity was a sin, she knew that, but still it felt good to be admired. But not one man had ever done something heroic for her. Now she was forced to look at Mr. McDonald in an entirely new light and she didn't like it one bit.

"You smell awful."

Sophia groaned. Ian had seen her covered in sheep dung. "Ian shoved me behind him and I slipped."

"What were you doing in the pasture?" Juliet asked. "You knew Ian was here for mating season."

"Why would I know about the mating patterns of sheep? I was in a hurry, so I cut across the pasture. I've done it before." Sophia slipped off her shoes and handed them to the maid. "These are ruined."

"I'm sure we can get them cleaned up. Why weren't you wearing your half boots?" Juliet took a rag from the maid and wiped at Sophia's cheek.

"I had to escape the house, Juliet. It was awful." Sophia took the rag from her sister and wiped her hands. "I didn't stop to think. Our guests arrived and Lord Bateman brought a lady with him. He's going to marry her. This is all my fault."

"I doubt that. Come upstairs. I'll have a bath prepared and find a change of clothes,"

Sophia followed Juliet to one of the spare rooms where soon a hip bath was set up. Water steamed from the bath. Sophia almost groaned. She couldn't wait to get the muck off her.

"Now tell me all. Who is this mysterious lady? And why this is your fault," Juliet said once they were alone.

"Miss Hamilton is her name. I met her in London." Sophia turned her back to allow Juliet to unbutton her gown. She peeled it off, leaving it in a heap on the floor. "Lady Catherine couldn't wait to get in a taunt about Lord Bateman's intentions."

Juliet loosened the laces of Sophia's stays. "Miss Hamilton? I don't remember her when we were last in Town."

"She is the daughter of a wealthy merchant. The rumor is that her father has settled twenty thousand pounds on her."

"Goodness! That is a powerful inducement, but how did you cause this?"

Sophia pressed her lips together and struggled to put the words together. Anyone else would think she was mad, but Juliet would understand. "I climbed the Fairy Steps yesterday."

Juliet laughed. "I thought you didn't believe in that nonsense."

"As you well know, there is evidence to the contrary. I thought if I made a wish it would make Lord Bateman's engagement a sure thing."

"Evidently not."

"It gets much worse. I was climbing the steps when Mr. McDonald appeared, demanding that I stop. We were both angry and I'm afraid I might have wished that he be stuck with me forever."

Juliet laughed.

"It's not funny." Sophia's shoulders sagged. "Lord Bateman was supposed to propose to me."

"He's an earl. Why would he propose to you?"

This was the outside of enough. Was she not worthy of an earl? She was the daughter of a baronet. Her dowry might not be large, but it was respectable. "Why does everyone think he will not propose?"

"Several reasons. You don't have a large enough dowry, for one. You don't have the appropriate connections, nor are you titled."

"We are daughters of a baronet."

"You always aimed too high. How many proposals have you turned down, Sophia?"

"None of that matters now. Lord Bateman singled me out in Town this Season. He made his intentions very well known. Why would he do that if he wasn't going to propose?" Lord Bateman had treated her carefully. He'd had feelings for her; Sophia could tell.

"Do you love him, then?"

Love did not enter into the equation for her future. "He's an earl. He has a town house in London and several estates. He comes from a very prestigious family."

"Sophia, all those things mean nothing. You should marry someone you love."

"I can spend more than ten minutes in his company without wanting to escape." She liked him well enough, she supposed. He was handsome. Not with the same rugged good looks as Mr. McDonald, but in a more refined way. She removed the rest of her clothes and dumped them into a pile. "You're going to need to burn these."

Juliet wrinkled her nose. "I think so. I'll have someone dispose of them."

Sophia stepped into the bath and sank into the heated water. She removed the pins from her hair and set them carefully aside so she could use them again. She reached for the soap.

"You were saying that you liked Lord Bateman enough. Marriage is forever, Sophia. You really should more than just 'like' him."

Sophia lathered her skin. "I'm not the same as you, Juliet. You and Anne have a capacity to love that I don't have."

"That's not true."

"Yes, it is. I'm too much like Father. I'm selfish and vain."

"Sophia—"

"It's fine. I know what my weaknesses are. I've accepted them. I know that if I marry for love, I'll end up hurting him as Father hurt our mother. I can't do it." Sophia blinked away the sting of tears and pulled in a controlling breath.

Juliet said nothing for a long moment. Sophia couldn't look at her sister and see the pity in her eyes. She was better off knowing her own weaknesses. She could plan her future without worrying about hurting the man she would marry. Many couples started with less.

"I'll leave you to finish your bath, Sophia. Ring for a maid when you are ready."

Sophia nodded.

Juliet moved to open the door, then paused. "I think you're wrong, you know. I think you have a great capacity to love."

Sophia stared at the door as it closed behind her sister, pondering Juliet's words. Juliet always thought the best of people, of her. In this case, Juliet was being overly generous. Sophia ducked her head under the water. She was too much like their father, like her brother.

Selfishness and cruelty ran in the family. Her father had treated her mother with coldness and disdain. Her brother had abandoned her and her sisters, leaving them to fend for themselves with no money or connections. Thank goodness for Nathaniel honoring his promise of a dowry. Sophia was terrified she was her father's daughter. It was better to control her own destiny than to leave it to the chance of falling in love. She was taking the practical approach to life. She would marry for material things and find her happiness in the delights of Society. It would be enough. She would make sure it was enough.

Chapter 5

Ian waited in Matthews's library, nursing the rest of his brandy. The hour was growing late and if they didn't leave soon, they'd be late for dinner.

He was not looking forward to the brief ride back to the Lodge, knowing he should come up with some sort of apology for shoving Sophia into the sheep dung. She'd been foolish to stomp into the pasture without looking to see if there were animals about. Ian was reminded again that she was no country miss. He hadn't thought much about her lack of knowledge when formulating his plan. He'd only cared that he wanted her.

"Has the cart been brought around?" Sophia asked, coming into the parlor.

Ian gulped. She wore one of Juliet's dresses. The sisters might resemble each other in beauty, but Mrs. Juliet Matthews was slight. Sophia was not. Her breasts jiggled like custard over the tight bodice of the dress. The dark color enhanced the pale cream of her skin. He looked down. Her toes peeked out from the shorter hem of the gown. "Where are your shoes?"

"Ruined. Juliet's feet are much smaller than mine. Nothing would fit." Sophia tugged at the skirt of the gown, not realizing that she was threatening to pop out of the bodice. "She is checking among the maids for a pair of shoes I can borrow."

Her hair was down and pulled back from her face. It hung in a dark, shining fall around her shoulders. He cleared his throat. It made her look younger, more innocent. "How long do you think she'll be?" He winced at the gruffness in his tone. "If we leave now, we just might make it in time to change for dinner."

Juliet came in behind them. "None of the maids had shoes your size. Your feet are a good deal bigger than everyone else's."

Sophia glared at her sister as her cheeks colored.

"You'll have to go home barefoot, Sophia. There is nothing the maid can do about your slippers. They'll have to be replaced. I'm not sure about the dress."

"You may burn that dress. It's an old one."

Ian cleared his throat. "Shall we go?"

Sophia hugged her sister and thanked her. She then followed him out to the park of Horneswood. He mounted the horse and reached a hand down to pull her in front of him.

"You cannot be serious. I cannot ride with you like that. It's improper."

He had no patience for this. "If you wish to get home quickly, it's the only way."

She crossed her arms, forcing her breasts to plump up over the edge of the gown. Lord forgive him but he couldn't look away.

"Surely Tony has some sort of conveyance we can use to get home."

"It will take too much time to have them bring the cart around. As it stands now, we shall have just enough time to change for dinner."

"Fine." She grabbed his hand.

He tugged on her arm, but she didn't budge. "You are supposed to help me. Put your foot in the stirrup."

"I've never done this before."

Ian hid his grin at her exasperated tone. Miss Sophia Townsend, who never had a hair out of place, was completely out of her element. He was enjoying this too much. "Move back so I can dismount."

Sophia stepped back on the stones, stumbling as they shifted beneath her. "This is ridiculous."

Tony came down the steps. "Stay there, McDonald. I'll lift her up."

"You'll do no such thing, Tony Matthews!"

Sophia shrieked as Tony lifted her up onto the horse. Ian grabbed her around the waist and pulled her close.

"Put your one leg over the pommel so you won't fall," he instructed gruffly. She smelled wonderful, like flowers and warm skin. She settled stiffly against him, wriggling a bit to get comfortable. Thank God it was a short trip to the Lodge.

Ian urged the horse forward, his arms on either side of Sophia. He forced his eyes forward and away from the view of her perfect breasts in front of him. He should receive a medal for his fortitude.

"Thank you, Mr. McDonald."

"For what?"

"For saving me from the sheep"

"How do those words taste on your tongue, Miss Townsend?"

"Sour."

He chuckled. "You shouldn't have been in the pasture in the first place." He still wanted to shake her for that one stupid act.

"Why can't you just accept my gratitude and leave it at that?"

He ignored the irritation in her voice. "Why did you come that way?"

"I didn't think. I've come that way before. It's the shortcut I always use."

Ian closed his eyes for a moment to avoid temptation. "Have your guests arrived?" he asked.

"They have."

"I'm surprised you left them unattended."

"Did you know that Lord Bateman is anxious to make your acquaintance, Mr. McDonald? I find myself wondering why."

"Many people want to meet me, Miss Townsend."

"That's an arrogant statement."

He whispered into her ear, "It's the truth."

Sophia pulled away from him, but not before he could feel the shiver that went through her. "Did you come here to meet Lord Bateman?"

"The reason for my visit is business. I came to mate my ram to one of Tony's ewes. Anything else is purely coincidence." She did not need to know that he was here to get Bateman to sell him land that abutted his property. He needed more land for his sheep, and it would also allow him to cut a road to shorten the trip to Dumfries. Bateman owned the land and did nothing with it. Rumor had it that Bateman was in dun territory. If so, he'd be more open to selling the property. This could work out to Ian's advantage. "Has his lordship proposed yet?"

She twisted around to glare at him for his tone. All he saw were her breasts.

"No, he has not."

"But you are expecting him to."

"I suppose."

There was a note of uncertainty in her voice that pulled at him. Ian couldn't stop his hand from brushing her hair back. The desire to touch her was overwhelming.

Sophia had little money and Bateman needed to marry a fortune to rescue the estate. Ian had seen them in London together. They made a beautiful couple.

Ian had noticed the marked attention Bateman had paid to Sophia. He'd welcomed her into the pack of friends he had in Town. Ian had called on Sophia several times to find Bateman already there, leaving flowers and gifts. Even he was inclined to think Bateman felt more than a passing attraction to Sophia. However, the rumors were flying about the lack of a proposal. If Bateman chose another woman to marry, Sophia would suffer the shame of being ruined because of his marked attentions.

They rounded the corner to the park of the Lodge and he guided the horse to the stable. "Take the entry at the back of the house, Sophia. You'll avoid your guests that way."

"I'll see you at dinner." She slid from the horse with the help of one of Matthews's grooms, then ran off for the kitchen entrance.

Ian dismounted and handed the reins to the same grooms. He went through the front entrance, removing his gloves and hat and handing them to the waiting footman. His hands still stung from wrestling the ram, but he'd survive.

Lord Bateman stood in the library doorway waiting for him. "I expected you to be here when I arrived."

Ian let the slight go by. Bateman might be used to preferential treatment from others, but he'd not get it from him. "I had business to attend to at the neighboring estate."

"I doubt your business was that important."

Ian moved into the library, ignoring the comment. The man never allowed him to forget who his father was. He poured himself a healthy splash of Nathaniel Matthews's fine brandy and sat down in one of the large leather chairs in the room. Bateman did the same, taking the seat across from him.

"How was your journey?" Ian asked.

"Long, but we are nearly there, perhaps three, maybe four days more." Bateman tossed his drink back and rose to set the glass down by the brandy decanter.

"Have you considered my offer?"

"So, we are to dispense with the niceties, McDonald? Your father would not have approved."

"I am not my father, nor do I work for you."

"The offer was too low."

Ian swirled the brandy in his glass, taking his time to mull over Bateman's comment. If Bateman thought he was like his father, he was in for a rude awakening. He hadn't gotten where he was by serving others. "The offer is fair."

"You know the difficulties we are facing with the estate."

"I'm aware of your financial difficulties, yes. It's rather common knowledge that the family lived beyond its means."

Bateman picked a piece of lint from his coat and returned to the leather chair. He said nothing for a long time. "The earldom has a history of living beyond its means. Unfortunately, it cannot continue."

"Then accept my offer for the land. It lies fallow. You aren't using it."

"I'm not going to give it away."

"Then I look forward to your counteroffer."

"Marry my sister and the land is yours."

Ian choked on his brandy. "Excuse me?"

"Catherine hasn't had any luck finding a husband, not to mention the fact that she doesn't have much of a dowry any longer."

Ian tossed down the rest of the alcohol. He walked over to the decanter. "And you'd marry her to me? The son of a steward? I would not have thought you would allow your sister to marry so far beneath her." He was tempted to refill his glass but resisted. He'd need his wits about him for the rest of this conversation. And there was more to Bateman's tale; he was sure of it.

"You're wealthy and probably the only one who can deal with her," Bateman said carefully. "You were her choice."

What a horrifying thought. "And if I don't marry your sister?"

"I'll sell the land to someone else, probably for a better price."

The glasses rattled on the table as Ian leaned against it, reflecting his nerves. While he needed that land to expand his operations in Scotland, marrying Lady Catherine Grayson did not figure into his plans. She brought the connections Sophia had, but she lacked one thing: He didn't desire her, not like he did Sophia Townsend. "Will it be enough to salvage the earldom?"

Bateman shook his head. "Miss Hamilton is worth twenty thousand pounds. I intend to make her my wife. This trip is to help her decide."

Ian fought to hide his shock. Bateman had certainly found a solution to his problem. "What about Miss Townsend? I noticed your attentions to her in Town recently. It was common knowledge that a proposal was expected."

"She is lovely, but far beneath me socially and not nearly wealthy enough." Bateman stood and tugged down on his waistcoat. "Then there is her age to consider. She is quite on the shelf."

"She's not decrepit. You're here enjoying her hospitality. She's expecting a proposal."

"It isn't as if I had a choice in the matter."

"Then why did you single her out? You know what the gossips will do to her."

"At the time, I had no idea how bad things were. She'll recover."

Ian suspected the more persistent creditors must have caught his attention. "You've pretty much doomed Miss Townsend to spinsterhood."

Bateman glared at him. "It couldn't be helped."

"Sell me the land. You'll instantly have money in your pocket."

"Take Catherine off my hands and you have a deal." Bateman left the room abruptly. Probably just as well; his last comment had Ian's fists curling. The man was damned rude. He tossed people aside as if they were rubbish.

Ian stared at the closed door for a long time. There was no way in hell he'd marry Bateman's sister. She was a shrew. There was no way he would endure that kind of torture for the rest of his life. He'd wait. Bateman would weaken, especially if he needed money that badly. Patience had worked for Ian in the past. Patience would work this time as well.

Sophia sat by the fire, away from the rest of the group. Lady Catherine, Lord Bateman, Captain Smith-Williams, and Miss Hamilton were playing cards. Anne was quietly talking to Nathaniel. Probably about the disaster dinner had been.

It was beyond a disaster; it had been a nightmare. Lady Catherine was either complaining about the food, her room, or the heat. Miss Hamilton, Lord bless her, had tried to smooth things over, but to no avail. Mr. McDonald had sat between Lady Catherine and herself but said little, keeping his own council, ignoring all attempts to draw him out. It was actually quite comical to see the tables turned on him.

Sophia had no intention of drawing him into conversation despite the fact that he stood nearby. He had unfinished business with her and she was in no hurry to continue it. She longed to talk with Lord Bateman, but he had patently discouraged all attempts at conversation. This was a very different man from the one she'd known in London. He was being downright rude to her.

It was fast becoming clear that Bateman was not renewing his attentions to her, but if he wasn't going to propose, why come to Beetham? It was clearly out of the way of his final destination. She glanced at Ian McDonald, standing like a stone nearby. He'd had a permanent frown on this face since dinner. Something was going on between the two men. How did they know each other?

"Miss Townsend, will you not play cards? I would gladly relinquish my seat," Captain Smith-Williams said.

"You're very kind, sir, but no, thank you."

"Do you have something against card games, Miss Townsend?" Lady Catherine pounced. "I don't believe I've ever seen you play."

So it was to be her turn to be the subject of Lady Catherine's ire. "I prefer other pursuits to cards."

Lady Catherine tossed the cards onto the table and rose. "Perhaps some music would be in order."

"Please, feel free to entertain us, Catherine," Lord Bateman said. "My sister is an exceptional musician."

Lady Catherine moved to Mr. McDonald's side, making her interest in him clear. There was fear and a bit of begging in his eyes as he glanced over at Sophia. She smirked but did nothing to rescue him. She was enjoying this a bit too much, considering the glare from Mr. McDonald. And why shouldn't she enjoy it? The earl and his obnoxious sister were here under false pretenses. She'd bet her last pound that Ian McDonald was in the middle of it.

"Mr. McDonald, would you sing with me?" Lady Catherine said in a low voice.

"I've no talent for music, my lady." His voice was soft but firm.

Sophia watched Lady Catherine turn her back with a sniff and make her way to the pianoforte. She began to play. The piece was difficult and Lady Catherine's hands seem to float quickly over the keys. Sophia felt a twinge of envy. She'd never learned to play.

Ian took the seat next to her, filling up all the space on the small settee and leaving her thigh to press against his. She tried to move over to give him more space, but there was nowhere to go.

"I can't believe you are hiding in the corner tonight. Usually you are the life of the party." McDonald's voice was low.

"You should have joined Lady Catherine at the piano. I've heard you sing. You aren't so bad."

He frowned at her. "When have you heard me sing?"

"When we were in London." She smiled. "You and Tony were drunk, I believe. Your voice wasn't half bad."

"That would explain why I don't remember it." He chuckled. She liked his laugh.

"Lady Catherine is very lovely."

"If you like that sort."

Sophia glanced at him through her lashes. "She plays well."

"I'm sure you play just as well."

Sophia laughed. "I don't play. Never had the inclination to learn. My sister is the musician in the family."

"Miss Townsend, will you not join me in entertaining the room tonight?" Lady Catherine said, standing at the piano.

Sophia's heart thumped. "I'm afraid I lack the talent. Perhaps my sister—"

Catherine moved to stand before her with the look of a cat about to capture a mouse. "Come, Miss Townsend, surely you possess some talent."

Sophia gasped at the insult. She felt Ian McDonald tense beside her.

"Sophia, if you wish to sing, I will play for you," Anne said quickly.

"Thank you, Anne, but I'm not inclined to sing tonight. Perhaps another time? There will be ample opportunity, I'm sure, during your visit, Lady Catherine." Sophia was not going to be bullied into performing when she had not practiced in weeks.

Lady Catherine sniffed and strolled back to the card table. Sophia fought the urge to slump in relief. The woman was worse than she was herself, and that was saying something.

"Well done, Miss Townsend," Ian said softly beside her. "Though I'm surprised you aren't playing cards."

"I was not in the mood for cards tonight." She had no desire to watch as Lord Bateman showered his attentions on poor Miss Hamilton. She wasn't jealous but resigned. Miss Hamilton was young, pretty, and, most of all, rich. She might be able to compete with the former, but she couldn't compete with money.

"I imagine you are very disappointed in these developments."

Sophia turned to Mr. McDonald. "What are you trying to say?"

"Only that Bateman seems to be drawn to Miss Hamilton of late."

She lowered her head. "Do you know Miss Hamilton well?"

"This is the first time I've made her acquaintance, but she seems a nice young lady. Rather quiet and proper, though. Do you know her from Town?"

Sophia looked down at her hands. She did know Theodora Hamilton, but she was not proud of her treatment of her. She'd ridiculed her on more than one occasion when in Town. Miss Hamilton was extremely rich but also extremely shy. "I do know of her from Town."

"Did you not like her?"

"I really didn't know her well." Sophia chewed her lip.

"There is something you aren't telling me about this. What did you do to Miss Hamilton?"

"The worst thing was ignoring her, if you must know. I'm not proud of my actions."

Ian snorted. "You admit it?"

She met Ian's warm dark eyes. "I know my own faults and when to be ashamed of them." Sophia looked across the room, where Catherine was berating Miss Hamilton for playing the wrong suite. "I'm afraid she's suffering worse treatment now."

Ian squeezed her hand. "At least you realize your mistake."

"I can see why Lord Bateman likes her. She's very sweet and proper, and she would be rather pretty if she wore the right styles."

"Very kind of you, Sophia," he said with a soft laugh. "But you left out the most important attribute Miss Hamilton possesses: an obscenely large fortune."

"No one can compete with that inducement. Miss Hamilton is still very young."

"Bateman probably prefers that she knows little of his world. Still, she can't be that much younger than you. How old are you?"

"I'm not yet twenty-seven and it's very ungentlemanly of you to bring it up."

"You, of all people, know I'm no gentleman. It will be extremely difficult to compete with Miss Hamilton's youthfulness and gentle beauty."

"And extremely large dowry. I will have to get by as best I can."

"By some standards, you are firmly on the shelf," Ian said. "Past your prime, as most would say."

Warmth flooded her cheeks. "How kind of you to point out the obvious, sir. If I'm on the shelf, what does that make you?"

"It's different for men. We usually do not reach our prime until later."

Sophia snorted. "That's a matter of opinion, sir."

"Don't be crude. I only meant that most men prefer to marry a woman closer to them in age."

"Unfortunately, there is a great deal of evidence to the contrary." Sophia glanced back at the card players. Lord Bateman leaned over to say something to Miss Hamilton. She blushed prettily.

"You do realize Bateman's pockets are to let. He has no choice but to marry a fortune." He glanced at her.

Sophia turned to face him. "I'd heard rumors of such in Town."

She had hoped the rumors weren't true. Given Bateman's attentions, she'd had cause to hope. Now reality was staring her in the face. Spinsterhood loomed over her like a vulture.

"You have other qualities, Sophia. You are vivacious and beautiful." Ian looked at Bateman. "He is a fool for letting you go."

Sophia turned to look at Lord Bateman. "He seems quite taken with Miss Hamilton. Besides, if he is as poor as you say he is, he is making a sensible decision."

"Am I hearing you correctly? You would prefer to marry for money rather than love?"

"Love does not put food on the table."

"I think I like this practical Miss Townsend."

Ian's voice was deep and low, his breath stirring the wisps of hair at the base of her neck. She fought the urge to shiver. "You forget that I've had my share of days when we wondered where our next meal would come from."

"I had forgotten that."

She nodded her head but said nothing. Ian's lips were so very close to her exposed neck. She fought the urge to shiver. "So you see, Mr. McDonald, it is no great loss that Lord Bateman has chosen another lady."

"You would have been bored with him within the week," Ian grumbled.

"That's a terrible thing to say." She stared back at Lord Bateman and noticed him watching her exchange with Mr. McDonald. She smiled at him. He smiled back. Funny that his smile didn't cause the little tingle of awareness Mr. McDonald's did.

"He spends most of his time at his club. I doubt you'd ever see him." Ian got that tick in his jaw.

"Sounds perfect, actually." Sophia would have her society events, balls, charity works, calls, and such. His lordship would be off doing whatever it was earls did during the day; the House of Lords and that nonsense. It sounded too perfect.

"What will you do now?"

"Now that I'm officially an old maid?" She laughed. "What do you know of Mr. Smith-Williams? Do you think he'll have me for my modest dowry?"

"I just met the man tonight. You don't mean to chase him, do you?"

Sophia turned back to watch the card game across the room. Catherine pinned her with a hateful look as she noticed how close Ian was sitting to her. Sophia smiled gently just to watch the woman's frown deepen.

"I've noticed that Lady Catherine watches you a great deal. I think she likes you."

"Lord, I hope not."

"She is a lovely woman."

"Until she opens her mouth."

"Is that fair?" She turned back to Ian. "I think she means to marry you."

Ian snorted. "Not without my cooperation, I'm sure. She is not the sort of woman I prefer."

"Really? What kind of woman would you desire in a wife?"

Ian leaned even closer. She could feel the warmth of his breath against the exposed skin of her neck. "One who shivers in response to my touch."

"Then I would be cautious if I were you. You never know when a lady might misconstrue the attentions of a gentleman."

His soft laugh stirred wisps of hair, causing her to shiver. "I seem to remember you shivering at my touch."

"I was wet and cold, sir."

"You're going to have to admit to liking me sooner or later." His tone rumbled gently in her ear.

"I refuse to discuss this further." Sophia kept her eyes on the card players, resisting the urge to look up into Ian's face. She could not let him see the heat his soft suggestion lit inside her.

"Sophia, you are a passionate woman. You should have a husband who is just as passionate. The last place you want to be bored is in the bedroom."

"Mr. McDonald, this conversation is getting much too personal for my comfort. Kindly put more distance between us, please."

Ian shifted to the other side of the small couch. It wasn't much, but it was better than him literally breathing down her neck.

"I'm just stating the obvious. A woman of a certain age has earned the right to explore her passion."

"What you are suggesting could get me ruined."

"It could if you aren't careful, but what are you saving yourself for?"

"That is positively scandalous. I cannot participate in such a thing." Sophia fought the urge to squirm under his regard.

"I did not take you for a coward."

"I am not a coward." She glanced at Lady Catherine. "Who would I choose to participate in this exploration of passion? You?"

"Of course." He grinned at her.

Sophia felt her heart flip in her chest at his boyish grin. The man was too handsome for his own good. "I don't doubt that you are more of an expert in this area than I."

"I wouldn't go that far."

It was then Mr. McDonald realized how Lady Catherine was glaring at them. Sophia put her mouth close to his ear, fighting the urge to crow as he squirmed. "Even now, as we talk, Lady Catherine Grayson has not taken her eyes off you. She's jealous of me sitting next to you."

"You cannot be serious."

Sophia sat back and smiled. "If Bateman is in dun territory, as you suggest, then she is also quite desperate. You are by far the wealthiest single man in the room."

"Your point, Miss Townsend?"

She had him now. "If you are not careful, you might find yourself in the parson's trap, my friend." She glanced at Catherine. "I can imagine she'll be quite persistent in her pursuit. She certainly was during dinner. She practically dominated the conversation."

"Don't be ridiculous."

"You don't know her as I do. She'll stop at nothing to get what she wants, and she always gets what she wants." Sophia patted his arm. "I'm sure you'll do just fine." She shouldn't take so much pleasure in his discomfort, but she did. It was all she could do to keep a serene look on her face and not give away her glee.

McDonald was quiet for a long moment. Sophia wanted to glance at him, watch his face as he thought through her comments, but she didn't.

"You need to marry. I know you do. If you go back to London for yet another Season at twenty-seven you'll be relegated to ape leader. You won't be able to compete with the younger women flooding the marriage market."

Sophia gasped. The harshness of the words cut her deeply. She hadn't thought Ian would hurt her this way. She strove to keep her voice light. She couldn't let him know how deep his barb had struck. "That is a rather harsh statement."

"I always tell the truth, Sophia. You can count on that."

"The truth is one thing; being cruel is another." She made to rise.

Ian grasped her arm, keeping her in her seat. "I apologize. That comment was uncalled for."

She yanked her arm out of his grasp. "At least we can agree on that." She smoothed invisible wrinkles from her dress. "I recognize that I've probably wasted more than a few opportunities to marry."

"Why is that?"

"I don't know. If you'll excuse me . . ."

"Stay. Please."

There was a tone in his voice that gave her pause. She sat back on the sofa and waited. She'd never revealed so much to another human being and now she felt as if she had walked into the room in her chemise. "Then at least can we change the subject."

"I am going to need your help." The words were low, spat out almost beneath his breath. "With Lady Catherine."

"Am I hearing correctly? You need my help?"

"I deserve that."

She smiled and patted his arm. "You do. I'm going to enjoy this moment." She could practically hear him growling under his breath. There was something quite uncivilized about Ian McDonald. "I have an idea," she said. "I'll protect you from Catherine's aggressive advances, but I want something in return."

"What do you want?" His tone was cautious.

"A boon. Don't worry; I'll let you know what I want when it's time."

"That's not quite fair, now is it?"

She met his gaze. "Do you want help fending off Lady Catherine or not? Because I can tell you right now, you have no chance of avoiding being trapped into wedded bliss without my help."

Ian stared at Lady Catherine for a long moment. "She would put her reputation at risk like that?"

"It depends on how much you're worth."

"That's rather mercenary, isn't it?"

"As women our only way to improve our lives is through marriage to the right gentlemen."

"Fine. I accept.

She studied Ian carefully. There was something else going on here. "You are up to something, sir. What?"

Ian grinned.

What more could he want? "Well, out with it."

"You could always marry me, Sophia. Not because you have to but because you want to."

Sophia fought to keep her countenance. "Marry you? A sheep farmer? A man who lives somewhere in the wilds of Scotland? I think not." She'd shrivel up inside living without Society. She'd rather be poor in London than wealthy in the back country of Scotland.

"I'd make sure you didn't care where we lived or how much money we had." There was that voice again. How did Ian manage to change his voice so that it played along her nerves as fingers on a harp?

"Impossible. You hate Town and you know how much I thrive in London. It would never work. We'd drive each other mad before the banns were read." She forced her voice to be practical.

He took her wrist in his hand, his thumb on her pulse. "While your mind may object, your body tells a different story. Even now your pulse is racing by my just being close."

"You go too far."

"Prove to me that you can resist this passion between us. Prove to me that you can marry someone whose touch you can barely tolerate."

Sophia stood. "I've had enough of this conversation. Good night, sir."

She had moved across the room to say her good nights to her sister when Lord Bateman stepped into her path. There was no way to avoid him, though she desperately wanted to.

"Miss Townsend, allow me to apologize for my marked attention to you in London. I had no idea you thought we had an understanding."

Sophia stiffened her spine as her heart sank. Having Ian tell her the truth was one thing; hearing it from Lord Bateman was another. "I, uh, had not thought—"

"Come on, old girl; we did have some fun."

Old girl? Did he seriously think of her as old? The next thing he'd probably do was slap her on the back like one of the men in his club. She struggled for the right words. What was wrong with her? She was always quick with a witty remark. "We did, indeed, sir. In fact, I cannot imagine how I might have misconstrued your attentions. The gifts, the flowers, the dances at every event; I was quite taken aback by the fun, as you called it."

"Miss Townsend—"

"Take care, sir, that you do not lead another young lady to misconstrue your attentions in such a manner. She might not be as understanding as I. If you will excuse me . . ."

Sophia brushed past him while making her way out of the room. She could feel the eyes of everyone on her back as she stepped into the hall. *I wish they'd never come.*

Chapter 6

Sophia could not sleep. The room was warm despite her leaving the window open to catch the breeze. Her mind wouldn't settle. Her brain played Ian McDonald's words from just a few hours earlier over and over again. He spoke of passion, something she avoided whenever possible. Passion only got a woman ruined, especially when it ruled both head and heart. The problem was this insane attraction to him. He represented everything she didn't want—an endless country lifestyle—yet she was drawn to him.

Sophia rose from her bed and pulled on a robe. She stepped into her slippers. She needed a really boring book to lull her to sleep. She stepped out of her room and into the hallway.

It must be past midnight. The house was finally quiet. Sophia tiptoed down the stairs without a candle, feeling her way in the dark. She stepped into the library and found a candle. She lit it and made her way to the shelves. Tonight called for something seriously boring, perhaps something on agriculture. She pulled out a book, thumbed through it, and put it back. She'd spend most of her time trying to understand the Latin words for plants. Definitely not for her. She moved down the stack and pulled out another dusty volume. The maids really needed to clean in here.

Sophia set the candle on the ledge of the shelf and opened a book. She glanced at the title page and giggled. *Travels of Scotland*: a suitably boring topic. She snapped the book shut and clutched it to her chest. She lifted the candle and made her way to the door just as Ian McDonald stepped inside.

"What are you doing here?"

"Sssh, she might hear you." He looked terrified.

"Who might hear me?"

"Catherine."

"She's long since sought her bed, Mr. McDonald. There is no reason to fear."

He shook his head. "I caught her going into my bedroom as I went to my room."

Sophia frowned. She didn't recall seeing anyone in the hallway, but then, the men were on the other side of the house. "Why were you up so very late?"

"Nathaniel and I were discussing our breeding experiment." Ian moved into the room. "Why are you in here?"

"I couldn't sleep and thought I'd read."

He moved closer to her, taking the candle from her hand and setting it on a nearby table. "What are you reading?"

Sophia clutched the book closer to her. "Nothing really. Just one of Nathaniel's books."

Ian chuckled. "Give me the book, Sophia. Please."

She clutched the book closer. If he saw the title, he might get the wrong idea. "It's just something really boring. I fully expect to be asleep before I get through page ten."

"Then you won't mind if I take a look?" He pulled the book from her hands. "*Travels of Scotland by a Unique Route.* I didn't realize you were interested in Scotland."

Sophia smiled. "I'm not. I imagined that a book about Scotland would be as dull as the countryside itself."

Ian flipped through the pages and moved farther into the library. "There's a wildness to Scotland you might find you like."

Sophia followed him. "May I have my book back, please?"

"I think you should stay here with me in case she comes looking for a book to read." Ian settled into a nearby chair. He flipped the book back open and began to read.

"It would not be good for anyone to find us alone here this late at night, Mr. McDonald."

"That would keep Catherine from her pursuit of me. Isn't that what we agreed to?"

"Not if it means risking my own reputation." She was not going to stay here and keep him company. It was late. It wasn't proper. She would just make do without a book. "Good night, Mr. McDonald."

Ian moved quickly to stop her. "Don't leave. Not yet." He stepped between her and the closed door.

There was a tone in his voice that tugged at her. Her emotions warred. She was really starting to like Ian McDonald. "I really must. It's late."

He gently brushed a strand of hair from her face. Sophia shivered and stepped back from him. She needed distance. His scent, his presence were filling her senses with mad ideas like kissing him again. She couldn't allow it to happen, yet she craved it. This had never happened to her before. "Don't."

He stepped closer. "You're trembling."

"I'm cold."

"Are you sure?"

"Mr. McDonald—"

"Ian. My name is Ian. Say it, Sophia."

"Ian."

He brushed her lips with his thumb. She couldn't control her response to his touch, but instead of crowing his success, he moved closer.

Sophia should have stepped back away from him, especially after the lecture she'd given herself just a few minutes before. Ian didn't hold her; he'd let her go if she really wanted him to. The closer he got to her, the more his scent made her senses swim. He radiated heat.

His nearness had never lured her like a moth to a flame before now, and she was tempting fate enough to be singed, but she didn't have the strength to walk away from him.

The buttons of his waistcoat brushed against her breasts, reminding her of how little she wore—just a robe over a thin nightgown. He lifted her chin and brushed his mouth against hers, so very softly that she couldn't stop the sigh that slipped from her. Never had a kiss stirred such feelings within her.

His lips were soft, warm, and oh so very tempting. Sophia had been kissed before. Frankly, she'd been kissed a great deal more than her older sister Anne realized. She'd become a rather good judge of men's kisses. Ian McDonald put the others to shame. His was neither too wet nor rough. His mouth was mobile but not too soft. This kiss was a pure temptation to sin.

Ian lifted his mouth from hers. Sophia slowly raised her eyes to his, her thoughts dazed, her mouth parted. His eyes were heated. His hands circled her waist and pulled her into his firm body.

Warmth surrounded her and seeped through the thin layers of her gown and robe. Her breasts tightened as they brushed against his waistcoat.

Oh my.

Her hips cradled his hardness through the thin layers. Her pulse raced; her breathing grew shallow. He had to kiss her again. She craved his mouth on hers, craved more of his taste, this passion bubbling through her like champagne, sweet and intoxicating.

Ian's mouth met hers in teasing little nibbles. Her hands found their way to his jacket and gripped the lapels. He wouldn't take the kiss deeper. She groaned against his mouth, all but begging him to take it deeper, take her deeper. She touched her tongue to his bottom lip.

That touch urged him into action. His mouth crushed hers, his tongue tasting, teasing, torturing her mouth. Sophia melted against him, like warm chocolate as his warmth embraced her.

Nothing had ever felt this good, this mesmerizing, this addictive. She didn't want him to stop. He could keep kissing her until she was a puddle at his feet. Who knew sheep farmers possessed such an incredible talent?

His hands moved over her body, leaving feverish trails as he learned her curves. His fingers brushed the undersides of her breasts, teasingly before smoothing the silky fabric over her hips.

Sophia wrapped her arms around Ian's neck. Her hands found the softness of the curls at the base of his neck, the crisp fabric of his cravat. She pushed her body up and into his, seeking more of his warm, hard body. She instinctively moved her hips back and forth against him.

Ian's hands grabbed her hips to still her. Slowly, he eased her down, his mouth gentling hers.

She eased down from her tiptoes and raised heavy-lidded eyes to his. She felt as if she'd run a great distance, her breath coming in shallow gasps. Still lost in the fog of desire, she said nothing, just stared up at this very surprising man.

He brushed a thumb tenderly across her cheek. "Sophia, sweetheart, you need to go upstairs before this goes much farther."

His words of warning were like ice water, waking her from this dream state in which she'd been. Sophia stepped back and glared at him. She didn't know if she was angry because he'd stopped or because she hadn't wanted him to stop.

"Don't be angry with me. You were an active participant." His voice was low, gravelly, as if he needed to clear his throat. He ran his hands through his hair, then picked up the book and handed it to her. He turned her toward the door and pushed her. "Good night."

Sophia took the book and clutched it against her as if it were a shield. She couldn't find her voice, her thoughts still tangled in the passion they'd shared.

She stepped out into the dark hallway, her brain still wrapped in the fog of passion. Heavens.

"I see we have the same idea, Miss Townsend."

Catherine Grayson came down the stairs in a diaphanous robe and gown that floated around her. Her golden hair was brushed and fell over her shoulders.

Sophia could feel the heat rise in her cheeks and was thankful it was dark. The last thing she needed was for Catherine to know what Ian and she had been doing in the library. "Yes. Are you having trouble sleeping as well?

"I always do in a new place. What are you reading?"

Sophia had to look down at the title. She'd completely forgotten about the book. "A book on travel. It's quite dull, actually. Would you like it?"

Sophia hoped she would take the book and leave Ian alone for the night. She must have supposed if he weren't in his room, he'd be reading in the library.

"Thank you, no. I think I'd prefer a novel tonight."

Sophia stepped out of the way to allow Catherine to open the library door. There was no way to warn Ian. Perhaps it was a fitting revenge for the way he'd stirred her emotions.

"Sophia?" His tone was full of questioning hope.

Sophia couldn't see his face, but Catherine could. The woman narrowed her eyes as she looked between Ian and Sophia.

"My, so many of us are having trouble sleeping. Perhaps you should mention to the cook that the food is keeping us all awake." Catherine's voice was pure ice.

Sophia said nothing as she watched the door close, leaving Ian alone with Lady Catherine. A sharp pain twisted in her chest. She didn't like this feeling. She hurried back to her room. Once she was inside, she turned the lock. She didn't want to tempt fate any more tonight.

* * *

Ian turned as Catherine Grayson closed the library door and clicked the lock. He'd never seen a woman stalk a man like this, and he'd seen some very unusual things in London. "Is it necessary to lock the door, Catherine?"

"I think so." She moved toward him into the room. "With so many others having trouble sleeping, I wouldn't want us to be interrupted."

Ian said nothing, just watched her, waiting for her to make her move. She made him uncomfortable in a way he'd never been before. Usually he wasn't the target of women of the Ton. While he was wealthy enough, he had his hands in too much trade to be husband material on the marriage mart. That position had offered him some protection.

He longed to tug at his cravat, edge around the settee to avoid her, and make his way out. He was fairly sure he could beat Catherine to the door, but it would only delay the inevitable conversation. He might as well get it over with now, then focus on what he'd come here to do.

"What were you and Miss Townsend doing in here alone at this hour?" Her movements were catlike as she traced her finger on the stitching of one of the leather chairs.

"I came down for a brandy and a book for the night. Miss Townsend was also seeking a book."

"You two were very chummy tonight in the parlor, but then she left early. Did you argue?"

"We always argue. I don't think she likes me very much."

"Good." Catherine smiled sweetly.

She really was a beautiful woman, he thought dispassionately, just not his type.

"I think you're mistaken, Catherine."

"Ian, what can you mean? I just want us to become reacquainted."

He looked down at her robe. "Do you always dress like that to become reacquainted with men?"

She at least blushed at that. "Fine. I'll be blunt."

"That would be preferable."

"I think we should marry," Catherine said, crossing her arms in front of her. "You are wealthy; we are not. An influx of funds would save the earldom and help us bring the estates up to par."

"Surely you could marry someone more suitable for that purpose. You are popular, pretty, and well connected."

"Rumors of the estate being in dun territory have flooded Town. My dowry is gone and the debts are so large that no man would take them on."

There was a note of defeat that pulled at his sympathy. She had not asked for this mess, yet she'd been tasked with repairing it. "So that leaves me, the son of your former steward. I'm flattered." He almost felt sorry for her. "Catherine, you don't have to do this. Marry who you want and let Bateman deal with the debts."

"I'll not abandon the family. My brother will marry Miss Hamilton, but while she is wealthy, it isn't enough. I have to do this."

Ian couldn't argue with her. She'd been spoon-fed the vitriol of their positions since she was a baby. "I'll not marry you, Catherine. Now, if you will excuse me, I will retire to my room."

"I could come with you."

"You don't want to do that."

"I do." She moved forward and wrapped her arms around his neck, pressing herself against him. "I really do."

"I don't." He pulled her arms from around his neck and gently set her away from him. "Go to bed, Catherine, and we'll forget this ever happened. Find someone to marry who cares about you. Let your brother solve his own problems."

Her eyes welled with tears. "I can't. His problems are my problems. We can no longer afford the town house in London. I won't be going back for another Season. I'll be stuck in the backwoods forever."

He'd never realized how dramatic Catherine could be. He didn't like it, which was surprising, given how dramatic Sophia was. It was different somehow.

Yet it was late and he'd had enough of female theatrics. "Good night, ma'am." He bowed and moved to the door. He unlocked it, the click of the lock sounding loud in the room.

"I'm not giving up on this, Ian McDonald," she said in a confident voice. "We will marry."

He turned back to her. "Not without my consent."

She smiled coldly. "There are ways."

The comment gave Ian pause. She was a great deal smarter than her brother. Could she really manipulate a wedding between the two of them? He hoped not. It would ruin his own plans.

He stepped out of the library. "Don't forget to put out the candle before you leave."

"You just wait, Ian McDonald. You just wait."

Her words haunted him as he made his way to his room. He locked the door behind him, resisting the urge to put a chair under the knob. He almost laughed at himself. Catherine Grayson was a tiny thing, and here he was terrified that she was going to do something that would force a marriage between them.

He'd have to resolve this with Bateman in the morning. The man was going to have to control his sister before she did something really foolish.

Chapter 7

Sophia reluctantly opened her eyes the next morning. She glanced at the mantel clock and groaned. It was only seven o'clock. She plopped back into the bed. She'd barely been asleep for three hours. Her eyes felt gritty. Oh, how she wanted to just roll over and sleep a bit longer, but no, she was wide awake now.

Damn Ian McDonald! His kisses had haunted her all night. That and the thought of him doing the same with Catherine Grayson. Lady Catherine definitely had plans for Ian, and Sophia could not understand why she cared so much.

The man irritated her to no end. He'd taken great pleasure in the past in tormenting her either with his inane comments about her behavior or his constant flirting. In fact, nothing had changed until the other day.

The day she'd made that stupid wish on the Fairy Steps.

Why did she have to let Ian McDonald get the best of her? That stupid taunt was going to ruin her life if she let it.

She knew Ian did not believe, but she wasn't so sure. The evidence was pretty convincing. First there was this uncontrollable attraction to him. If he was in the room, she was drawn to him. Then Lord Bateman arrived with an almost fiancée. He was supposed to marry her. Even the episode in the pasture seemed to give Ian the upper hand. Who knew he was hero material?

Sophia sat straight up in bed. "Oh dear God." She threw the covers off and began pacing. "No, oh, please, no." It was all adding up.

Stopping in the middle of the room, she covered her face with her hands. The attraction, the kissing, all of it was the result of the wish. She'd not just ruined her chances but Ian's as well. They were doomed to be together forever.

Sophia resumed her manic pacing. There had to be a way to undo this. Surely Anne, her sister, would know. She'd have to confess and ask her. Sophia couldn't be stuck in the countryside of Scotland forever. She didn't care how well Ian McDonald curled her toes in passion. It was not going to happen.

If she couldn't resist Ian's advances, wish or no wish, she'd end up his wife. The man was too honorable. She couldn't allow herself to give in to the temptation that was Ian McDonald.

But were the backwoods of the Lake District any worse than the backwoods of Scotland? She would still be stuck with the same problem: a spinster in the middle of the damn country and bored to tears.

Sophia stood and rang for her maid. There was no sleeping now. If she were lucky, she'd have a few moments with Anne to discuss the wish situation. Her father had always wanted them to work problems from both ends to arrive at a resolution.

The maid arrived quickly. "You're up early, miss."

"Is my sister awake?"

"Not yet, ma'am. The only other person up and about is Mr. McDonald."

Of course he'd be an early riser; he was a blasted farmer. "Is he in the breakfast room?"

"Yes, miss."

"Help me dress. I'll have the light green day dress with the ivory fichu." She'd rather start with Anne, but things weren't working out that way, so she'd improvise. It was time to put Mr. McDonald in his place.

Her maid dressed her hair simply and within fifteen minutes, a record for her, she was making her way downstairs to the breakfast room. There he sat, alone, with his breakfast and his newspaper. Sophia sighed. He was fiercely handsome with his wild, dark hair and blue eyes. Just looking at him made her heart thump in ways neither Lord Bateman nor any other man had ever stirred. Her reaction to his touch put impossible thoughts in her head. She stiffened her spine. She would be strong. She was a Townsend. She could do this.

Ian sipped his coffee and read through the latest copy of *The Scotsman* he'd brought with him. The house was quiet and with any luck it would remain that way. He'd like to be out and about before Lady Catherine and Sophia were up. He didn't need a repeat of last night. He had trouble dealing with one woman, Sophia. He didn't need another to add to his misery.

Not that he wouldn't enjoy spending more time with Sophia. Her passionate response had fueled his dreams. He wanted more of her. Needed more of her.

Catherine, on the other hand, scared the hell out of him. What possessed the woman to be so straightforward? He'd definitely have to talk to Bateman about her behavior. She was also wily enough to trick him into a compromising position. He was going to have to convince Sophia to keep him from being alone with Catherine. The woman was positively ruthless.

Not that he could blame her or any other woman for feeling desperate. Women didn't have the flexibility men did when it came to earning a living. They either became governesses, companions, or married their future. It was the way of the world, though completely unfair.

He didn't want to be a part of Catherine's plans. He wanted Sophia.

"Good morning, Mr. McDonald," Sophia said.

Ian got to his feet as the object of his thoughts breezed into the room. "Good morning to you as well." The green dress made her skin glow. Her dark brown hair was simply dressed. She'd been in a hurry this morning.

"I was hoping to catch you before you went out and did something farm-related." She took the seat to his right.

"Would you like tea or coffee?" he asked.

"Tea, please."

Ian eyed her smile with apprehension. She was definitely up to mischief. He motioned the footman to fetch a fresh pot of tea for Sophia. She looked tired, as if she'd not slept well, and he was pleased inwardly. He wasn't the only one who'd lost sleep last night. "You are up early. Don't tell me the book on Scotland kept you awake."

"It was fascinating reading."

She eyed his toast and he pushed his plate toward her. He wasn't much for breakfast anyway. He waited until she'd bitten into the toast before saying, "I take that to mean you spent a good deal of the night considering our conversation."

She nodded, chewing quickly, then swallowing. She had a crumb in the corner of her mouth and he couldn't stop staring at it. She licked her lips.

Ian cleared his throat.

"Yes, a great deal of thought, but I have a question for you first."

The footman came with a fresh pot of tea, a few cups, and cream. "Just set it on the table. We won't need anything further," Ian said to the footman. He waited until the man had left the room. "You were saying you had a question."

Sophia poured herself a cup of tea, adding milk and sugar. A good deal of sugar, Ian noticed. She stirred and sipped, then sighed, her eyes closed. There was a look of pure pleasure on her face.

"Sophia?"

She held up a hand. "Tea first."

"I take it you don't care for early mornings," he said gently. Truly, he'd never seen Sophia awake and dressed before midmorning.

"I hate mornings." She sipped more tea, clutching the cup between her slim hands.

"Are you able to ask your question now?"

She set the teacup down and nibbled a piece of toast. "Where was I?"

This was a side of Sophia Townsend he'd never seen before. Usually she was haughty, with a sharp tongue. This morning she still had the sharp tongue, but she was softer, more honest. "You had a question for me."

"The other day at the Fairy Steps, before the storm hit. Do you remember the air feeling strange? Cold?"

It was an odd question. "A storm was blowing in. The air usually cools prior to one."

"So you don't remember anything strange happening?" Sophia picked up another piece of toast.

Ian thought back to that day. "Not really."

"Do you remember making a wish?"

"I remember you wishing for something. What is the point you're trying to make, Sophia?"

She said nothing for a long moment. "It's of no matter."

Given the disappointed expression on her face, it was more than a little matter. Ian couldn't rid himself of the feeling that there was something else going on in her head. "Are you sure?"

She looked up at him and blurted out, "I'm not going to be able to help you fend off Lady Catherine's attentions."

Ian struggled for a moment at the change of subject. This was the last thing he'd expected. "Am I allowed to know the reason why you won't?"

"After what happened in the library, I do not think it would be wise for us to spend so much time together."

She was afraid and it was his own fault. He'd pushed her into things she wasn't ready for. "If I promise not to kiss you again, will you help?"

Sophia nibbled more toast and watched him for a long moment. "Do you think you could keep that promise?"

His brain screamed *hell no*, but he said, "I can control my baser instincts if you can." He picked up his coffee and drained it. "I need your help. Catherine is determined to marry me."

"If she loves you—"

"Love has nothing to do with it." The words came out harsh and blunt. "She isn't above tricking me if necessary."

"That's absurd. What woman would do that?"

"A desperate one."

"So the rumors about their finances are true, then."

"I'm afraid so. Catherine is facing the same fate as you. Stuck in the country with no dowry and no hope."

"Thank you for putting that fine point on the subject." Sophia made a face at him but then grew serious. "If Lord Bateman marries Miss Hamilton, won't that solve Lady Catherine's problem?"

Ian debated telling Sophia the whole of it. It really wasn't his secret to tell, but Sophia was involved to some degree. "Bateman's situation is much worse than most know. Miss Hamilton's dowry will cover only a portion of the debt."

Sophia propped her chin on her hand. "I almost feel sorry for Catherine. Her life is going to change in so many ways, none of which are very pleasant. Don't look so surprised, Ian McDonald. I am capable of sympathy when the need arises."

"If you say so, though I've seen no evidence of it."

"You are impossible."

"It's nice of you to sympathize with Lady Catherine, but what about me? Will you help me hold her at arm's length?"

Sophia poured another cup of tea and dumped in more sugar and a splash of milk. "Do you like tea or just sweet?" he asked.

"I like both at the same time, if you must know." She sipped and wrinkled her nose before setting the cup down. "What do you propose we do to protect you from Lady Catherine?"

"We could become engaged."

"Out of the question. No one would believe it."

"Of course they would."

"I don't know how you ever succeed at anything; you obviously do not understand strategy. No one will believe we are engaged because you are a sheep farmer. Everyone knows I had planned to marry—"

"Someone with a title. You could pretend to be in love with me." She shook her head.

"Then what do you suggest?" He couldn't keep the sharpness from his tone. He was losing patience with Sophia's snobbery.

"We'll have to work up to the engagement. For now, I think you should court me. Flowers, chocolates, and love notes."

Ian pushed away his plate. "I'm not writing any love notes."

"Can't you write?" Her voice was all innocence.

"That sharp tongue is going to get you into trouble one day, Miss Townsend."

"Well, then, no love notes." She smiled at him. "If you are courting me, you'll have little time for Lady Catherine."

It wasn't a bad plan. "What about Lord Bateman?"

She waved a hand. "He's made his decision. There's nothing I can do about it."

Ian studied her for a long moment. He wished he could tell what was going on in that brain of hers. She was cunning for sure, but there had to be something more behind this. "What do you get out of this?"

She smiled serenely. He felt his gut tighten, but he thought it was more from fear than lust.

"I get the pleasure of thwarting Lady Catherine. She is not going to like this one bit."

"There is one other consideration before I agree to this plan of yours. Your family."

Sophia suddenly became very interested in the pattern on the china in front of her. "This has nothing to with them."

"Matthews is going to assume all this courting will lead to an engagement. I have business dealings with him and Tony. I don't want this to get in the way of those."

She rolled her eyes at him. "Really, Mr. McDonald, let me deal with Nathaniel and Tony. Things will be fine. We won't let the situation go that far. Besides, I have a history of being fickle. You'll be safe; don't worry."

There was something in her tone that gave him pause. "You could always just marry me, Sophia."

She raised her eyes to his, shocked. "No. Thank you."

"Why not? If last night was any indication, we should be quite compatible."

She blushed, her cheeks fiery. "A gentleman wouldn't bring that up. But now that you have, we shall have to prevent incidents like that from happening again."

He was a glutton for punishment regarding this woman, but he had to know. "What would be so wrong with being married to me? Is it that I lack a title?"

"It's more that you live so far away from any sort of civilization, honestly." She grimaced. "Talk about a fate worse than death."

A sharp pain at her retort shot through him. "Thank you."

She had the grace to look chagrined. "You know I didn't mean it like that."

"What did you mean, Sophia? Honestly, I really want to know."

She said nothing at first. She fiddled with her cup of tea and sighed heavily. "I apologize if my remark hurt your feelings."

"Apology accepted, but you didn't answer the question. Am I some mongrel to be avoided by the ladies of the Ton?"

Sophia's eyes met his and hers widened. "I—uh—I mean, you are a fine gentleman, sir, but uh—"

He leaned close enough to her to smell the floral scent of the soap she used and lowered his voice. "I could make you want to marry me."

She laughed nervously. "You could try, but you wouldn't succeed."

"Such confidence. Which is surprising, given your response to me last night in the library. Shall we make a wager on it?"

She had the grace to look wary. "What did you have in mind?"

"Instead of pretending to court you, I will do it for real. I wager I can make you want to marry me."

"This is a joke, isn't it?"

Ian shook his head. "No joke."

She narrowed her eyes. "So you think I can be manipulated into marriage through passion?" She laughed. "You, sir, are going to lose this wager."

Ian smiled. "Here are the terms: If I succeed in getting you into my bed, I win and we marry."

"You have a fairly high opinion of your skills, sir."

"I've not had too many complaints thus far."

Her blush deepened. "And if I win?"

"I'll leave you alone. I'll be out of your life entirely." It heartened him a bit to see the surprised look on her face. Would she be sad to have him out of her life? He hoped so; in fact, the wager depended on her feelings being more engaged.

"What about your business dealings with Nathaniel and Tony?" Her voice was hesitant.

"I can deal with them without spending time with you. I shall be more at my estate for the next few years while I develop this new breed. There is always the post, Sophia. So do you agree to the wager?"

"I suppose I must. It would be inhuman to allow Lady Catherine to be saddled with you for the rest of her days." Sophia reached for the last piece of toast.

Ian fought to keep the pain of her comment from showing. He'd learned that Sophia Townsend threw verbal knives at the targets that mattered most. He'd take consolation in that knowledge. He pointed to his plate. "You've eaten my breakfast. I'll gladly ask for more if you're hungry."

She delicately dabbed at her mouth. "I always eat when I'm nervous."

Ian fought the urge to smile. This was the woman he always sensed beneath all her bravado and sarcasm. "I make you nervous?"

"That is not what I said."

Ian drained his coffee and stood.

"Where are you going?"

He came around the table to her. "I'm going riding before the rest of the party wake up and spoil the day for me."

She frowned at him. "You don't like my guests?"

"Not particularly." He smiled at her. "If you'd like to ride with me, I'll gladly have someone saddle your horse."

He could tell she was seriously considering it, but then she shook her head. "Thank you but no. I must come up with activities for today."

"Suit yourself." He bent down and kissed her mouth quickly. "I'll see you later, then?"

"What?"

He chuckled. "You have dark circles under your eyes. Why don't you sneak back upstairs for a nap before the rest of the house wakes? You look exhausted." He kissed her mouth again and left her sitting at the table staring after him.

Ian's kiss still lingered on her lips several hours and a nap later. Sophia made her way back downstairs, still feeling as if her head was in a fog. She was beginning to regret her decision to take Ian up on his wager. The wish would make keeping him at arm's length hard enough. Add to that the time they needed to spend together to thwart Lady Catherine and Sophia knew she was in trouble. He was like chocolate to her at this moment, decadent and irresistible.

Things would have been so much easier if she had held her tongue and wished for marriage to Bateman. Unfortunately, marrying him now would mean living in reduced circumstances. While he might go to Town for the House of Lords, his wife might have to stay behind because of the cost. Truly a fate worse than death.

Sophia entered the drawing room to find Miss Hamilton staring out the window.

"Good morning, Miss Hamilton."

Theodora Hamilton turned to look at her. Her face was blotchy. Sophia wasn't sure she was capable of dealing with an emotional Miss Hamilton without additional tea. Sophia moved to her side. "Are you unwell? Shall I ring for a maid?

"I'm fine," she said, pulling at her handkerchief. "It's Crispin. Captain Smith-Williams."

Sophia felt her heart rate pick up. Could there be trouble in Bateman's paradise? "Captain Smith-Williams?"

"I shouldn't say anything," Miss Hamilton said quietly.

Sophia took the girl's hand and led her to the couch. "Come and sit with me. You'll feel better when you tell someone."

"My father and Lord Bateman have come to an understanding. I'm to marry Lord Bateman."

Sophia felt her heart sink. "Has Lord Bateman proposed?"

Theodora shook her head. "We barely know each other. That's the reason I am on this trip to Carlisle—to give us a chance to get to know each other."

Sophia fought back a twinge of guilt at the chance to manipulate Miss Hamilton and win the challenge. "He is a very nice man."

"He is, and that is what makes this so difficult."

"What?"

"I love Crispin," Theodora said. "I have for a long time."

"Surely your parents will want you to marry where you love."

"We are in trade, Miss Townsend. It is my father's greatest wish to have a peer in the family." Theodora dabbed her eyes. "To make matters worse, Crispin and I have argued. He wants to elope before we reach Carlisle"

"Why don't you?" Sophia couldn't stop the words from leaving her mouth. Encouraging Miss Hamilton suited her perfectly.

"Papa will cut off my funds if we do. He doesn't approve of Crispin."

"The captain appears to be quite gentlemanlike. What does your father have against him?"

"He's not titled. He is the third son of a baron. Father sees the Ton accepting us if I marry high enough." She sniffed again. "Papa also thinks Crispin is only interested in me because of my dowry."

Miss Hamilton's father was a wise man. Such a large dowry was a huge inducement. Sophia patted Miss Hamilton's hand, suppressing the inner urge to crow. "It will all work out."

"How? How am I to make everyone happy?" She wiped her eyes with a handkerchief. "I must do my duty to my family."

Sophia wanted to tell her to please herself, but the reality of the situation was that without money, the couple didn't stand a chance of survival. It would be a hard life of dealing with the ruination that an elopement would cause. Theodora was pretty and rich, but her parents being in trade was a strike against her. Sophia experienced an unusual feeling of compassion for Miss Hamilton. "I don't know what to tell you, Miss Hamilton. I do know that whatever decision you make should be for your own happiness."

"Catherine told me that there were rumors that Lord Bateman was going to propose to you."

"He paid a great deal of attention to me when I was lately in London, but there will be no proposal. He has made that perfectly clear. You have captured his heart."

"I doubt that, Miss Townsend. Do you love him?"

There was the question of the hour. She wasn't sure what she felt for Lord Bateman. "I liked him well enough, I suppose."

Miss Hamilton clasped her hand and Sophia felt odd at being comforted. "But you really should love him if you are to marry him."

"It's different for me."

Why had she said that? Why had she even thought it? The last thing Sophia wanted to do was bare her soul to a young woman she barely knew. She searched for the words to cover up her gaff.

"There you are, Theo. I've been looking everywhere for you." Catherine came into the room. She was dressed in a light yellow muslin suitable for the heat. Her hair was perfectly arranged.

Sophia and Miss Hamilton rose from their seats. Sophia felt as if she'd escaped the gallows. There would be no unburdening of her soul to anyone. "Good morning. I trust you slept well?"

"Yes, finally. The room was so very warm last night. I could hardly tolerate it. I had thought we'd have relief from the summer warmth this far north."

Sophia exchanged a look with Miss Hamilton. "The weather has been unusually warm of late."

"I assume by your dress that we have nothing planned today? It's just as well. It is very hot."

Sophia smoothed her hands down the front of her day dress, which was wrinkled from her nap. Why had she not thought to change? "I thought an outing later in the day would be more comfortable for everyone. The woods around the Lodge are lovely. Perhaps a stroll?"

"I cannot stay cooped up in this house all day." Catherine turned to Miss Hamilton. "Theo, dearest, have you been crying?" She took the girl's hands and glared at Sophia. "Have you said something to make Miss Hamilton cry?"

Sophia stepped back from the venom in the young lady's voice. "I have not."

Miss Hamilton looked up at Sophia like a frightened kitten. "Miss Townsend and I were just discussing a book she'd read that she found hysterically funny. They are tears of laughter."

"I didn't hear any laughter."

Sophia smiled sweetly. "We were just changing topics when you came in, weren't we, Miss Hamilton?"

Miss Hamilton gave a quick nod. The girl was positively cowed by Catherine.

Catherine dismissed Sophia with a wave of her hand. "It's of little matter. I thought we'd walk the gardens this morning, Theo."

"Is Lord Bateman joining you?" Sophia asked.

"No, he's not. There was some agricultural thing going on. My brother and Mr. McDonald traveled to a nearby estate."

"They must be at Horneswood. My sister lives there."

"Come, we shall walk outside, Theo. Miss Townsend, will you be joining us?"

"I'm sorry, but no. Enjoy your walk." She probably should go to protect Miss Hamilton, but the girl would have to learn to fend for herself once she married the earl.

Lady Catherine paused and turned back to Sophia. "Miss Townsend, what is Mr. McDonald to you?"

The question took her by surprise. "I don't know what you mean."

"He seems to spend a great deal of time in your company. Do you have an understanding?"

Sophia hesitated. She'd agreed to help Ian in fending off Lady Catherine and here was a perfect opportunity. "There is no understanding as yet."

"Do you think he will propose?"

If Sophia was honest, he'd done so at least twice in the last two days, but those didn't count. She really wasn't sure if he was mentioning the word for real or teasing. "I think he might."

Lady Catherine's lips pinched together as she snapped her mouth closed over her words. She practically dragged Miss Hamilton to the front door and outside to take the air. Why did Lord Bateman come to Beetham if not to propose to her? Why stop at all?

Beetham was not directly on the route to Carlisle for them, so this was a special trip. Lord Bateman was practically engaged to Miss Hamilton, yet he had called here. None of this made any sense.

More interesting was the fact that Theodora Hamilton was in love with her captain, yet set to marry into an earldom. Sophia couldn't believe she'd choose to marry for love rather than for the title and all it entailed.

If she could urge Miss Hamilton to follow her heart, would that leave the door open for Bateman to propose to her? He would probably find another heiress to take Miss Hamilton's place. Men thought women interchangeable. Honestly, Sophia wasn't sure she wanted to bother with Lord Bateman at this point. The man was beyond fickle.

Still, it wouldn't hurt to help Miss Hamilton and her captain find happiness either. Perhaps Lord Bateman would have a change of heart, given how much fun they'd had together in London. Sophia knew she should be crowing at this new development, but she couldn't. Lady Catherine's comments about Ian tugged at her. She didn't like that the woman was so predatory toward him, as if he were one of his own prize sheep.

Chapter 8

Ian forced himself to smile, even though Catherine was plastered to his side. He could barely lift his fork without his arm rubbing against hers. It was not pleasant.

Nor was the smirk that seemed to remain on Sophia's face as she sat across from him. When she wasn't smirking at him, she was in deep conversation with Captain Smith-Williams.

Why did Sophia have to have the talent of making every man in the room want her? Jealousy was a bitter taste in his mouth. He didn't like feeling like this. Not one bit.

"Tell me, Mr. McDonald, what did you and the other gentlemen do today?" Lady Catherine asked. "It must have been important to have you gone all day."

Lord Bateman paused in his conversation with Miss Hamilton. "It was quite informative, Catherine. We shall have to adopt some of these agricultural improvements on our own estate."

Bateman had been excited to see what new developments they were testing on the Matthews estate. Ian had already implemented them on his own estate. Bateman quickly needed pencil and paper to jot down ideas.

"You mean raise sheep?" Sophia said.

"It's a good possibility for our northern estates. We will be able to put the land to use and help the tenants," Lord Bateman said. "Mr. McDonald seems to think we can turn things around."

Sophia shot him a look. "That is good news indeed, Lord Bateman."

"Tell me more about your estate in Scotland, Ian," Catherine said. "I love Scotland. It's so wild and beautiful."

"I live in the lowlands, far from the highlands."

"Sir Walter Scott writes so lovingly of Scotland," Mrs. Matthews said from the end of the table.

"He has romanticized it quite a bit, ma'am." Ian set down his fork. "But I must admit there is something mystical about Scotland, even the lowlands. The lush green of the hills that roll down into the pastures; the small stone buildings of the villages can be beautiful. The people are stubborn but also very generous."

He looked across the table at Sophia, who appeared to hang on his every word. "Edinburgh is every bit as majestic and entertaining as London. Have you been to Edinburgh, Miss Townsend?"

She shook her head. "I've not had the pleasure."

"It's a beautiful old city," Miss Hamilton said. "My father has business there and takes us with him. The shopping is just as nice as in London."

Ian picked up his fork.

"You are not from Scotland, are you, Mr. McDonald?" Sophia asked.

"I was born in England, but my father's family is from Scotland."

Bateman set down his glass. "Mr. McDonald's father was our steward for the longest time. I don't know if you realized it, but Mr. McDonald spent his childhood at Bateman Abbey."

"Indeed, I had no idea," Sophia said, glaring at him.

The fat was in the fire now. Ian had forgotten to inform Sophia of his connection with Bateman. He shot a glance at Nathaniel Matthews, who was also glaring at him. Damn.

"Tell us about Bateman Abbey, my lord. Is it beautiful?"

"It's more old than beautiful, Miss Townsend." Bateman looked down the table at Ian. "Wouldn't you say, McDonald?"

"It's been many years since I've been there; I could hardly say." The place held nothing but bitter memories for him. After the death of his mother, his father had declined quickly. He'd died, leaving Ian to make his own way in the world. Though the old earl had funded his education, Ian had paid back every shilling. There was no way he'd be beholden to that family.

"Where is it located?" Sophia asked.

"In the midlands, near Northampton. It's been in the family since the sixteenth century."

"Is the house in ill repair?" Miss Hamilton asked.

"It is in need of some repairs. I imagine it needs a few modern updates to make it presentable again."

"The house is very large, with an abundance of windows. The gardens are immense," Lady Catherine said. "One could walk for hours on the grounds and not see a single soul."

Sophia glanced at Lord Bateman. "It sounds lovely."

Ian watched as Sophia wove her magic around Bateman. The gloss of her dark hair, that full lower lip she had a tendency to bite, those dark, dark eyes that could turn into pools of melted chocolate when she wanted them to.

"It is lovely," Bateman said.

Ian watched the looks that passed between Bateman and Sophia and felt his heart sink. How easily those two had fallen into their camaraderie again. All Sophia ever seemed to do with him was argue.

"Let's hope you can keep it that way, Brother," Lady Catherine said bitterly.

The entire table looked at Lady Catherine, but she stubbornly refused to return the glare.

"Nothing like speaking the truth, is there, child?" Lady Danford said. "Cleanses the soul."

Laughter surrounded the table and Ian felt sorry for Catherine. Her cheeks colored and she lowered her head. In that instant he could sense the fear in her for her future. He could understand how she'd feel that way. He'd felt something similar when he'd been at Bateman Abbey.

"I imagine it takes a great deal of upkeep for an estate that size," Ian said. "I believe your estate is about the same size, Mr. Matthews."

"With the help of my wife, we were able to turn things around."

Ian smiled. He loved this story.

"Your wife?" Bateman said, looking at Anne sitting next to him.

"My husband greatly exaggerates my abilities," Anne said with a smile. "He was more than capable of turning the estate around himself."

"But not motivated until I met you," Nathaniel said.

Envy was one of the many emotions coursing through Ian. He looked at Sophia, who was smiling sweetly at her sister. Another facet of her personality he liked.

"Stop, Mr. Matthews, you make me blush," Anne said.

"You two are going to spoil my dinner with your silliness," Lady Danford said. "In my day, we didn't discuss such things at the table." Laughter filled the room again. Ian turned back to his wine.

"My brother tells me that you've purchased an estate near our own in Dumfries, Mr. McDonald. Which estate did you purchase?" Catherine asked.

"I believe he purchased the Donald estate just south of ours, Catherine. Is that the one, McDonald?" Bateman said.

"Yes. It is." Ian choked down another bite. "It is rather an old house."

"Several centuries old, I believe," Catherine said.

Sophia set down her glass. "Mr. McDonald, you've described Scotland as a magical place. Is it a castle?"

"Of sorts."

"How can it be a castle of sorts?" Sophia said with a laugh.

Ian rested his arms on the table, his eyes pinning Sophia in place. "Like any castle, it has its old ruins, ghosts, and secret hidden places, but it lacks a tower."

"I didn't think you were the type to believe in ghosts, Mr. McDonald," Sophia said.

"You see all manner of interesting things in Scotland." He picked up his fork.

"I've heard of a mystical place right here in Beetham," Miss Hamilton said. "It's called the Fairy Steps. Is it close?"

Sophia choked on her wine.

"Are you well, Miss Townsend?" Lady Catherine asked. "I've not heard of such a place. Tell us more, Theo."

"I don't know much. I found it in a book I was reading."

"It's actually quite close," Mrs. Matthews said. "We can walk to it from The Lodge."

Sophia cleared her voice. "The Fairy Steps played a part in my sister's marriage to Mr. Matthews."

"How romantic!" Miss Hamilton said with a smile.

"Depends on whom you talk to, Miss Hamilton," Nathaniel Matthews said.

Ian watched Mrs. Matthews blush prettily.

"Shall we walk there tomorrow?" Sophia Townsend asked.

"I would like to, Miss Townsend," Miss Hamilton said.

"Then we shall." Sophia smiled indulgently at Miss Hamilton.

Ian picked up his fork and pushed at his food. Something was amiss. Sophia had always been indifferent to Miss Hamilton. Now they were close? He'd corner her later to find out what was going on.

The gentlemen were left to their port after dinner. Sophia followed Anne as she led Lady Danford into the parlor. Dinner had not been a total success, but she'd held her own, and Catherine Grayson had been embarrassed. Sophia was feeling quite pleased with herself.

"I think we need music tonight," Lady Catherine said with a smile. "I know you lack the talent, Miss Townsend, but, perhaps Mrs. Matthews will indulge us."

Sophia ground her teeth. Why hadn't she paid more attention to her music lessons? "Anne, would you mind playing for us?"

Anne tucked a blanket around Lady Danford's legs and patted her hand. "I should be delighted to play for you. Do you intend to dance?"

"I think a dance would be delightful," Miss Hamilton said with a smile.

Sophia sat across from Lady Danford, silent.

Lady Catherine moved to the piano and thumbed through the music. "Do you have a waltz, Mrs. Matthews?"

Anne moved to the piano. "I'm sure we do. Here is one."

"Do you think we'll be able to walk to the Fairy Steps tomorrow, Miss Townsend?" Miss Hamilton asked.

"I think so," Sophia replied.

"You're going to climb those steps, child?" Lady Danford asked.

"Not necessarily to make a wish, but I don't mind taking the ladies to see it." Sophia knew that climbing the steps again would not lead to breaking the current wish. She'd only anger the fairies, and as she'd not seen a single fairy, she didn't know if she believed in the legend.

"Perhaps a wish would be just the thing, girl," Lady Danford said.

"I don't believe in wishes and fairies. If one of the other young ladies wishes to try to climb the steps for her heart's desire, why should I prevent them?"

"Perhaps it's dangerous to climb such uneven steps, Miss Townsend."

Ian's deep voice came from behind her. "If I remember correctly, you stumbled several times on the steps. I was afraid you might be injured."

Sophia turned to face him. "I was in a great hurry to avoid the storm, sir."

"Perhaps we gentlemen should accompany the ladies to prevent any accidents."

"You are most welcome to join us. I'm sure certain ladies in the group would be happy to have your help in climbing the steps."

"Mr. McDonald, are you accompanying us tomorrow? How delightful. Brother, say you'll come as well," Lady Catherine said. "Finally we are to have an adventure on this trip."

Sophia fought the urge to roll her eyes. "I'm sure we can drum up some more adventures for you during your visit."

"We've not been riding yet," Miss Hamilton said. "I do love riding."

"Then we shall add that to the list of things to do while you are here," Sophia said.

"We should dance now. Mr. McDonald, would you do me the honor?" Catherine asked.

Sophia watched as Ian offered the lady his arm and led her to the center of the room. He smiled down at Catherine Grayson. They were well matched, his dark good looks to her paleness. Sophia didn't like the emotions churning inside her as she watched the couple move across the floor.

Lord Bateman and Miss Hamilton moved past her as they danced to the music. She didn't feel the same tug of jealousy now as she had with Ian. This mad tumult of emotions was so unlike her. She didn't like it one bit.

"If you're not careful, she'll waltz away with him," Lady Danford said from behind her.

"Who do you mean?"

"Lady Catherine has her eye on Mr. McDonald and she is determined. If you're not careful, she'll steal him away from you."

Sophia turned to Lady Danford. "What makes you think I have feelings for Mr. McDonald?" She was sure she'd given nothing away.

"I'm old but not blind. I see the way you two watch each other when each thinks the other isn't looking." Lady Danford cackled. "It's a game as old as time itself."

"You are mistaken, my lady," Sophia said. "Mr. McDonald is just a friend."

"Now you go on with that friendship nonsense. That man undresses you with his eyes every chance he gets. There's no friendship there."

"Lady Danford, please keep your voice down," Sophia whispered furiously, thankful the waltz was a lively one.

"Miss Townsend, may I have the pleasure of this dance?" Captain Smith-Williams said, appearing at her side.

"Captain, thank you." Sophia dipped into a curtsy and took his arm as he whirled her into the mix of the dancing couples.

"Do you like to waltz, Miss Townsend?"

"I do indeed. And do you enjoy it?"

He nodded with a smile, and for the first time Sophia could see why Miss Hamilton was so taken with him. During the short time the man had been at the Lodge, he had seemed to glower at all of them. Tonight was different. He smiled easily, and his smile was infectious.

"You seem happy tonight, sir. I don't think I've seen you smile since arriving."

He tightened his grip on her hand in response. "There is reason to hope for the future, Miss Townsend."

"In what way?"

"I cannot say exactly."

"Perhaps hope is the reason you smile. If it is, I'm happy for you."

He whirled her around and they came to a stop as the music ended. Sophia clapped along with the rest of the partners.

"If you will excuse me, Miss Townsend."

"Of course, thank you." Sophia moved to the side. Ian bowed to Catherine and came to stand before her.

"You dance well, sir. I didn't know you liked dancing," Sophia said.

Ian grimaced. "I hate it, but it is a necessity in society."

"Very true. Lady Catherine and you are well matched."

Sophia fought the smile at the expression on his face.

"Don't start, Sophia."

"Start what?"

"Miss Townsend, would you do me the honor of dancing the next with me?" Lord Bateman said, walking toward her.

"I would be delighted, my lord." She smiled up at Ian as she took Bateman's hand.

*   *   *

Ian watched as Bateman danced with Sophia, her face lit with pleasure. Miss Hamilton was dancing with the captain. He could see the partiality she had for her captain. He wondered if this would make it easier for Sophia to win Bateman's hand.

Jealousy was making him insane. Bateman was a practical man. He'd simper and dance to Sophia's attendance but he'd marry Miss Hamilton's hefty dowry.

"You look lost in thought, sir," Catherine said beside him.

"I beg your pardon?" Ian did not take his eyes off Sophia.

"Could you be any more obvious, Ian?"

"What do you mean?"

"Sophia Townsend is a social climber. You could do so much better if you would acknowledge the connection between *our* families."

"I have no desire to broadcast to Society that my father was your steward." Ian glanced at Catherine. Her eyes were pinned on her brother. She was scowling. "Do you like Miss Hamilton?"

"Miss Hamilton is a nice young lady. Much nicer than Miss Townsend."

Ian chuckled. "You mean you can manipulate her more easily than Miss Townsend. If Bateman does marry Miss Townsend, what will you do then, Catherine?"

"He won't marry her. He cannot afford to."

Ian felt sorry for Catherine again. She had little control over her circumstances.

"I know that look. Do not pity me," she grumbled.

"If you took the time to get to know Sophia, you might like her."

"Not likely."

"Come, dance with me. It will cheer you up." He offered his hand. She took it and he led her into the dance. She was quiet, still watching Sophia dance with her brother.

"I just don't see it."

Ian also looked over at the couple. "What are you looking for?"

"I don't understand what men see in Sophia Townsend. She's not good Ton."

Ian said nothing. He was rather interested in discovering the reason for that as well.

"She's pretty, but in an ordinary way. She's too opinionated."

"Yes, she is." However, he liked that she didn't put on airs like other young women.

"She's also too old. She's nearly twenty-seven."

He didn't think that was too old for a woman, but he kept his opinion to himself.

"You like her, don't you?" Catherine finally asked.

"Yes, I do. I like her very much, but I've known her for quite a while." He whirled her around. "She is better upon a deeper acquaintance."

"She could cause this family to fail. If Geoffrey marries her, we are ruined." Catherine gripped his hand tighter.

"Surely things aren't as bad as all that."

"Do you know why we are going to the estate in Carlisle?"

"A chance for Bateman to get to know Miss Hamilton before he marries her?"

"To sell it." Catherine's eyes welled up with tears. "It is my favorite place and soon it will be gone, like the other estates."

Ian glanced around helplessly. He hated it when women cried. He never knew what to do. "Catherine, don't." He escorted her outside to the garden and handed her a handkerchief. "I didn't think things were as bad as that."

"Geoffrey doesn't want anyone to know. He's quite desperate."

He grabbed her shoulders to keep them from falling. "Catherine."

"Just hold me."

He wrapped his arms around her as she sniffed. "This isn't proper."

"For heaven's sake, does everything have to be proper all the time?" She sighed. "Not once has Geoffrey asked me what I wanted. He's suggested I marry, but the men he suggests are older than the stones of Bateman Abbey. I cannot do it."

Ian felt uncomfortable. He didn't know where to put his hands. He stood stiffly with Catherine resting against him. He glanced into the drawing room and found Sophia standing by the window, staring at them. He met her eyes and she angrily turned away.

Ian cursed silently.

He pushed Catherine upright. She'd seen Sophia in the window. There was a sly bit of a smile on her lips. He was done being the dupe. "Dry your eyes and control yourself. We should return to the party."

"You could kiss me."

He put more distance between them. Enough was enough. "Excuse me, Lady Catherine. I'm returning to the house."

"Ian, don't be an idiot."

Ian glared at her. "I suppose I deserve that, given you've made a fool of me. Keep your theatrics for men foolish enough to believe them. It won't be me."

"Ian—"

"Good night."

Ian stomped back into the house and tried to bury his anger. He'd fallen for it again. Some stupid act to capture him. He was too damn easy a target.

"Mr. McDonald, are you retiring for the night?" Sophia asked from behind him.

There was something in her voice. He couldn't pin it down but, honestly, his temper was too high to puzzle her out. He turned to her. "Meet me in the garden at midnight."

"Are you insane?" she whispered as she looked around to see if anyone else had heard.

"Just do it."

"Why?"

"Come to the garden at midnight and find out."

Chapter 9

Sophia paced her room, still dressed in the gown she'd worn to dinner. She'd sent her maid to bed knowing she was going to meet Ian McDonald.

She couldn't believe she was actually contemplating it, but seeing him with Catherine Grayson on the terrace that night had pricked something inside her. It had hurt more than she cared to admit.

The clock in the entrance way chimed the midnight hour. With every clang of the clock, she grew more nervous. Why had he commanded her to see him?

She'd been staring at the couple for a few minutes before he'd noticed her. He'd been tender with Catherine Grayson. He'd handed her his handkerchief and comforted her. It reminded her of how Ian had been with her during the storm. He'd held her, comforted her, kissed her. He'd soothed her, and no one had done that for a very long time.

She'd stood there waiting for him to kiss Miss Grayson. She could see Catherine lean against his broad chest, clutching his jacket. And still she watched, as if they were on a stage performing, her heart thudding painfully, a cry caught in her throat.

"Stupid man," she muttered. It would serve him right if she didn't obey his order to meet him in the garden.

But Sophia knew she would go. Some hypnotic force pulled them together thanks to her stupid wish, and she couldn't stop herself. It was like watching herself from outside her own body. She didn't want to do it, yet she did. It was like eating fresh strawberries. They were so sweet, so delicious that she couldn't stop eating them. Until she was sick.

The chimes of the clock ceased and the house settled down quietly for the night. Sophia blew out the candles in her room and went to the window to look out onto the garden. Was he there? Waiting? Would he kiss her again?

"This is nonsense," she muttered to herself and turned to leave the room, but a movement caught her eye.

A couple moved from the shadow of the house and crossed the lawn.

Had Catherine found Ian before her?

The couple moved to a bench near the roses and sat. The man took the woman's hand and pressed his mouth to it. They talked quietly. Sophia squinted her eyes, trying to make them out, but the dark was too deep in that corner of the garden. If it was Ian and Catherine, she had no desire to interrupt their tête-à-tête. There was another movement in the garden. This time a single figure stopped in the green and looked up at her window. Ian.

She ducked behind the curtain and watched him. The faint light of the moon lit his face with ghostly shadows, highlighting the edges. He stared as if he knew she was looking back, unable to make the decision whether to come down.

Sophia felt a nervous energy flow through her. It was fear, excitement, and something else she couldn't put her finger on. She'd not felt it before, this urge to move forward and go. She stepped away from the window and moved away silently.

She peeked out. The corridor was empty, the house quiet. She tiptoed quietly into the hallway and silently moved down the stairs, avoiding the step that creaked in the old house. Normally she'd go through the library, but Miss Grayson's penchant for late-night reading kept her from taking the shortest route. The front door would be locked for the night. The parlor was the best choice.

She reached the parlor door, which was partially closed. She heard a noise behind her and stepped into the room. The familiar groan of the wood of the one step on the stairs echoed in the hall. Who else was roaming the house at this hour?

Sophia moved across the parlor out to the gardens. Soundlessly, she stepped out onto the terrace. Light from the library lit the stones in front of her. Where was Ian?

A hand touched her bare arm and she almost screamed. Ian placed his hands to his lips and took her hand. He led her into the darker part of the yard toward the stables and into the trees lining the park of the Lodge.

"What are you doing?" she whispered.

"Captain Smith-Williams and Miss Hamilton must have had the same idea," Ian said quietly against her ear. "They have the bench."

"Someone else is in the library," Sophia whispered quickly.

"It's Catherine. She's probably waiting for me."

"Then why are you meeting me? Shouldn't you go to her?"

"No." His voice was a harsh whisper.

The bushes brushed at her skirts as he took her away from the house. "Where are we going?"

"Where we can have a conversation and not be overheard." Ian's voice was a bit louder now that they were farther from the house.

The nervous energy inside her urged her on, but Sophia still hesitated. It was one thing to have a midnight tryst in the garden near the safety of the house; it was another to allow a man to pull her deeper into the woods. She pulled her hand away from his. "I don't think this is a good idea."

Ian stopped and she practically ran into him. "Then why did you come?"

Why had she come? Sophia had been questioning her actions since watching Ian with Catherine from the window of the parlor earlier that evening. "I don't know."

He was silent for a long moment, watching her as if she were going to run like a schoolgirl back to the house. "We are almost there."

Ian started walking, once again pulling her behind him. Sophia tripped on a tree root and he was there to catch her, placing his arm at her waist. She could feel the warmth of his hand through the thin fabric of her dress.

"Why didn't you change into something warmer?" he asked.

"I couldn't tell my maid to set out another dress because I had a midnight assignation, now could I? The gossip would be in the village before we came down for breakfast tomorrow morning."

Ian chuckled. "There's the Sophia Townsend I know."

"Please tell me we are almost there. These slippers are not made for a romp through the woods."

Ian stopped at the ruins of the old cottage. Moonlight turned the old stones a silvery gray. Sophia touched the gate with her hands, memories flooding her mind. Thoughts of good times and bad. She didn't miss the lack of funds, but she did miss being together with her sisters. Now they were married and starting their own families, they had little time for her.

"Do you know this place?" Ian asked, noting her reaction.

She smiled. "I lived here with my sisters when we first came to Beetham. Anne was Lady Danford's companion. To this day, I swear the old lady played matchmaker for her and Nathaniel."

"Good memories?"

"For the most part." She followed the stone fence with her hand. "Why have you brought me here?"

"I thought to explain what you saw," Ian said. "Catherine was upset when you were dancing with Bateman."

Sophia snorted. "Really, Ian, I thought you were better able to detect feminine wiles than that. Catherine wasn't upset. She was angry."

"Upset, mostly. Her life is changing and she cannot control it."

"Life just happens to women whether we want it to or not." Catherine's life was not that different from her own. "She should be used to it."

"It is not as bad as all that, Sophia. You have choices."

She said nothing. She had been given many choices and she'd passed them up, waiting for something better that just hadn't happened. She sagged against the fence, feeling an urge to cry. "I saw Miss Hamilton in the garden with the captain before I came down."

"Captain Smith-Williams is in love with Miss Hamilton."

"She returns those feelings. Her father has promised her to Lord Bateman in exchange for her very large dowry. If she marries the captain, she will be cut off without a penny." Sophia stared up at the stars. "It all sounds like a bad play, doesn't it?"

Ian chuckled. "It does at that. May I ask you something? And will you be completely honest with me?"

"That will depend on the question, Mr. McDonald."

"Why do you not marry for love?"

The question startled her. "Haven't we had this discussion already?"

"No, we've discussed Lord Bateman in particular. This is a more general question."

She glanced up at him. "Couples have been marrying without love for centuries. Marriages for dynastic purposes suited both families well."

"Do you really believe that?"

"Mr. McDonald, the only way a woman can move upward in this world is through marriage. We cannot inherit. We cannot work for a living wage. What other choices do we have?"

Ian looked up at the sky. "That sounds cold to me, and lonely."

"How can it be lonely when there is Society? I'll have friends, entertainments. My life will be full."

"Will you take a lover, Sophia?"

"That, sir, is none of your business."

"You have a passionate nature. How long will it take for you to become bored with your husband's attentions? What will you do when he turns to his mistress for affection because he doesn't find it at home? That is what these types of marriages are about."

"You think I do not know that? My own parents were a prime example." She spat out the words.

"Then why will you settle?"

His questions were hitting too close to the mark and there was no way she was going to unburden her soul to Ian McDonald. Sophia pushed away from the fence. "I'm going back to the house."

"You're afraid."

"And what, pray, am I afraid of? Or do you judge me a coward for trying to better my place in this world? Is that what the issue is?" She placed her hands on her hips. How dare he judge her for her decisions when men made those choices all the time?

"You're afraid of real emotion, Sophia. You think you want London Society, shopping, and a large house full of servants, but those are just things. Things that can easily be taken away, like that." He snapped his fingers in her face. "But feelings like love scare the hell out of you."

"Don't be coarse."

"I'm being honest."

She covered her face with her hands, suddenly very tired. "It's late and we are both cross." Sophia turned and made her way up the lane to the house. She hugged her arms to her chest against the chill and the anger in Ian's voice.

She couldn't argue with his logic, but he thought her afraid of the wrong emotion. It wasn't love she feared but the loss of it. She couldn't bear it if she drove love away like her father and brother had. It was so much better for everyone involved if she didn't love her husband. A cool distance would protect them both.

"Sophia, wait!" Ian called after her.

Sophia kept walking, ignoring the stones cutting through the thin soles of her evening slippers. It had been foolish to come out here. She should have expected Ian to berate her.

He grabbed her arm. "You should not walk back to the house alone. It's not safe."

Sophia jerked away from his touch. "Even the brigands have gone to bed."

"I won't allow you to traipse through the woods alone." He took her arm and placed it on his.

She resented it, but she let him take her arm and guide her back toward the house. "You are wrong, you know."

"Am I? I'm not so sure."

Sophia ground her teeth but didn't say anything. She could never fool Ian. She hated that he saw through her façade.

"What is so special about London?"

"It is not Beetham. It is not the wilds of the Lake District, where the air smells of cattle and smoke. It's not the constant tittle-tattle of the village about mundane topics."

"London smells worse. It's noisy. The air chokes you. A man can't hear himself think from the noise."

"There are the museums, the theater, the musicales and balls. There is a rich society. There is conversation about politics, art, and music."

"You have those things in Beetham and other communities."

"How can I make you understand? It is the city itself. There is a heartbeat to London. The fast pace, the noise, the smells. All of it merges into this almost living, breathing being." She met Ian's eyes. "I don't expect you to understand."

He squeezed her hand. "I feel the same about Scotland."

"London is the first place I've ever been where I felt alive, Mr. McDonald." She climbed the few steps and crossed the terrace to the parlor. "I don't know if I can live anywhere else. Good night."

"You are wrong, you know," he called after her. "That's just part of the story, and London is just a place. You know in your heart I'm right."

Sophia couldn't stop herself from pausing in the doorway. She turned and looked back at Ian. The moon caught the anguish on his face. Even in this, she was hurting him. She didn't want to hurt him. He cared for her. It had been a very long time since anyone besides her sisters had actually cared about her, about her thoughts, her feelings.

He approached her, his hand out. "Do you think your mother wants you to end up like her? Do you think Anne does?"

She closed her eyes against the prick of tears. He chose his arguments well. "I am my father's daughter, Ian. I know only how to hurt others. Good night."

"Sophia—"

She couldn't look back. If she did she'd be in his arms and crying like a baby. She walked away from him, away from the emotion in his voice. It was better to shorten the pain now than subject him to a lifetime of it. She walked to her room, tears silently falling from her eyes.

Ian cursed as he watched Sophia go into the house. Never in the three years he'd known Sophia Townsend had he seen her reduced to tears. Yet he'd done it. He followed her into the house and reached the top of the stairs just as she closed the door to her bedroom. In the dark gloom of the corridor, he heard the click of her turning the lock.

He tapped on the door and whispered, "Sophia, let me in."

Silence.

"Please."

"Ian, what are you doing outside Sophia's bedroom?"

Ian jumped and turned. Nathaniel Matthews stood behind him with his arms crossed.

"She was upset. I was checking on her." Ian sounded like a green youth. "What are you doing awake at this hour?"

"There was a great deal of noise in the hallway. I thought I'd investigate."

Ian stepped away from the door. "I'll just be getting to bed, then. See you in the morning."

"McDonald?"

Ian turned and winced at the look on Nathaniel's face. Why did dealing with Sophia Townsend always end up making him look like the fool in a bad play?

"You can bang on her bedroom door after you marry her. And for God's sake, quit looking so desperate."

Nathaniel walked back down the hall to his room. Ian closed his eyes and groaned. He'd really bungled it this time. He walked quietly back to his room.

She'd said something peculiar. She had said she was like her father. What did that mean? He'd have to find out. Perhaps Anne would tell him. He didn't dare go to Nathaniel. The man would just laugh at him.

He was done for the night with emotional women.

Chapter 10

Sophia stood at the window of her room and stared, unseeing, at the garden. She didn't want to go down to breakfast. She didn't want to face Ian after their conversation last night. He and his probing questions had slipped behind her mask.

The last thing she needed was his pity. Worse yet, he thought he could repair her. What was it about men that made them feel they had to attempt to find a solution to every problem a woman had?

She was more than capable of dealing with her own issues.

But that wasn't the worst part of it. She'd let Ian see a side of her few ever had, She'd been vulnerable, weak.

He would exploit it. Men always did.

A knock sounded. Sophia turned and watched as Anne came into the room and closed the door behind her. "Good morning."

"You look awful."

"Nothing like having someone else confirm what you saw in the mirror." Sophia stepped away from the window. "Did you need something?"

"Nathaniel told me Ian was outside your bedroom door last night." Anne moved deeper into the room. "Might I remind you that our family already has a reputation for improper behavior?"

As if she didn't know. "Might I remind you that I have no intention of adding to that image? Seriously, Anne, I was upset. He angered me and was trying to get back into my good graces. I had no intention of letting him in."

"What of Lord Bateman?"

"Lord Bateman is planning to propose to Miss Hamilton and her immense fortune. He made his feelings quite clear to me last night." The *old girl* comment still rubbed.

Anne moved to the other chair by the fire. "Sophia, I'm so sorry. You must be devastated."

"There was no understanding, Anne."

"There most certainly was on my part. He called on you, brought gifts and flowers. He singled you out in Town. Everyone was talking about the match. And he comes here and doesn't propose? Think of what that will do to your reputation."

"As we are not likely to be in Town anytime soon, that hardly matters. He has to marry a fortune, Anne. His estate is in ruins."

"Then the rumors are true?"

Sophia nodded. "Hence Miss Hamilton."

"But she is in love with the captain. Where does he fit into all of this?"

"How do you know she is love with the captain?"

"Anyone with eyes can tell she is more than just partial to him. Neither of them is good at hiding their feelings. I'm surprised Lord Bateman allowed the captain to accompany them to the north."

Once again Sophia had underestimated her sister's capacity for observation. "Captain Smith-Williams has no money. If Miss Hamilton marries him, she loses her dowry. I feel sorry for him. He has to stand back and watch the woman he loves as she is courted by another man. The man her father wants her to marry."

"None of this makes sense."

"No, it doesn't."

"Lady Catherine is quite taken with Mr. McDonald."

Sophia snorted. "She quite taken with his purse. She is determined to marry a wealthy man and he's the only one nearby." Sophia glanced at Anne, noting the look in her eyes, and quickly looked away.

"Does that bother you?"

"Why should it? Ian can marry where he wishes. He has funds and an estate." Sophia kept her voice even.

"It does bother you. You care for him."

"He is a friend. It does not mean I want to marry him. He lives in Scotland, with sheep."

"You live in Beetham with sheep."

"And I hate it."

"Do you really?"

"I meant no offense."

"None taken. We are sisters. We should be honest with each other."

What did she mean by that? "I loved my time in London."

"You loved being the center of attention."

Sophia gasped. "That's a horrible thing to say!"

"But honest."

Anne had her there. "Fine. I loved being the center of attention. What is wrong with that? I love dancing. I love the music, the theater."

"The shops."

"Yes! Exactly. I see nothing wrong with those things."

Anne patted her hand. "There is nothing wrong with it, but those are trivial things."

"So?" Sophia wasn't sure she liked where this conversation was going. Anne had a way of seeing inside her head that she didn't like.

"I think you hide behind those trivial things to protect yourself. If you aren't careful, you'll find yourself alone and bitter because you let so many opportunities go by."

"I have no intention of letting opportunities go by."

Anne gave her that look, as if she were calling her bluff. She hated that look.

"Come downstairs to breakfast, Sophia. For better or worse, our guests await. Do you know how long they will be staying?"

"Too long, I'm afraid." Sophia shook out her skirts. "I had no idea Bateman was such a boor." Or Catherine such a witch, but she kept that to herself. They were too much alike for her to point fingers.

"You were too busy being dazzled by the attention in London. I never liked Lord Bateman, and his sister is just as bad. But as they are our guests, we must make the best of it."

"Perhaps the heat will drive them north," Sophia whispered into Anne's ear as they walked to the staircase. "Or the rain. Do you think rain would drive them away?"

"Until Lord Bateman achieves his objective, nothing will drive them away."

"What do you mean?"

"Good morning, Mrs. Matthews, Miss Townsend," Captain Smith-Williams said cheerfully as he passed them on the stairs.

"Good morning, Captain. I trust you slept well." Anne's voice was all politeness.

"Indeed."

Sophia waited as he disappeared around the corner to the morning room. "Explain."

"Anyone can see Bateman is here with a purpose. I think it has something to do with Mr. McDonald. So does Nathaniel."

"But what?"

Anne shook her head. "I don't know."

Sophia thought back over what Ian had said and her conversation with Bateman. Was Bateman's objective to marry his sister to Ian? Was that what he meant? But why here? Why not just call on Ian in Scotland? Or have him come to Carlisle? Ian had a close connection to the family if his father had been the family's steward.

She'd not once seen Ian while she was on Bateman's arm. He had been there, he would occasionally dance with her when she wasn't engaged, but the more she involved herself with Bateman and his friends, the less she saw of Ian.

Why would Bateman throw his sister to someone who was so far outside their circle? Except for money. For the first time in the years she'd known Lady Catherine, Sophia felt sorry for her.

They were in the same predicament. As much as it pained her to admit, they were both trying to achieve the same objective: finding a husband who met their qualifications and securing their futures. Lady Catherine had the advantage of connection on her side. Sophia couldn't even claim that.

Ian greeted Captain Smith-Williams as he came into the room. The man looked relaxed, but Ian felt tired. After being caught by Nathaniel, Ian felt like a fool. Luckily, only Nathaniel had witnessed his foolishness.

No more letting Sophia tie him in knots.

Mrs. Matthews entered the room and he got to his feet. "Good morning, ma'am."

She smiled and motioned to the footman for a pot of tea. "Please be seated. I wouldn't want your breakfast to grow cold."

Ian sat and stared at his cup. Usually, his mornings were spent with coffee and the business news, before anyone else was up. Here he was expected to make small talk before coffee. It did not bode well.

Sophia stepped into the room and paused, as if she wanted to turn around and flee. She seemed to relax when she realized he wasn't alone in the room. What had he done to make her afraid of him? He watched her straighten her shoulders and enter the room. He drew to his feet. "Miss Townsend."

"Mr. McDonald."

"Good morning, Mrs. Matthews and Miss Townsend," Captain Smith-Williams said brightly. "I trust you both slept well. It is a beautiful day, isn't it?"

"Yes, thank you," Sophia said quietly.

Ian almost growled into his coffee. The man was too cheerful to have spent a frustrating night alone. Ian wondered how long the captain had spent in the garden with Miss Hamilton.

Sophia walked to the sideboard to fill a plate. She toyed with the eggs and kippers but decided on just toast. She sat down across from Ian, next to her sister, and glanced at him.

He felt his face flush. Ian forced himself to pick up his fork and eat. He hated that so many people were in the room. He wanted to talk to Sophia alone, find out what had upset her so.

Sophia wasn't one of those missish girls who cried over every little thing. That she was visibly upset meant something. That she'd let slip the mask she insisted on wearing in public meant more. He had definitely touched a nerve. "Are there plans for today, Mrs. Matthews?"

"I thought Sophia could show you all the Fairy Steps. It's quite famous in the area."

"Is it a long walk?" Captain Smith-Williams asked.

Sophia smiled at him. "Not at all. It's quite a lovely spot. You can see for miles from the top."

"I look forward to it, then."

Ian said nothing.

"It's quite a magical place, Captain," Sophia said. "The fable goes that if you climb the steps without touching the sides of the stone, a fairy will grant you a wish."

"I didn't think you believed in magic, Miss Townsend," Ian said.

Sophia smiled at him. "I don't really, but you have to admit, Mr. McDonald, it is romantic."

"The steps had a much more practical purpose," Anne said. "They used to bring the coffins from Arnside down them to be put to rest at St. Michael's."

"Gruesome place, then," Captain Smith-Williams said.

Miss Hamilton entered the room. Ian and the captain got to their feet. He missed breakfasting alone. All this standing and sitting was growing tiresome.

"Please don't get up for me," Miss Hamilton said.

Ian watched as she smiled at the captain, who smiled back. It hurt to watch them, knowing she would marry another. He knew just how the captain felt, but it didn't make it easier. "I hope you slept well, Miss Hamilton," Mrs. Matthews asked.

"Indeed. This country air is perfect for sleeping. I didn't awaken once all night."

Ian noticed the look exchanged between Miss Hamilton and the captain. Something was afoot.

"Miss Hamilton, you should join in. You love historical places," Smith-Williams said.

"I would like to join if you do not mind, Miss Townsend."

"I'd be delighted. We shall make a party of it. Shall I have our cook prepare a basket for us?"

"That sounds delightful, Sophia," Anne said as she stood. "Allow me to take care of it."

"Thank you, Anne."

"Will Lord Bateman also be going?" Smith-Williams asked.

"I'm sure he will, sir," Sophia said with a smile. "I promised him when we were in London that I'd show him the steps."

Ian watched as Anne left the room, then turned his attentions back to Miss Hamilton and the captain. They were staring at each other like lovesick calves. What else had happened on that garden bench?

He glanced at Sophia, who shrugged, then tossed his napkin on the table. "If we are to have an outing this afternoon, I need to get to Horneswood so that I can be back in time to join you."

"Checking on your sheep, Mr. McDonald?"

"But of course, Miss Townsend. One should never ignore an investment. Would you care to join me? I thought you rather liked sheep."

She blushed. "No. Thank you."

"If you'll excuse me, then."

Bateman entered the room as Ian was leaving. "Where are you off to so early, McDonald?"

Why did providence insist on throwing this man into his path again and again? "Horneswood."

"A word before you leave." Bateman moved toward the library, clearly expecting Ian to follow. The scene that would erupt if Ian didn't comply was just not worth it, especially with only one cup of coffee under his belt.

"Close the door," Bateman ordered as they entered.

Ian shut the door with a bit more snap than was polite. "What is this about, Geoffrey?"

The use of Bateman's first name irked him. Good. Ian was tired of the man trampling all over Society, expecting preferential treatment. He thought he was the bloody king of England.

"I thought you were going to tell Miss Townsend the truth about why I was still here."

"I was. I just haven't gotten the opportunity yet."

"No need, now. The chit figured it out."

No wonder she was upset last night. He was an idiot. Bateman probably had put his foot in his mouth again, assuming Ian would jump right on his orders. Why not? Everyone else did.

"Have you given any thought to accepting my offer in exchange for the land you want?"

"If you mean marrying your sister, Geoffrey, the answer is no." Ian put more emphasis on Bateman's given name and enjoyed the way his face tightened with anger. "You should also speak to her about her behavior. It's quite unbecoming for a young lady to throw herself at a man."

Bateman chuckled. "When my sister makes up her mind that she wants something, she is very single-minded."

"As I've noticed," Ian said dryly. "Have you considered my offer?"

"It is too low."

"It is more than adequate. I doubt you'll receive a better one. The land is isolated between our two estates."

"But if I choose to sell the estate in Dumfries, the land would go with it."

"Do you plan to sell?"

Bateman seemed bored with the conversation. "I've not decided yet. It was to be part of Catherine's dowry. Would that induce you to marry her?"

Ian tightened his jaw. "No."

And there was the real reason Lord Bateman had descended upon the Lodge and its inhabitants. Ian felt the need to apologize to the Matthews family for having been manipulated by Bateman and his schemes.

Ian forced himself to relax. "How much money do you need?"

"Do you think to save the estate for me?"

Ian lifted his shoulders. "I was just curious, that's all. The estate did quite well when my father was steward." He took pleasure in the anger in Bateman's face.

Bateman took a long time to answer. "This has been a long time coming. We've lived beyond our means for years."

"Most do, I find."

Bateman threw him a questioning look.

"How bad is it?" Ian had a feeling he knew what was coming. It was a common tale in Society, where many people lived beyond their means and gambled away what little hard cash they had. He'd never seen the point of it all. Life was so much more peaceful when you could pay your creditors on time.

"I might have borrowed money from some of the more unsavory lenders in London."

"Bloody hell, what were you thinking?"

"I was funding Catherine's Season. I was hoping she could catch some old gent with a great deal of gold. Unfortunately, no one wanted her."

"Do you have any care of your sister? Or anyone besides yourself, for that matter? Tell me you didn't go to one of those cent-per-cent men."

"No choice."

Ian walked into the room. The man was either stupid or desperate. "What could possibly require you to do that?"

"We have an image to maintain. If we didn't show up in Town for the House of Lords, people would suspect."

God save him from keeping up appearances. "That explains why you need so much money."

"I'm desperate. We've sold everything we could."

"Do the lenders know where you are going?"

"Do I look like an idiot? I chose the Carlisle house because we never go there. We came this way to throw them off in case they followed us."

"I suggest you marry Miss Hamilton. She is probably your only hope."

"Maybe her father can come up with more money, for his grandson?"

There was no saving Geoffrey. "I'm late for an appointment."

"You could buy the loans from the lenders. I'd rather owe you than someone who is going to break my legs if I don't pay."

Ian paused. "And why would I do that?"

"You owe the family. Don't forget, my father funded your education."

"An investment I paid back with interest." Ian grounded the words out.

"You'd be nothing without that education my family provided you."

Ian curled his hands into fists to prevent himself from slamming them into Bateman's face. He could barely stomach the condescending tone in the man's voice. "I owe you nothing, Bateman, but I do have some advice for you."

Bateman lifted his weak chin, waiting for the answer.

"Learn to hide, because I'll not invest my hard-earned money to bail you out of trouble."

Ian left the man sputtering in the library. Bateman had nerve to ask him to pay off those loans. The man should have known better. He owed the Bateman family nothing. They'd made his life a living hell while he lived there. Yes, the old earl had recognized his gift for numbers, but he also had manipulated it for his own amusement. He'd also worked his father into an early grave and left his mother without a pension. Ian made his way to the stables for his horse, just as Lady Catherine was also arriving.

"You're up early."

"Ian. Good morning. I like a ride before breakfast," Catherine said. "It's cooler during this time of day. Where are you off to?"

"Horneswood. On business. Perhaps I'll see you later." He moved past her to enter the stables.

"Ian . . ."

He paused, waiting for her reply.

"I'm sorry for my behavior these past few days."

"Apology accepted."

"Geoffrey has told you our problems, then?"

"Yes."

"So you will help us?"

"I'm afraid I'm not able to. You should discuss this further with your brother. If you'll excuse me ..."

Her face danced between anger and disappointment. She would suffer more than her brother. She'd be sold into marriage to the highest bidder.

"I told Geoffrey you were a waste of time, but he thought you'd have more loyalty to the family for what we've done for you."

Anger seethed within Ian. "Do not call my loyalty into question, madam."

Catherine's face flushed.

Ian knew he should apologize, but he was done with both Bateman and his sister considering it their due that he was to save them in their present circumstances.

He moved into the gloom of the stables. "Is my horse saddled and ready?"

"Yes, sir."

Ian followed the man outside and accepted the reins.

"Keep an eye on the sky, sir. It may rain today."

"Thank you, I will. It would be a relief from this heat."

"Yes, sir."

Ian set off for Horneswood. He hoped work would settle down his thoughts and allow him to work through his emotions to reach a decision. That was what he needed right now. Hard physical work always eased his mind and his body when he had issues to work through.

Chapter 11

S ophia had led the small party through the woods, past the cottage, and up to the top of the Fairy Steps. The day was warm, but in the shade of the forest surrounding the Lodge, the air was refreshing. A light breeze cooled their skin from the heat of the day.

The walk so far had been uneventful. Bateman had quickly claimed Miss Hamilton's arm. He had his oh-so-very charming mask back in place. Lady Catherine held on to Ian with a death grip. Sophia had taken Captain Smith-Williams's arm as they trailed behind the group.

"Is it much farther? This heat is almost unbearable."

Sophia had to grind her teeth against the whine in the woman's voice. "Not much farther, Lady Catherine," Sophia repeated for the seventh time.

"Do you walk this way every day, Miss Townsend? It seems like such a long journey," Miss Hamilton said. "Though the woods are lovely."

The woods were lovely, Sophia had to admit. The bright greens of summer were starting to fade to a subtler color. Soon the canopy of trees would be painted with the shades of gold, orange, and red of autumn. She'd never appreciated how pretty this area was.

"I think I could stay here year-round," Crispin Smith-Williams said.

"It is nice. I don't know why I hadn't noticed before," Sophia said.

"We tend to take for granted that which is right under our noses."

She looked at the captain. "Very true." And perhaps too late. Ian looked to be enjoying himself with Catherine.

"Do you love him?" he asked.

"Excuse me?"

"Lord Bateman. Do you love him?"

Sophia looked at Bateman walking with Miss Hamilton. He was charming her right out of her half boots. Theo laughed at something Bateman said and Sophia felt the arm beneath her hand tense. This must be torture for the poor captain. "No. I don't think I do. Lord Bateman is very charming. Can be very charming."

"But you were expecting a proposal."

Would this rumor ever die? "No, sir, I was not."

He shot her a glance as if he didn't believe her.

"Fine, perhaps I was . . . just a little bit. He was paying a great deal of attention to me." She followed Smith-Williams's glance to Theo Hamilton. "If you love her so very much, you should act before it's too late."

"It is complicated."

"Captain, it is always complicated, but if you love her—"

"What would we live on? Her father would cut her off if she married me."

Sophia had to concede that point. "Then let her go."

Captain Smith-Williams pulled them to a stop so suddenly that Sophia had to grasp his arm to keep from falling. He held her there while the others moved farther ahead.

"I'm supposed to show them the way, sir."

"Just one moment. I have to tell someone the truth."

She looked up into his earnest face. "Captain, please don't unburden yourself—"

"She might be carrying my child." He said the words so softly and so quickly, Sophia wasn't sure she heard him.

"Pardon?"

"You heard me."

Sophia's head was spinning. This put a different light on things entirely. She honestly did not know what to say. Theo Hamilton—with child!

"I need your help, Miss Townsend. I cannot let Theo marry another man while carrying my child. It's not right."

"How could you let this happen?"

He shrugged and his cheeks flushed.

"Oh, right." She should have known this from the way her sisters had acted with their prospective husbands.

"Will you help us? Theo seems to think you can."

Good heavens, this was an interesting turn. She'd never supposed that having a house party would equate to the plot of a gothic novel. Sophia patted his hand. "I don't know what I can do, but I can try." He squeezed her hand and lifted it to his lips. "Thank you, Miss Townsend."

"Shouldn't we have gotten to the steps by now?" Lady Catherine's voice cut through the intimacy of the moment.

"They are just up ahead." Sophia released her clasp on the captain's arm and moved toward the front of the group. She pushed through a few of the bushes until she could step out onto the flat top of the hill that formed the steps. "Here they are: the Fairy Steps."

"What a lovely view of the village from here. Miss Townsend, is that Beetham?"

"Yes, Miss Hamilton. That is Beetham."

"I should like to walk into the village before we leave."

"We shall do that tomorrow then, my love," Bateman said as he kissed Theo's gloved hand.

Captain Smith-Williams looked ready to punch Bateman in the nose. Sophia felt as if the entire outing was spinning wildly out of control.

"Shall we try to climb the steps?" She kept her voice bright.

"Oh, let's!" Miss Hamilton said. "What did you say the fable was?"

"If you climb the steps without touching the wall, a fairy will grant you a wish."

"Up or down? Does it matter if we climb up the steps or down?" asked Ian.

"I don't think it matters either way, Mr. McDonald," Sophia replied.

"Miss Townsend, have you climbed the steps without touching?" Lady Catherine asked.

"I have, Lady Catherine."

"And did you get your wish?"

"Not as of yet, ma'am," Sophia said with a laugh.

"How do we reach the bottom so we can climb up?"

"There is a path down the hill just through those bushes, Captain. Be careful, it is steep." Sophia watched as the party went down the hill to try to climb the steps.

"Not going to give it another go, Sophia?" Ian asked.

"No, my days of believing in magic are over."

They stood together watching the group struggle down the hill. "Think someone will climb the steps?" she asked.

"It's doubtful. Not on the first try."

Sophia smirked. "We did it."

Ian looked down at her and smiled. "We did, didn't we? If I remember right, you shouted your wish at me."

"Please do not remind me." She liked Ian when he was like this: friendly, comfortable. She could become used to the camaraderie, the teasing. If she were to be honest with herself, she could become used to his kisses.

"What are you thinking now?"

Sophia felt her face heat. "Nothing, really."

"Your blush gives you away. You were thinking about me."

"Your arrogance astounds me. I was thinking how comical it would be to see Lady Catherine land on her bum on that hill."

"Wicked girl."

"Miss Townsend! We made it? What next?" Miss Hamilton was on the first step.

"Now you must climb to the top without touching the side walls. If you touch them, you won't get your wish."

"I'm determined to get my wish." Theo placed her foot on the bottom step. She took a step and wobbled.

Captain Smith-Williams and Bateman both jumped to her aid. They stood glaring at each other like two bulls.

"What's that about?"

"Ian, please don't let them come to blows. Trust me, we do not need the truth coming out now."

"We will talk about this later."

"Go, quickly before things get worse."

Ian quickly made his way down the hill to defuse the situation. What the hell was wrong with those two? By the time he got down the hill and back around to the bottom of the steps, Captain Smith-Williams had backed away, allowing Bateman to assist Miss Hamilton.

"You have to make her stop, McDonald," the captain said.

"Captain, I see no harm in her climbing the steps."

"But if she falls—"

Ian glanced between the two. "She'll be fine with Bateman. He won't let her fall."

Captain Smith-Williams looked deflated.

"Captain, are you climbing?"

"I think I'll join Miss Townsend at the top."

Ian glanced up at Sophia as the captain made his way back up the hill, his shoulders slumped. He pitied the man; he really did. Ian turned to Lady Catherine, who had her foot on the first step but looked unsure.

"Lady Catherine, are you going to climb the steps as well?"

"I will, if you will assist me. I'm afraid I might fall."

Ian's own choices were limited. He could either allow Catherine to try to climb the steps herself—a dangerous proposition—or risk Sophia's ire. Catherine won. He didn't want to be the one who carried her back to the house if she fell.

"What do I hold on to? These steps are so uneven!" Catherine complained.

"You have to find your balance Tilt yourself forward toward the next step to keep from touching the sides."

"You've done this before?"

"Once, with Miss Townsend."

"And did you get your wish?"

"No." Nor was he likely to.

Catherine took the steps slowly, now that she'd heard Sophia had managed to climb them. Ian could feel her determination. She wobbled on a few of the steps but finally made it to the top.

The breeze picked up as they stepped on the flat part of the rock that formed the ledge at the top. The air was cooler. He looked at Sophia. God, he wished she was his.

Catherine turned in his arms. "Do you feel the breeze?"

"I think there's a storm coming. We'd best get back."

Catherine looked disappointed.

"Did you make a wish?"

She shook her head. "What good would it do?"

Considering her situation, she had a point. "Come, we should join the others." He offered her his arm and led her back toward the group.

Miss Hamilton was laughing, joking about having to touch the wall to keep from crashing into Lord Bateman. Catherine released his arm to join Miss Hamilton.

Bateman looked bored as he moved to stand next to Ian.

"Did she climb without touching?" Ian asked him.

"No, and she almost had me falling backward down the steps."

"Lucky for all of us you didn't."

"I imagine that more than a few problems would be solved if I fell."

"Now you are being macabre."

Bateman nodded. "A distant cousin would inherit the mess I've made."

"Think where that would leave your sister, man."

"Are there refreshments? I'm so very thirsty," Lady Catherine said.

"I had the housekeeper pack us a basket of refreshments. I thought we'd sit under the trees in the shade." Sophia ushered her guests to the area where a footman had spread a cloth and set out treats. As the rest of the group moved to help themselves to water and cold beer, Ian stopped beside Sophia. "What is going on with Captain Smith-William?"

"I'll not discuss it here."

As she kept that serene smile on her face, he couldn't tell if she was delaying because of their company or because she didn't want to talk to him. Ian opted for the former. "Meet me in the garden tonight then, at midnight, after the house settles down?"

Her smiled faded. "Ian, what if we're seen? I cannot risk it."

"Then come to my room. We have much to discuss."

"And that is a better option? The garden is safer." Sophia got that stubborn expression in her eyes. "The captain told me in strict confidence."

Ian looked down at her in amazement. "Sophia, you've never let that prevent you from telling all before."

"You are incorrigible."

Ian spotted Lady Catherine coming toward him with a glass. "I thought you'd like some beer," she said.

"Thank you, Catherine."

"Someone must look out for you," she said with a smile.

Ian turned back to Sophia only to find her moving toward the picnic. She accepted a glass of wine from one of the servants and sat beside Captain Smith-Williams, who was some distance away from Bateman and Miss Hamilton.

"Perhaps the captain has focused his attentions on someone attainable."

Ian looked down at Catherine. "That's a rather harsh statement."

"My brother is determined to marry Miss Hamilton. Her father is in trade, but the family is of good society."

"You do not think Miss Townsend is of good society?"

"I've already told you what I think of Sophia Townsend."

"I'm surprised your brother would consider lowering his standards to court Miss Hamilton."

"Really, Ian, you surprise me. If her father hadn't settled such a large sum on her, she wouldn't be here."

"So you are for a dynastic marriage?"

"I have no choice but to believe in the institution." Catherine stared at her brother for a long time. "His position as earl won't allow him to earn a living."

"Be realistic, Catherine. Had he taken care of the estates, neither of you would be in this position."

"Father had a hand in it as well."

"He did, but your brother has held the position for a good while and hasn't done anything to solve the problem." Ian looked down at his cousin. "Do yourself a favor and find a nice man to marry."

"I thought I had."

Chapter 12

Ian waited in the garden for the midnight hour. The house was quiet and dark, as the guests had finally succumbed to country hours.

In the distance, lightning flashed in the night sky. He wondered if they'd get rain tonight and, if so, how long he could keep Sophia with him.

His conversation with Catherine at the picnic by the Fairy Steps had weighed on his mind. She was determined that they marry and did not appear willing to take no for an answer.

Dinner had been another strained affair as Captain Smith-Williams sunk lower into his blue mood and Lord Bateman pursued Miss Hamilton. Catherine had hung on Ian's arm, not letting anyone get a word in edgewise. He'd been glad to sneak away and call it an early night.

He was looking forward to time alone with Sophia.

The glass door leading to the terrace off the parlor opened. He could see the shape of a woman. He stepped into the shadows in case it was Catherine. The last thing he wanted to do was fight off her attentions.

"Ian?"

Sophia's voice could barely be heard over the sounds of the crickets and frogs. Ian stepped out of the darkness to meet her. "I'm here." He kept his voice to just barely above a whisper.

Ian took her hand and led her to the path leading to the old cottage. Given the summer warmth, most of the guests would be sleeping with their windows open. Anyone would be able to hear them if they were too close to the house.

They walked silently into the woods away from the house. The air was cooling as a breeze from the oncoming storm stirred the trees. "I don't know how long we have, Sophia. There is rain coming."

"This won't take long."

She pulled her hand free as they reached the old stone fence where the cottage used to be. The moon colored everything in a silver light.

"Captain Smith-Williams seemed upset during dinner tonight."

Sophia sighed. "It is a mess. Miss Hamilton may be pregnant."

"So he has compromised her." He wasn't surprised. The two could barely stand to be apart from each other. If she was with Lord Bateman, Smith-Williams was lurking close by.

"I'm afraid so. She's been promised to Lord Bateman by her father. Her mother is already planning the wedding."

"Then why has she continued the charade? Surely if she's given herself to the captain, Miss Hamilton couldn't possibly marry Bateman."

"It's not that simple, Ian. There is a great deal of money involved. Do you see Lord Bateman relinquishing that amount of money because his fiancée is in love with someone else?"

Sophia had a point. Bateman needed cash. It would also cause more problems for him if Bateman didn't have the influx of coin from Miss Hamilton's generous settlement. "So she is pregnant."

Sophia smiled. "That's not what I said."

"Is she pregnant? Or not?"

"I do not know for certain and neither does the captain, I'm afraid."

"It might be too soon to know."

Sophia laughed nervously. "And how would you know about that?"

Ian brushed a strand of hair from Sophia's face. "Women's cycles are common knowledge, and I'm good at math."

"This is highly inappropriate."

"You're embarrassed."

"These are not things we should be discussing."

Ian laughed. "You are embarrassed. I didn't think that was possible."

She pushed away from him. "I think I shall return to the house."

"Sophia, stay, please. We have to solve this."

"No. We do not. This is Miss Hamilton and the captain's issue."

He looked out into the night sky. "It isn't just their problem. It is mine as well."

"Yours? How so?"

"Bateman is deeply in debt. So much so that even Miss Hamilton's money won't be enough to settle the debt."

"I had no idea it was as bad as that. Poor Lady Catherine."

"Indeed. Bateman has already asked me for money. A great deal of money."

"You are not a relative; why would he do such a thing?"

"He suggested that I owe the family. Bateman's father paid for my education."

"But you've repaid it, correct?"

Ian nodded. "If it were only that simple. My connection to the family is a longstanding one. Bateman's debts are very large and he's borrowed from some very unscrupulous money lenders."

"Dear God, what possessed him to do such a thing?"

"Desperation, I guess," Ian said. "I can marry Catherine or I can pay off the lenders."

"You do not have to do anything unless you want to."

"If he doesn't marry Miss Hamilton and her pound notes, he'll need money from me."

Sophia's jaw dropped. "You have that much money?"

It was his turn to blush. "I do."

"I had no idea sheep were so profitable."

Ian ignored her derisive comment. "Perhaps you should ask Miss Hamilton if she's increasing."

Sophia snorted. "That would be a pleasant conversation. 'Tell me, Miss Hamilton, are you enceinte?' No, thank you."

Thunder rumbled in the distance. Sophia looked up at the sky as lightning flashed. Ian could feel her tensing.

"It's miles away."

She nodded but didn't relax.

"Do you want to go inside?"

"I'm fine. As you said, it's miles away."

He studied her in the limited light. "Do storms make you nervous, Sophia?"

"Sometimes." She wrapped her arms around herself.

He wanted to fold her into his arms, keep her safe, keep her happy. But if Bateman were free, would she pursue him? "If Miss Hamilton were to marry her captain, would you pursue Lord Bateman?"

She looked at him. "I don't know. This is a side of him I had no idea existed."

"What do you mean?"

"In Town, he was charming, attentive. He brought presents, flowers and candy. He took me to Gunter's for ices. It was hard not to like being on his arm."

"It was all a game."

"Indeed." Sophia gave a bitter laugh. "I was completely fooled by him. I was flattered by his attentions. What woman wouldn't be?"

"He has shown his true colors here, I think."

"How could he be so very cruel as to come to my home and not propose?"

"Had he made you any promises?"

She shook her head. "There was the hope of a proposal, of a connection, given his attentions. I was persuaded to believe he might propose. I fear I gave too much credence to the gossip."

"He doesn't deserve Miss Hamilton. She's a lovely young lady."

Thunder rumbled closer, shaking the ground a bit. The wind picked up, pulling at Sophia's skirts.

"We should return to the house." Sophia turned to go.

He grasped her hand. "Don't go yet. Stay and watch the storm with me."

Sophia looked down to where Ian's hand engulfed hers in a warm clasp. A strong hand, yet gentle. Thunder rumbled again as the storm moved in. She wanted to stay, give in to the pleading note in his voice. "We really should go back to the house."

He tugged on her hand, pulling her close. Her skirts fluttered around his legs. "Why do storms bother you?"

She watched lightning flash in the sky. "It's silly, really. I was so young. Mother was so sick. She died, and we all had to go into the room to say our farewells. Everyone was so busy that no one missed me. I wandered outside and got caught in a storm."

"You've been afraid since?"

She nodded. The thunder rumbled and she felt that panicked feeling. "Let's go in."

"We are safe enough." His voice deepened. He tugged her closer. "Ian McDonald, what are you doing?"

His thumb rubbed against her hand. He grasped her other hand and raised it to his lips. "Trying to keep you here. We've barely spent any time together."

She fought a shiver as he kissed her hand. "We weren't supposed to be spending time together."

"How else could I seduce you?" He pressed his mouth to her palm.

Sophia tugged on her hand. "No seductions."

He pulled her hands and she fell into his arms, her body pressing against his. "This is better."

"Ian—"

He nibbled her fingertips, then released her hands to wrap his arms around her waist and pull her close. He sweetly pressed his mouth to her forehead and tucked her into his body. "Watch the storm with me. I'll keep you safe."

She nestled against his chest, succumbing to the feeling of being cared for. The wind grew stronger, blowing her hair in her face. Ian pushed the strands away gently. Her heart melted as she relaxed against him.

Sophia had never felt cherished as she did in that moment. It was a unique feeling, one she'd never expected to feel. She hadn't known what she was missing. She now understood why her sisters had fallen in love. To have someone to rely on, protect her, care for her, could be so seductive.

She matched her breath to the slow rise and fall of Ian's chest. His heart beat constantly beneath her ear. The storm moved closer, but she didn't feel afraid. She knew she was safe with Ian. Lightning flashed closer and she jumped.

Ian placed a finger under her chin to lift her face to his. His mouth teased hers, his lips barely touching her own. His lips were warm and soft. He didn't press to deepen the kiss; instead, he called to her with his mouth. The gentle, teasing movement of his lips, the warmth of his hand at her waist, seduced her with tenderness.

She was used to men sneaking a kiss and a grab. She was prepared for the grabbing hands, the crushing mouth. This kiss swept away all her hesitation, all her fears.

Ian lifted his head and pressed a kiss to her forehead, then tucked her back into his arms and held her close. "Watch the sky. See how the lightning dances?"

Thunder rumbled closer, lightning flashed. Sophia tensed, and when she did, Ian's arms tightened. She felt protected, something she hadn't felt in a very long time. The lateness of the hour closed around her. Her eyes grew heavy as Ian's warmth wrapped around her.

"No sleeping yet."

"I'm not." She yawned out the words.

"Perhaps we should go in. You cannot keep your eyes open."

She smiled and burrowed into his shoulder, breathing in the smell of soap and man. "It is after midnight."

"I will escort you back to the house if you wish."

Sophia shook her head. "Let's not go yet."

Ian chuckled. "I knew I could convert you to liking storms."

"I'm not converted. The storm is still miles away."

The wind strengthened, blowing her skirts around their legs. "Ian, may I ask you a question?"

"You may ask me anything, love."

Her heart skipped at the endearment. "Why are you in Beetham?"

He was quiet for a long moment, just moving his hand up and down her back in a soothing manner. "Matthews and I are trying to breed sheep to produce better wool."

"Did you know Lord Bateman would be here?"

His whole body tensed for a second before he resumed gently stroking her back. "He might have mentioned it. I don't remember."

Ian lifted her face to meet his. Sophia couldn't make out the look in his eyes in the dark of the night. She licked her suddenly dry lips. "We had better go back to the house."

His eyes were on her mouth. "Not yet. There's still time."

He bent his head. This was no simple, sweet kiss. His mouth moved more firmly on hers. The hand on her back pulled her closer. His other hand tilted her face up to meet his mouth. His fingers slipped into her hair and she felt some of the pins give way.

Heat flowed through her veins like warm sugar, pooling low in her belly. She squirmed her hips against his own, needing more of something. Every thought of propriety faded as his kiss deepened. Her hands crept up to grasp his coat, needing something to hold her upright. His tongue licked at the seam of her lips, wanting entry.

Sophia parted her lips and was sunk into the whirling storm of passion as Ian took the kiss to a deeper, darker place. Her blood moved sluggishly through her veins. A delicious lethargy filled her.

It was warm, sweet, and addicting. She touched her tongue to his, mimicking his movements, and one of them groaned. It might have been her.

The wind pushed her body against his so close her breasts crushed against his hard chest. His hand moved to her hip to still her movement.

Rain hit her face with a cold splash, startling her out of her passionate haze. Rain. Thunder crashed, shaking the ground with the noise. And suddenly it was like a bucket of water had been poured over them both.

One moment Ian was lost in Sophia's kiss, the next he was drenched by cold rain. It came in sheets. Sophia was already running for the house.

"Sophia, wait!"

He caught up with her quickly, grabbing her hand and leading her through the forest, trying to take advantage of the canopy of trees. "Come."

Thunder rumbled. Lightning flashed. Sophia's hand was icy in his own. She had to be freezing. His coat was soaked; there was no point in covering her with it.

"Ian, slow down," Sophia said as she tripped over a tree root.

He caught her before she fell. He wrapped one arm around her waist and urged her forward. "You are freezing."

"Quite an observation. Can we just hurry?"

He winced at the derision in her voice. He pushed past the bushes and moved the lower tree limbs out of the way as they ran for the terrace. "Please tell me you left the door unlatched."

"Of course." Her skirts were plastered to her legs. She picked them up so she could move more freely. "But I don't know if anyone locked it behind me."

"The servants were all abed."

"Yes, but Lady Catherine might be roaming the house, as she is wont to do."

"Or Miss Hamilton and the captain."

He wanted Sophia to come to him all on her own, not because she was forced to do so by propriety. The terrace was in sight. The library was dark. "Almost there."

Sophia said nothing. He could hear her breathing, labored from running through the woods. She did little complaining, which was surprising. They reached the terrace and his foot slipped on the stone. She steadied him.

"Be careful."

He turned the handle. The door opened silently. He pulled Sophia inside and closed it, locking it behind them.

"Do you think there is anyone else out there?"

He shook his head. "I doubt anyone ventured out but us. The storm has been brewing for hours."

"Yet we got caught in it," she said through chattering teeth.

"You should go upstairs and get dry before you catch your death."

Lightning lit her face as she watched him with a waiting expression. He wished he could read her mind, understand the question behind her expression. Did she resent the kiss? Did she regret it?

He wasn't sure he wanted to know the answer to that question, but he was also unable to stop himself from lowering his mouth to hers once more, to taste her.

Her lips were cold from the rain but waiting for his kiss. As his lips met hers, parted hers, she leaned into the kiss. He caught her shoulders in his hands to keep them from falling.

He could lose himself in Sophia Townsend. He'd always suspected it, though he knew she wasn't for him. Her body pressed against his as if she craved his touch. He pulled her closer, enveloping her in his arms. She felt so very good there, pressed against him.

His body heated until he no longer felt cold from the drenching rain. He moved his mouth across hers. She tasted of clean rain, smelled like sunshine and flowers. It was seductive and addictive at the same time.

Her hands crept up around his neck and sank into his hair, pulling him closer. He deepened the kiss. This time he couldn't stop his hand from moving over her breasts. Through the layers of her wet clothing, her nipples were hard. He cupped and squeezed gently, brushing his thumbs over each one.

She gasped, then pushed her breasts further into his hands.

He could have her. He could seduce her and bury himself inside her as he'd dreamed of doing. His cock urged him on, needing to be inside her, feel her tight, soft body clasping his. But if he took her, made love to her now, would she be his?

He eased the kiss back from that dangerous edge. Yes, he could have her now, but he wanted her forever. This was not the way. Not the time.

"Ian." Her voice was soft, breathy, pleading.

It took all his inner strength to step back from her and put precious inches between them. "Sophia, love, go upstairs."

"But—"

"Now, before I cannot let you go."

He knew his voice was gruff, harsh even. He could tell by the expression of shock on her face. It had just dawned on her how close they had come to the point of no return. She'd be angry in the morning, when she had time to think about it.

Sophia stepped back and away, her skirts and shoes making squishing sounds.

"Good night, Sophia."

Ian couldn't keep the longing from his voice, even as he knew he'd given away how he felt about this woman. The room was too dark for him to make out her face, which was probably for the best. He didn't want to see regret.

She left him alone with his thoughts.

He'd pushed too hard, too fast. He knew that now. He might have lost her forever.

Chapter 13

The breakfast room was full the next morning. Lord Bateman ate his full plate of food with gusto. Lady Danford was nibbling her toast and sipping tea. Servants bustled in and out of the room, replenishing food and pouring tea.

Sophia moved her food around her plate with a fork. Why had she gone out to meet Ian? Why had she allowed him to kiss her? Lord knew she wasn't going to marry him.

But she didn't want to marry Lord Bateman either, it seemed. She was beginning to think she wasn't meant for this dynastic marriage nonsense after all.

Nathaniel stepped into the room and motioned for coffee. "Does anyone know why the carpet in the library is wet?"

Sophia felt her face flush red but she kept her head down toward her plate. The last thing she needed was for Nathaniel to learn she'd been out after midnight with his business partner.

Lady Danford studied her, her eyebrows raised. Sophia felt her face flush again. "It was raining very hard last night."

Nathaniel looked at her.

"The storm woke me."

Ian stepped into the room and broke the quiet that followed. "Good morning."

"McDonald. You wouldn't happen to know why the carpet in front of the library door is soaked, would you?" Nathaniel asked.

Sophia took a bite of toast and chewed, afraid to glance at Ian, afraid she would give them away.

"I have no idea. I did take a walk last night to help myself sleep, but I was inside before it started raining. Perhaps I left the door ajar." Ian filled his plate and sat down across from Sophia.

"This penchant for late-night walking is curious, McDonald. Have you always had trouble sleeping?" Bateman asked.

"Not always, but given the heat, I find a walk in the cool air very refreshing."

Sophia tried to not choke on her tea. Ian's eyes twinkled with humor. At least he wasn't going to throw her to the wolves now, even though it would suit his purposes to do so.

That very thought gave her pause. He could have ruined her by stating they'd been together last night, but he hadn't. In fact, he could have done it several times over but still hadn't.

"What thoughts have you frowning so fiercely, Miss Townsend?" Ian asked.

Her cheeks heated yet again. Three times during one breakfast was quite enough. "I was just going over our activities for the day."

"What activities have you come up with to entertain us, Miss Townsend?" Lord Bateman added. "I've had quite enough of sheep watching, I daresay."

"I thought we'd have an archery contest. The ladies against the men. I've had targets set up in the back garden."

"Archery? Interesting. Not usually your cup of tea, is it, McDonald?"

"We'll have to see, Lord Bateman. Are you up for a wager?"

"No wagers. You'll be on the same team," Sophia said with a rush.

"What fun is there in that, Miss Townsend?" Ian's eyes twinkled with humor.

"For once I agree, McDonald. I think a wager is in order."

Sophia pushed away from the table. "You two can do as you wish."

"Do you expect me to be present at this event?"

"And miss an opportunity to torture you?" Sophia smiled sweetly at the disappointed look on her brother-in-law's face. "Don't worry, Mr. Matthews, I invited Tony and Juliet. He shall play in your place."

She breezed out of the room, feeling as if she'd made a lucky escape, especially dodging the question about the wet carpet in the library.

"Sophia, there you are. Why are there piles of hay in the back garden?" Anne asked, coming down the stairs.

Sophia pushed herself away from the wall. "Archery. The ladies are challenging the gentlemen."

"You are putting a weapon in the hands of Lady Catherine? What time is this supposed to happen? I want to make sure the boys are safe."

"I thought around teatime would be ideal."

"They should be down for their naps."

"I thought we should do something together while the earl is here."

Anne paused before going into the morning room. "Sophia, what were you and Mr. McDonald doing outside in the storm last night?"

Sophia opened her mouth to answer, but the low, censoring tone of Anne's voice cut through the lie that was ready to trip off her tongue. "Uh . . . Well . . . How did you know?"

"Young Nat heard a noise and woke me. I thought it was the storm. I saw you both running toward the house. What's going on, Sophia? I thought he was beneath you."

Sophia searched for the words. "I never said he was beneath me."

"You call him 'the sheep farmer.'"

"True." Sophia couldn't find words to correct her sister. She *had* called him that. It was what he was. But now Ian was so much more. He was funny, tender, good.

Sophia fought the urge to squirm under her sister's pointed stare. Anne always had a way of seeing past her tales. "Sophia, take care. If you do not wish to be with him, stop meeting him in secret. If you're discovered, he will be made to marry you."

"We were only talking."

"In the woods. At night. Unchaperoned."

"It is not the way it looks."

"It rarely is, Sophia. Mr. McDonald is a gentleman. He is well aware of the rules Society places on us all. He'll do his duty."

"Anne—"

"Don't play with the man, Sophia. You won't like the consequences."

Sophia watched Anne disappear inside the morning room. She listened as Anne greeted everyone cheerfully.

"Miss Townsend, do you lurk outside of the morning room for a reason?" Lady Danford said as she stepped into the corridor. "Is this some new method of spying on the earl?"

"No, ma'am." Her cheeks heated. "I was just going upstairs."

Lady Danford looked her up and down. "Of course you were.

What was going on in the breakfast room? I could cut the tension between Mr. McDonald and Lord Bateman with a knife."

Sophia smiled. "Just some friendly competition, I suppose. You know how men can be."

"But what of the mysterious puddle in the library? Do you think it was lovers sneaking about at night?"

"I—uh—I honestly don't know, Lady Danford."

Lady Danford patted her hand. "Don't worry, girl; I won't tell."

Sophia had to close her mouth. Good Lord, was nothing a secret in this house? She made her way upstairs to her room before someone else could claim she had seen her last night with Mr. McDonald.

"Miss Townsend, a word. Please," Miss Theodora Hamilton said from her bedroom doorway.

"Of course, Miss Hamilton."

Sophia stepped into the girl's room. Her trunk was open and her things were folded inside it. "Miss Hamilton, are you going somewhere?"

"I don't know how to tell you this, but Crispin and I are leaving tonight. I cannot marry Lord Bateman." Tears filled her eyes and she pressed a hand to her stomach.

Sophia closed the door so they would not be interrupted. Captain Smith-Williams had been correct; Theo was pregnant. "You are—"

"Carrying Crispin's child; yes, I am. We love each other, Miss Townsend."

Sophia sat on the bed, a bit stunned. Miss Hamilton had looked so prim and proper. "But your father: won't he disown you? How will you live?"

"We've both worried over that for so long, but we cannot be happy without each other. My father will understand in time. This trip has gotten us most of the way there. Mr. McDonald has also agreed to help us. He has a vacant farmhouse available for us."

"You never intended to marry Lord Bateman, did you?"

"He is yours, if you want him."

"I'm sure he'll go back to London and find another heiress to marry." Sophia wasn't altogether sure she wanted Bateman anyway. He'd shown himself to be a bigger snob even than she. "I'm rather glad it's not you, Miss Hamilton."

Theo looked wounded. Sophia cursed her sharp tongue and took the girl's hand. "I only meant that you deserve so much better than he. Your captain loves you so."

Theo smiled. "He does. And I love him. We will be poor but happy."

Sophia squeezed Theo's hand. "I'm happy for you both." She was also a bit envious. She was going to end up a dried-up spinster, while Theo would be happy living with her captain. "What can I do?"

"If we leave too soon, it will cause suspicion. I need to know exactly how long Lord Bateman and his sister plan to stay. I've tried to coax a date from them but have been unable to do so. I don't want Lord Bateman to come after us."

"Do you think he will?"

"There is twenty thousand pounds at stake, Miss Townsend."

The matter-of-fact tone in Theo's voice told Sophia that she knew exactly why Bateman had chosen her. Sophia wanted to hit him. How could a man treat a woman thus? Yet they'd been doing it for centuries. "You are right. Let me see what I can find out. I will let you know, but you must have an alternative plan."

"I told Crispin you'd help us."

"Lord Bateman will suspect you are going to Gretna Green and will immediately head in that direction. You should avoid it at all costs."

"How will he know we took the Great North Road?"

"I shall tell him, of course. It would help if you put it in the note you must leave, breaking off the engagement."

"Good point."

"What point is that, Theo?" Lady Catherine asked. "I knocked, but you were so wrapped up in your conversation I don't think you heard me."

Sophia moved off the bed to stand in front of the packed trunk. "Lady Catherine, I trust you slept well."

"I did. Thank you." She moved into the room. "Theo, dear, why is your trunk open and your things in it?"

"I . . . uh . . . uh . . ."

Sophia fought the urge to roll her eyes. The girl couldn't lie if her life depended on it. "I was asking her to show me the dress she'd worn the other night. I wanted to look at the trims. I'm thinking of adding something similar to one of my gowns."

Sophia willed Theo to follow her lead. "Yes. The, uh . . . yellow muslin." Theo moved to the trunk and dug through it to pull out the dress. "I purchased these trims in London."

Sophia took the dress and spread it on the bed. "They are very fine. I love the embroidered detail. What do you think, Lady Catherine? Should I convince the shop in the village to order something similar?"

Lady Catherine looked skeptical and said nothing for a long moment. "I should like to go downstairs for tea. Theo, dear, will you join me? I'm fairly certain my brother is already awake."

"Of course, my lady."

"My dear, you are soon to be my sister—please call me Catherine." Theo followed behind Catherine as they left the room. "Are you joining us, Miss Townsend?"

"Thank you, no. I must see to the preparations for our archery contest today."

"Archery? How intriguing. Are we to compete against each other?" Lady Catherine asked.

"I thought we would challenge the men. So much more interesting, don't you think?"

Lady Catherine and Theo moved down the stairs and into the morning room. Sophia made her way back to her room.

Theo and Smith-Williams were going to elope. Lord Bateman would be free to capture another naïve heiress. For once Sophia was thankful that she didn't have a large dowry, especially the way he treated women. Nothing was turning out as it was supposed to. She just wished everyone would leave.

"When are these people going to leave my house?"

Ian chuckled as he watched Lord Bateman take aim and release his arrow toward the target across the yard. "I suppose he will leave when I succumb to his demands," Ian replied.

"Do I even want to know how much?"

Ian chuckled. "No. You do not." He clapped his hands as he noticed where the arrow hit, very near the center of the target. "Well done, my lord."

"I thought to show you how it is done. Matthews, I think you are next."

"If I must."

Ian waved his hand to shoo away a fly buzzing around his head. It was hot, but not as hot as it had been just a day before. He glanced over at the ladies, who were doing quite well and stood to beat them soundly.

Lord Bateman glanced over at them as well. "Matthews had better up his game if we are to win this tournament."

"I doubt he cares either way," Ian said.

Bateman plopped himself down in one of the many chairs scattered under the nearby trees. "Whose fool idea was this? It's too damn hot to be outside."

"I believe that would be your hostess, Miss Townsend." Ian accepted a glass of beer from a servant.

"I thought the hike to those damn stone steps was bad enough."

"If you disdain the company so much, why stay?"

Bateman sipped his beer. "Miss Hamilton has not agreed to marry me yet."

Ian watched as Miss Hamilton stood for her turn to shoot. "I'm sure she'll change her mind. How could she resist such an offer?"

"I don't need your sarcasm, McDonald."

"No, you just need my money," Ian downed his beer and picked up his long bow. He selected an arrow from the quiver and checked it.

"Don't be crass."

"I'm being honest."

"Where is Captain Smith-Williams? I thought he'd be part of this match."

"He's calling on my brother for some reason," Nathaniel said. "It's the reason I was called to play."

"Damned inconvenient. He's probably the only one of us who's a worthy shot. They are probably going to trounce us thoroughly."

"I think my ego can handle it. Matthews—how about you?" Ian said with a grin. He released his arrow and waited for it to complete its journey. It struck closer to the center than Bateman's arrow. "I think that will do."

"Good shot, man," Nathaniel said.

"How are we doing, gentlemen?" Sophia asked, joining them in the shade.

"It's damned hot," Bateman complained.

"It's summer, my lord," she teased. "Who has the highest score?"

"McDonald, I think," Bateman said. "But I shall change the odds. What say you? Will you wager that I'll be able to split your last arrow?"

"A foolish wager from this distance, but if you insist . . ."

"We have almost completed all the rounds; I shall have tea brought out." Sophia turned to go.

"It's too hot for tea," Bateman complained.

"There will be sandwiches and cakes as well, my lord. Or perhaps you'd like more beer?" Sophia said.

"Perhaps you could have tea brought deeper into the shade, Sophia. It's cooler there," Nathaniel said.

She smiled. "A perfect idea. Gentlemen, if you'll excuse me." Sophia moved across the yard to speak with the servants.

"It's really too bad Miss Townsend's dowry is so small. She'd make a good countess." Bateman motioned for a servant to bring more beer.

Ian stilled, waiting for Nathaniel to say something.

"A great shame, I'm sure, for you," Nathaniel said in a measured tone.

"She'd be a much easier catch than that mouse, Miss Hamilton. Probably a great deal more fun in the bedroom too," Bateman continued.

Ian ground his teeth. The man was driving him mad with his complaining. "Well, you've made your choice"

"I'm sick of people assuming I had some choice in this," Bateman whined.

Ian leaned his long bow against the table, holding the quiver of arrows. "You have had more choice than most, my lord." He emphasized the last two words.

"Gentlemen, perhaps we should go inside. Billiards?" Nathaniel suggested.

Ian backed down from the argument he so wanted with this wastrel. Given the comments made about Sophia, it was a better choice. The spoiled boy he'd known growing up at Bateman Abbey was little changed. It was doubtful he'd ever change.

"McDonald, come and let me show you how billiards is done," Bateman said with a smile.

Ian glanced under the trees, where the ladies were gathering. "Thank you, but I think I'll have some refreshments with the ladies."

Bateman looked in the same direction as the women took their seats at the tables, laughing and sipping lemonade. "Perhaps you are right."

Ian chuckled as Bateman moved to the shade and accepted a glass of lemonade from a servant. He bent down to talk to Theo Hamilton, who blushed and looked away.

"What will it take for you to succumb to Bateman's demands?" Nathaniel asked. "At this point, I'll give you a fortune to make him go away."

Ian couldn't stop the bark of laughter that erupted. "Good joke, Matthews, but as the man wants me to marry his sister, I doubt anything you could add would meet his demands."

"Those are his terms?"

"Needless to say, I've refused. Repeatedly."

"I can understand why."

With that, Nathaniel turned and walked into the house.

Chapter 14

Sophia watched with a frown as Nathaniel went back into the house. "Anne, your husband's ill humor is beginning to wear on me."

"He hates all the pretentiousness. I can't say I blame him."

Guilt washed over Sophia. She had brought this into their peaceful home. "I'm sorry, Anne."

"You couldn't have known it would turn out like this."

Sophia thought back to the conversation she'd had earlier with Theo Hamilton. "Anne, would you excuse me for just one minute?"

"Of course. It's only your party."

"I won't be a moment."

Sophia dashed across the yard to meet Ian, who was strolling toward her. She paused and waited for him.

"This is a surprise," he said.

"I wouldn't get your hopes raised. I have news I thought I should share."

"News?" Ian offered his arm and Sophia took it. "What sort of news?"

"It involves a baby." She grinned at the look of surprise on his face.

"Good work, Miss Townsend. How did you manage to discover this news?"

"She also told me of your plan to help them."

"I had to."

Sophia's heart made the funny kind of lurch it always did when Ian was near. There was such kindness in him. "I want to hear what you've planned." She glanced around her. "But not here. We cannot risk being overheard. Later."

"Tonight?"

She nodded. "I'm sorry you gentlemen lost the archery tournament."

"No you are not."

She laughed. "You are right. What has upset Nathaniel so badly?"

"Your houseguests are wearing on his nerves."

"Today has been a good day. Lady Catherine has been quite charming so far."

"You seem surprised."

"I am, rather."

"Miss Townsend, my brother has had a wonderful idea!" Lady Catherine approached them with a bow.

"And what is that?"

"He proposes a rematch with the top two players. I believe that would be the two of us."

Sophia felt a bit of unease. Perhaps it was the glee in Catherine's eyes. "I thought we'd have tea."

"Are you afraid of losing, Miss Townsend?"

Sophia did not like the tone of Lady Catherine's voice. "Not at all. I simply thought it would be nice to take a break from the heat." She strove to keep her voice light and cheerful. Lady Catherine had the light of competition in her eyes. She was not going to back down from this battle. And it was indeed a battle.

"Miss Townsend, weren't you the one who thought of this idea?"

"Perhaps the tournament should be the best gentleman against the best lady," Ian offered.

Sophia almost leaned against him in gratitude. She was hot and tired. Lady Catherine was a fierce competitor, causing Sophia to have to focus completely on the game rather than enjoy the day. Catherine had a way of taking something fun and making it much less so.

Lady Catherine lifted her chin and glared at Ian. "I don't believe we were asking if you'd like to join in."

"Lady Catherine, is that necessary?" Ian interrupted. "This is just a foolish game."

"You only say that because you bested me. There are reputations at stake," Lady Catherine said through gritted teeth.

Sophia quickly spoke, hoping to ease the tension. "Lady Catherine was one of the top archers in school. Her reputation for archery is legendary."

"I had no idea, Lady Catherine," Ian said with a smile. "If you will permit me to get you something to drink, I would love to hear all about it."

"I must defend my title!" Lady Catherine insisted.

There was no way around it; Sophia was going to have to shoot one more round. "Very well. Shall we begin once everyone has had tea?"

Lady Catherine smiled victoriously. "I look forward to it." She strolled off to rejoin the party.

"I'm surprised you did not allow her to win," Ian said.

"I had no idea she was such a stick about this honor. We are just a small country party."

"She's gathering her arrows. You'd best ready yourself."

Sophia agreed and went to retrieve the arrows she'd left in the target, marking that she'd won. The targets, bales of hay with paper bull's-eyes pinned to them, faced the back lawn which rolled down to the small creek that separated the Lodge from Horneswood, where her younger sister lived. She picked up several arrows from the other ladies as she strolled behind the targets. She could see Lady Catherine practicing her stance.

If Sophia beat Catherine again there was no telling how long she'd have to stand out here and shoot arrows before Catherine could win. No, she'd allow Catherine to win.

Sophia shielded her eyes from the glare of the afternoon sun as she watched Anne's two boys, Nat and Fred, playing in the yard near the kitchen. She turned away and began to walk toward where everyone was sitting, making sure to stay clear of the area where they'd been shooting. She frowned as Catherine picked up an arrow and positioned it. Surely she'd wait until Sophia cleared the area before taking aim.

Just at that moment, little Fred took off across the yard toward his mother. For one second, Sophia froze in fear. "Freddy! No!"

Fearing that Catherine hadn't seen the little boy, Sophia took off running, hoping to catch him before he was harmed. She heard shouting behind her but kept her eyes on her nephew. A sharp pain seared her upper arm and she stumbled but caught herself. She reached the boy and scooped him up in her arms.

"Auntie Sophia! Down! Down!" he cried.

The boy cried and wiggled, trying to get away. Pain, so harsh that she caught her breath, lanced through Sophia's arm. "Hush, love. We can't run across the range. You might get hurt."

"Freddy, are you all right?" Nathaniel said, he and Anne rushing up to them at once. He was out of breath from running from the house. "I saw it happen through the window. I thought he'd been hit."

Sophia handed the wriggling boy to his father. "He's fine, Nathaniel."

Nathaniel gathered the baby in his arms and hugged him. "Thank you. I knew I could not get to him fast enough."

"Sophia, your arm," Anne said, touching her sleeve.

Sophia knew she shouldn't look. She knew if she looked, she'd faint, but she couldn't stop herself from glancing at her arm. Her sleeve was ripped and blood dripped down her arm to her hand. Lord, how she hated the site of blood, especially her own. The edges of her world went black.

Suddenly, Ian was there, his arm around her waist. "I've got you."

Sophia sagged against him. "I hate blood."

"Apparently not enough to keep from dashing into the path of an arrow."

His arms felt warm, safe. "I couldn't let Freddy get hurt. He was running right into the line of Lady Catherine's arrow."

"Mr. McDonald, please take her inside."

Sophia could hear the shaking in her sister's voice. "I'm fine, Anne, really."

Lady Catherine ran to join the group. "I am so very sorry. I had no idea the boy was going to dart into the range like that. Why wasn't his nurse with him?"

"Lady Catherine, we will discuss that later. Please allow us to see to Miss Townsend's wound." Sophia was shocked at the anger in Ian's voice.

"Really, I'm perfectly fine."

"Does this mean you withdraw, Miss Townsend?" Lady Catherine demanded.

Sophia couldn't believe her gall. "Yes, Lady Catherine, I withdraw. By all means, declare yourself the winner."

Lady Catherine grinned and walked away.

"Please tell me they aren't staying much longer," Nathaniel said to Anne before adding, "Let's get her inside."

Sophia allowed Ian to lead her into the house, following Nathaniel and Anne, who still hadn't let go of their young son. "All this fuss for a scratch."

"It's bleeding rather heavily for a scratch, Sophia." Ian's voice was dark. "You could have been seriously injured."

"Better me than Freddy."

"Take her into the library. The light is better there by the window, Mr. McDonald."

"Anne, I'm fine. It is just sore." She felt she had to lighten the mood. Everyone acted as if she were dying. The worst thing she'd suffer was Catherine's triumph at being declared the victor. Honestly, it was just a stupid game.

"Prepare yourself for some coddling, Sophia," Ian said.

"I wish they wouldn't."

"You saved their child from being hurt."

"Of course I did. He's my nephew. Does everyone think I'm so heartless that I'd allow my nephew to be hurt? Why was Catherine shooting the blasted arrow in the first place?" She twisted her arm, wincing, to look at the gash. It wasn't deep but was long and still bleeding. "Didn't she see me?"

"I don't think she was paying attention."

There was something in his tone that made her think he was lying. She looked at him. "You think she did it on purpose."

"She had to have seen you on the sideline."

"Of course. But she couldn't have seen Freddy. The children were playing on the lawn, well away from where we'd set up for archery. The nurses had strict instructions to keep the boys away until we were done." She'd tried to think of everything. She knew the two boys wouldn't be able to resist the bows and arrows.

"But we'd broken up and gone for tea, so their nurse would have thought it was safe to allow the boys to join their mother."

She didn't like where his thoughts were going. Was Lady Catherine vindictive enough to try to hurt her intentionally to win the tournament? It was a game, a lark. It was a silly house party that no one in the Ton need ever know about. It made no sense. Unless she was jealous of Ian's attentions to Sophia. She could clear up the confusion on that score at least.

It could all have been so much worse. They were using standard arrows with fairly sharp points rather than the duller ones the children usually played with. "I don't think I will ever plan another house party as long as I live."

Ian brushed her hair back from her face. "You took years off my life, running off like that just as she was releasing the arrow. I don't like it when you're hurt."

Sophia let that comment pass unremarked upon, tamping down the thrill his words stirred inside her.

He brushed a kiss to her forehead. "I had no idea you could be so fast on your feet, Miss Townsend."

Sophia pushed him away and laughed as he landed on his bum on the carpet. "Never underestimate me, Mr. McDonald."

Ian laughed from his position on the floor. "Trust me, Sophia, I've never underestimated you at any point in our relationship."

She stilled. "We don't have a relationship."

He stood and tugged his jacket before bracing his hands on the arms of the chair in which she sat. "Oh, I think we do." His mouth touched hers gently. "Even if you do not recognize it."

Sophia said nothing, but her eyes widened.

Ian couldn't stop himself from gently rubbing a piece of dirt from her cheek. "I have to say this before your sister comes back in to clean and wrap the wound."

Her lips parted, and the temptation to kiss her soundly over-whelmed him. To hell with it! He bent down and took her mouth the way he wanted to. His tongue delved into her warm mouth, coaxing a response from her.

Sophia's hands found their way to his hair as she clung to him, mimicking his own actions, taking what she wanted from him. His heart pounded in his chest, and it was all he could do not to pull her into his arms, lay her on the floor, and sink into her. Ian wanted this woman with a passion that defied anything he'd ever known.

What had begun as friendship and a wish for a wife who could be his partner in the future was now very different. His feelings ran deep, much deeper than he thought he could feel.

He could hear the doorknob rattle as someone turned it. He quickly pulled away to stand by her chair. "Do not doubt when I say this," he said, his voice gruff even to his own ears. "Lord Bateman will have to live with disappointment."

Sophia gasped as Anne bustled in, followed by a maid carrying a bowl of water and the items needed to patch up Sophia's arm.

"Did you give her a brandy, Mr. McDonald? I think she needs it. She looks pale."

"Don't talk as if I'm not here, Anne. You know how I hate that," Sophia grumbled.

"If your tongue is sharp, you must be feeling better." Anne motioned for the maid to set down the water and rags.

"I'll get the brandy." Ian walked to the table holding a decanter and glasses. He poured two glasses. One for him, which he downed quickly, and one he carried back to Sophia. "Drink it slowly."

"What, and not follow your example?" She tossed the contents back and gasped, then coughed. Tears came to her eyes.

"I warned you."

Sophia glared at him. "Don't you have anything better to do than to stand here and watch me?"

"Sophia is right, Mr. McDonald. Please let me tend to her." Anne took his arm. "I think it would be easier if you were to wait outside. Better yet, could you help Mr. Matthews with our guests?"

Ian was torn. He wanted to stay to comfort Sophia. Hell, he wanted another kiss, but that wasn't going to happen anytime soon with her sister there to protect her. "I should speak with Lady Catherine."

"No!" Sophia said quickly.

"Whyever not?" Anne wrung out a rag and dabbed the wound. Sophia hissed from the pain. Ian fought the urge to go over to her.

"It was an accident. I don't want Lady Catherine to feel as if we blame her," Sophia said.

Anne put her hands on her hips. "I most certainly do blame her. She had no business shooting that arrow while people were milling around."

"Don't worry, Mrs. Matthews. I'll take care of it." Ian walked back outside to find the party rather quiet. Miss Hamilton and Captain Smith-Williams were still seated, talking quietly together.

"Please tell us Miss Townsend is all right, Mr. McDonald," Miss Hamilton said quickly. "She was so brave to charge after her nephew like that."

"She is fine. Lucky, really. It was only a surface wound. Where are Lord Bateman and his sister?"

"They walked away from the house toward the stables. Lady Catherine was rather upset," the captain said.

Ian exchanged a look with the captain. He didn't like where his suspicions were leading. Surely Catherine had not done it on purpose.

He walked quickly toward where Smith-Williams had indicated. The two were standing close together, arguing. Ian could hear the anger in Bateman's voice. It didn't surprise him.

"Bloody hell, Catherine, are you trying to ruin everything I'm doing here?

"It was an accident."

"Damned if it was."

"She's taking all of Ian McDonald's attention away from me."

Ian edged closer to the pair, keeping himself hidden by the bushes surrounding them.

"Catherine, your stupidity is going to cost us. Do you want that?"

"Do you think I'm going to sit around and wait for you to convince Miss Hamilton to marry you? We are desperate, Geoffrey. Someone has to fix things. You are obviously not up to the task."

"I've already approached Ian and he's refused to marry you. At this point, I can hardly blame him."

"There are other ways to bring about a marriage. He's rich as Croesus. It's not as if I'll have to live with him very long."

Ian stood perfectly still in shock. What the hell did that mean?

"What do you mean by that, Catherine?" Bateman's voice was low, flat. "Do you plan to do away with him once you are married?"

She laughed. "How Machiavellian of you, Brother. I'm doing no less than what you plan to do—marry someone you care nothing about for her money, then dumping her in the country."

"I care about Miss Hamilton. She is a very nice young lady."

"You will be bored with her within three days after the wedding. If you can even convince her to marry you. I can't seem to tell who you wish to marry, her or Miss Townsend."

"Leave Miss Townsend out of this."

"You can always take Sophia Townsend as your mistress. She really isn't worth doing much else with."

"Enough, Catherine."

Catherine laughed. "How will you feel having Ian McDonald as a brother-in-law? Father always said he was so much smarter than you."

"I've had enough of this conversation. Don't do something foolish if you know what is good for you, or you'll find yourself stuck at home with no money," Bateman warned.

Ian ducked out of sight as Bateman stormed past him and back toward the rest of the party. Ian had never thought Catherine could behave like this. She'd been such a sweet child growing up; spoiled but sweet.

Catherine took a deep breath and then followed her brother back to the party.

Ian stood in the woods for a long moment, mulling over what he'd heard. It was almost too much to take in. Bateman was jealous. Catherine was determined to marry him. He'd thought he'd put her off that path. Obviously not.

That she'd hurt another intentionally was the shocking part of it. He'd never thought she would go that far. He had underestimated her.

He moved deeper into the wooded area in order to circle back around the garden. He'd only raise suspicion if he returned on the same path as Bateman and his sister.

As he approached the group, Catherine was smiling and laughing, as if nothing had occurred. Bateman approached him before he could reach the chairs.

"McDonald. A word."

"Certainly."

"How is Miss Townsend? Was she seriously wounded?"

Ian couldn't doubt the sincerity in Bateman's voice. He wasn't as unmoved as he'd led Catherine to believe. "It was just a flesh wound. I have no doubt she'll recover quickly."

Bateman was visibly relieved. "Catherine did not do this intentionally, McDonald."

Ian played along. "Of course it was an accident. They happen sometimes."

"Yes. That's very good. I'm glad she'll recover and the boy was unhurt."

Ian waited. Bateman clearly had something else on his mind.

"How much longer are you intending to stay in Beetham, McDonald?"

"I've not yet decided. My business with Horneswood is taking longer than I expected. Why do you ask?"

"I've been giving more thought to your offer to buy the land."

"Yes?"

"I've decided to accept your offer. How quickly do you think you can produce the money?"

Ian quickly masked his surprise, especially given the conversation he'd just overheard. "I will put a note into the post directly for a draft from my bank. I can have it for you in a few days. For the agreed upon amount?"

Bateman nodded his head. "We will be traveling to Carlisle. Do you think you can have the draft directed there?"

"I'll bring it myself when I travel back to Dumfries. When do you think to leave Beetham?"

"In a few days, I think. Catherine is—restless." Bateman held out his hand. "Thank you for your help."

Ian clasped his hand. "Even if it comes from the son of your old steward?"

"That was bad form of me, to treat you thus."

Ian silently acknowledged the somewhat backhanded apology. "Shall we join the rest of the party?"

"Yes."

The two men walked back to the others. Tea and cakes had been cleared away, but lemonade was being provided to the guests. Sophia had not returned. Ian followed behind Bateman and accepted a glass from one of the servants.

"Mr. McDonald, you've returned to us. How is Miss Townsend?" Catherine asked from a chair in the shade. "I hope she's not seriously wounded."

"She is not," Ian said. "It was just a scratch."

"I'm surprised their nurse allowed those boys to run about in such a way. She should be reprimanded thoroughly," said Lady Catherine.

"That is for Mrs. Matthews to decide," Captain Smith-Williams said sharply. "You should not have fired with anyone in the vicinity."

Catherine's face grew red. "How many times do I need to apologize for this?"

"As many as it takes, I suppose," the captain said.

"Shall we move onto another topic?" Miss Hamilton suggested. "I hope we shall hear you play tonight, Lady Catherine. Your talent on the pianoforte is second to none."

"Thank you, Miss Hamilton. I should be delighted."

Ian set down his glass of lemonade. He'd had enough of Bateman and his sister to last the next ten years or more. "If you all will excuse me, I have some business to attend to."

"But Mr. McDonald, you just joined us."

"Leave him be, Catherine. If he says he has business, he has business," said Lord Bateman. Catherine shut her mouth and glared at her brother.

Ian didn't hesitate to make his escape. He needed to get the letter regarding the sale off to his attorney. He wasn't going to allow Bateman to change his mind.

Chapter 15

Sophia forced herself to focus on the bookcase in front of her as Anne cleaned the wound. It stung so badly she wanted to cry out, but she pressed her lips together to keep silent. She'd never had a high tolerance for pain.

What had possessed Catherine to fire the arrow when she'd seen Sophia in the area of the targets? While no one could have predicted Freddy running into the path of the arrow, Sophia knew Catherine had seen her. The rules were clear: no shots were even to be set up while anyone was in the area. Certainly Catherine had known the rules.

Sophia winced as Anne dabbed brandy on the cut. "Ouch."

"If I don't get it clean, it will fester," Anne said sharply.

Anne's face was grim, her hands trembling slightly.

"Freddy is all right."

Anne swallowed. She blinked rapidly to fight back tears. It had been a long time since Sophia had seen her so upset. She wouldn't fall apart in front of the staff. Sophia glanced at the maid. "You may go."

"Yes, ma'am."

Sophia waited until the door closed behind her before speaking again. "It's a flesh wound, Anne. It is nothing serious."

Anne bottom lip wobbled. "I know. I can't imagine what would have happened if Freddy had been hit."

Sophia covered Anne's hand with her own and squeezed. "It did not happen. None of us would allow that to happen."

"Thanks to you, Sophia." Anne set down the rag and reached for the bandage. She wrapped the fabric around Sophia's arm before tying it off. "I think this dress can officially be tossed in the rubbish bin. I hope you weren't too attached to it."

"It was one of my favorites." Sophia brushed at her skirts. "I suppose I'll just have to wander into the village and order another one. I'm sure Nathaniel won't mind paying this particular bill."

Anne laughed. "Sophia—"

"Anne. Don't." Sophia grasped her hand. "I owe you a huge apology. I've been such a brat since we got back from London."

The look of shock on Anne's face caused her to chuckle. "I guess you didn't expect an apology."

Anne shook her head. "No, I didn't, but I'll accept it."

"I can't believe how I've treated you over the years, all because I was so jealous of you."

"Why would you be jealous of me?"

Sophia took a long moment to form her words. She had been envious of her sister for so long, she wasn't sure where to start or how to explain. "It goes back so far I don't even know where to start."

"The beginning is usually a good place."

"My earliest memory of Mama was hearing her tell me to behave more like you." Sophia winced as she settled her arm more comfortably in the big leather chair.

"Surely that's not true."

"Father was worse. I have no talents except for shopping and sarcasm, and perhaps beauty."

Anne laughed.

Sophia sighed. "You play and sing. You were able to step in as hostess for Papa when Mama died. You took care of us when our brother threw us out. All during that time I made things so much more difficult for you. For that I am so very sorry."

Sophia waited quietly as Anne took in her words. "It was so silly, but I feel talentless beside you."

"You are not talentless."

Sophia laughed. "I lack musical talent. I can neither paint nor draw. I am good with a needle."

"You have more talent than that. You coax flowers into the most beautiful arrangements."

"Thank you for that." Sophia laughed. "A talent that comes in so handy."

"Of course it does. There is nothing wrong with being able to make your house beautiful with flowers." Anne pulled a chair close. "What brought on this change of heart?"

Sophia pulled in a deep breath and thought about the question. Why had she changed? The only answer to the question was Ian. He saw something in her that she hadn't seen in herself. "Ian McDonald."

Anne tilted her head. "What has he done to foster such a change?"

Sophia laughed. "I have no idea. He sees something in me that I had no idea existed."

Anne smiled and grasped her hand. "It has always existed. I never doubted it."

"You were the only one." Sophia stared out the window at their guests beneath the trees. "I am so sorry I ever invited Lord Bateman and his sister. I knew she was troublesome, but I didn't expect this level of rudeness."

"Her behavior is unpardonable, but we shall chalk it up to experience unless she is becoming part of our family."

Sophia stared through the window as Lord Bateman leaned down to talk with Miss Hamilton. "I don't think he ever planned to marry me." She turned back to Anne. "And I'm resigned to that. In fact, I'm thankful he doesn't want to marry me."

"Has he proposed to Miss Hamilton yet?"

Sophia shook her head. "She is too good for him."

"She loves Captain Smith-Williams."

"Yes, she does. How do you know about that?"

"Someone has been telling Nat stories about scary pirates and now he has nightmares. I've been up with him most nights. I've seen them walking through the garden together after dark."

"She might be pregnant."

"I'm not surprised, but will she marry Lord Bateman if she is expecting another man's child?"

"Her parents haven't given her much choice. Her father is determined to have a peer in the family. He does not approve of Captain Smith-Williams. She will likely be cut off if she marries him."

"It is a difficult decision." Anne stood. "You should rest. I also insist that you stay in your room tonight. I'll have a tray brought up."

Sophia really wanted to face down Catherine after the arrow incident. She glanced out the window again and saw Ian with her. She felt a pang of something she hadn't ever expected to feel in relation to Ian. She liked him—a great deal. She thought he might like her too. She wasn't sure she wanted to sit and watch Catherine Grayson fawn all over him. "I think you are right. I think I will rest. It has been an eventful day."

Anne stood and brushed out her skirts. "I should see to the rest of the party. Nathaniel is in no fit state to deal with them."

"I'm sorry, Anne. Perhaps you can convince them to have an early night." Sophia doubted it.

"Never fear. I can handle it. I've handled worse."

Sophia turned back to the window as Anne left the room. The library was gloriously quiet.

"There you are. Feeling better?"

Nathaniel Matthews came into the library.

"I'm better, thank you."

He moved to the window to gaze at their guests. "Please tell me how to make them leave."

Sophia laughed. "They should not be here for very much longer."

Nathaniel glanced back at her. "How would you know that?"

She smiled. "Just a hunch really."

"I take it Lord Bateman is not going to propose."

She sighed. "No, he is not, and honestly, I'm very thankful. He needs a great deal more money than I have."

"I have never understood why men allow themselves to be put into that position. My own father fell victim to gambling and living beyond his means."

"We have all lived the consequences of our parents' actions." It felt strange having this conversation with Nathaniel. Usually he was her severest critic. He took pleasure in baiting her.

"I'm glad you made your peace with your sister."

"I take it you overheard our conversation?"

He nodded. "You do realize that she has always had your best interests in mind."

"Despite the way things have appeared, I've always known. I just didn't show it."

"I am here to help you upstairs to your room before our guests come into the house."

"We are all guided by Anne's hand."

Nathaniel laughed. "I would not have it any other way."

Sophia stood and took his arm.

"Perhaps Ian McDonald would suit?"

"You really are trying to marry me off, aren't you?" She studied his face, looking for humor. He was serious. "You aren't joking."

Nathaniel shook his head. "He likes you a great deal. He has for a while."

"He's a sheep farmer, Nathaniel."

"He's extremely wealthy. You could do worse."

She did like Ian McDonald. She liked him a great deal. She didn't want to delve deeper into her feelings for him. He was handsome. He was rich. He liked sheep. Those three things didn't seem to fit together in her mind. She liked Town. She wasn't sure she could settle in the middle of the country and breed. She would miss the theater, the shopping, the musicales, and the gossip. "Since Mr. McDonald hasn't proposed, my response is not important."

"He will propose."

Sophia glanced up at Nathaniel. Her heart skipped a beat at the thought. "How are you privy to this information?"

"The man has it bad. Anyone can see it."

She wondered how Lady Catherine felt about that. If Nathaniel noticed, the entire party knew it. Her brother-in-law was not the most observant person.

"Would you say yes?"

Would she? If anyone had asked her just days ago, she would emphatically have said no. Now, she wasn't so sure. Ian was attentive, protective, and fun. She was addicted to the feel of his mouth on hers, his touch on her skin. "I don't know."

Nathaniel squeezed her hand. "At least you didn't say no. Thank you for giving me hope that perhaps you might someday marry."

She elbowed him in the ribs.

Dinner was a quiet affair. Sophia was noticeably absent from the party. Mrs. Matthews had insisted that she spend the evening in her room. Ian missed her. It wasn't because he was forced to communicate with Lady Catherine. It wasn't the knowing looks Nathaniel was giving him, as if he knew a secret Ian wasn't privy to.

Ian stood as the ladies made their way to the parlor so the gentlemen could enjoy their port. He took his seat again and accepted a glass from the butler. "How is Miss Townsend? Recovering from her ordeal?"

Bateman swirled his glass. "I do not understand why she had to run in front of the target while my sister was practicing."

"She was protecting my son." Nathaniel practically growled the words.

"Where was the child's nurse?"

Ian met Nathaniel's glance and shook his head. There was no point in arguing with Bateman.

"Lord Bateman, when you have boys of your own to contend with, you'll understand why the nurse was not able to contain the boys' excitement when the saw the opportunity to shoot arrows."

Captain Smith-Williams laughed. "I'm surprised she held them back that long. As a boy, I would not have been able to resist the lure of archery."

Ian had to agree. The lure of weapons was irresistible.

"I noticed you weren't present for archery, Smith-Williams," Bateman said.

"I've taken an interest in the work Mr. Tony Matthews is doing at Horneswood." Crispin Smith-Williams tossed down his port.

"It's not as if you have an estate to work with, Smith-Williams." Bateman practically spat out the words. "Why waste your time?"

Ian stiffened as anger coursed through him. He shot a glance at the captain. "I don't know, Bateman; if you'd taken more of an interest in what your tenants were doing, you might not be in the position you're in."

The room was silent and he knew he had gone too far, revealed too much, but damn, the man could goad him better than anyone else.

Bateman stood. "I think I'll join the ladies, where there is more civilized conversation." He stormed out of the room.

Captain Smith-Williams stood as well. "Gentlemen, if you will excuse me, I think I will also join the ladies."

Nathaniel waited until they were alone before speaking. "Well done, McDonald. You've managed to chase them both away."

Ian swirled the last of the port in his glass. "The man irritates the hell out of me. He always has."

"Has he agreed to sell you the land?"

"As a matter of fact, he did today. I've already sent a post to my attorney to draw up the papers."

"Now maybe he'll leave, and take his sister with him."

"With any luck, he will." Ian laughed.

Nathaniel tossed back his port and placed the glass on the table. "Do you still plan to marry Sophia?"

"If she'll have me."

"Why Sophia Townsend?"

Ian laughed. "You're joking surely?"

"No. I'm not."

Ian fought the urge to squirm under Nathaniel's regard. "You've known I've wanted her to be my wife for a long while now."

"Yes, but I never heard your reasons."

"She is beautiful, smart, and very popular in Society."

"In other words, you're looking for an ornament for your arm."

When Matthews put it that way, it didn't sound so well. "I like her a great deal."

Matthews was quiet for a long moment. "McDonald, you are aware that while Sophia is of age and doesn't need my permission to marry, I am still the closest thing to a male relative."

"She has a brother—"

"Who is away. According to Anne, you've been meeting her alone in the garden after everyone has gone to bed. Is she ruined?"

Anger welled up. "You overstep."

"As is my right." Nathaniel sighed. "I have a reason to be concerned. Your reasons for marrying her are shallow at best. You like her and she'll look good on your arm. If I were to discuss this with my wife, she'd refuse you entry to the house."

"You mean your wife would expect a love match? Has she talked to her sister? Sophia has no intention of marrying for love."

"Sophia has never been in love to know what she wants," Matthews said. "You, on the other hand, should know better."

Ian wasn't going to admit his feelings to Matthews before he said anything to the lady in question. "Again, you overstep."

"Do not ruin the girl if you've no feelings for her. I don't want to have to pick up the pieces and deal with two unhappy Townsend women." Nathaniel stood and walked to the door. "If you don't love her, leave her be. Don't drag her reputation through the mud just because you need an arm decoration. Find some chit from Town."

Matthews walked out of the dining room, leaving Ian alone. Damn him. Ian felt like slamming his fist on the table. The last thing he wanted to discuss with anyone was how he felt about Sophia Townsend. Hell, he knew he had it bad, but love? He wasn't sure yet.

She was a pain and a bit of a snob, but there was also goodness in her. He'd seen the kindness in her. But in the eyes of Society, he was well beneath her.

To his mind, the nature of his birth mattered little. His father's job as a steward had enabled him to have a decent education. He'd taken that education and made it work. He'd studied law. He made important contacts. He was able to increase his fortune through his partnership with Nathaniel Matthews.

By this time, Ian had acquired so much wealth, no one questioned who his parents were. Then he'd met Sophia Townsend. She was beautiful, vivacious, and had an ease in Society that he lacked. She would make a good partner in helping him move to the next phase in his career. Love didn't have to enter into it. They had passion and a friendship of sorts. Wasn't that enough?

Feeling better about the issue of Sophia, Ian stood and straightened his coat. He just needed more time; that was all. A few more days and he'd be able to propose. He'd make her his wife and they would be back at his estate outside of Dumfries before the month's end.

The plan was sound, well planned, as were most things in his life. It would work. He was sure of it.

Chapter 16

Sophia had had enough of staying in her room. Last night she'd sat quietly by the fire, trying to ignore the throbbing pain in her arm while listening to the party downstairs. Someone was playing a jig and she could hear the sound of boots on the wood floors. They were having a high old time while she sat in her chair trying to read.

She had her maid change the bandage for a much smaller one and dressed in a light blue dress with shorter sleeves to accommodate the injury. It felt better today, so no more staying in her room. It was also past time to face Lady Catherine. While she'd told Nathaniel and Anne the injury was an accident, she wasn't so certain. Lady Catherine was much more competitive than she'd given her credit for. She could have done the deed on purpose.

As she made her way down the hall, Sophia practically ran into the object of her thoughts. "Lady Catherine, good morning."

"Miss Townsend, how is your injury?"

"It's fine, thank you."

"I'm glad you are recovering from the accident." Lady Catherine made to move by her to go downstairs.

"Was it an accident?" Sophia forced her voice to stay light. "You seemed very intent on winning the archery tournament."

Catherine laughed. It sounded hollow, fake. "You have a creative imagination. I only wanted a rematch to help the time go by. It's been deadly dull since we've arrived."

Sophia didn't believe her. "I'm sorry your visit hasn't met your expectations."

"I daresay we'll make up for it when we celebrate my brother's wedding to Miss Hamilton."

"I daresay you will."

Sophia watched Lady Catherine make her way down the corridor to the morning room.

"She is furious with you, Miss Townsend," Miss Hamilton said, coming up behind her.

"I can't imagine why. I've not done anything."

"You've captured Mr. McDonald's attention. She came here with the intention to marry him."

"Do you think she really cares for Mr. Matthews?"

"She cares for his wealth, just as Lord Bateman cares for my dowry more than he cares for me."

"Miss Hamilton, that's not entirely true. He treats you with care. I think he likes you a great deal." Sophia couldn't believe the words were coming out of her mouth.

"It doesn't matter. In just a few days I'll be Mrs. Smith-Williams, thanks to Mr. McDonald."

"I thought you had decided on a date since you were already packing your things."

"I would leave right now if it were up to me. Crispin has other ideas. I hope to speak with him about it today."

"I'm very happy for you, Miss Hamilton."

"Thank you. Coming from you that means so much. I hope you find your true love as well, Miss Townsend."

Sophia didn't answer but watched as Miss Hamilton also made her way to the morning room for breakfast. Sophia took the steps at a slower pace. Did she have a true love? She honestly didn't know. She had thought she liked Lord Bateman, but there were things about him she didn't care for. And having Lady Catherine as a sister frankly scared her.

Then there was Mr. McDonald. According to Theo, he'd gone out of his way to help the couple. Sophia was dying from curiosity to know just what Ian had arranged. She'd had no idea he could be so romantic.

She couldn't deny that she enjoyed his company. He was witty, with a cutting sense of humor. He was ruggedly handsome, but he could be tender as well. His touch set her on fire. In his arms she felt a desire she'd never known, but was this love? She didn't know.

It was a tangle that was best solved after tea. She entered the morning just as Miss Hamilton took her seat. The three gentlemen at the table stood at her arrival.

"Miss Townsend, how are you this morning? We missed you last night," Lord Bateman said with a smile.

This was a new development. "Thank you, sir, I'm much better."

"It was very brave of you to rescue your nephew, but I assure you he was perfectly safe."

"Accidents do happen, my lord. I'm just thankful it was me and not my young nephew." Sophia took a seat and accepted a cup of tea from the footman. She added sugar and took a sip.

"Is your arm giving you pain, Miss Townsend?" Ian asked.

"Not at all, sir."

"Shall I fix you a plate?"

"I'm sure Miss Townsend is capable of getting her own plate if her arm isn't paining her, Mr. McDonald." Lady Catherine's voice was so sharp that everyone in the room looked at her in shock. "I'm only repeating what Miss Townsend said."

Sophia replaced her cup in the saucer and stood. "You are so right, Lady Catherine. I am perfectly capable of preparing my own plate of food." She glanced at Ian and the tick in his jaw caught her attention.

She placed eggs and ham on her plate and returned to her seat. She picked up her fork and pushed the food around.

"Are you not hungry?" Ian's voice was so soft she was sure no one else noticed it.

"I'm fine."

"What are the plans today, Miss Townsend? Or are you unable to provide entertainment for your guests?" Lady Catherine's voice was sharp as cut glass.

Sophia drew in a breath and pushed down her anger. "I thought we'd walk to the village. There are some fine local shops."

"How quaint! I think it's a splendid idea," Miss Hamilton said with a smile. "I should like to find a new pair of gloves for my mother."

Lady Catherine smiled indulgently at Miss Hamilton. "Then that's what we shall do. What time should we be ready to leave, Miss Townsend?"

"In a few hours."

"That should give us enough time to prepare for the walk," Miss Hamilton said.

"Is it a far walk, Miss Townsend?" Captain Smith-Williams asked.

"It's not far at all, perhaps two miles down the lane. Most of it is shaded by the wood until we get to the church. You are welcome to join us, Captain."

"I would love to join you, but I'm afraid I've already committed to another engagement."

"Should we accompany you on this shopping trip?" Lord Bateman asked.

Ian pushed his plate away. "Please do not include me. I hate shopping."

Sophia grinned at him. "Come now, Mr. McDonald. Surely there is someone you wish to purchase a present for? Some memento of your visit here?"

"I'm afraid not, Miss Townsend. I too have some business to attend to."

"Then shall we meet in the entryway in a few hours?" Sophia said.

"I look forward to it, Miss Townsend," Miss Hamilton said pleasantly.

"It appears you are our only chaperon, my lord. Are you sure you wish to accompany three women shopping?" Sophia teased.

Bateman bowed. "I should be honored."

Ian pushed his plate away and stood. "If you'll all excuse me, I've work to do."

Sophia watched Ian leave the room. "Goodness."

Bateman laughed. "Someone needs to remind him that all work and no play makes for a very dull gentleman."

Lady Catherine snickered. "You might want to take some lessons from him, brother dear. He's much wealthier than we are."

Bateman glared at his sister.

"I hope it's not too hot," Lady Catherine grumbled. "Can't we take the carriage?"

Sophia bit the inside of her cheek to keep an inappropriate comment to herself. "I assure you, Lady Catherine, it is a lovely walk."

"What's a lovely walk?" Lady Danford asked as she entered the room.

"Lady Danford, good morning. We are walking into the village for a bit of shopping. Would you like to join us?" Sophia said with a smile.

"As much as I'd love too, I'm afraid these old bones won't allow me. You young people go along on your adventure." Lady Danford motioned the footman for her tea and toast. "I would have you pick me up something in the village, if you would, Sophia."

"I'd be happy to."

"I'll write it down for you."

"Yes, ma'am," Sophia said. She finished her tea and toast. "I will check with you, Lady Danford, before we leave for Beetham."

"Thank you, child."

"If you will all excuse me . . ." Sophia stood and made her way from the room.

"Miss Townsend, a moment?" Theo Hamilton stopped her in the hall. "If I could have a word in private?"

"Of course." Sophia took her hand and made her way down the corridor to the empty back parlor. "No one will bother us here. It's rarely used."

Theo Hamilton was twisting her hands. "I think we have a date for our elopement. I need your help. I'm afraid Lord Bateman suspects something is going on between Crispin and me."

Sophia wasn't surprised. The two couldn't keep their eyes off each other when they were in the same room. Bateman had to have noticed. "Do you think he would stop the elopement?"

"Yes." Theo covered her face. "Father promised him the dowry upon the wedding day. This trip was supposed to give us a chance to get to know each other, but—"

"You'd already given yourself to the captain."

"It happened before I was acquainted with Lord Bateman. Papa is so set on having an earl for a son-in-law."

"And Lord Bateman has his mind set to gain your dowry." Sophia did not hide the derision from her voice.

When Theo nodded, she took the girl's hands and led her to a small sofa. "Do you love Crispin?"

"Yes, more than anything."

"Even more than your parent's approval? It is likely you will be disowned. You will have to become accustomed to a very different lifestyle."

"But I'll be with Crispin. Mr. McDonald has been kind enough to give him a position on his estate. We won't have much, but we won't starve either." Miss Hamilton smiled. "I'll have to learn to cook."

Sophia laughed. "That is something I do not want to do. Anne did a bit while we lived in the cottage and she enjoyed it."

"I'm sure it won't be too very hard."

Sophia grew serious for a moment. "If you think Lord Bateman suspects you are not going to marry him, you should spend more time with him on our walk."

"Crispin will be angry."

"If your father has made promises to Lord Bateman, he can make things ugly. It's best to pretend that all is well, don't you think?"

"You are right, I'm sure." Miss Hamilton squeezed her hand. "I hope I shall see you soon in Scotland, Miss Townsend, when you marry Mr. McDonald."

Sophia's jaw dropped in shock "Oh, uh . . . I have no intention of marrying Mr. McDonald."

"But I've seen you together in the gardens."

Sophia pulled her hands free as her face heated. "It was nothing really. He's not made his intentions known to me."

"Would you marry him if he asked?"

Sophia paused. Would she? The thought wasn't as odious as it had been several days ago. "As he has not posed the question, I've not given it much thought."

"I saw you kiss him."

Sophia's cheeks heated. "It means nothing."

Theo Hamilton stood. "For what it's worth, Mr. McDonald is a good man. Crispin and I will never be able to thank him enough for all he's done for us. I think he cares for you a great deal." She squeezed Sophia's hands before she left the parlor.

Could Ian McDonald like her well enough to marry her? Could she marry him? She liked him more than she thought she should. Right now she liked him more than she did Lord Bateman. But marriage was forever. If she married Ian, she'd be wealthy, but she'd be giving up everything that had been important to her for a long time. Could she live without the prestige that a title would give her? Could she settle for just being Mrs. McDonald? It sounded droll.

"There you are."

As if summoned, the man of her recent thoughts came into the small parlor.

"I thought you'd left for Horneswood."

"I was hoping to catch you before I went. What was Miss Hamilton doing in here?"

"Telling me that she suspects Lord Bateman is catching on to her feelings for Captain Smith-Williams."

Ian frowned. "They haven't been very secretive about it. He's a bit dim but not that much."

"True. They can't keep their eyes off each other. Lord Bateman is bound to notice at some point." Sophia returned to her seat and motioned for Ian to join her. "What are your plans today, as you will not come with us to the village?"

"I need to complete my work at Horneswood. I shall only be here a few more days."

Sophia's heart did a funny lurch. "You leave so soon?"

The squeak in Sophia's voice caught his attention. She wouldn't meet his eyes. Could it be that she was finally changing her mind about him? "Would you care, Sophia?"

"I've enjoyed your company."

"You've enjoyed our intrigues."

She smiled. "That's true. Can't you stay just a few more days to see our plans play out?"

"I won't leave until Miss Hamilton and Captain Smith-Williams are on their way. I'll need to be here to deal with Lord Bateman. He is not going to be happy."

"Theo thinks her father has already signed agreements with Lord Bateman," Sophia said. "Do you really think he'll make trouble?"

"He is counting on her dowry to save his estate. He is going to be very angry when she marries Smith-Williams."

Sophia shivered beside him.

"He may be more open to a match with you then." He kept his voice even, hoping he wasn't giving away how important her comments were to him.

"I seriously doubt it. He'll just find another heiress to replace Miss Hamilton."

He took one of her hands in his. Her skin was so very soft and delicate, the color of cream. "I'm glad you realize he wouldn't make you happy, Sophia."

He allowed his thumb to brush across the underside of her wrist, unable to resist touching her in some way.

"Happiness in marriage is a gamble at best."

"You don't really believe that, do you? Your sisters married for love."

"My sisters were very lucky in their choice of husbands. I doubt I should be so lucky."

"Even with a fairy wish?"

Sophia laughed. "You know as well as I that there is no magic where love is concerned."

His thumb moved in circles against her skin. "Didn't you wish for us to be stuck together forever?"

"That had nothing to do with love and everything to do with driving you mad." She pulled her hand away from his touch. "Don't."

"You like it."

"I shouldn't."

He brushed his thumb against her lower lip. "There isn't anything wrong in liking to be touched."

"Are you trying to ruin me?"

Ian paused. It would be the quickest way to gain his goal, but no. He didn't want her forced to be with him. He wanted her to come all on her own; to want him. "Perhaps just a little."

Color flooded her cheeks, but she didn't flinch away again from his touch. Ian pulled her into his lap.

"What are you doing?" She grabbed his shoulders as if she were going to push away, but she didn't.

"I am going to kiss you senseless." His mouth took hers before she could say anything else. He caressed her face, his fingertips barely grazing the surface of her skin before sinking into her thick, soft hair. Her scent flooded his senses with a seductive combination of flowers and warm female skin. His blood thickened as he deepened the kiss.

Sophia relaxed into his arms as she parted her lips to accept his. She wound her arms around his neck and eagerly pressed her body to his. She was beautiful and he had to hold on to his sanity or take her here on the couch. She was passionate, responding to his kiss by tasting him back, fueling the fire.

He lifted his mouth from hers and stared into her eyes. They were slumberous, her mouth swollen from his kisses, her body sprawled across his lap. She looked rumpled and delightful. "I should let you up."

Sophia's eyes cleared of passion and sat up so quickly, she elbowed him. He caught his groan. "This is highly improper. Anyone could have come in." She moved over to the other side of the sofa. "We must stop doing this."

Ian chuckled. "It's the wish."

"It is not the wish."

"Then what is it?"

Her eyes filled with tears and he instantly regretted his words. There was no way she could be feeling what he felt. Hell, he couldn't even name his feelings.

"We must stop, Ian. Nothing can come of it."

Ian looked down to compose himself. She stopped him at every step, but now was not the time to make her see his feelings were real. "Meet me here tonight. We have to go over the plans for Miss Hamilton and Captain Smith-Williams. I'm going to need your help."

"Of course. Midnight, correct?"

He took her hands. "Be careful with Lord Bateman today. Make sure he does not suspect anything."

"I will."

He kissed her, softly. "I will see you tonight."

Chapter 17

Sophia came down the stairs, tying the peach ribbons of her bonnet under her chin. Lady Catherine, Lord Bateman, and Miss Hamilton waited for her in the entryway. "I'm so sorry I kept you all waiting."

"Will your sister be joining us?" Lord Bateman asked.

"Mrs. Matthews will not be joining us," said Sophia. "Shall we begin?" She stepped outside, leading the group through the small park to the lane.

Miss Hamilton came up to her. "It is so beautiful in this part of England. I had no idea."

"The Lake District is very beautiful. Our estate north of here is very pretty," Lady Catherine said. "This is nothing compared to the hills and lakes."

"I've not been north of here, Lady Catherine. I'm sure the landscape is stunning." Sophia squeezed Theo's hand. "I hear Scotland is also very pretty. Have you ever been?"

"I've not, but my brother has."

"Scotland is quite the wilderness," Lord Bateman said.

"I've always wanted to go," Miss Hamilton said. "Sir Walter Scott's books paint such a beautiful picture of what it must be like."

Sophia laughed. "Sir Walter's Scott's Scotland is fiction. The reality is probably quite tame."

"I'm not sure I agree, Miss Townsend. In my experience, Scotland is quite savage."

"Lord Bateman, this is 1822. Surely there are no savage places left in the country." Sophia laughed again. "Besides, the king himself visited Scotland only last month. I doubt he would visit if it were that savage. Do you mean to tease us?"

"To what purpose, Miss Townsend?"

Sophia glanced behind her. "What do you mean, Lady Catherine?"

"Do you think my brother exaggerates?"

Miss Hamilton spoke quickly. "What sort of shops shall we find in Beetham, Miss Townsend?"

Sophia was happy for the escape. Lady Catherine seemed ready to pounce on every word. "There is a fine leather shop. I love the gloves there."

"Here. In Beetham? They cannot be as good as the ones we purchase in Town," Lady Catherine said. "Where in London did you shop? There is a glove maker on St. James's Street that I prefer."

"Thank you for the recommendation, Lady Catherine. I will look for the shop when next I'm in Town."

"That won't be for a long while, will it, Miss Townsend? If I understood your sister correctly, that is. Didn't she say it would be a while before you returned to London?"

Sophia winced. Why did Lady Catherine have to bring that up, now of all times? Nathaniel's refusal to take her to London still stung. "Then it's a good thing I've found a glove maker here in Beetham, isn't it?"

"Is there a book shop, Miss Townsend? I would love to have a new novel for the journey," Miss Hamilton asked.

Sophia swallowed her gasp at the slip.

Lord Bateman pounced. "What journey is that, Miss Hamilton?"

"Why, the trip to your estate, my lord," Miss Hamilton said quickly, too quickly given the way Lord Bateman's eyes grew hard. "You did say it was more than two days' journey, did you not?"

Sophia held her breath and waited for Lord Bateman to answer. She glanced over at Theo, who was pale. Sophia squeezed Theo's hand in support.

"I did indeed, Miss Hamilton. You did not read anything on the journey here."

"We had so much to discuss, Brother. There was no time," Lady Catherine said. "Theo, dear, we shall pick out some books together. Then we can trade when we've completed them."

"What a good idea, Lady Catherine," Theo said in a rush.

Sophia could feel the tension leaving Theo's arm as she relaxed. It had been a close thing. "What type of book would you prefer, Lady Catherine? A romance? Or an adventure?"

"I think a romance. Can you recommend one?"

Sophia laughed. "My sister is the reader. I would be happy to have her recommend one for you. The bookshop in Beetham is usually well stocked, thanks to the influx of visitors to the Lake District."

"Small villages are so delightful, with their eclectic collections of little shops and tradespeople," Miss Hamilton said.

"It has made staying in Beetham tolerable, but I will miss London a great deal." Sophia took in the stone buildings and narrow streets that made up Beetham. There were no museums, no musicales, no theater. She missed the hustle and bustle of the City. The pace in Beetham was slow and steady, year after year. London's pace was exciting.

"Are you certain you cannot convince Mr. Matthews to return to London next year?"

"He is quite determined, Lady Catherine." She was going to have to come to terms with being a spinster. Nothing had gone as she had planned.

"You may yet find your way back to Town if you marry, Miss Townsend."

Sophia ignored Lady Catherine's remark as the party entered the village at the far end, by the church. She felt she deserved the comment, considering how many times she had issued similar cutting remarks to others. She glanced around as people milled around the shops and the public house at the end of the lane and resigned herself to never escaping Beetham.

"How quaint," Lady Catherine said. "Shall we start with the glove shop?"

"Yes, let's. I would love to purchase gloves for my mother. Which shop is it, Miss Townsend?" Theo asked.

"Just there, past the bakery."

"Is there a place where a man can get a pint, Miss Townsend?" Lord Bateman asked.

"There is a public house, my lord. Just down the lane, where the carriages are."

"Then if you ladies will excuse me, I shall leave you here to shop." Lord Bateman bowed before he left for the pub.

Sophia watched as he crossed the lane. She hoped Theo had covered her blunder well enough not to raise suspicions, but she doubted it. Lord Bateman would keep Theo close until he could wed her. It was going to be very difficult to escape his notice.

"Miss Townsend, are you coming?" Lady Catherine said.

"Yes. Of course." She followed the two ladies into the glove shop, which was small and well lit but cramped. Gloves of various colors lined the wall and the shelves in the windows, blocking some of the light. Sophia hovered near the window to ease the discomfort the closed-in space gave her. She might like shopping, but she hated the boxlike feeling of the small shop. She watched as Lady Catherine helped Theo find a suitable pair of gloves for her mother. It occurred to her that Lady Catherine would be hurt when Theo eloped with the captain. Despite her condescension, Lady Catherine truly liked Theo. What was there not to like? She was so nice to everyone.

"Miss Townsend, I found the perfect pair," Theo said with a smile. "The leather is very soft."

"I may have to agree with you, Miss Townsend. This shop has some very fine gloves," Lady Catherine said.

"Shall we go?" Sophia asked once they had paid for their purchases. She led them out of the shop.

"Miss Townsend! How delightful. I was hoping to run into you."

Sophia groaned. Mrs. Dellwood hurried across the street, her high-pitched voice echoing off the stones.

"Mrs. Dellwood, I did not see you there. May I present Lady Catherine Grayson and Miss Hamilton? Lady Catherine is Lord Bateman's sister. Mrs. Dellwood is the vicar's wife."

"I'm delighted to meet you both. I had hoped Mrs. Matthews would throw a party that would allow us all to get to know one another."

"I'm afraid there's been no time for that, ma'am."

"Indeed, Mrs. Dellwood, our stay is a short one. We've only planned to stop for a few days," Lady Catherine said.

"Well, I'm sure there will be plenty of time for parties when your brother marries Miss Townsend."

Sophia felt her cheeks heat. How had this bit of gossip reached Beetham? "You are mistaken, Mrs. Dellwood."

"I do not think so, Miss Townsend. My cousin says Lord Bateman paid very close attentions to you. How happy your sister must be to know you will be so well married."

"I would not put stock in speculative gossip, Mrs. Dellwood," Lady Catherine said coldly.

Sophia watched the color fade from Mrs. Dellwood's cheeks at

Catherine's blunt statement. Sophia was trapped. If she supported Mrs. Dellwood, it would give credence to the gossip. If she defended Catherine, it would make any future relationship with Mrs. Dellwood difficult. "We should let you get back to your errands, Mrs. Dellwood."

"Yes, of course. Please give my regards to Lady Danford and Mrs. Matthews," she said.

"I would be happy to, ma'am."

Sophia ushered the ladies away from Mrs. Dellwood and on to the bookshop.

"I cannot believe she brought up that gossip," said Catherine. Sophia bit the inside of her cheek to stop the tirade she saw was building up. Catherine had been there. She'd seen the marked attention her brother had paid to Sophia. Now she was pretending it had never happened?

"Your brother spent a great deal of time with Miss Townsend prior to her leaving Town. I can see how that could be misconstrued," Theo said gently.

"Shall we go into the bookshop?" Sophia desperately wanted this topic to go away. She didn't need Theo defending her to Lady Catherine. Theo would only come out the loser in the battle. She was just too sweet.

"This discussion is not over, Miss Townsend," Catherine said as she made her way past Sophia.

"There is nothing to discuss. Your brother made his choice."

"I suppose this means you'll pursue Mr. McDonald, then."

"I'm pursuing no one, and if I were, it would be none of your concern."

"I would caution you about Mr. McDonald."

Sophia fought the urge to roll her eyes. What could this woman possibly say about Ian that she didn't already know?

"You'll never be accepted in the social circles to which you aspire if you marry him."

"It doesn't stop you from pursuing him." The words were out of her mouth before she could even think. Oh, how she wished she could grab them out of the air and stop them.

"It's different for me, as the daughter of an earl. I shall be accepted no matter what."

Lady Catherine breezed into the bookshop, leaving Sophia standing there with the door open. She would be so very glad to see the last of Lady Catherine Grayson.

Ian sat in the library in Horneswood with Tony Matthews and Captain Smith-Williams. The mating of his ram with several of Tony's ewes was complete. Once Smith-Williams eloped with Miss Hamilton, all the reasons keeping Ian in Beetham would be gone, save one: Sophia.

"When do you think we should elope?" Smith-Williams said. They had been strategizing over the best way to get Miss Hamilton away from Bateman.

"Bateman is getting suspicious of the attention you are paying her," Ian said.

"I've tried to stay away," the captain replied.

"Even when you are in the room, you are watching her. You don't even try to hide your emotions."

"I remember what that was like," Tony said with a smile. "You aren't much better, McDonald."

"Is there some lady who has caught your eye? Miss Townsend, perhaps?" Smith-Williams asked.

Tony laughed. "The man has been infatuated with her for the last three years. It's been fun to watch."

"I'm glad I could provide you with some entertainment, Matthews."

"Turnabout is fair play, McDonald," Tony said with a smile. "You watched me deal with my affections for my wife in amusement."

It was a true enough statement.

"For what it is worth, I think Miss Townsend likes you a great deal, McDonald. I've seen you kissing her quite a bit."

Ian felt the color rise in his face.

Tony's eyebrows rose. "Are you setting out to ruin my sister-in-law?"

Ian tightened his jaw. "I've had enough of this conversation. I'm not out to ruin anyone. Can we get back to the matter at hand? Captain Smith-Williams, you will announce tonight that you intend to leave the party tomorrow for Lancaster. You have business there."

"And if they ask what business?"

Ian sighed. He should have known a military man would have no imagination. "You could visit a member of your old regiment, perhaps."

"That will work. Then I come here, correct?"

"Yes. I've already mentioned this to my wife. We will have a room prepared for you. How do you plan to prevent him from being seen from the Lodge?"

"You'll have to stay in the house. I would like several days to pass before having Miss Hamilton join you. This should keep Lord Bateman from becoming suspicious."

"I will talk to Miss Hamilton tonight, then, before dinner to let her know the plans."

"No. She will not be able to hide her feelings. It's best to tell her as little as possible."

"I can't have her think I've deserted her, McDonald."

Ian needed a drink; he hated this type of thing. He would rather get everything out in the open and deal with it. Unfortunately, with Miss Hamilton possibly pregnant with Smith-Williams's child, things could not be out in the open. "She will know you aren't deserting her. I just think it would be better if she thinks you are going to Lancaster to make way for your future together."

"Ah. Makes sense. Good plan." Smith-Williams stood. "I shall return to the Lodge and begin to pack my things. I'll inform Mrs. Matthews at dinner tonight that I intend to leave in the morning."

Tony rose to his feet. "We shall expect you tomorrow, then, Captain."

"I cannot thank you both enough for your kindness."

Ian walked over and poured himself a brandy as the captain left the room. He raised a glass toward Tony, who shook his head. He downed the contents, letting the alcohol sooth his nerves. Was Bateman worth this?

"Why are you doing this, McDonald?"

Ian shot a questioning glance at Tony. "Can I not want to help a man in love with a woman?"

"Not without an ulterior motive."

"I helped you with no ulterior motive." He walked back to the large leather chair and plopped into it. "Miss Hamilton is carrying the man's child. What else am I supposed to do?"

"You gave him a position at the estate."

"I needed someone there to look after the place. He needed a job. As a military man, he will be well suited to the position."

"You wanted to snatch a wealthy heiress from Lord Bateman so he would be forced to sell you the piece of land you want."

"He's already agreed to sell me the land."

"Then to snatch the man's chance for recovery out of his hands."

Ian fought the urge to squirm. As usual, Tony knew him too well. "I can't deny I will gain some pleasure in beating an old opponent."

"Because of Sophia?"

Ian shook his head. "Bateman and I have a long history of competition. We were raised together."

Tony sat back in his chair, shock showing on his face.

"My father was steward to Lord Bateman's father. They attended school together, and when my father was down on his luck, as he usually was, the old earl offered him the position of steward. Bateman and I attended school together up until University. I attended Cambridge rather than Oxford. We parted ways there."

"I take it you were highly competitive."

"The old earl used to take great pleasure in holding up my accomplishments to his son." Ian had hated those moments. They had always come as backhanded compliments, with a jab at his own father being too poor to provide his son with a quality education. It had pushed him to be better than Bateman. He might not have the title, but he had the wealth.

"Does Sophia know any of this?"

"I've never denied being the son of old Bateman's steward."

"I'm talking about your need for revenge."

"It's not revenge."

"Then what is it?"

Ian remained silent. Tony could be relentless when he knew he was in the right. "I don't know."

"Was what Bateman's father did so very bad? He funded your education."

"And made me feel beholden to him for it." He spit the words out as if they were poison. "He made me feel as if I would owe him something for the rest of my life. Do you have any idea what it is like to have to grovel every single time you meet someone? To bow and pretend they are so much better than you when you know damn well they are not? To have to take charity because your own father was too foolish with money to provide enough for his own children?

Have you had to accept charity when all you wanted to do was slap the hand away and walk out of the room?"

Ian waited for Tony to speak. He'd revealed too much, but he could not stop the words from bubbling out of him like lava from a volcano. Perhaps he'd kept things bottled up for too long.

"What happened when your father died?"

Ian closed his eyes. "I had to beg him to keep us on so that my mother would have someplace to live while I finished school. He denied us. All those years of holding me up as an example was just another whip to beat his son with. He wasn't proud of me. He didn't even care. Mother died of consumption shortly after I moved her to Cambridge."

"So ruining Bateman's chances to marry Miss Hamilton will make you feel better? Bateman will just go find another heiress."

Ian knew that, but at least he'd get a bit of his own back.

"You can't get revenge from a dead man."

"Seeing Bateman brought as low as my father had been will make me feel better. He will taste what it is like to beg for something." Ian poured more brandy into the glass and tossed it down. It burned his throat and hit his stomach with a sour pain, but it offered him a modicum of calm. "I apologize. I did not mean to burden you with ancient history."

"You've held this in for a very long time, Ian."

Ian walked to the window and looked out. Tony had done well for himself. He'd pushed past his demons, given up gambling, and married the girl he loved. His life was comfortable, peaceful. "Do the demons still haunt you?"

Tony did not answer right away. "The old temptations are still there. I miss the chance to cheat fate and win, but it doesn't rule me as it once did. I have way too much to lose now to ever risk giving in to the temptation."

"This will be over in a few days. Once Smith-Williams and Miss Hamilton are married, Bateman will have to start over finding another heiress."

"And you think taking this from him will hurt him?"

"He is in dun territory and he's borrowed money from some unsavory characters. It is the reason he wants to marry Miss Hamilton." Ian ran his hand through his hair. "She is the key to it all."

"What of Sophia? Do you think he'll renew his attentions to her? She liked him well enough in London, or so I hear."

"By then it will be too late, I will bind her to me." The words came out harshly.

"What are you planning?"

Ian said nothing as he looked back at Tony.

"You mean to seduce her. Then what?"

"She'll have to marry me." As he said the words, he instantly regretted them. He didn't want Sophia to have to marry him. He wanted her to want him, to feel some part of what he felt for her. But time wasn't on his side. In just two days, the elopement would take place and he'd have no further reason to stay. There was no more time for wooing.

"Ian, you don't want to do this. Trust me when I say it. It will not endear her to you."

"I have no choice." He looked back out the window at the rolling hills surrounding Horneswood. It was peaceful here, soothing. It reminded him of home. He was so exhausted, ready for this entire mess to be done. "I won't take the chance that Bateman might turn to her when the elopement happens."

"Have you told Sophia how you feel about her?"

Ian couldn't keep the blank look off his face as he stared back at Tony.

"You poor, dumb sod. You have no idea, do you?"

"What in the hell are you talking about?"

"You love Sophia Townsend."

Ian turned back to the window in shock. He had not thought himself capable of such an emotion. He'd spent so much time working his way into Society and out of poverty, he had not had time to think about the gentler emotions. Did he love her? Certainly he wanted her. Desired her. Cared for her. But he wouldn't call it love. He wasn't capable of the emotion. It would better serve him to allow Tony to believe it was love that drove him to want Sophia for his own.

Tony moved to stand beside him in the window. "Because you are neither confirming nor denying, let me leave you with this, my friend: Examine why you wish Sophia to be your wife, then ask yourself if she deserves better."

Ian stiffened as he realized what Tony was implying. Sophia did not deserve to be a pawn in the game he was playing with Bateman. He'd stubbornly ignored the guilt that seemed to accompany his plans for her. She deserved her dream, something he'd never be able to give her. Ian met Tony's knowing look.

"I think you have your answer."

Chapter 18

Sophia waited for the downstairs clock to chime the midnight hour yet again. Rain beat on the windows, and for once she was happy not to be meeting Ian outside. The air had turned decidedly cooler. She pulled her dressing gown around her, wishing someone had thought to lay a fire tonight.

Dinner and the evening had been tense affairs. Captain Smith-Williams had announced he was leaving in the morning at first light.

He hadn't told Theo. Sophia could see the tears in her eyes and squeezed her hand tightly. She'd spent the rest of the evening trying to keep Bateman away from Theo lest she reveal the whole plan. This had to be a part of the scheme; Captain Smith-Williams would not leave Theo behind.

Unfortunately, because Ian had not bothered to communicate any of the details of his plans to her, Sophia had no way of knowing. It was just one of the many bones she planned to pick with him tonight. How dare he make these plans without at least telling her something. It was fortunate she could improvise when called upon.

The clock finally chimed, signaling midnight. Sophia crept from her room, checking the corridor for night wanderers. This house party seemed to be full of them. She silently moved down the steps, avoiding the places where the wood had a tendency to creak. She moved through the dark entryway and down the corridor toward the back parlor. There were no lights in the library nor the front parlor. The house was still.

She eased the door to the back parlor open and slipped in, closing it as silently as she could.

"Lock it behind you."

Sophia jumped at the sound of Ian's tightly controlled, soft voice.

"Good heavens, you scared me. Is it really necessary to lock it? Everyone is abed."

"Lock the door, Sophia."

There was something dark and dangerous in his voice. He stood in the shadows by the window. She could make out the shape of him but not his face. His voice was low, demanding, and there was something else as well that she could not name. She turned the key in the lock and walked toward him. "Are you all right?"

"I'm fine." The answer was terse.

Sophia should have felt afraid. It was a dark, small room. Ian was acting strange. And yet she didn't fear him. He wouldn't hurt her.

She stepped closer to one of the chairs near the window. She couldn't make out his face but sensed the nervousness in him. In all the time she'd known him, she'd never seen him like this. She sat in the chair and folded her hands, forcing herself to be calm. "Shall we discuss the plans you've made? I take it Captain Smith-Williams's departure in the morning has a bit to do with it."

He turned to look out into the garden. "He will stay at Horneswood tomorrow night and we will get them away the day after. You mustn't tell Miss Hamilton. I don't believe she'll be able to keep the secret if tonight is any example."

"She might surprise you."

"What has happened?"

"She almost gave the whole thing away but she recovered quickly. She played her part well. I don't think Lord Bateman suspects a thing."

"Even more reason to keep her out of it. We cannot afford a slipup now."

"I think Lady Catherine suspects something."

"Why would she? She seemed relieved to hear Smith-Williams was leaving." Ian started to pace in front of the window. "Did she say anything while you were out?"

Sophia thought back over the confrontation with Catherine and her warning about Ian. "We ran into Mrs. Dellwood. She was full of gossip about how Lord Bateman was here to propose to me, after paying such marked attention to me in Town."

"I suppose Catherine set her to rights on that subject."

"Indeed she did." Sophia squinted her eyes, trying to see his face.

She wished she had lit a candle. She wanted some bit of light so she could see his expression. "She warned me about you."

"What did she say? Exactly."

"She said if I married you I would not be accepted in good society."

"Given the society you kept in Town, she's right."

Sophia tucked her legs beneath her in the chair. There was something in his voice. "Is there something else you should tell me, Ian?"

"What else did she say?"

"When I asked her why she was pursuing you if that was how she felt, she said as the daughter of an earl, she'd not be subjected to the same prejudice I would. Odd, don't you think?"

"Very."

"Marriage to her would be very good for your position, Ian. You'd be in the best of Society. It could open many doors for you."

He moved swiftly to her chair and loomed over her, his face close. She could see him now, his eyes nearly glittering in the darkness. Her pulse skipped, but she forced herself to be still, to wait for what he would say next.

"I don't want her."

"I don't know why not. She's beautiful, titled. Comes from a good family. You've plenty of money, so that's not an issue."

"She's not you." He sounded as if he had been forced to say it. "She's not you."

His words flowed over her like sweet honey. She'd been holding her breath, hoping to force him into admitting that he felt something for her. Her heart thudded in her chest as this big, handsome man touched her face with a gentleness that belied the harshness of his words. His thumb rubbed against her chin, as if addicted to the feel of her skin. She could say nothing, do nothing but gape up at him wondering when he would kiss her.

When had he become so important to her? She pulled in a deep breath to settle her nerves, and the spice smell of him, man and soap, enveloped her. When had she become so addicted to his touch, the scent of his skin, his commanding presence in the room?

"Ian . . ."

She couldn't keep the longing from her voice. She needed him to touch her. Not just the soft-as-a-feather caress of her face but his mouth on hers. She needed those drugging, soul-searching kisses he was so good at. She needed to feel his body pressed against hers, his hardness countering her softness.

But he didn't kiss her.

A sense of rejection caused her to pull away from the touch of his hand. She turned her face away from him, refusing to look at him, her skin heating with embarrassment. He would think her fast now, unworthy of his honorable intentions. All the horrible words her father had yelled at her flooded in from her subconscious. She fought the urge to push out of his arms and run upstairs.

"What is going on in that brain of yours now, Sophia?"

"You don't want me."

He chuckled, a low, rasping sound. "Far from it, sweetheart, but I want you to have a choice." He knelt down in front of her chair and framed her face with his hands. "If we do this, you will have to marry me. There won't be any going back."

Sophia knew what *this* was, and for once in her life, she didn't fear it. This man wanted her. He saw all her weaknesses and foibles and still wanted her for his wife.

Did she love him? She searched his eyes for an answer, but it was too dark in the room to really read his emotions. Could she marry him?

The question left her feeling as if she was teetering on a precipice. If she let go, she'd be giving up the dream of marrying a man with a title, the London Society she loved, and the life she had always planned for herself. If she let go, she'd be in Ian's arms for a lifetime. She would always know why he'd wanted her, married her.

"If we marry, would you stay faithful to me?"

"Would you stay faithful to me?" he whispered. "It works both ways."

Sophia didn't even hesitate. "I would be faithful."

"So would I." He kissed her.

Sophia's hands framed his face. His whiskers were rough against her fingertips. She brushed her thumb over his lips. "There is something I need to tell you first. It might change your mind."

"Nothing will change my mind, sweetheart."

She didn't believe him. "Do you mind sitting there? It will be easier to tell if you aren't touching me."

His teeth flashed white in the darkness. "So, my touch affects your ability to think. That is good to know." He moved to the chair across from her, watching her.

Sophia had thought his closeness robbed her of thought. She could feel his eyes on her. She was now the one who was tense, hesitant. She cleared her throat. "If we are going to do what I think we are, I have to tell you what happened when I was fifteen."

"Oh, we are going to do what you're thinking. I guarantee it."

She shivered at the confident heat in his tone. "You might want to wait before you say that."

"Does this have something to do with why you are afraid of closed-in spaces?"

She nodded. "Things were very different after my mother died. There was less attention paid to us girls. We were left to our own devices far too much."

"What of your governess?"

"Our mother took charge of our education, and when she passed, Anne took over. Father couldn't be bothered with hiring someone to educate girls. We were a drain on his resources. His only hope was for us to marry well."

"Did he dote on you?"

She smiled. "He did. He frequently told me I was the prettiest of the sisters and it would be me who would change our fortunes. Looking back now, I realize my sisters had every reason to hate me. I lapped the attentions up like a kitten with a bowl of milk."

"As would most girls of that age."

"There was a boy working in the stables. He was tall, well built from working hard, with dark brown eyes and sun-bleached hair. He was there every morning when I went for my rides." She clenched her hands together tightly before continuing. "One day he was waiting for me in the stables. I was hoping he would steal a kiss."

"But he stole more than that?"

She shivered. "He tried. He kissed me. I liked it. He pulled me into one of the back stalls. It was dark. He kissed me again and I kissed him back. I didn't see any harm in it, until he took things further." Sophia stopped, her throat clogging with tears. Even after all these years, the memory still flooded into her as if it was yesterday. She rubbed absently at her arms, as if she could wipe away how dirty she'd felt.

"Did he rape you, Sophia?"

"No." Her voice caught on a sob. She rubbed at the tears with the palm of her hand. Why did it still make her feel like this? Would she ever get past it? "My father came in. One of the maids heard me struggling and sent for my father."

"What happened next?"

"He beat the boy within an inch of his life for daring to touch me."

"You saw him do this?"

She nodded. "I couldn't stop crying. Then he turned on me."

Ian sat up angrily. "Did he beat you?"

"No. My father would never lay a hand on me. It was so much worse than that. He looked at me and told me I was dead to him. He ignored me. I walked around that house without him acknowledging my presence ever again."

"Why tell me this now?"

"If we are to marry, you will want children. You'll want to . . . you know."

"It's called making love, and yes, I want that very much."

She wiped at her face. "I don't want to disappoint you. I've never been able to stand the touch of another man until you. You should know what you are getting if you marry me."

"Would you have told this to Lord Bateman?"

"I don't know. I was rather hoping I could just endure and think of something else until it was over."

"Trust me, you won't be thinking of anything but how you feel." Ian rose from his chair and knelt in front of her once more. He took her hands and pressed kisses into her palms. "Come upstairs with me, Sophia. Let me show you how it can be, how it's supposed to be."

"What if I can't do it?"

"We'll figure it out. We'll take it slowly. It will happen when it happens, but it will happen."

"You sound confident—a bit too confident."

He pressed his mouth to her hands again. "I have never felt this way about another woman, Sophia. I have wanted you for three years. I have waited those three years for you to want me back. We can figure out the rest of it together. Come with me now. Let me love you."

Ian stood and pulled Sophia up out of her chair and into his arms. He'd wanted to touch her while she told him about what had happened to her but knew if he did, she would not be able to finish the story. She needed to exorcise the memory. He'd learned words spoken eased the fear and the pain that went with them. He needed her not to be afraid tonight.

Sophia tucked her head under his chin and snuggled into his arms like a child, but she felt nothing like a child. Her curves, unhindered by the layers of undergarments women wore, were soft against his body. He fought the urge to rush, to mold his hands to those curves and press her even more deeply into his body. He hadn't thought it was possible to want her more.

He'd always sensed a vulnerability deep within her. She'd hidden it well from the rest of the world, but not from him. He'd always seen that piece of herself she held back from others. Now he knew the cause of that vulnerability. He treasured her all the more for it.

Tonight would be difficult for both of them. Sophia had her fears to overcome and he'd have to fight his own nature to take what he wanted and just give tonight, cherish her as no one else ever had done.

Ian kissed her forehead. "Sophia? Look at me, sweetheart."

Slowly, she raised her eyes to his. In the dim light, he could see the fear. He felt it in the sudden tension in her body.

"May I take you back to your room?"

"So we aren't going to—"

He kissed her, wooing her with his mouth, coaxing her passion. She responded quickly and in kind. She wanted him; that he was sure of. "Eventually."

He stepped away, needing a bit of distance to calm his own yearning to take her there. She'd had one bad experience. This one had to be special, something to erase the terrors from the past, a sweet memory to replace the bad.

Ian took her hand and led her across the room. He unlocked the door and stepped into the corridor.

They crept up the stairs and Ian paused outside her room. "Are you sure?" He had to ask once more. He was determined to give her the choice at every step of the way. She would have the choice to say no and he'd abide by it, no matter what.

Sophia nodded and headed to her room. He followed behind her and closed and locked the door behind him.

Despite how very feminine Sophia was, the room was rather sparse. There were no lacy comforters, or tons of pink pillows and such. The room was a soothing blend of blues and browns. There were a few brightly colored pictures painted by her nephews near the dressing table. A box of ribbons was open on the floor by the only chair in the room. The bright colors spilled out onto the dark carpet.

Sophia stood by the chair looking terrified. Her hands clenched and unclenched at her side.

"We need a fire," Ian said.

"Do we have to?" Her voice was breathy and high.

"Yes, we do. It is cold in here."

"The rain brought cooler weather."

"You're rambling on about the weather, love."

"I'm nervous."

He walked up to her and brushed her hair from her shoulders. "I am too."

Her eyes met his in surprise.

"I want this to be special for you. You've been hurt rather badly by another man. I want to give you a memory of how it should be like, of how good it can be."

"You've put yourself up for the impossible. I hope you realize that."

"I think I can convince you."

"Really?"

"Or die trying."

Ian took her hands and wrapped them around his neck. He ran his hands down her arms to pull her against him. "You're shivering."

"You're very warm. A veritable furnace, Ian. How is that possible?" She snuggled closer, wiggling her hips against his groin.

He grasped her hips to still them. This was going to be a great deal more difficult than he'd thought. He prayed he had the patience and stamina to get through tonight without making things worse.

Sophia was still for a long moment. He lifted her chin and kissed her. "Perhaps we should just go to bed to sleep."

Her eyebrows raised. "Really? But I thought—"

"We have plenty of time," he said as he walked over to the bed. "Give me your robe."

She slipped off her dressing gown and quickly climbed into the bed, pulling the covers up to her neck. "Are you leaving, then?"

Ian shook his head as he tossed her discarded robe over the chair. He bent to the fireplace and stirred the embers, adding more coal until the fire started to warm the room. Turning to the bed, he pulled the tails of his shirt from his evening trousers and pulled it over his head. He tossed it on the chair with her robe.

Sophia watched him with rapt interest. He fought a grin. He undid the buttons of his falls and removed his trousers, leaving his drawers in place. He sat on the bed and slipped off his stockings and tucked them into his shoes.

Finally, he lifted the blankets and slid in next to her. It was a small bed and she was pressed up against him. Ian pulled her into his arms. "Are you all right?"

She snuggled down into him, resting her head on his shoulder. "This is nice."

Ian sighed. He deserved a medal for his restraint. Sophia yawned, her jaw cracking. "You need to sleep."

"So you will stay?"

He kissed her softly. "I'm not going anywhere."

She closed her eyes. He could feel sleep finally take her in the weight of her body on his. It wasn't what he'd planned for tonight, but it was what Sophia needed. He tenderly brushed her hair from her face. She was so beautiful, and she would finally be his.

Chapter 19

She was warmer than she'd been in a long time, covered by a large, heavy blanket. She pushed against it and hit skin. Ian's skin. Her eyes opened and she found him over her, watching her, his eyes warm and filled with humor.

"Good morning, love. I wondered when you'd awaken."

She frowned. "What are you doing?"

"Trying to make love to you. You fell asleep last night." He grinned at her. "It was a very memorable night."

Sophia brushed her hair from her face. She wasn't her best when she awoke. "You're naked."

"Not quite."

"You lit a candle."

He waggled his eyebrows at her. "The better to see you with, my dear."

She looked down at her nightgown, now bunched up around her waist. She moved to push it down, but Ian pressed his body to hers. He was aroused. He had her trapped underneath him. She could feel the panic rise up. She pushed at him. "Get off me."

Ian moved to lie beside her. He propped himself up and gently brushed her hair from her face. "Shh, love, it's all right. It's just me wanting you, wanting to love you."

"What time is it?"

"Very early in the morning. The servants aren't even stirring yet."

"Then you have time to sneak out to your room before you are seen." She held herself perfectly still.

Ian kissed her gently. "Is that what you want? For me to leave you?"

Sophia didn't know what she wanted. She was terrified she would not be able to put the past behind her and respond to him the way he deserved. She'd be ruined and he would be stuck with a wife who couldn't enjoy this part of marriage. She was afraid if she didn't go forward, she'd be ruled by the past for the rest of her life.

"What is going on in that head of yours?"

"I don't want to disappoint you. If we stop now, you won't have to marry me."

He stilled. "Sophia, I'm marrying you regardless."

"But if we stop now, I won't be ruined."

"I'm not marrying you because I've ruined you. What I feel for you is much, much more than that." He lowered his head to hers in frustration. "I'm just going to have to show you."

Sophia closed her eyes as his mouth met hers in a deep kiss. This was no gentle kiss but one of passion. He held her face in his hands as his mouth slanted over hers again and again, each kiss pulling her deeper into passion until she could no longer form words, much less think.

Her blood thickened and pooled low in her stomach, but her heart pounded. She felt lethargic and excited all at once. She mimicked the movements of his tongue against hers, tasting him back. He tasted so good.

He came up for air. "I need you to promise me something."

"What?"

"Promise me if you have any bad moments, you'll tell me."

She nodded her head. Her hands touched his bare shoulders. The skin smooth as satin but firm with muscle. "Kiss me again."

His mouth moved down her neck as she gasped for air. "Ian?"

"Yes, love?" He toyed with the buttons down the front of her night shift.

"What are you doing?"

"Freeing you from this mountain of fabric you wore to bed." He finished the last button and went to spread the fabric open, revealing her breasts.

Sophia clutched the edges together, feeling shy, fighting the fear that was welling up inside.

Ian eased to the side and looked down at her. "Am I going too fast?"

"A bit." She pulled the covers up over her breasts.

He pulled them back down. "I want to see you."

She pulled the covers up again. "Why?"

He paused to look at her. "You are the loveliest thing I have ever seen. Your skin is like cream, so smooth and so soft. Your dark hair has a life of its own." He touched her hair. "See how the strands cling to me? Fascinating."

She relaxed her hold on the blanket. "Can you kiss me again? It seems to make me not think about it so much."

"With pleasure." His mouth teased hers again, then captured hers in a deep kiss.

Sophia let go of the blanket and reached for Ian as the kiss heated. She felt his hand gently push away the cotton fabric and cup her breast. She pulled away and gasped.

"Easy, love." He left his hand on her breast, brushing his finger-tips gently over her skin.

Sophia closed her eyes as his mouth traced her neck to her shoulders. His hand brushed the fabric away as his tongue dipped into the hollow at the base of her throat.

What was happening to her? Never had she felt anything like this, as if she was going to fly apart. He nuzzled her breast, then pulled it into his mouth. She squealed.

"Shh, love. We don't need everyone to come in."

"That would not be a good thing."

He laughed. "No, it would not. Can we take off the night rail now?" He tugged the gown up and over her head and tossed it on the floor. She clutched the blanket to her chest, feeling shy but, strangely enough, not scared. She brushed Ian's hair from his forehead.

"No bad moments?" he asked.

"Not yet." She lifted up and kissed him again, her hands in his hair. The blanket fell between them. The brush of Ian's chest against hers felt so good, there were no words to describe it.

"Slowly, Sophia, slowly."

"I don't want to go slow now, Ian. I feel so—I can't explain it."

"I knew you'd be passionate."

"Kiss me again."

He lay her back onto the bed, his mouth finding hers in one scorching kiss after another. She moved restlessly beneath him, needing more, but she didn't know what she wanted. More of his mouth on hers. More of his hands touching her. She returned kiss for kiss.

"More, Ian. More."

* * *

Ian reined himself in with all the control he had left. Sophia's excitement was intoxicating. He longed to be inside her, deep inside her. She moved restlessly against him. If it killed him, he would make it good for her—and it just might.

He pulled her breast into his mouth and suckled. Her skin was so very soft. Her scent wove a spell over him. He was never going to get enough of her. "You are so very soft all over." He pressed kisses under the curve of her breast. "So very pretty." His mouth moved down her stomach. His tongue dipped into her navel.

"Ian!" She jerked away. "That tickles."

"Good to know." His mouth moved farther down her body.

"What are you doing?"

"Kissing you all over." He pressed his lips just above her curls. He could smell her unique scent strongest here, earthy and sweet with her arousal. He moved between her legs, moving them wider.

"No!"

Ian paused. "No? You might like it, Sophia."

She shook her head, her eyes wide.

Ian moved up her body and took her mouth in his until she was mindless again. He trailed his hand into her curls and gently touched her, circling her sex in delicate circular motions. She pulled her mouth away and gasped.

"All right?" he asked.

"Oh God." She gasped, arching into this hand.

"If you like that, you're going to love this." He pushed one finger inside her.

Sophia squealed and he covered her mouth with his to keep her quiet. She took control of the kiss, hot, completely wild. Her hands moved his body until she found him. She gripped him tight and it was his turn to gasp.

"Sophia, sweetheart, easy."

"Did I do something wrong?"

"If you keep that up, this will be over before it starts." He kissed her hand and placed it around his neck. He nuzzled her neck again, then covered her with his body, his cock nestled between her thighs. She felt so very good. She pressed her hips to his and shook her head.

"I want you, Ian."

"Are you sure?"

Sophia nodded.

"That means you'll have to marry me. There won't be any getting out of it. You'll be mine."

Sophia reached up and kissed him. "For someone who is bent on ruining me, you are putting up a good fight."

"I just want you to be sure, sweetheart."

She kissed him again, "I am sure. Love me, Ian. Just love me."

Emotion overwhelmed him. His eyes stung. He tenderly touched her face. "I do."

Her eyes widened. "What?"

"I love you, Sophia."

Her eyes welled with tears. "How can you love me? I've been horrible to you."

Ian brushed the tears from her cheeks. "How could I not love you? You keep me on my toes." He bent down and captured her mouth with his. Never had he felt so much for a woman. This woman was special. He whipped her passion up until she was squirming beneath him. He positioned himself at her entrance.

"This may hurt, my love."

"I don't care. I need you, Ian."

"Hold on to me."

Sophia wrapped her arms around his neck, her legs around his hips. He pushed into her, slowly, completely, until he was fully seated deep inside her.

Tears ran down her cheeks. Her eyes were tightly closed.

"I'm sorry, so sorry to have to hurt you." Ian kissed her tears away. He held himself still, waiting for her tense body to relax. His mouth found hers with teasing kisses, each one deeper than the last, until she started to respond. His mouth trailed down to her breasts, pulling each one deep into his mouth.

"Ian?"

"Yes, love."

"It feels so strange. I am full of you."

He kissed her mouth again. "That's the way it works."

His hand reached between them to touch her sex and coax her passion back to full bloom. She pushed up against his hand and pushed him deeper. Deeper and past his control.

He pulled out slowly and pushed in again, watching Sophia's face. If she winced, he would stop, or try to. He wasn't sure he could. She felt so damn good, so warm, soft as velvet around him.

She gasped and opened her eyes in surprise. "Do that again." He flexed his hips again. Sophia's eyes went soft like melting chocolate. "Again." Ian repeated the move, and this time she lifted her hips to meet his. It destroyed the thin thread that was his control. He braced his hands and flexed again and again as he moved within her. He'd never felt anything so amazing. Beneath him, Sophia gripped his arms as she gasped and found her pleasure. The inner spasms pulled at him until he pushed into her with one final thrust and collapsed upon her. He lay there, stunned, drained of all energy until Sophia poked him.

"I cannot breathe."

"Sorry." He lifted himself from her and rolled over to his back. He pulled her back into his arms. He was never letting her go. Ever. He pressed his mouth to her forehead, unable to find the words to describe the pleasure he had experienced. She was his, forever. "Sleep, love." He kissed her again and let his eyes drift shut as sleep took him.

Chapter 20

Sunlight streamed into the room when Sophia next woke. The actions of the last night flooded into her mind, dousing her good mood. What had she done? Was Ian still in the bed next to her?

She silently edged her foot to the other side of the bed, feeling for Ian. He was gone. She didn't know if she should be happy about that or upset that he'd stolen away without saying a word to her. She felt the linen sheets. They were cool, which meant he'd been gone for a while.

Sophia pulled the covers overhead. How had she let the man slip through her defenses? He would demand that they marry. He'd hinted at such in the back parlor last night. One touch and she had weakened. A few kisses had her throwing all her plans out of the window. He was as addictive as chocolate.

Someone knocked at her bedroom door. Sophia panicked. Dear Lord, she was nude! She sat up and frantically searched the room for her nightgown. Finding it in a heap on the floor, she scrambled out of bed. "Just one moment, please!"

Once she was dressed she called, "Come in."

Calm. She needed to be calm.

Her maid entered with a tray of tea and toast. "I've brought your tea and breakfast as requested, miss."

Sophia frowned. "I didn't—"

There was a funny look on the maid's face. Clearly someone had let Cook know Sophia would be taking breakfast in her room. *Ian.* How thoughtful. "Thank you."

Sophia smoothed her hair, feeling self-conscious. Could the maid tell what had gone on in the bed? The bed! She glanced at it. It didn't look as if two people had wrestled in it.

"Should I set out a dress for you today?"

"My riding habit, please." Sophia picked up a piece of toast and nibbled.

"The other ladies are also riding this morning."

So much for riding alone and thinking through this mess she'd made of her life. But given her penchant for thinking too much, it was probably better that she joined the ladies. "I think I'll join them."

"They are already downstairs so you'll have to hurry."

Sophia was dressed, coiffed, and ready to ride in record time. She descended the stairs to make her way to the stables. Perhaps the ladies would already be gone. She could use some time to formulate her reaction when Ian forced a confrontation. And he would. His honor would demand nothing less.

"There you are," Anne said, coming out of the front room. "You slept in this morning."

Sophia could feel the heat rise up in her face. "I suppose I was tired."

"Lady Catherine and Miss Hamilton just left for the stables. Perhaps you can catch them."

"I had planned on it."

"Please promise you'll keep them out riding for a few hours."

Sophia laughed. "I will try. With any luck they will be gone in just a few days." Lord Bateman would have no reason to stay once Miss Hamilton eloped with her captain.

"I hope so." Anne quickly covered her mouth with her hand. "I did not mean for that to sound so insulting. They are your friends and this is your home."

"I'm ready for our guests to be on their way just as much as you are."

Anne gave her a sly look. "Including Lord Bateman?"

"Yes, even him. There is something about him that doesn't ring true. I was entirely wrong about his interest in me."

Anne nodded. "The right man will come when the time is right."

Sophia wasn't so sure any more. She also wasn't sure she would have a choice in waiting for the right man now. "Perhaps."

"Go meet the young ladies before they find their way back here to drive me mad. I'm going to enjoy my quiet house."

"Where are the gentlemen?"

"Nathaniel took them shooting near Horneswood, thank goodness. They should be gone most of the day. If you keep the ladies out until the noon meal, I shall have several hours of peace and quiet."

"I will do my level best." Sophia moved down the stairs with a bit more energy than previously. She wouldn't need to see Ian for most of the day. By then she could prepare the proper response for their confrontation. She had no doubt he would confront her. He wouldn't leave well enough alone.

The main question was marriage. That had not been a decent proposal. She expected flowers. He must get down on one knee. It must be the perfect time. A casual comment right before they were together did not count as a proposal. He'd said he loved her. Men had been spouting about being in love with her since her first Season. They tossed the word about so freely that she did not put much faith in it. The words rolled of their tongues easily when they wanted something. Unless he confessed his feelings with a proper proposal, Sophia wasn't taking anything he'd said last night seriously.

"Miss Townsend, I'm so glad you could join us." Theo came forward and grasped her hands.

Sophia bowed. "Lady Catherine."

"I'll inform the stable manager to saddle your horse."

"Thank you." Sophia waited until Catherine entered the stable before turning back to Theo. "Are you well?"

"Crispin is gone. He left early this morning."

"But not for long." Sophia gripped Theo's hands. "You must hide your feelings, Theo. No one must suspect."

"I will. I promise."

"We should be able to leave shortly. It will be just a few minutes," Lady Catherine said as she rejoined them.

Sophia put on a bright smile. With Theo being sad the captain was gone and Lady Catherine's dour mood, she felt as if she had to liven things up. "What would you like to see? The woods and pastures are lovely around this area. We could ride down to the river and back. That would give us some pastures to let the horses have their heads."

Theo blanched. "I'm not very good with horses; something staid is best for me."

"I should like a run," Lady Catherine said. "But as you know the area best, we will leave it to you."

Sophia glanced at Theo, who shrugged. Lady Catherine was acting very strange. "Then we shall ride down by the river. It's quite beautiful, no matter the speed at which you ride."

Sophia left them to mount their own horses while she went to find her mare. She mounted the horse and took the reins from the groomsman.

"Be careful near the river, miss. We had a great deal of rain last night. It will be high."

"We will. Thank you."

Sophia took the lead and directed the ladies out of the park and down the lane toward the woods. She crossed to a field that led down to the pastures that edged the river.

It was a cool but bright morning. Autumn was finally edging out the warmth of summer. Soon the leaves would change and fall. Once Lord Bateman and his party left for his estate to the north, Sophia's life would return to days filled with busy nothings. There would be a few social occasions for the holidays, but for the most part, life would be quiet. She had nothing more to look forward to except for Mrs. Dellwood's excellent gossip from her sister in London.

Lady Catherine guided her horse up next to Sophia's. "It is beautiful here, peaceful even. I don't know why you ever leave such a place."

It was an odd comment. "Do you not like Town?"

"It is exciting when one is there, but I find it exhausting."

Sophia smiled. "It invigorates me. I love the fast pace of it, the multitude of events, the new people to meet."

Theo finally caught up with them. "Are we stopping for a while?"

"Just for a moment," Sophia said.

"I'm surprised, Miss Townsend, that you've not found some gentleman here to marry, as your sisters have done," Lady Catherine said.

"Like you, I would prefer to marry someone who can ensure my happiness. I've not met someone here who would do that."

"Happiness in marriage is more a matter of wealth and connections."

"Lady Catherine, you don't really believe that, do you?" Theo asked.

"I think you must take into account your temperament. Not everyone is the same, Theo," Sophia said gently.

"I think I will meander back to the stables," Theo said, tactfully changing the subject. "By the time you ladies have your runs across the pasture, I should have time to get to the stables."

"Are you sure you can find your way, Miss Hamilton?"

"I believe this old girl knows her way home, but I remember how we came, Miss Townsend."

Theo turned the horse around and ambled back the way they had come.

Once she was out of earshot, Lady Catherine turned to her. "Now that Theo is gone, I would like to speak with you privately."

"Of course."

"I would warn you about Mr. McDonald. He is not all he seems."

Sophia's heart gave a lurch. Had Catherine seen Ian leave her room? Had she heard them? Sophia couldn't remember if she'd made any noise, but the bed had certainly creaked. "I'm afraid I don't know what you mean."

"He's paid marked attention to you during our visit."

"He's been a friend for three years. He is a business partner of my brother-in-law."

"You've also shown some favoritism toward my brother."

Sophia swallowed her irritation. It would do no good to argue with Catherine in the middle of this field. "That is public knowledge, as well you know. But your brother has made his interest in Theo known to us all. I've abided by that decision."

"Because you could not have my brother, I wondered if you'd set your cap for Ian McDonald instead. If you have, I should warn you that he is already spoken for."

Sophia fought hard to hide her astonishment. "Is he indeed? By whom?"

"My brother is at this moment arranging a match between Mr. McDonald and me. Ian is interested in a piece of land my brother owns that joins our estates."

"Mr. McDonald has an estate near Lord Bateman?"

"It was his father's."

Sophia couldn't hide her astonishment. "Mr. McDonald has inherited an estate?"

Catherine laughed. "I believe he purchased it some years ago. It's a very small house needing a great deal of work. His father was the steward for the late earl, then for Bateman when Father passed. There were some money problems that forced him to seek a position. My father, being a generous man, allowed the family to move into the house until Ian's father died."

Sophia hid her surprise. "I knew Mr. McDonald's father was a steward, but I had no idea of an estate. Is this the one in Dumfries?"

Lady Catherine nodded. "My father doted on Ian while we were growing up. Held him up to my brother on a regular basis. I believe this is the cause of their rivalry to this day."

"I had noticed their animosity." Sophia's mind was spinning. She now realized Ian had said very little about his family.

"I'm a much better choice for him than anyone else," said Catherine. "He gets the land he wants and ties to an earl that can open doors for his business and possible political career. I'm hoping Ian will officially propose so that we can announce it with Bateman's engagement to Miss Hamilton."

Sophia found her voice. "Thank you for telling me, Lady Catherine. I wish you every happiness."

"You are very gracious."

Sophia pasted a bright smile on her face. "Shall we race?" She needed the wind to sting the tears from her eyes.

"Thank you for being so understanding, Miss Townsend." Lady Catherine was all smiles. She urged her horse into a gallop. Sophia did the same.

The wind whipped Sophia's bonnet from her head and tore at the pins in her hair. She paid no mind to Lady Catherine. She had to get away from the woman, even though her words echoed in her head. What a hateful woman!

Sophia had so many questions. Why would Ian make love to her if he were going to marry Lady Catherine? She understood the reasoning. With his wealth and Lady Catherine's connections, it would be an equitable match.

Sophia felt used. She urged the horse to run faster, wanting to put a buffer between the confident words of Lady Catherine and her pain at being abandoned by Ian.

Her saddle slipped to the right as something beneath her snapped. Sophia clung to the horse's mane, trying to slow her down. If she fell at this pace, she could be killed. She slowed the horse a bit, then felt the saddle give way, throwing her off into the tall grass.

Sophia rolled to a stop against a tree, unable to catch her breath.

Every bone ached as she waited for Catherine to join her. Surely the woman would come to see if she was well after such a nasty fall.

Minutes went by. Sophia raised herself up on her arms. Pain radiated up both her arms from her wrists. Lord, she hurt. She frantically searched for Catherine, but she was gone. Sophia lay back again. Perhaps Catherine would send for help. She must have seen Sophia fall.

She crawled away from the tree to find a softer place. She would just lay here for a few minutes to catch her breath. It was her last thought before darkness overtook her senses.

It was much later in the afternoon when Ian finally returned to the Lodge. He'd forgotten that Nathaniel was taking the men shooting that morning. No breakfast, little coffee, and rather chilly weather while waiting for birds to fly by was not how Ian wanted to spend his own morning. He would have been happy just to stay in bed with Sophia in his arms. Last night had been one of the best of his life. It had killed him to leave her sleeping in her bed and sneak back to his own room. They could not marry fast enough to suit him. Of course, he'd have to ask her properly, bended knee and all that. She would expect a proper proposal.

It bothered him that he had admitted his feelings for her but she had said nothing. It said a great deal that she'd let him into her bed, but that wasn't as binding as a betrothal. Ian knew he still had some hurdles to jump with her. It was these thoughts that had distracted him into missing all but one of the birds. Bateman had crowed over his lack of ability with shooting, making the morning even more of a trial to endure.

Finally they were back at the Lodge, and all Ian wanted to do was find Sophia and finish settling things between them. He dismounted his horse and handed the reins to the stable boy.

Bateman approached with a determined stride. "A word, McDonald."

Ian noticed that Nathaniel had already made his way to the house. Probably just as well, given the harshness of Bateman's voice. "Of course."

"Is it too much to ask for you to actually pay me the respect I deserve?"

"Come, Bateman, do you really want me to answer that question?"

Bateman shook his head. "I have to ask once more if you've given any thought to marrying my sister."

Ian covered his shock by leaning against the side of the stable. This was not what he'd thought Bateman wanted to discuss. "I respectfully decline your kind offer."

"Why"

"Lady Catherine and I do not suit."

"So you'd doom Catherine to a life of drudgery?"

"I believe that would be your doing, not mine, Bateman." The man was outrageous to blame his sister's lack of suitors on him.

"By the by, I know of your plans to help Miss Hamilton to escape my clutches."

"What plans would those be?"

Bateman sneered. "To help her elope with her poor captain. Yes, I know all about her feelings for Captain Smith-Williams. Giving him a position isn't going to change anything."

"I have never understood this need to assume that the world operates at your leave. I didn't give Smith-Williams the position to thwart your plans to marry Miss Hamilton. I needed a man of his caliber and he needed work."

"Do not interfere with my marriage to Miss Hamilton. You will not like the consequences."

"More threats, Bateman?" Ian chuckled. "After all these years, haven't you realized that threats don't work with me?"

"Mind my words, McDonald."

Bateman stomped off toward the house. Ian watched him until he disappeared. He'd have to tweak his plans to get Miss Hamilton out of the house now. Bateman would be on his guard. Sophia would have to tell Miss Hamilton to be more cautious with Lord Bateman. Ian couldn't risk giving her the message himself with Bateman suspicious.

He pushed away from the wall to return to the house. He wanted to find Sophia, kiss her senseless, then propose again when they weren't so distracted by passion. Of course, if he kissed her, he'd be lost again. He glanced up to see one of the younger grooms leading a horse with a side saddle back to the stable. Something bottomed out in the pit of his stomach.

"Whose horse is that?"

The young man answered, "Miss Townsend's. Found the horse in the rear pasture grazing."

Panic rose in him as he saw the way the saddle sat on the horse. It had slipped. "Where is Miss Townsend?"

The young man shrugged. The stable master came up beside him. "The other young ladies came back several hours ago, stating that Miss Townsend wanted to ride a bit longer. She typically does this." He reached out for the reins of the horse and inspected the saddle. "Looks like something gave on the saddle."

"So she was thrown?"

"Can't really say, sir. From the looks of the saddle, she might have been. Miss Townsend is a right good horsewoman. She might just be walking back."

Ian knew in the pit of his stomach that something was very wrong. He pulled the reins of his own steed from the stable boy's hands. "Do you know in which direction they rode?"

"She was going to take the young ladies down by the river. I warned her it would be muddy and wild."

Ian mounted his horse. "See what you can find out about that saddle and what gave way. I'll search for her."

"You want me to send someone with you?"

"No, but if Miss Townsend comes back, please send someone out for me."

"Yes, sir."

Ian rode off in the same direction Sophia had taken earlier that day. He'd traveled down the lane and into the wide open green spaces by the river looking for any hint that she might have gone in this direction. Fear choked him. She could be dead. She could be lying anywhere, hurt and alone. What had possessed her to ride off by herself when the ladies returned to the house?

Blue netting rustled in the breeze just ahead of him. Ian stopped the horse and dismounted. It was Sophia's hat. The netting had caught on the tall grass. He picked up the hat and looked around. "Sophia?" His voice echoed in the hollow. He trailed the reins in his hands as he searched. "Sophia!"

"Ian?"

Ian heard her voice just ahead of him. He picked through the tall grass toward a stand of trees. She sat in the deep grass against a tree. "Sweetheart, are you all right?"

"I'm fine, I think. Just battered. Did Lady Catherine send you?"

"No. She is at the Lodge. Was she supposed to?"

Sophia leaned her head back and closed her eyes in pain. "I don't know."

"Where are you hurt?" He knelt beside her. "Did you break anything?"

She shook her head, then groaned. "I hit my head pretty hard, knocked the breath out of me, but I don't think anything is broken."

"Have you tried to stand?"

"Too dizzy."

"You could have been killed."

"Something snapped on the saddle. I felt it give and was able to slow the horse down before I fell." She closed her eyes again. "Can I go home now?"

"Of course, love." Ian's hands shook as he brushed the hair from her face. "Let me help you stand."

He placed his hands underneath her arms and lifted her against him. She gripped his shoulders and stood still, white as a sheet. "Dizzy?"

"Not as bad as it was earlier."

"Do you want to try to walk a bit? Or I can bring the horse to you."

"Let me walk. It will ease the stiffness. I think I'm going to be covered in bruises."

"If that's the worst of it, be thankful. How long have you been here?"

"I have no idea. I was waiting for someone to come."

"I'm beginning to think you are prone to accidents. First the incident in the pasture, then the arrow, and now this." He had to clear his voice twice before he could get the words out.

"All of which can be attributed to you, sir. Perhaps it's the fairies getting their revenge."

Ian pressed his mouth to her hand. "A much more romantic thought than blaming me. Now let's get you home."

They walked slowly to the horse he'd left grazing as he rushed to her. He held the reins. "Let me lift you up. Sit astride the horse and I'll mount behind you. Hold on to the pommel if you feel dizzy."

"I'm covered in mud. Why didn't you tell me?"

"Be thankful for the mud. It probably kept you from breaking something. Here we go." He lifted her to the horse and settled her in the saddle. Her skirts bunched up, revealing her slim legs to the knee. He mounted behind her, a difficult task as the horse didn't care to have two people riding him. Ian took the reins and turned the horse around to return to the Lodge. "What possessed you to go riding alone like that?"

"I usually ride alone."

Ian noted the coolness in her tone. "You could have been killed."

"As if you would care."

Ian wished he could turn her around, see her face. "What the hell does that mean?"

"Lady Catherine told me all about your upcoming marriage to her. After all the time you spent lecturing me on marrying for material things, you go and marry her for a piece of land."

"I am not marrying Catherine."

"She then proceeded to tell me about your father, steward to her father."

"You knew that." He should have told Sophia about that himself, but damn it, he'd wanted her to like him for who he was today, not for who his father had been. "Does that really matter?"

Sophia stiffened against him. "I would have rather heard it from you."

He knew there was more. "What else did she say?"

"She was rambling on about land and revenge. I've always suspected the animosity between you and Bateman but never knew why. Were you envious of him and his title? Of his position?"

"I never envied Bateman. His father would use me as an example to his son. 'Why can't you be more like Ian?' Bateman hated it and he hated me." Ian could still hear the taunts in his head. Taunts about his parents, his birth, and how unworthy he was to have the gifts the earl provided.

"So helping Miss Hamilton is a way for you to get back at Lord Bateman? Ruin him?"

"It won't ruin him; he'll find some other poor, unsuspecting young heiress to marry."

"You admit this."

"Of course. You mentioned the word *revenge*. I don't see it as revenge. I'm doing very little to hurt Bateman. If I'd wanted revenge, I could have ruined him years ago."

"For what? Revenge because of some schoolboy taunts? I don't understand you."

"You are making more of this than you should."

Sophia didn't speak. He had thought perhaps she was done with the topic, but at last she said, "We are all just players on a chessboard to you."

The sadness in her voice tore at his heart. "That's not true, Sophia."

"What piece am I? Let me guess: depriving Lord Bateman of another conquest."

"Sophia, you do not understand—" Ian struggled for the right words to say to her but couldn't find them. He could feel her slipping away from him and was desperate to stop it.

"I think I finally understand, all too well."

Ian gave in to the anger that bubbled inside him like lava. She had no idea what she was talking about. Nor did she realize she had already sealed her fate.

"I have one more question, sir."

They were back to being formal again. "What is it?"

"Was making love to me last night part of your grand plan? Ensure by any means necessary that I would have no chance to marry Bateman, or any other man, for that matter?"

Her words were the last straw. "Do you actually believe I'm capable of manipulating you in that manner? Good God, I told you I loved you!"

"Men utter those words all the time when they want something from a lady."

"This man doesn't." He halted the horse, fairly vibrating with anger. She had called into question his very honor. "We will be married, Sophia. It's too late to go back on that now."

"No. We will not."

"What if you're with child?"

Sophia laughed, a hollow sound. "Even I know it doesn't always happen the first time. Look at my sisters."

"I'll go to Matthews. He'll make you marry me."

"Go right ahead, Mr. McDonald," she said snidely. "I doubt it will work any better for you than it did for him and my sister."

Chapter 21

Sophia felt Ian nudge the horse to move again. She wanted to cry, not because of how badly she ached from her fall but from Ian's betrayal. She'd been so careful all these years to hold men at a distance. She knew firsthand how badly they could use a woman, but she had let him in. Let him into her heart and her bed. She was such a stupid fool.

It was better to focus on why her saddle had given way. She always checked the saddle before getting on her horse, but today she hadn't. She'd let Lady Catherine ask the groom to saddle her horse while she talked with Theo. She stiffened in shock. Great God, could Catherine be behind this? For what purpose?

They reached the stables in just a few minutes. It surprised her how close she'd been to home. She let the stable master lift her down from the saddle and settled her skirts around her. "Has my mare returned?"

"Yes, ma'am." The stable master looked at Ian, who had also dismounted. "You were right, sir. The strap that runs underneath the horse had been cut with a knife just enough to make it give way with pressure."

"Someone did this on purpose?" Suspecting that someone wanted her hurt was one thing; confirmation was something different. "Are you sure?"

"Yes, ma'am. The cut is clean and there was a knife near the stall where the horse was kept."

Sophia looked up at Ian. "It was Lady Catherine."

"Sophia, you cannot go about accusing people without cause."

"She had opportunity. She went into the stables while I was talking to Theo."

The young groom spoke up. "The lady is right, sir. I found Lady Catherine in the stable by Miss Townsend's saddle."

"Did you see her with the knife?"

"No, sir. I found it later, in the hay."

"There. Is that not proof?" Sophia said.

"Sophia, we cannot go accusing Lady Catherine of sabotaging your saddle." Ian turned to the stable master. "Please set the saddle aside for now. We'll discuss this later. I should get Miss Townsend up to the house so we can see to her injuries."

"I'm not injured so badly that we can't continue this conversation."

"Nevertheless, we are letting the staff get back to work." He took her arm and led her to the house. "Let me handle this."

"Why? So you can protect your precious Catherine?"

"She is not *my* Catherine."

She jerked her arm away from his touch. She had to put some distance between them, get away to think, to decide what she would do now. First Ian's betrayal and now Lady Catherine seemed bent on hurting her.

"Sophia, let me help you."

"I think you've done enough, thank you. But I have one request."

"Anything."

"Say nothing to anyone about this."

"I have to tell Nathaniel, Sophia. The woman is a guest in his house. Who knows what she'll do next."

Sophia whirled around, then paused as dizziness washed over her. "Theo. We have to protect Theo."

"Bateman is suspicious of her feelings for Smith-Williams. He may try something that will keep her here."

Sophia frowned. "Like what?"

Ian's telling look said it all.

"He wouldn't. He's a gentlemen," Sophia said.

"Desperate men do desperate things, Sophia."

"As well I know." She turned toward the house.

"I think we should discuss the elopement. You are still willing to help with that, aren't you?"

"I'm not so shallow that I'd allow my feelings for you to shadow Theo's happiness."

"Thank you—I think."

"Well, what is the plan?"

"We'll sneak her out of the house tomorrow while everyone is changing for dinner. It will be when Bateman will least expect it. He'll think she'll go tonight or tomorrow night."

Sophia had to admit to herself that it was a good plan. "What do you need me to do?"

"She will hide in your room after tea, claiming she has a headache. Once the gong sounds, you'll collect her and take her down the back-stairs and to the stables. I'll have the cart waiting for you both. You'll drive her to the Wheat Chaff Inn on the edge of the village. Smith-Williams will meet you there with her bags. They'll take the mail coach for Lancaster."

"Lancaster? That is the opposite direction from Gretna Green." Sophia shook her head. "It would be faster to take the North Road. It's but what, three days' ride?"

"Yes, and the first place Bateman will search when he finds she is gone. Remember, this is twenty thousand pounds slipping through his fingers."

He had a point, but she wasn't going to concede it to him will-ingly. "From Lancaster where do they go?"

"They shall sail north to Scotland. Marry and meet us at my estate in Dumfries."

"Us? You are dreaming. There is no us." Sophia turned to go.

"Sophia, wait. We have to discuss this."

"There is nothing to discuss. If you will excuse me, I'm covered in mud and ache all over. I want nothing more than a bath and a cup of tea."

"We are not done with this conversation."

"As far as I am concerned, we are." She picked up her skirts and forced her legs to move faster. If Ian continued to talk to her, she'd give in. Even in this short time discussing Theo's elopement she was ready to forgive him. Perhaps she'd hit her head harder than she thought. She reached the steps leading into the house and paused. This was going to hurt.

Ian appeared next to her to assist her. "At least let me help you into the house."

"Don't touch me."

Ian released her and stepped away. "As you wish. But do not think that this discussion is over. We will be married."

"There will be no wedding."

"That's not what you agreed to last night."

"I would hardly call what you said last night a proposal, nor did I accept it."

Ian leaned close, so close she could feel the heat of his body. "You accepted my proposal when you let me deep inside your body. You cried out with your pleasure, Sophia. Don't deny it."

Heat suffused her face. "Don't be coarse."

"What do you expect from the son of a steward, my dear? It's in our nature to be coarse." His voice was cold.

"That was uncalled for."

"It's what you're thinking, isn't it? The man you gave yourself to is so far beneath you. How will you hold your head up in Town now? What have you always told everyone? You'd marry a man with a title? It seems it is as easy to fall into the arms of a commoner as it is a peer."

The barb hit very close to home. "I'm not listening to this."

"Mark my words, Sophia, you will be my wife."

"And you are going to have to learn to live with disappointment." She took a few steps and turned around to face Ian. He stood there looking at her with an odd expression on his face. If she didn't think him capable, she would have guessed he was in pain. But that wasn't possible. A man who could manipulate people as easily as he did not feel pain.

"I'm assuming you'll be leaving once you've completed your ruination of Lord Bateman."

He winced. "Don't forget that you're helping with that."

"I'm helping a friend find happiness. My motives are pure."

"Are you sure about that?"

"I would ask that you please leave me alone. We shall be polite in company, but no more. I expect you to leave once this business is done."

"Sophia, please don't do this."

The pleading in his voice was almost her undoing. She forced herself to climb the steps and enter the house with her head high and her eyes dry. She started to slowly climb the staircase to her room, gripping the banister tightly as she moved from step to step.

Anne rushed out of the library. "There you are, Sophia. We have been so worried."

"I'm fine."

Anne moved quickly to her side. "You are not. You're hurt. What happened?"

"My horse threw me."

Anne gripped her waist to assist her up the stairs. "Funny, but Lady Catherine didn't mention you falling."

"I just want a hot bath and to lay down."

"Should I send for the doctor?"

Sophia shook her head. "I'm fine, just bruised. I just want some time alone."

Anne nodded but asked no further questions, for which Sophia was thankful. She didn't feel like rehashing her argument with Ian now. The last thing she needed was for Anne to realize Sophia had succumbed to Ian's charms. She'd never hear the end of marriage if that occurred. Nathaniel would make sure Ian married her.

After settling Sophia in her chair by the fire, Anne left the room. "I'll have a bath brought up along with your maid. I'll make your excuses at dinner tonight. Rest, Sophia. You'll feel better in the morning."

Sophia nodded because she was supposed to. She realized she wasn't going to be better for a very long time.

This day could not get any worse. Ian stumbled into the house feeling as if he'd been punched in the stomach. At this very moment, all he wanted was to get drunk and not feel the pain of Sophia's rejection. He'd asked for it. He'd pushed her into intimacy without really knowing how she felt about him. He'd revealed his feelings to her thinking she'd not give herself to him unless she felt the same. Women just didn't view lovemaking the way men did.

He should have known. Sophia Townsend had been running him in circles for the past three years.

Ian made his way to the library without seeing another person. He poured a brandy and tossed it back. The burn made his eyes water. He filled the glass again and tossed that back as well.

"If you aren't going to savor it, let me get you the cheaper brandy. Or I could get you whiskey, if you're seriously looking to get drunk."

Ian finally realized he wasn't alone in the room. Nathaniel sat behind his desk, ledgers spread out in front of him. Ian poured a bit more brandy in the glass and plopped down into one of the leather chairs in front of the desk. "I should have listened to you when you warned me about the Townsend women."

Nathaniel laughed. "What has happened now?"

"The list is too long to discuss now. Suffice it to say that Sophia now hates me more than ever."

Nathaniel got up and poured himself a brandy. "I can't have you drinking alone."

Ian took a sip from his glass. The first two drinks had deadened the pain a bit; this one he could savor.

Nathaniel took the chair opposite him. "I overheard Sophia tell Anne that she had been thrown from her horse."

"My hands are still shaking. She was thrown because someone cut into the girth of the saddle. It snapped while she was galloping through the pastures near the river."

"Good God, she could have been killed! How badly was she injured?"

"She hit her head and is badly bruised but all right."

"If she had to fall at least she hit the hardest part."

"Too true."

"There appears to be something else amiss with our guests. Lord Bateman came back from shooting and was slamming doors left and right."

"He is about to be even angrier." Ian couldn't keep the smile from his face. He was going to enjoy every moment of Bateman's comeuppance.

"As it is happening in my house, perhaps you should enlighten me."

Ian wasn't sure where to start. "You know most of it." He was suddenly filled with a nervous energy. "Bateman wanted me to marry Lady Catherine in exchange for the land I offered to purchase."

"That's rather medieval of him, isn't it? She's not chattel."

"I think it was her idea."

"Why?"

"Money. She knows me from when my father was steward for the old earl. She knows I'm rich. She thinks she can help me move up in Society or politics."

"She has a point, if you're interested in that sort of thing." Nathaniel set down his glass. "I didn't think you were interested in social climbing and politics."

"I've not ruled out politics. Catherine is desperate because Bateman's pockets are to let. There will be no more trips to Town or fine gowns until Bateman is solvent again."

"Which will happen when he marries Miss Hamilton and her thousands of pounds."

Ian nodded. "I think Catherine sabotaged Sophia's saddle. She had the opportunity."

"But what was her motive?"

"I don't know. There has always been an animosity between the two women. They were constantly competing for the same gentlemen in Town."

"And here."

Ian had to concede that point. "I've made my partiality to Sophia well known to Catherine. This might have been her way to get Sophia out of the way."

"By attempting to kill her? That is a bit extreme, isn't it? Besides, Catherine has no need to feel desperate if Bateman is marrying Miss Hamilton."

Ian looked down at his boots, still covered in mud from rescuing Sophia. "He's about to be extremely disappointed."

"She's going to refuse him?"

"She is eloping tomorrow with Captain Smith-Williams."

Nathaniel drained his brandy and slammed the glass down on the desk. "Then why travel with him? She's been leading him on this entire time."

"She wanted to please her parents. She thought she could go through with it until she found out that she was carrying Smith-Williams's child."

"No more bloody house parties after this."

"Actually, intrigues are why people attend house parties."

"I assumed people would behave in a civilized manner."

Ian felt his face heat. The brandy in his stomach churned a bit. The last thing he wanted to discuss was his relationship with Sophia, especially with her brother-in-law.

Reading Ian's guilty expression, Nathanial groaned. "Not you as well! If I didn't know your intentions were honorable, I'd punch you in the nose right now. Tell me you have a date for the wedding."

"Sorry, but no. Sophia and I have some matters to work through yet."

Nathaniel covered his face with his hand. "I can't tell Anne this."

"Don't tell her about our suspicions about Lady Catherine either. Sophia doesn't want anyone to know."

"I'll try, but I'm not making any promises. Anne has the uncanny ability of knowing when I'm keeping something from her."

"Do your best." Ian drained the last of the brandy in his glass. "I am going to go change for dinner." He left the library and slogged his way up the stairs feeling extremely tired. The last thing he wanted was to face everyone at dinner, but he had to keep up appearances.

God, how he wished he could go home and leave this mess and pain behind him.

"Mr. McDonald, if I might have a word?"

Lady Catherine stood in the doorway of her bedroom. She was already dressed for dinner, which made him realize how late it was.

"I really should get ready for dinner."

"This won't take long." She stepped inside the room.

"It isn't appropriate for me to be in your room, Catherine."

"It will be even less appropriate if I'm overheard, Ian. Please?"

Ian stepped into the room but stopped her from closing the door all the way. "Leave it partially open."

"If you insist." Catherine folded her hands in front of her and gave all the appearance of innocence.

Given what he knew of her character, she was far from it. "What is this about, Catherine?"

"I saw you leaving Miss Townsend's room this morning."

The pieces of the puzzle finally fell into place for Ian. "Sophia has agreed to be my wife. Will you wish us well?"

"If you are marrying her to protect her virtue, you are a bigger fool than I thought you were. Sophia Townsend was ruined years ago. Everyone in Town knows about it."

Ian had never wanted to strike a woman as he did as Catherine spewed her venom. "Is there anything else?"

"Well . . . no. Isn't that enough?"

Ian studied her for a long moment. "How far are you willing to go to get your way, Catherine?"

"I'm sure I don't know what you mean."

"Why did you sabotage Sophia's saddle this morning?"

"You cannot be serious. How would I know how to sabotage a saddle?"

"You had ample opportunity. A knife was found in the hay near where the saddle was stored. Why would you do this? She could have been killed."

Catherine's face turned red. "I wish she had. What is it about Sophia Townsend that draws men like flies to manure? Even my own brother succumbed to her charms until I revealed the truth about her to him."

"What have you done, Catherine?"

She laughed. "I've protected my family. Bateman wanted to marry her, did you know that? She would be related to me. I'd have to see her every day. It was unthinkable."

Ian stepped close to her, so angry he had to close his hands into tight fists to keep from wrapping them around Catherine's neck. "Stay away from Sophia Townsend."

"You can't hurt me, Ian. You have no proof."

"Do not underestimate me. I will ruin you so badly that you'll be ostracized from your precious Society. How do you think they will feel about you when they find out you attempted to murder one of their own?"

Ian left the room, slamming the door behind him. Bateman needed to know that his sister was mad, but unfortunately Bateman wouldn't listen to him.

Ian entered his room and called for a bath. This trip was turning into a nightmare.

Chapter 22

Sophia kept to her room most of the following day. She was covered in bruises from the fall but had recovered sufficiently. She just wasn't up to seeing Catherine or facing Ian and his insistence on marrying him.

What was it about unsuitable men that drew her attention like a bee to a flower? She'd done so well avoiding them over the last few years, at least until Ian. Though, if she admitted it to herself, she couldn't put him into the mold of an unsuitable mate. He was handsome, wealthy, and a gentleman, regardless of his parentage. He was more of a gentlemen than most of the peers she'd met in London. Ian was the rare breed of self-made man in a Society that enforced conformity. He stood out because he was different.

She'd miss his friendship the most. She didn't think men were capable of having a woman as a friend until she'd met Ian. She'd also miss his teasing. He kept her from being too serious about herself. Sophia hadn't realized how much she needed that until now.

She walked to the window and looked out. She had to face the real reason she'd pushed Ian away yesterday. She'd didn't know if she could live without the acceptance of Society. Her whole life had centered on acceptance. She had to have the right wardrobe from the most popular modiste and the right friends from the most appropriate families. It was all about her connections and how she could improve them.

Sophia wrapped her arms tightly around herself. She had just ruined her best chance at happiness by pushing Ian away. He'd made her realize that none of that mattered. How stupid and blind she'd been not to see what was right before her. For three years he'd waited patiently for her to realize it and now it was too late.

Or was it?

Sophia turned from the window to cross the room. She would find him. Apologize to him. Make him realize she needed him.

She was just about to step out when Anne came into the room.

"Anne, what is it?"

"Tell me it isn't true, Sophia." Anne fairly trembled with anger.

Sophia took a step back toward the bed. "I would if I knew to what you were referring."

"The list is rather long at the moment."

Sophia sat down on the bed. "Might as well tell me all and get it over with."

Anne looked as if she didn't know where to start. Sophia gave her a few minutes to collect her thoughts.

"What is going on between you and Lady Catherine? Nathaniel told me she was the cause of your being thrown from the horse."

"She's never liked me; you know that."

"And that excuses her behavior?"

"She is used to getting her own way. She doesn't think the rules apply to her."

"You could have been killed! I've half a mind to throw her out of my house on her bottom."

"She will be gone soon enough."

"That is all you have to say on the matter? I cannot be so forgiving."

Sophia didn't want to discuss why she felt more pity for Catherine than hatred. "What else?"

"Miss Hamilton and Captain Smith-Williams are eloping."

"I know nothing about it, and that's all I'm saying on the subject." Sophia wouldn't say a word until she knew Theo was safe from Bateman.

Anne wasn't having any of it. She looked as if she wanted to strangle her.

"Was that the end of your list?"

"To think that all of this was going on under my own roof. One final question: What about Ian?"

Anne had saved the most difficult matter for the last. "What about him?"

"Is it true that you and he—"

"That is none of your business."

Anne covered her face with her hands. "I understand. The man has loved you for three years, Sophia. Please tell me you aren't just playing with him because you couldn't have Lord Bateman."

"I can't believe you think me capable of such a thing."

Something in Sophia's voice caught Anne's attention. "Then things are all right between you?"

"Things are muddled at the moment between us."

"Can you mend them?"

Sophia couldn't meet her sister's eyes without bursting into tears. "I hope so."

Anne stepped forward and wrapped her arms around Sophia. The dam broke and she sobbed into Anne's shoulder. "I've been such a bacon-brained idiot."

"It cannot be that bad."

Sophia nodded her head. "I said some hateful things, Anne. I insulted his heritage. I let him think he wasn't worthy of me. That he was less than a gentleman."

"You must talk it over and mend it. Though I imagine you'll have to do some groveling. And I know how much you hate to grovel."

"What if he gives up on me?"

"He won't." Anne handed her a handkerchief. "Dry your eyes and come down for tea."

Sophia shook her head. "I can't. Not yet. I'm barely able to move after yesterday's fall." It was not exactly the truth, but she needed to be there for Theo, who would be here shortly to hide until they could sneak down the backstairs and out to the stables. "Then there is having to face Lady Catherine."

"Now that I understand, I can hardly wait until they leave. Get some rest. I'll send up tea and those cakes you like. But you will have to face them all at some point."

"I know. One more day. That's all I need."

Anne left the bedroom. Sophia lay back on the bed. Could Ian forgive her? Would he still want her? She hoped so. Oh, how she hoped so because she was desperately afraid she loved him.

Ian stood in front of the library window at Horneswood, staring out across the pasture at the Lodge. He'd almost gone to her the night before but thought better of it. He hated how they'd parted but wasn't surprised by it. He should have been honest with her, but in his defense, it hadn't mattered to him. What mattered was the man he was now.

He worried about her injuries. She'd said she was fine, but he needed to confirm that for himself. There were discussions to have. Decisions to make. After this business with Bateman was over, Ian would give her one last chance to rub her heel into his heart and then he was done. He'd begin to put her behind him and find happiness somehow.

"When do you return to Scotland?" Tony asked from behind him.

"Day after tomorrow, I believe. Once I'm sure Smith-Williams and Miss Hamilton are safely away."

"What about Sophia?"

"We will see. She has no desire to marry me and I've no desire to keep allowing her to hurt me. It's time to go home." He could hear Tony approach the window but said nothing else. Even saying those words aloud hurt.

"That's not the advice you gave me two years ago when I was suffering a similar emotion about Juliet."

"Juliet loved you."

"You don't think Sophia loves you?"

Ian gave a harsh laugh. "I don't know what to think anymore."

Tony clasped his shoulder. "Do you honestly believe Sophia is capable of letting you into her bed without feeling something for you?"

Ian glanced at Tony. "How did you know?"

Tony smiled knowingly. "What is it about those Townsend women that entrap and enthrall us so? And just when they have us where they want us, they do the complete opposite of what we expect."

"I've been patient for three years." Three long years of being Sophia's friend when he wanted so much more.

"Then a few more days won't matter."

"I doubt very seriously it will make any difference. She made her feelings very clear. She is the most stubborn woman I've ever met."

"Yes, she is," Tony said.

Ian glared at him.

"You forget she was set to marry me way before she met you," Tony said.

Jealousy had Ian tightening his hands into fists. He forced himself to relax. What had he become? He did not like this side of himself.

"It was a year before she met you," Tony continued.

"I do not want to hear about this."

"We all have things in our past."

"I care nothing for her past. She should care nothing for mine."

"Social status and family connections are everything to Sophia."

"I am not that person anymore."

"It's different for women, especially women from the upper class. Sophia was brought up to improve the family fortunes by marrying well. She was taught that connections with peers were important. You are judged by Society by who your friends and family are. She was groomed to make the appropriate connections."

"Can't she see that none of that is important?" Ian's frustration boiled over. "I don't understand any of it."

"Sophia isn't going to be able to set aside something she's spent her whole life believing just because she fell in love with a man who cares very little about it."

Ian pushed down the words that stirred hope inside him. He just wasn't sure about anything except that he was done being her whipping boy. "It's not just that. This business with Bateman; she's accused me of manipulating her to get back at him for past wrongs."

"Wasn't that the reason you set out to help Smith-Williams and Miss Hamilton?"

Ian had to concede that Tony was correct, but somewhere along the way his motives had changed. "Yes, in the beginning, but not now."

"Did you tell Sophia that?"

Ian scrubbed his face with his hand. "I tried."

"What romantic gestures have you made?" Tony asked.

"I know nothing of romance."

Tony laughed. "Then I suggest you learn. Women love the stuff. Flowers, gifts, and compliments will go a long way in winning her back."

"What do I do?"

"I have no idea, but I know someone who does." Tony moved to cross the room and whisper to one of the maids working in the entryway. "My wife will know how to fix this."

Would this humiliation never end? "Just let it be, Matthews."

"And see two of my closest friends unhappy? What's going to happen when you visit and see each other again? I for one hate uncomfortable situations. Trust me on this: Juliet will know what to do."

Ian moved back to the brandy table. Ten o'clock in the morning and he was drinking. This was what Sophia had brought him to.

Juliet entered the library. She smiled at Ian and then said to Tony, "You wished to see me?"

"Love, our friend here needs your help."

"Why would Ian need my help?"

"He's trying to woo Sophia back into his life. Evidently they had a wicked row and now aren't speaking."

Juliet glanced at Ian. "But you fight with each other all the time. Why is this time different?"

Tony whispered into Juliet's ear. She flushed. "Oh. You are going to marry her, aren't you?"

"I've asked and she's said no."

"My guess is that he bedded her and just assumed they'd marry. It's a common mistake."

Ian felt his face heat. "It wasn't like that."

"Ian, please tell me you got down on one knee and proposed," Juliet said.

"Uh, no. Was I supposed to?"

"Men." Juliet moved to take the chair in front of the desk Ian had vacated. "My sister is different from Anne and me. She will want all the romantic trappings so that she can tell her friends and her children about the day her husband proposed. It's very important to Sophia that this be done right and proper."

"How am I supposed to know what is the right way to do this?" Ian asked.

Juliet got up and went to the bookcase, looking for a particular volume.

Ian glanced at Tony. "What is she doing?"

"Getting you a book to show you how to do this properly."

"There are books about this stuff?"

"Evidently."

Finally Juliet found the book. She opened it, thumbing through the pages until she found the right one. "Sophia wants romance. She's had an image in her head of how her wedding proposal should be."

"She's had at least half a dozen proposals already. Why should mine be different?"

Tony laughed loudly. "You poor, dumb sod."

Juliet glared at her husband. "They never did it correctly to Sophia's mind." She walked over and handed him a slim volume. "Quote something from this."

Ian looked at the book and groaned. "Not poetry. Anything but poetry."

"In the three years you've known Sophia, have you ever sent her flowers?" Juliet asked.

Ian shook his head as he thumbed through the book. This was drivel. He couldn't do it.

"Candy? Gifts?"

He continued to shake his head. "I've never sent her anything."

"I suggest you start, then. If you wish to win my sister's heart, you're going to have to do all of those things, and do them better than any other man has. She's been courted by the best and the most romantic, yet she turned them down. Try not to foul this up."

Ian looked at Tony. "And this will work?"

"I have no idea. I didn't have to do any of that."

"That's because Juliet already loved you." Ian sighed and snapped the book shut. This was going to take some creativity and thought. After another moment's thought, he said "Can one order flowers in Beetham?"

Chapter 23

"Theo, please quit pacing; you are making me daft," Sophia said as she glanced once more at the clock. Theo had left tea with a headache but come to her room to wait until the gong sounded. Then they would be on their way.

"What if we are seen leaving the house?"

This was the tenth time she had asked that question. Sophia was already sick of the intrigue game. "We will not be seen. It will be fine. Mr. McDonald has taken every contingency into consideration. Now try to rest. You have an arduous journey ahead of you."

Theo nodded and finally went to stretch out on the bed. Sophia sat in the chair by the fire, staring at the clock. It did no good to watch it, but she had to anyway. Part of her would be glad when Theo and her captain were on their way. Bateman and his sister would leave soon after and the house would be quiet again.

Ian would leave too. That thought hurt. She picked up the note he had sent earlier to let her know the plan was underway and things were going well. It included final instructions on where they were to meet the captain and what would happen afterward. If things went smoothly, they should be home in time for dinner. Sophia ran her finger over his signature. It was as bold as he.

She tossed it back down on the small table by the chair. The note was also a terse list of instructions. There was nothing personal there. Had she expected any? Well, she'd hoped for something more personal, but then, she'd ruined that as well.

When this was over she was going to sit him down and have a long chat with him about proper proposals and how to court a woman. She would also beg his forgiveness for making him feel less than he was.

If this elopement went horribly wrong, what would they do? Theo would have to confess that she was carrying another man's child. Bateman would have no choice but to release her from any agreement.

The outcome would be no different, it occurred to her. Theo's parents would still disown her. She'd still marry her captain. Bateman would still need a rich wife. Theo's reputation would still be ruined. Then why go to all this trouble?

Oh yes, this was about belittling another person. She'd be sure to let Ian know how stupid he was to dream this up. She might know all the details of why Ian felt he had to do this to Lord Bateman, but they would have a firm discussion on not doing it again. If she was going to have to give up her time in London for the backwoods of Scotland, he was going to have to make some concessions as well.

The gong sounded below. Theo's head popped up. "Is it time?"

"Let's give everyone a few minutes to get to their rooms," Sophia said.

They sat still as church mice watching a cat, listening to the stairs creak as the others went up to their rooms. Doors closed and servants shuffled along the hallway. Finally it was quiet. Sophia looked out; no one was in the hall. Sophia silently closed the door. "Come. We can go now."

Theo rose and tied on her bonnet. She gathered her reticule and a book. Sophia pulled on her pelisse and a bonnet. "We are taking the servant's stairs and going out through the kitchens. The fourth step creaks, so have a care."

"What if one of the maids see us?"

"They'll keep quiet." Sophia was more worried about Lady Catherine. The woman was smart. She had to know something was up. Thankfully, Sophia's little tumble off the horse had given her a good excuse for being in her room. Now, if only Theo hadn't raised suspicions. She opened the door and peered out again. "Come."

Theo followed her out and they walked silently down the corridor to the backstairs. There was no carpet on these steps. "Be as quiet as possible."

Sophia gently placed one foot on the wood step, then another. Theo did the same. They reached the dark, narrow landing with almost no noise. Sophia pushed Theo ahead of her.

"What are you doing?"

Lady Catherine stood at the top of the steps. Sophia's heart sank. She thought quickly. "Go now. Wait in the kitchen for me," she whispered to Theo. Then, in a louder voice, "Lady Catherine, I thought you'd be changing."

"Obviously. Where are you and Theo going?"

"A quick trip to the village for ribbons. Theo left the ribbons for this gown in London. Do you want to come along?" Sophia kept her voice as sweet as possible, though it killed her to do so. This woman was a witch of the first order.

"Ribbons? The gong has just sounded. Why would you go now?"

Sophia searched her brain for a quick answer. "Theo's headache was so much better and she knew you were all leaving soon."

Lady Catherine frowned. She didn't believe her.

"You are most welcome to come with us," Sophia said.

"I've no desire to visit the village again."

"Well, then, we shall see you at dinner." Sophia turned to go down the backstairs.

"There is something going on. Don't think I don't know it, Sophia Townsend."

Sophia laughed. "I never took you for the type to see intrigues were none existed."

Lady Catherine huffed and stomped off. Sophia wasted no time going down the stairs. If Lady Catherine told her brother, the game would be up. She rounded the corner and went into the kitchen. The staff looked up in surprise. Sophia grabbed Theo's hand. "We must hurry."

They left the house from the kitchens and took the long way around to the stables. The stable boy had the cart ready for them. He assisted them both and handed Sophia the reins. "Anything else, ma'am?"

"No, thank you," Sophia said absently. "Wait!"

The boy paused at the open door of the stables. "Ma'am?"

"Please do not tell anyone in which direction we are going."

He grinned. "Yes, ma'am."

Sophia guided the cart out of the park and onto the lane toward the village. If Lady Catherine was watching them, she would not suspect. She urged the horse to go faster.

"My goodness, Miss Townsend, that was a close one," Theo said, her hands gripping her book tightly. "How ever did you come up with that story about ribbons?"

"Many years of dealing with sisters," Sophia said. She kept glancing behind her, expecting to be followed. Lord, she was nervous. It had been a close thing.

"How far to the inn?"

"Several miles. We must go through town to get to it," Sophia said anxiously.

Theo glanced behind them. "Do you think anyone will follow us?"

"I don't know. I'm hoping Catherine believed the story I told her." Sophia guided the cart onto the main road into town. It was late afternoon, so there was little traffic. She could see the village up ahead. "The Wheat Chaff Inn is at the other end of Beetham. The captain and Mr. McDonald should be there waiting for us."

"What if they are not? We can't just go into an inn unaccompanied."

Theo was a dear girl, but she was grating on Sophia's nerves. "They will be there." If they weren't, there would be hell to pay from her. "Not long now."

Never again would Sophia involve herself in someone else's business. She had learned her lesson well.

They traveled through the village, Sophia waving at a few of their acquaintances. Then she saw her. Damn. It was the vicar's wife, Mrs. Dellwood.

"Miss Townsend, what are you doing in the village at this late hour?" Mrs. Dellwood's high-pitched voice carried through the street.

Sophia slowed the cart.

"We can't stop!" Theo whispered frantically.

"We have no choice." Sophia turned to Mrs. Dellwood. "Good afternoon. I thought I would give my friend, Miss Hamilton, one last look at Beetham before she leaves on the morrow. She was quite taken with the village when we were here last."

"Indeed, I wanted to see it once more," Theo said inanely.

Sophia fought the urge to groan. If Mrs. Dellwood believed this lie, she was more beetleheaded than anyone thought.

"How lovely. I will let you go on your way. Please give my regards to your family, Miss Townsend."

"Thank you, I will. Good day, Mrs. Dellwood." Sophia urged the horse forward.

"That was close."

"We aren't out of the woods yet, Theo. She is the biggest gossip in the village, though with any luck you will be long gone and never have to worry about it."

"She's not too bright, is she?"

Sophia laughed. "No, she isn't, but she means well, I suppose."

There were no other incidents; soon Sophia pulled the cart around the side of the old inn, so that it couldn't be seen from the road. The inn was a rambling stone house. There were several horses and carriages in the side yard. She looked around for Ian, uncertainty curdling her stomach. Now what?

Sophia had expected Captain Smith-Williams and Ian to be there waiting for them. She wished now she had some sort of timepiece. She had no idea if they were early or late. She had not expected to run into Lady Catherine or Mrs. Dellwood.

"What if he doesn't come?"

Theo pressed her hand to her stomach. She'd been doing that a great deal of late.

"He'll be here." Sophia kept scanning the few people milling about in hopes of spotting them. Finally, Ian stepped outside of the inn and came forward. "See, they are here."

"You are right on time," Ian said softly as he took the reins and helped first Sophia down, then Theo. "Captain Smith-Williams is waiting in one of the private parlors, Miss Hamilton."

"Thank you."

Sophia watched as Theo rushed to the front of the inn. She glanced at Ian, feeling nervous and uneasy. She didn't quite know what to do with her hands or what to say. Would he be rude to her? He had every right to be rude after the words they had exchanged.

"Did you encounter any bad moments?"

She could tell nothing of what he was feeling from his tone or his face. Her heart gave a sad little lurch. She really had ruined things. "Lady Catherine found us sneaking down the backstairs."

"Did she tell anyone?"

"I made up a story of coming into the village at the last minute for ribbons. I invited her to join us, but she declined."

"Thank goodness or you'd have been in trouble."

"I would have thought of something, rushed Theo out the back door of the shop while Catherine wasn't looking. I also ran into Mrs. Dellwood."

"She will tell everyone she saw you."

"It will not matter because Theo will be gone by then," Sophia said. "Should I return to the Lodge?"

"Not yet. We shall see the couple off and travel back together. Smith-Williams and I traveled in the coach from Horneswood. I shall need a ride back."

Sophia nodded. Given his coolness, she would not bring up her decision. He'd probably withdraw his proposal after she'd been such a shrew. Perhaps it was just as well. She would just have to become used to spinsterhood and caps.

"Come, let's say our good-byes. With any luck, they will be well out of Beetham before we get back to the Lodge."

Sophia took his arm and allowed Ian to lead her into the inn and to the private room, where Theo and the captain waited. They broke their embrace as they entered the room.

Theo rushed to Ian and kissed his cheek. "Thank you so much for everything, Mr. McDonald."

Captain Smith-Williams shook his hand. "I shall see you in Dumfries in two weeks' time, sir."

"I'll have the cottage ready for you both," Ian said with a smile. "It should be smooth sailing from here."

Theo touched Sophia on the sleeve. "I shall never forget your kindness to me this past week. I hope we shall see each other again very soon."

Sophia squeezed Theo's hands. "I wish you both every happiness."

Smith-Williams cleared his voice. "Come, love, we must be away."

The couple left the room. Silence filled the air, making Sophia uneasy. She knew Ian was watching her. She moved to the window to watch the captain help Theo into the coach. The carriage left, heading south to Lancaster as Ian had directed.

"I thought we would wait here until closer to dark before leaving, Miss Townsend."

They were back to formality. "That should still give us time to change for dinner."

"We'll have to come up with some sort of story as to why Theo is missing dinner."

Sophia turned from the window and found Ian seated at the small table with a cup of tea. "Is there another cup?"

"Of course, but the pot is almost empty. Shall I ring for more?"

Sophia shook her head and accepted the tea from Ian. She sat in the chair across from him. It was all so proper. "I had thought to tell everyone that Theo had a headache, but now that Lady Catherine saw us leave, that won't wash."

Ian stared at her pointedly and she found herself trembling. She set down the cup quickly before she spilled the tea all over herself. She smoothed her hands on her gown. "Do you have a suggestion?"

Ian watched as Sophia tried to decide what to do with her hands. She was nervous and clearly uncomfortable being alone with him. They could not return too quickly to the Lodge, but sitting in this parlor sipping tea and being polite had not been a good idea either. He didn't know what to do with the time between saying good-bye to Smith-Williams and Miss Hamilton and returning to the Lodge.

"Miss Townsend, is the tea not to your liking?"

"Please, Ian, can we dispense with formality?"

"You were the one who designated our places in Society, Miss Townsend." He emphasized her name. "Unless you've changed your mind?"

She glanced at him in shock. "I do not want to discuss that now."

"I agree. All that was needed to be said has been said." He couldn't keep the flatness from his tone.

She heaved a heavy sigh and twisted her hands in her lap. "That's not true. There is something to say."

"Go on."

She wouldn't meet his eyes. "I owe you an apology. I had no right to call your parentage into question, no right to make you feel less than you are. I am sorry."

Ian let the words sink into his brain and his heart. It was a small consolation, he supposed. "Apology accepted."

"Then we can be friends again?"

The hope in her voice almost killed him. "Perhaps after a time."

She nodded, accepting his rejection, then turned back to her tea.

Silence once again boomed through the room. The urge to pull her into his arms and kiss her senseless was riding Ian hard. He could make her want him. He could stir her passions until she admitted how she felt, but would it be the truth or would they just be words uttered easily to make him feel better?

Damn, this was hard! He had not thought just sitting here with her alone would be this difficult. If Juliet was right, he'd have to bide his time and woo her as he should have in the first place, instead of letting his other organ guide him into doing what he most wanted to do.

He watched the clock as she finished her tea. "I think perhaps we can leave now."

Sophia stood and brushed out her skirts. She took his arm as they left the parlor and out the door to the cart she had brought.

Ian assisted her, then climbed in and accepted the reins from one of the servants. "How do you suggest we get back to the Lodge?"

"We can take the road past the church and avoid the main road through Beetham. It will lead around toward Horneswood."

"I know the way." He urged the horse forward and took the street that led to the church. It was getting late, the sun sinking low, casting dark shadows on the road. They had no lamp on the cart, so they needed to be there by dark. "I should have thought to bring a lantern."

"We should be fine. No one takes these roads this late."

They passed the vicar's cottage and St. Michael's. Ian turned the cart onto the smaller lane leading back to the Lodge. The evening had grown cooler and Sophia shivered beside him. "Do you want my coat?"

"I'm fine. Thank you."

Ian hated this awkward silence between them but could think of nothing to say. No, that wasn't the truth. He could think of a great deal to say but didn't want to bring up the topic on his mind. She clearly had no desire to discuss it either, given her silence.

"Do you think Bateman will be angry?" Sophia finally asked.

"I think he'll be bloody furious."

"You'll have your revenge then."

"Sophia, it wasn't about revenge."

"If you say so."

Ian glanced at her. "You don't like them any better than I do, so why do you care?"

"Lord Bateman was kind to me, until his sister ruined it," Sophia defended.

Ian let a few minutes pass in silence. "You never did tell me what she said to you that day the horse threw you."

"She told me the reason Lord Bateman decided not to marry me was because of the rumor that I had been ruined."

He could hear the hurt in her voice. "Does it matter now?"

"Now that I know the man? Not really, but I don't want anyone thinking less of me."

"Anyone who knows you would not."

"Why would Catherine do that to me? I've never really liked her, but I've never been rude."

"She is jealous. You move through Society with an ease she can only imagine. People want to be around you. Your personality draws them to you like a moth to a flame."

"More like a fly to a spider."

"You are not as bad as that, Sophia."

She glanced up at him. "Thank you."

They spent the rest of the trip back in easy quiet, now that some of the tension between them had been dispersed. Ian guided the cart to the front of the stables and handed Sophia down. "Help me get the horse into the stables and we can go up to the house together."

"Of course." She accepted the reins and watched as he disconnected the cart. It must have been time for the servants' supper because no one was in the stables, which was probably for the best. He took the reins from Sophia. "I'll just put him in his stall."

Sophia nodded, glancing nervously at the stables.

"Stay here if you wish."

He guided the horse to the stall and gave him some oats. He closed the stall and hesitated. It was done and he felt nothing. The land didn't really matter now. Only the woman who waited outside mattered.

"Where is Theo Hamilton, McDonald?"

Ian looked up and found Bateman facing him with a gun. Bateman pulled back the hammer, the sound echoing in the stillness.

"I suppose she's on her way to marry the man she loves," Ian quipped.

Bateman moved closer. "Do you have any idea what you've done?"

Ian kept his eyes on the gun, hoping Sophia would have the sense to stay outside. Bateman must have been waiting for them to return. "I have a fairly good idea."

"Why?"

"Do you really have to ask that?"

"This is about the land? A stupid piece of land I already agreed to sell you?"

"That you'd barter your sister for but not sell outright. That's part of it, yes."

"I didn't take you for someone interested in fairy stories, Mc-Donald."

Ian looked around the stable for something with which to disarm Bateman. "Some people deserve their happily ever after."

"That's romantic nonsense."

"Surely you'd allow Miss Hamilton to marry the man she loves."

Bateman raised the gun with a curse. "You have stolen a fortune from me, McDonald. Now how shall I make you pay?"

Chapter 24

Sophia shivered in the growing darkness. "Ian, hurry up. I'm cold." She paused, listening for his voice. "Ian?" How long should it take to put a horse in a stall? She walked into the stable.

"Sophia, get back, now." Ian's voice was dark, terse.

"No, I think Miss Townsend should join the party, don't you?" Bateman said as he grabbed her arm tightly. "Come, Miss Townsend, celebrate with us."

She twisted her arm, glancing between Bateman and Ian. "Release me!"

"Ever the shrew, I see. How do you tolerate her in bed, McDonald?"

Ian said nothing. Bateman trailed the barrel of the gun down her throat, the metal cold against her skin. Sophia went still and swallowed her panic. Oh dear God, what had they done? She fought the panic and the fear and tried to pull herself together. She needed to think, to come up with something that would allow them to escape.

"She's not part of this, Bateman. Let her go."

"And have her run to the house to alert Matthews? I think not. Where did they go?"

"Of whom are you speaking?" Sophia said as calmly as she could.

"Tell me, bitch!" Bateman screeched in her ear.

"Gretna Green," Sophia muttered. "If you hurry, you can catch them. It's only been an hour."

She closed her eyes, hoping he believed her. Please God, let him believe her.

"I don't think Mr. McDonald would be so careless as to send them the obvious way, Miss Townsend. Try again." Bateman jammed the gun into her bruised side.

Sophia couldn't stop the groan of pain from escaping.

"Bateman, she doesn't know. Let her go." Ian edged closer to them.

"Stop right there or I'll shoot her right in front of you."

Ian stopped. "You don't want to do that, Bateman. Think of your sister. Think of your family."

"Without Miss Hamilton, there is no estate." He tightened his hold on Sophia and she squeaked. "You have no idea what you've done to me, do you, McDonald?"

"I have a good idea, but she is not part of this. Let her go and you and I will deal with it."

Bateman laughed. "Finally, something you care more about than money. How does it feel to see me touch her thus?" He ran the gun over the neckline of Sophia's gown. She shivered as the cold metal touched her skin.

Sophia struggled against him as Bateman hauled her closer to him. He smelled of sweat and panic. She met Ian's blue eyes across the stables as Bateman pulled her back into the shadows.

"I should have a taste of her just to see what I was missing. All of London wondered if the ice princess was as cold as she pretended to be."

His mouth found hers and Sophia almost gagged. She placed her hands on his shoulders and tried to push him away, but his grip was too tight. His tongue ravaged her mouth and she felt nausea rise up. She finally wrenched her mouth away from his and wiped it.

Bateman chuckled darkly at the look of anger on Ian's face. He could do nothing to help her as Bateman dragged her farther into the stable.

"I will kill him unless you cooperate with me, Miss Townsend," Bateman warned, his breath hot on her skin.

Hysteria was crashing into her in waves. She fought her way through it. She had to gather her thoughts. She focused on Ian, trying to read his eyes. He was trying to tell her something, but she couldn't figure out what. He mouthed one word: *faint.*

Faint? She never fainted. Ever. She fought again.

"Stay still or this will hurt more," Bateman said. His arm was around her waist, his hand cupping her breast and squeezing hard.

"I will scream this place down if you touch me like that again."

Bateman laughed. "Go ahead and your precious commoner will be dead before your relatives can reach us. Of course, you and I will be gone."

"You wouldn't!"

"What, use you? Of course I would. Half the men in London will be lining up after me. Though they may not want you when I'm done."

"You disgust me." She spat out the words, not caring if she angered him further. Sophia wasn't sure what he wanted her to do, but she was sick of being touched by this idiot. Fear was quickly being replaced by anger. She wiggled an arm loose and elbowed him hard in his stomach.

Bateman's hold on her loosened and she shoved at him before running to Ian.

Ian caught Sophia as she crashed into him. He tried to push her behind him, but she was having none of it. She was trembling and pale as ivory. "Get behind me. He still has the gun," Ian urged.

"He'll shoot you, Ian."

There was a tone in her voice that caused him to take his eyes off Bateman. "You'd care?"

She nodded.

"Then trust me." He shoved her away from him and went toward Bateman. He kicked at the gun in his hand. Bateman screamed with pain and let the gun drop. It went off as it hit the ground. Sophia screamed.

Bateman took that moment, when Ian was distracted by Sophia, and punched his jaw. Ian's head went back, pain radiating through his face. He cursed.

"My boxing lessons paid off," Bateman sneered.

Ian punched him in the gut, then crashed his fist into his jaw. Bateman went down on his back on the stone floor with a groan.

Ian stood over the man, lying out cold on the floor. It was over. He looked around for rope and quickly tied the man up. The gunshot should have people scrambling around them soon. "Sophia, go fetch Nathaniel. He'll know how to contact the magistrate."

She said nothing.

"Sophia?"

"Ian, it hurts."

Ian rushed over to her, his heart in his throat. The gun. How had he forgotten the gun? She pressed her hand to her side as blood bloomed on her pelisse. "Sit here, sweetheart. Let me see what happened."

"I don't know how I was hit," she whispered. "I feel cold."

"Stay with me, love." Ian picked her up in his arms. "Let's get you to the house."

"Bateman was going to kill you."

"I told you, men do desperate things."

"It's over, then," Sophia said, her voice weak.

"Yes, love, it is over." Ian looked down at the woman in his arms. She'd fainted after all. He hurried to the house, bursting through the front door and shouting loudly for help.

Suddenly, the room was filled with people. Mrs. Matthews took charge, directing him to carry Sophia to her room. He lay her on the bed. He touched her cheek. It was cool under his touch. "Is she going to be all right?"

"Out, Mr. McDonald," Anne said brusquely as the housekeeper came in with a basket of bandages.

Ian found himself standing outside the door as it closed in his face.

"Where is Bateman?" Nathaniel asked beside him.

"In the stables. He had a gun."

"He shot Sophia?"

Ian shook his head. "It's my fault. I kicked the gun from his hand and it went flying. The hammer had been pulled back and it went off. Sophia must have been hit." Ian scrubbed his face with his hands. "It's all my fault."

"Pull yourself together, man. Let's deal with Bateman," Nathaniel said harshly.

Seeing Bateman again was the last thing Ian wanted, but it needed to be done. "Should we call the magistrate?"

"I am the magistrate," Nathaniel muttered. "Damned if I know what I'm supposed to do with him—or you, for that matter."

Ian said nothing as they walked back to the stables. Bateman had come to and was shouting for help.

"Matthews, at last! Untie me at once. I want this man brought up on charges."

"On what charges, Lord Bateman?" Nathaniel's voice was calm. "I didn't think it was against the law to assist in an elopement."

"He took what was rightfully mine."

"Miss Hamilton is a person, not property," Ian said angrily. "He attacked Sophia. He was going to rape her in front of me."

"I did no such thing. She threw herself at me. She's been throwing herself at me ever since we were last in Town."

Ian had had enough. He went for Bateman's throat but was swiftly blocked by Nathaniel.

"Enough!" Nathaniel said. "If word of this is made known it will ruin Sophia."

"He should pay for what he did!"

"Ian, think clearly," Nathaniel said.

"What if she dies?"

"Dies? I did nothing but kiss the girl," Bateman snarled.

"Your gun fired and she was hit," Ian shouted.

"You kicked it from my hand," Bateman shouted back.

"Both of you, stop. Now," Nathaniel snarled.

Ian stepped away from Bateman, afraid that if he got close enough he'd kill him. Fear, anger, and guilt washed over him like a cold rain. He'd really wrecked things now, and it was going to cost him more than he was willing to give. It was going to take Sophia away from him forever.

"If I prosecute him, Sophia's name will be dragged through the muck. I can't do that."

"But he shot her," Ian exclaimed.

"I did not shoot her and the gun wouldn't have gone off if you hadn't kicked it out of my hand," said Bateman.

"What was I supposed to do, allow you to shoot us both?"

Nathaniel held up his hands for silence.

"The last thing any of us wants is a scandal." Nathaniel turned to Bateman. "I want you and your sister packed and gone tonight. Within the hour, if possible. You will not speak of this incident to anyone. If I hear the slightest bit of gossip, I will make your culpability in this mess known. Do not darken my door again. Understood?"

"That's it?" Ian shouted. "That's all you're going to do?"

Nathaniel glared at him. "You are as much to blame as he for Sophia's injury."

Ian backed down as waves of guilt rushed over him. Bateman shoved past him on his way back to the house.

"Come back to the house, Ian." Nathaniel's voice was gentle now. "You need a drink."

Ian felt as if his gut had been torn from the inside out. He followed Nathaniel back to the house. Catherine was waiting in the hallway.

"What has happened? Why is my brother insisting we leave? Where is Theo?"

Ian glared at her. "Where should I begin? Captain Smith-Williams and Miss Hamilton are on their way to be married."

"They are eloping? I knew I should have stopped Sophia Townsend when I saw her in the corridor."

"As opposed to sabotaging her saddle so that she'd be thrown from her horse?"

Catherine went pale. "I told you, I had nothing to do with that."

"Pardon me if I don't believe you, Lady Catherine," Ian said snidely. "I suggest you pack your things. You and your brother are leaving. Now."

"I will ruin you both in Town. You won't find anyone who will do business with you."

Ian curled his fists. Never had he wanted to hit a woman as much as he did now. "Do so and you'll regret it. I have enough evidence to ruin both you and your brother. You won't be able to show your faces in Town ever again. I suggest you gather your things and go."

Ian was done with Catherine Greyson. He stalked past her and went into the library.

Nathaniel followed, after giving the servants instructions to ready their coach and escort Bateman and his sister off the property. "The doctor should be here shortly," he said as he entered the library.

Ian stared out of the window into the night. How much time had passed? He had no idea. "I can't lose her, Nathaniel. Especially not by my own hand."

Nathaniel pushed a glass of brandy at him. "She's not going anywhere."

Ian sipped the brandy; it burned his throat and settled in his stomach like fire. He deserved this pain. "I have to see her."

"Let her sister see to her first. Wait until Lord Bateman and his sister leave. I don't want any further confrontations."

Ian turned back to the window, feeling lost. How arrogant and stupid he had been to risk Sophia's life. He knew Bateman would be angry at losing Miss Hamilton and her money, but he was sure he could handle it. Now Sophia was hurt yet again because of his thoughtlessness. He had no chance of winning her now. "Perhaps I should go too."

"Where?"

"I don't know. Home. Horneswood." Somewhere far away from Sophia.

The door of the library opened. Ian whirled around, sloshing the brandy he'd forgotten was in his hand.

Mrs. Matthews moved into the room and looked at her husband. "I take it you've ordered our guests to leave?"

"They have an hour."

"Nathaniel, it's night. Where do you think they will go?"

"I do not care. They will not remain under this roof."

She nodded.

Ian stepped forward. "How is Sophia?"

"I think it was a ricochet. There was no bullet, but the doctor will have to verify. She's resting."

"Then she will be all right?"

"She will recover, yes." Her voice was cool. "How dare you involve her in this nonsense, Mr. McDonald?"

Ian stepped back from her anger. "It was wrong of me, I know."

"First she is thrown from her horse and now this." Anne had her hands on her hips. "What's next?"

"Easy, love. I think McDonald has already beaten himself up pretty well over this," Nathaniel said, taking his wife into his arms.

"She could have been killed."

Ian set down the glass. He knew what needed to be done now. "If you'll excuse me, I'll go."

Nathaniel looked at him. "Where?"

"I'll stay at Horneswood tonight." Ian looked at Anne. "I did not mean for this to happen. I'd rather die than see Sophia hurt in any way."

"What will you do?" she asked.

"It's time for me to go home. Thank you for your hospitality."

Anne pulled out of her husband's arms. "What am I supposed to say to Sophia when she asks for you?"

"The truth. That she finally got what she wanted: me out of her life."

Ian left the library and the house. He walked across the pasture to the small bridge over the creek that separated Horneswood from the Lodge. The pasture was empty but full of memories. That was all he had left.

Sophia glanced up as the door opened, hopeful that Ian would step through. She was disappointed as Anne entered. Would he not come to her?

"I just saw the doctor out. He says you will be fine."

"Such a fuss over a scratch."

Anne sat down on the bed beside her. "The bullet grazed a fairly large scratch into your side. The doctor wants you to stay in bed and rest for a few days. We are to watch for fever, but he thinks you will be fine."

"Can you send Ian up?" Sophia finally asked.

Anne took her hand and squeezed it. "He's gone."

Tears filled her eyes. "What? Why?"

"He thought it best after all that had happened. He's the cause of this, Sophia. If he had not meddled in Bateman's affairs none of this would have happened."

Sophia yanked her hand away. "You told him to leave? How could you?"

"I did not tell him to leave. He went on his own. He feels responsible."

"He is not responsible. It was an accident."

"Ian McDonald had no business involving you in this mess."

"*This mess* would not have happened had I not invited Bateman and his sister to stay," Sophia said. "It's my fault, not Ian's." She struggled to sit up but collapsed back from the pain. "He cannot leave yet."

"Lie still before you rip out the stitches the doctor put in you," Anne said sharply.

Sophia closed her eyes as she realized Ian didn't have any reason to stay. She'd never told him how she felt. She'd never tried to convince him that she'd been horribly wrong about everything. "I want him to stay."

"Why?" Anne's voice was soft, gentle.

Sophia opened her eyes and blinked away some tears. "I love

him, Anne. I love him and it's too late. I have said some terrible things to him. You cannot imagine how bad."

"Why would you do that?"

"I have been so foolish. I thought I wanted a title. Lord Bateman was going to be the perfect husband."

"Yes, and look how that turned out."

"He was not the man I thought he was." Sophia wiped her face.

"What about Ian?"

"Somewhere in all the teasing and arguing, I fell in love with him."

"Did you tell him?"

Sophia shook her head. "I was afraid. I've wanted a certain kind of life for so long, I couldn't let it go."

"And now?"

"Now I don't care where we live as long as we're together, but it's too late." Sophia turned her head into the pillow and sobbed. It was too late.

Chapter 25

The flowers arrived the next day; not just one bouquet but dozens. They filled every corner of Sophia's room as she recovered. They overflowed into the rest of the house. There was no note, but she knew they were from Ian. The following day gifts arrived: chocolates, books, and trinkets. Where he'd found them all, Sophia could only imagine. She hoped he would come the next day, but that day dawned and no more gifts arrived. Sophia was finally able to get out of bed and dress. She'd never gotten the fever everyone feared.

Now the skin around her wound was itching and she was sick to death of being in bed and her room. She wanted to go to Ian. She missed him. She needed to touch him, assure him that none of this was his fault.

The flowers and gifts were painful reminders of the fact that he'd left without saying good-bye. At first she'd hoped he'd arrive and ask her to marry him again. But as the day wore on, Sophia's hope wilted like the flowers in the vases around her. He would not come.

Juliet peeked into the bedroom and smiled. "Are you supposed to be out of bed?"

Sophia tucked her feet beneath her, wincing from the twinge of pain the movement caused. "I will go mad if I have to stay in that bed for a second longer."

Juliet closed the door behind her and looked around. "Goodness, where did all the flowers come from?"

"There was no note."

Juliet took the seat across from Sophia. "They are from Ian, aren't they?"

"He's never sent me anything before." Sophia narrowed her eyes at Juliet. "You've been meddling. I can tell. You cannot hide that look from me. What have you done?"

"I might have mentioned that he should spend more time courting you as you should expect to be courted if he wished to win you." Juliet glanced around. "I think he outdid himself."

"Is he at Horneswood?" She tried to keep her voice casual, but the break in it gave her away.

"You love him, don't you, Sophia?"

Sophia nodded and looked around her. "I was in despair until the flowers started to arrive. A Scotsman would not spend this much money to assuage his guilt."

"Indeed." Juliet gave her a pointed look. "He's leaving tomorrow for his home."

Sophia's heart sank. "Without seeing me?"

"I'm afraid the next move must be yours."

"What do you mean?"

"Ian blames himself for your injuries. He blames himself for everything and doesn't think he deserves you."

"It was an accident— if anything, he saved me." She shivered at the thought of Bateman's hands on her. "How do I convince him?"

"Anne is going to kill me for this, but we have to get you out of this house and to Horneswood before Ian leaves. Are you able?"

Sophia clasped her sister's hands. "Tell me what to do."

Juliet pulled a book out of her pocket and set it on the table. Sophia frowned. It looked familiar, but Juliet was always carrying books.

"What is your plan?"

Juliet smiled a secret smile. "You are going to seduce him, of course."

Sophia sat back. "What? I can't do that!"

Juliet glared at her. "Are you going to tell me that you've not already lain with Ian? Because if you do, I will call you a liar."

Sophia felt her face flush. "Fine, but how are we going to get him back to the Lodge?"

"We aren't. You are going to seduce him at Horneswood."

"I cannot call on a man."

"You're calling on your sister, not Ian," Juliet grumbled. "The only thing I'm worried about is whether you will be up to it due to your injury. Can you walk all the way to Horneswood?"

"I'll be fine," Sophia said. She wasn't sure she would, but she would have to be.

"We are much less formal than Anne; we keep to country hours. You'll need to be in Ian's room by eight o'clock. I'll leave a nightgown for you to wear."

"You want me to be waiting in bed for him? Are you mad?"

"Do you want Ian or not, Sophia? This is going to take courage and audacity to accomplish. You will be so thoroughly ruined when it's over that he'll have to marry you."

"I don't want him to *have* to marry me. I want him to ask."

Juliet sighed. "He thinks you don't love him, Sophia. No man would ask again under these circumstances. They have their pride. Way too much of it, if you ask me."

"Fine. I'll be waiting in his room, but then what? I have no clue where to start."

Juliet grinned. "That's why I brought this book." She opened the book to a specific page. "I suggest this maneuver. Men really love it."

Sophia took the book and looked at the picture. "Dear God, her mouth is on his—"

"Yes, it is. Notice his smile? Trust me, this will work."

Sophia looked at her sister with a whole new respect. "May I keep this?"

Juliet shrugged. "Just don't let Anne see it."

Sophia laughed. "Do you really think she cares at this point? You're both married."

"But you aren't. Yet." Juliet stood and looked around at the flowers. "I think I'll take some of these home with me. We can have the maids put them in Ian's room while we dine."

"How am I supposed to sneak out of the house?"

Juliet looked at her. "Don't be dim, Sophia."

"Fine. I'll take a tray in my room and retire early. I'll sneak across the back pasture."

"Come in through the kitchens and up the back stairs. I'll have my maid waiting there for you to show you to Ian's room."

"I hope he won't be up too very late."

Juliet smiled. "He won't have a reason to. I'll have Tony completely occupied."

"Juliet!"

"One of the grand benefits of marriage, my dear." Juliet waggled her eyebrows. "Now, if he puts up a fight, drop the nightgown."

"Stand there completely nude?"

Juliet rolled her eyes. "Really, Sophia, you act as if you've never done this before."

"It was only once before, and it was dark. Besides, if I drop the nightgown he's bound to see the bruises and my wound and that won't be good either."

Juliet tapped her chin with her finger. "Good point. Leave the nightgown on. There won't be much to it anyway."

Sophia looked at her sister in a combination of awe and horror. How did she know about these things? Did marriage teach you this much?

Juliet came and took her shoulders. "Above all, Sophia, be honest with Ian. Tell him you love him and that he's the only man for you."

"What if he leaves the room?"

Juliet smiled. "Don't let him. Use any means necessary to keep him there. He wants you badly, so it won't be too hard."

"And you're sure this will work?"

"Positive," Juliet said. She took Sophia's hands. "He aches for you. Tony tells me he is miserable without you. Trust me. He loves you."

Sophia nodded, feeling tears prick behind her eyes. Lord, she was sick of crying over this man.

"Which flowers do you want in his room?" Juliet asked.

Sophia stood slowly and pointed to the bouquets she wanted. Juliet went for a maid to help her with them.

Anne stepped into the room when Juliet had returned and was directing the maid to remove the flowers. "What are you doing?" she asked her sister.

Juliet glanced at Sophia. "Taking some of these flowers home. It seems a shame to waste them."

"Waste them? How?"

"Anne, it hurts to look at them. I thought Juliet could take some and enjoy them before they wilted completely," Sophia said.

Anne rushed to her side. "I'm so sorry. You should have said something to me."

"I didn't want to trouble you."

Anne smiled sadly. "Well, now that you are up and around in your room, you can take dinner with us downstairs tonight."

Sophia heart beat frantically in panic. "I don't think so, Anne. I'll have a tray."

"But you need to rejoin the family at some point."

"Just one more day and I will. Please."

Anne gave in and kissed her forehead. "Get some rest after Juliet leaves."

Juliet looked at Sophia as Anne left. "That was a close call."

"Yes, it was. Are you sure I can do this, Juliet? I have no clue what I'm doing."

Juliet hugged her sister. "You won't have to do much. Just stand there looking beautiful and tell him you love him. Ian will do the rest."

Ian sat in the parlor, trying to avoid the way Juliet and Tony were looking at each other. "Could you two please go upstairs?"

"Ian McDonald, I have no idea what you're referring to," Juliet said as Tony nuzzled her neck.

Ian glared at her, then looked down at his book. He'd been reading the same damn page for two hours, but he couldn't go to bed. Sleep had evaded him for days now. Every time he closed his eyes he saw Sophia with blood on her hands. He dreamed of blood on his own hands. The sooner he returned home and got away from everything that reminded him of her the better he'd be.

"Perhaps he's right, dear. You look very tired," Tony said.

"I shall go up, then." Juliet kissed Tony before she said, "Good night, Ian. Sleep well."

Ian frowned at her as she left. "She is up to something."

Tony laughed. "I hope so, for my sake."

"You two make me ill. Can't you save that stuff for the bedroom?" Ian grumbled. In truth, he was envious of their relationship. He knew it hadn't always been that way. He was glad Tony had found his Juliet, but honestly, how much more of this was he supposed to have to take?

Tony grew serious. "What time do you leave in the morning?"

"I thought I'd go after breakfast. It will take a day and a half to get there from here."

"Where will you spend the night?"

"Somewhere around Clifton, probably. Shouldn't you be going up to your wife?"

"So you can drink yourself into oblivion? Why don't you stay longer? Go talk with Sophia."

"She doesn't want to see me or she'd have sent for me."

"Why would she do that? You know as well as I that a lady cannot be seen pursuing a gentleman."

"I hate all that nonsense."

"Then you should not have picked Sophia to fall in love with. She is extremely attentive to all things proper. You will have to make the first move."

"Did Juliet say how Sophia was?"

"She is up and about. Her wound is healing nicely and she didn't take a fever, so we have that to be thankful for."

Ian toyed with his book. "I'm glad. I hope she finds every happiness."

"She will if you stay and call on her."

Ian shook his head. "She deserves better. She said so herself."

"I don't believe Sophia thinks that and neither do you. Give her a chance, Ian. Don't throw away your own happiness without even trying."

"I have tried." He stood, taking the book with him. "I'm just not sure I could do it again and lose."

Tony nodded in resignation. "Good night, Ian. Rest well."

Ian trudged up the steps, wishing he'd grabbed the brandy while he was still downstairs. There was no way he was going to be able to sleep tonight. The idea of spending the next day and a half in the carriage alone with his thoughts didn't thrill him either. But he had no choice. It was time to go home and get on with life, get on with the business of putting this behind him.

Every other time he'd dealt with disappointment, he'd had his work to get him through. This time would be no different. He opened the door to his room and glanced at the fireplace. Someone had lit the fire. He tossed his book on a nearby table. He pulled off his jacked and removed his waistcoat. He set them out for the servants to pack in the morning. He pulled lose his cravat and added it to the pile.

He moved to a chair and removed his boots. It was then that he noticed them: flowers. They filled every corner of the room. His heart thudded in his chest. He stood slowly and turned to the bed.

His heart skipped and then beat faster. Sophia was asleep. Her dark hair flowed around her. She was wearing some sort of diaphanous gown that left a good portion of her legs bare and hinted at the rest. He could see the fading bruises from her fall from the horse, another reminder of the consequences of his actions.

Ian moved to the bed and shook her gently. "Sophia. Wake up."

She made a noise and then stretched. Ian had to swallow hard to force himself to look away as she arched her back. "Ian, you're here, finally." Her voice was roughened by sleep. "What took you so long?"

"What are you doing here?"

The harshness of his voice must have gotten through to her for she frowned and sat up with a wince.

"Shouldn't you be in bed?" he asked.

Sophia smiled. "I am in bed."

"Not mine but yours."

"Yours is more comfortable."

Ian could feel his control slipping. He moved to the other side of the room to put some distance between them. "You should be in your own room at the Lodge. Please tell me you didn't walk over here by yourself."

She slipped from the bed. The gown, if one could call it that, dipped low in the front and was so thin he could see her nipples pushing tight against the fabric. It hugged her curves, leaving little to his imagination. One side fell from her shoulder, revealing the upper curve of her breast.

"It wasn't that far."

"Your injury . . ."

"Is fine."

She moved closer to him, so close that her scent engulfed him. His hands itched to touch her.

Sophia ran her finger down the open collar of his shirt before pulling the edge of it from his trousers. "We have unfinished business, Ian."

He swallowed hard as her husky voice wrapped around him. "We do?"

She moved slowly around him, her hand lightly touching his body. "You sent all those lovely presents, but you didn't come calling so I could say thank you." Her breath touched his neck as she spoke.

Ian could feel himself harden. "I didn't think you'd wish to see me."

She laughed as she moved to stand in front of him. "Foolish man. I adore you. Why wouldn't I wish to see you?" Her hand found him through his trousers and squeezed.

Ian grabbed her waist, careful of her injury. "You had better mean this."

"Why?"

"Because if I take you now, I won't be able to let you go again."

Sophia smiled. "Good. I don't want you to let go ever again."

He froze as he looked down at her. In the dim light of the fire, her eyes were filled with an emotion he'd never thought he'd see directed toward him by her.

"I love you, Ian, and I'm so very sorry I hurt you."

He blinked away the moisture in his eyes as he looked down at her beautiful face. "I love you too, so much."

Her hand touched his cheek and he pressed his mouth to it.

"Will you marry me, Ian? Be my husband?" Sophia asked.

Ian couldn't stand it any longer. He crushed her against him and buried his face in her hair. "I thought that was supposed to come from me."

"I didn't want there to be any doubt about where this will end after I have my wicked way with you."

He laughed as he kissed her.

Sophia opened to him like one of the flowers around the room. Her fingers tangled in his hair, her mouth opened for his, and she gave herself to him as she'd never done before. Ian came up for air and lifted her into his arms in order to carry her to his bed.

"One of us is overdressed," she whispered.

Ian pulled off his shirt and shucked his trousers and smalls in record time. "Now I think you are the one who is overdressed."

Sophia hesitated. "I think I should leave it on."

The vulnerability in her voice was his undoing. "They are just bruises, Sophia. They'll fade."

"I didn't want to remind you."

Ian climbed into the bed and stretched out beside her. "We have had a time of it, you and I."

"Mostly me, I'd say. I'm the one covered in yellow and purple splotches."

"Then I'll just have to kiss each and every one to make sure they heal properly." His hand found the edge of the gown and pulled it up and over her head. He tossed it aside and looked down at her. She was beautiful. Her breasts were full, her nipples hard. He moved his hand reverently over her body. "You are so incredibly beautiful, my love."

Her eyes moistened. "Love me, Ian."

"I always have. I always will." His mouth found hers in a soul-seeking kiss as her hands explored his body. His hands were doing their own exploring, cupping her breasts, caressing her soft belly, before reaching the curls at the juncture of her thighs. She was warm and wet for him. "I hate to rush you."

Sophia gasped. "We can do it slower later."

Ian grinned as he moved over her. She tensed. "Easy, love. It won't hurt this time"

"I don't care. I just want you inside me."

Ian sank into her tight body and groaned. "I love you." His mouth found hers as she wrapped her legs around his hips. She moved with him as he thrust into her, relishing the way her body clasped his. "This isn't going to last long."

She pushed up against him. "Ian—"

His hands reached between them to touch her sex and push her toward climax. She gasped as she tightened around him and they both tumbled into paradise.

Ian rolled off her and tugged Sophia into his arms. He kissed her forehead and gently brushed her hair from her face. "I'm going to love having a wife."

"I'm going to love having you for a husband, even if you're a sheep farmer."

"No bad moments?"

She shook her head as she looked up at him. "You?"

Ian looked at her beautiful face in the firelight. "There can be no bad moments when I'm with you, my love."

Chapter 26

They were married one month from the day Sophia proposed to him. Ian stood waiting for his bride to walk down the aisle of St. Michael's on a bright autumn morning. Frost covered everything with a sparkling glaze as he'd taken the carriage with Tony to the church. Finally, Sophia would be his.

She had made him do things the right way, including proposing on bended knee complete with a betrothal ring. She'd made him wait until the banns were read. As she put it, "someone in the Townsend family has to do things correctly." He suffered through it all by visiting nearly every weekend from Dumfries and taking her back with him to see her new home—properly chaperoned, of course.

Things with Sophia had to be just right and proper, and that suited him just fine. She could save her improper behavior for when she was in his bed.

He was worried about how she'd feel about living in Scotland, so far away from London. She never mentioned it, but he knew she'd miss the entertainments. It was why he'd chosen to take her to Edinburgh for their wedding trip. He was looking forward to spoiling her there.

The church was filled with autumn leaves and late blooming flowers. Most of Beetham had gathered to see the proud Sophia marry her sheep farmer. Even Captain and Mrs. Smith-Williams had returned to Beetham for the grand event. Lady Danford and Anne sat in the pews near the front. Juliet would stand with Sophia. Tony stood with him. It didn't matter that he had no family of his own to attend the wedding. The Matthews-Townsend clan had always made him feel like part of their family. He was truly blessed.

Finally, the doors of the church opened and Nathaniel led Sophia down the aisle. She took his breath away. Her gown was ice blue and glowed in the candlelight of the church. Ian had to blink away the tears. This beautiful creature was his to have and to hold, to treasure, to love forever. How in the hell had he gotten so very lucky?

As Nathaniel placed her hand in his, Ian gently kissed it.

"Ian, I forgot about the wish!" Sophia whispered.

"What wish, darling?"

"The one I made at the Fairy Steps. I wished that you'd be stuck with me forever."

Ian laughed, eliciting quizzical stares from everyone in the church and a frown from Vicar Dellwood. "I'd forgotten about that. I guess wishes do come true."

He squeezed her hand as they faced the vicar and the ceremony began. He would remember to tell this story to his children and his grandchildren one day. He would tell them the story of how he didn't think magic existed until he met a stubborn, sharp-tongued lass who had changed his life forever.

Photo by Richard Pfaff

Eileen Richards's stories are filled with what she loves: snarky humor, love, laughter, and lots of village gossip. She lives in North Carolina with her husband, a greyhound named Honey, and a bunch of exotic fish. Eileen has two grown sons, a fabulous daughter-in-law, and the most beautiful granddaughter. Of course, she is a bit biased.

Visit her on the web at eileenrichardsauthor.com.

An Honorable Wish

Wish

A Lady's Wish

EILEEN RICHARDS

LOVE MAY BE THEIR GREATEST GAMBLE...

Tony Matthews spends his time in London's most notorious gambling dens, frittering away his fortune. But when his latest victory leaves a man ruined, Tony knows he's reached his lowest point. Determined to make amends, he returns home to his family's country estate with plans to settle down and marry at last. And he hopes the lovely Juliet Townsend will help him—if only he can keep his disgrace a secret.

Juliet's secret wish has always been for Tony to love her. The only bright spot in her dreadful London Season was dancing with him—before he disappeared to the card rooms. Now, he's returned, but has he truly changed? Or will gambling always be his mistress, even if she becomes his wife? And does Juliet dare risk her heart by finding out?

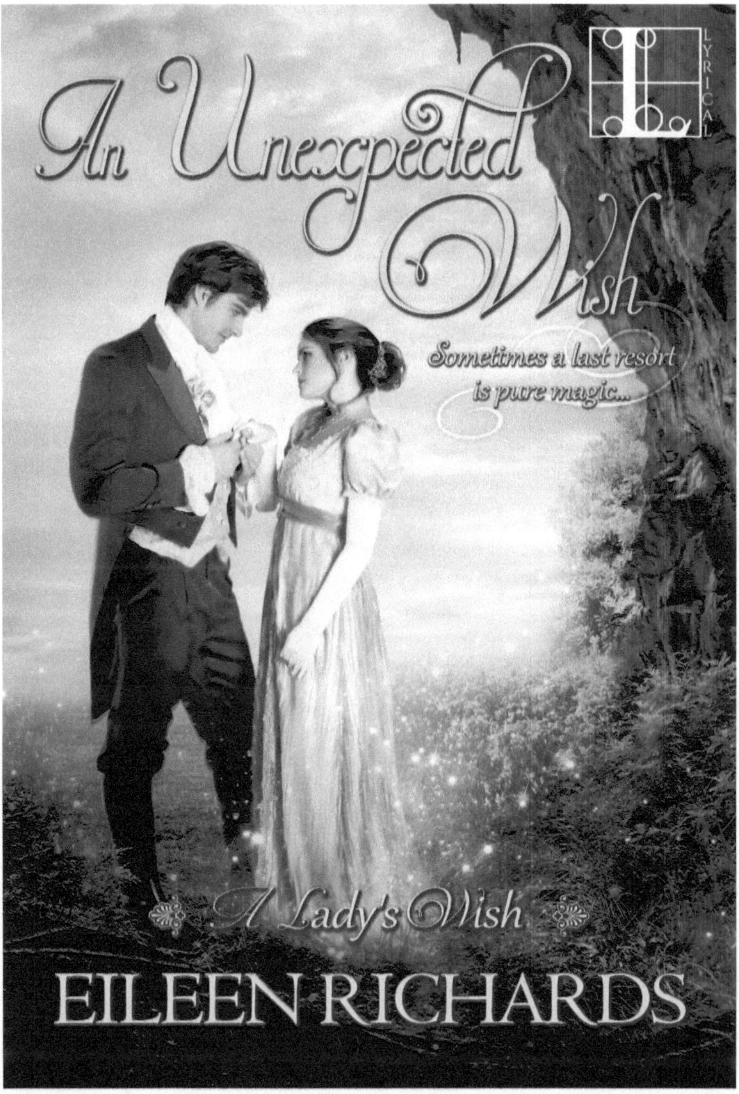
LYRICAL
An Unexpected Wish
Sometimes a last resort
is pure magic...
A Lady's Wish
EILEEN RICHARDS

See how the romantic trials and tribulations of the
Townsend sisters began in Eileen Richards's

AN UNEXPECTED WISH

Keep reading for a special look.

A Lyrical e-book on sale now!

Chapter One

"I hereby decree the word *spinster* be stricken from all manner of speech." Anne Townsend waved her makeshift wand from her perch at the top of the Fairy Steps. She cleared her voice in her most royal manner. "Furthermore, the word shall be stricken from every document in my fair kingdom!" The small village of Beetham shimmered in the gold cast of the late autumn sun, completely unaffected by her pronouncement.

Typical. She threw the stick down the uneven stones she'd just climbed.

Plain, practical, boring Anne
Was too plain to catch a man.
If she caught the eye of one,
To her sister he would run.

The truth of the hurtful childhood taunt stared back at her every blasted day. She was plain. She'd never attracted any man she deemed suitable. It wasn't as if she was being picky. He just had to be reasonably wealthy, reasonably handsome, reasonably witty, and not stupid.

Therein lay the difficulty. No man had met all the requirements. If he was handsome, he was either poor or witless. If he wasn't handsome, he had funds and was as old as the Fairy Steps.

It was of little matter. A modern woman made the best of things. Modern women didn't settle for some old shriveled-up man. And she would be a modern woman if it killed her.

Five years ago, the lure of magic in the Fairy Steps had stirred her romantic heart. A wish could fix anything: poverty, loneliness, and love. God, what a ninny she'd been.

The only thing that fixed poverty and loneliness was money.

Daily her sisters, Sophia and Juliet, whined about their lack of funds. They argued over hair ribbons. They complained about their old, unfashionable dresses. Her sisters had no inkling of the trouble they were in.

They needed fuel for the approaching winter, food for larder, and coins to pay the two servants Anne couldn't do without. It took blunt. Blunt was what she needed more than anything.

If the confounded fairy showed up today, Anne wouldn't hesitate. She'd wish for the ready. Pots of it.

Anne closed her eyes and embraced the rare moment of peace. No arguing, whining, bickering, nagging, tormenting, or complaining. Just beautiful, glorious silence.

A cold gust of wind blew the tendrils of hair from her face and chased a shiver up her spine. Dried leaves rattled behind her as they skated across the rock. A twig snapped behind her.

Her eyes flew open. She wasn't alone.

Anne's heart pounded so hard she could hear it thumping in her ears. Hair lifted on the back of her neck. Anger warred with fear. Anger won.

She picked up a good-sized limb from the ground and gripped it with both hands. "Show yourself, coward."

"Speak your heart's desire, my lady." An odd, otherworldly voice filled the air. The breeze kicked up again.

Anne tightened her grip on the tree limb. She threw her shoulders back and stood taller. She wasn't going down without a fight.

"You climbed the steps properly and earned a wish, you have." The voice cackled.

She lowered her arm. Blast, this was nothing but a prank. Probably some child bribed by Sophia. She'd box the child's ears and send him on his way. She'd deal with her sister when she got home. "The joke is over. Come on out."

"'Tis a magical place you've found, as well you know for the many times you've climbed these steps." The crackling voice sounded old, not childlike.

"Enough!" Anne was sick to death of being the whipping boy.

A wizened, bent old woman with a twisted cane shuffled out of the trees at the foot of the stairs. "Always you must see to believe."

"You must think me dicked in the nob, madam. There are no fairies."

Anne threw the limb into the bushes behind her. "Be gone now, and tell my sister Sophia to try harder next time."

"How hasty and untrusting you young people are. Make your wish, child."

Anne studied the old lady. She looked like one of the Gypsies who came around at harvest time. How much coin had she bilked out of Sophia for this prank? "Fine. I wish you to be gone."

The old woman cackled. "I should take you up on that, but your heart speaks differently. It speaks of struggle and loneliness."

What did this woman know of her life? "I'm sick of this game. Good day, ma'am." Anne turned toward the path.

"Wish for anything, my lady. Wish grandly." A gleeful, wicked light gleamed in the old woman's eyes. She lifted her cane and jabbed it toward Anne. "Little wishes are for little souls. They are not for the likes of you. Now wish. You are wasting my time."

Well, rats, she might as well wish for something. It would shut the woman up, everyone would have their fun, and Anne could go home.

"Perhaps a prince? Grand properties? Great beauty?" the old woman teased.

Anne dropped her hands and glared at the old hag. "You are bamming me."

"Anything is possible, miss." The old lady cackled. "You'll never know, if you don't believe."

Anne had the old woman now. She'd make the wish so impossible, so farfetched, that it couldn't be fulfilled. No fairy magic could conjure love. Everyone knew that. The mad woman would look like a fool. "Very well. I wish for a handsome man so rich that he will be able to provide a Season in Town for my sisters. He must also be passionately in love with me."

"Done!" the old lady crowed.

"You cannot be serious!" Anne turned to glower down at the old lady who had just taken the fun out of the game, but found no one there. "Well, rats, where did she go?"

Dried leaves danced where the old bat had stood. Maniacal laughter echoed in the wind. The old witch probably knew the game was up.

"How foolish do they think I am?" Perfect. Now she was talking to herself. Her sisters were going to drive her crazy. "Wishes, indeed."

"Were you granted a wish? Or are you the fairy?" A deep male voice, filled with laughter, echoed up the stone steps.

So much for peace and tranquility. Suddenly the Fairy Steps were the most popular place in Beetham.

With a huff, Anne leaned over the edge of the steps. Her mouth fell open. At the foot of the steps, seated on a large black horse, was the most handsome man she'd ever seen. Gorgeous, dark wavy hair curled around his high collar. Blue eyes danced with laughter. A navy blue coat had been tailored just right to fit his broad shoulders. Tight-fitting buckskin breeches outlined muscular legs. *Thank you, Providence, for buckskins*, thought Anne.

She swallowed to ease the dryness in her throat. "Excuse me, sir, did you pass an old lady on your way up the path?"

He smiled and those crinkles appeared around his blue-blue eyes. Anne fought the urge to swoon. Seriously? No man made her swoon. She looked down at his face again and fought the urge to gape.

"Depends. Are you the wisher or the fairy?" The elegant tone of his voice echoed a bit against all that stone.

Anne was done with being the ball for the bat. It was outside of enough. She crossed her arms over her chest. "Sir, if you didn't pass her, then just say so."

His smile fell and he shook his head. "An unbeliever."

"There is nothing wrong with being sensible."

"You are right, of course. Perhaps the fairy will grant you a wish for some fun in your life."

Good Lord, Anne hoped the fairy didn't hear that statement. She'd probably take it on as a challenge. Sophia was forever accusing Anne of extracting all the fun out of life. "Who are you?"

She cursed her propensity to speak before thinking. His face grew hard at her rudeness. Anne pulled her shawl tighter around her shoulders. Her embarrassment aside, no one came to Beetham without a reason for being here. It was ten days from London and so far off the main road, it rarely showed up on a map of the area.

"Nathaniel Matthews, at your service, ma'am." He touched his hat.

Oh no, he definitely had a reason. Anne's heart tripped in her chest. Her stomach clenched. He wasn't here for pleasure. He was here to stop the engagement.

"You're Lady Danford's grandson."

"Yes, ma'am. She is my maternal grandmother."

His tone hit her like the cold November wind blowing off the steps. She shivered and wrapped her shawl a bit tighter around her.

"Why are you at the Fairy Steps?" She narrowed her eyes at him. "You're lost."

He had the grace to blush. "It's been a while since I've been here."

What man couldn't find his way home? Men were supposed to be good at directions. It was probably more likely he was too busy to call on his grandmother. Did he not know how lucky he was to have her? "Take the path back to the lane. The Lodge is down farther, to the right."

His dark eyes flashed. "Thank you, Miss—You didn't tell me your name." His tone, saber sharp, cut through her skin to the fear she buried deep. This was not a man to cross.

"Anne Townsend." She dipped a curtsy.

"Thank you, Miss Townsend." He tipped his hat again. "Perhaps we shall see each other again?"

"I'm sure we will, sir." He reined in his horse and turned toward the lane. Anne watched him disappear into the woods. *Blast.* As if things couldn't get any worse, she'd just angered the one man who could make or break the match that would save her family. She just couldn't keep her mouth shut.

Nathaniel followed Miss Townsend's directions and arrived at the Lodge in short order. His brain had a natural aversion to coming here. Too many bad memories.

The dark gray stone house looked like the set of a bad play filled with ghosts and tragedy. He could vouch for the tragedy. It was tragedy that brought him here the first time.

Too many images filled his head. The sound of a gun being fired. Pity on the face of the man who'd ruined his father so completely that a gunshot wound to the head was the only answer. The fear and uncertainty of what would happen to him and his brother. There was nothing he could have done to stop those events. He hated that he couldn't avoid the memories, couldn't move past them.

Lady Danford, his grandmother on his mother's side, had brought Nathaniel and Tony to the Lodge. Yet even her kindness couldn't remove the pain of those awful years. Her husband had been knighted and had left her a comfortable sum when he passed. With no other heir, the house would one day be Nathaniel's.

As much as he loved his grandmother, he hated what the house represented: his father's weak mind and foolish decisions. Decisions that would have left Nathaniel and his brother to fend for themselves if not for their grandmother. Decisions made trying to keep up with the Ton. Decisions that left Nathaniel no choice but to sell the house in Sussex to pay his father's debts.

Nathaniel wouldn't be staying long.

"Sir, we were about to send a search party for you!" the footman said as he approached.

"Has the carriage arrived with my trunks?" Nathaniel dismounted and handed over the reins to the worried footman.

"Yes, sir," the footman said as he led the horse away.

Damn, his ability to get lost was well known and once again affirmed by the servants. Nathaniel pulled down on his jacket and girded himself to enter the house. Though much of it had been completely redone, it hadn't wiped away the images in his head. Like a hammer to his skull, they hit him hard as he entered.

He shoved the bad memories deep as he found his grandmother in her overdone, floral drawing room. Dust motes danced in the late afternoon sunlight that was streaming into the room. "I see you are holding court as usual, Grandmother."

"There you are. I thought I was going to have to send someone after you." Lady Danford's tone was sharp, but her smile was warm. She reached out a hand to him.

Nathaniel clasped it and raised it to his lips. Her skin was cool and papery. "I thought you at death's door from the sound of your letter."

"You're gone for nearly a year and treat me to impudence." She sat back in her chair and pulled her coverlet about her legs. "Come kiss me and tell me why you have stayed away so long."

He pressed a kiss to her papery cheek. "Beetham doesn't have a port."

Lady Danford laughed. "I've missed you, Son."

He studied her for a long moment. The years had taken their toll. He'd lost his parents, but she'd gained two grandsons to care for. He took a seat near her and crossed his legs. It was time to get to the point of his visit; the only reason he'd come back to Beetham.

"I take it I was summoned because my brother, Tony, is in some sort of trouble." Nathaniel leaned back in his chair, his hands folding and unfolding. "I've paid his gambling debts from Cambridge."

"He's a young man. You remember what that's like, don't you?" She smoothed the coverlet over her legs.

Nathaniel winced. "I'm not that old."

"Good heavens, your own father had more of a life than you do." Her voice was sharp.

"Don't compare me to him," Nathaniel said rather sharply. *Damn.* Lady Danford watched him closely. "Forgive me, ma'am," he muttered.

"Still haven't let that go?" She shook her head. "Nathaniel, Son—"

He stood and paced to the window, staring out. "We aren't discussing this." The last thing he wanted was a discussion of his cowardly father.

"Our past always comes back to haunt us in one way or another." Lady Danford's voice was soft but firm. "At least until we deal with it and move on."

Nathaniel let the comment pass. It was a reoccurring argument. "Has Tony been giving you any trouble during his visit?"

"No more than usual." Lady Danford picked up her embroidery. "He's infatuated with one of the local young ladies."

"Next week it will be some other girl." Tony changed women like most changed stockings. Nathaniel could hardly keep up. "You brought me this far from London because he's involved with a local girl?"

"He's driving me to distraction," Lady Danford huffed. "He's spouting that god-awful poetry he writes. All that education to write bad poetry."

"A quality education," Nathaniel quipped.

"You had the same, and you didn't turn out that way," she grumbled.

Thanks to his father's propensity for gambling away every shilling they possessed, Nathaniel had been head of the family at sixteen. He had been forced to grow up fast and figure out how to rebuild the family fortunes. It left little time for poetry. "Who is the young lady?"

"Sophia Townsend. She is the prettiest girl in the county, until she opens her mouth."

Nathaniel's bark of laughter filled the room. "So I take it you don't approve."

"The girl is a twit."

He fought the urge to chuckle further. "Townsend? Would she be related to Miss Anne Townsend?"

"Anne is her older sister." Lady Danford eyed him speculatively. "How do you know Anne?"

"I happened upon her on my way here," he said casually. He didn't need another person making note of his inability to get from one place to another without getting lost.

"She gave you directions to get home, didn't she?" Lady Danford cackled.

Nathaniel felt the heat rise in his face again. Hell, this was worse than when he was a child. "I did *not* get lost."

His grandmother rolled her eyes. "Where did you find her, then?"

"At the Fairy Steps." He flicked a string off his sleeve. Truth be told, he'd wanted to find the steps first, hoping for a moment of peace before going to the Lodge and facing his demons.

"She must be hiding from her sisters again."

Good to know he wasn't the only one who hid from his family. "What's wrong with this chit that Tony is interested in, if her own sister hides from her?"

"I'll let you decide when you meet her." Lady Danford motioned for a footman. "Bring tea and wake Tony. A good dousing of cold water should do the trick."

"He's still abed?" Tony had obviously been spending too much time with gentlemen. "Things will be different when I get him to Town."

"And you call Tony a dreamer." Lady Danford's tone was acerbic. "He'll be out every night with the rest of the young bucks."

Nathaniel sighed heavily. Tony's spending habits were eating into the cushion Nathaniel had worked hard to build with his investments in the textile business. If Tony wasn't going to contribute, he'd have to marry well. "What are this girl's connections?"

"Her half brother inherited the title, but doesn't support his sisters." Lady Danford had a white-knuckled grip on her cane. "I have no patience for such a lack of responsibility."

Nathaniel had no doubt she would use her cane on this missing brother if she could. "Who is he?" He'd been so distracted by his meeting with Miss Townsend that he hadn't connected her to *that* Townsend family. Surely she wasn't related to—

"He's a baronet. Sir John Townsend. The family is very old."

Nathaniel set down his teacup with a rattle. Hell, it couldn't be. All the way up here?

"Mind the china, Son. I have no desire to replace it."

What did he do to deserve the continuing irritation that was Sir John Townsend? Or his relations? Sir Walter, the elder Townsend, might as well have put the gun in his father's hand after winning everything Nathaniel's family had. Sir Walter had died before Nathaniel could confront him with what he'd done. Now Sir John was bent on continuing down the same path as his father. Nathaniel couldn't allow that to happen. He couldn't let another man suffer what he'd seen his father suffer at the hands of Sir Walter, not that Sir John seemed to be experiencing the same success his father had.

And Tony's marriage would join the Townsend family to their own. Over his dead body.

"Are you sure he's not providing for his sisters?" Nathaniel didn't know why he felt the need to try to salvage something of Townsend's reputation. The man couldn't be so bad as to not take care of his own family. But perhaps Townsend was following in his father's ruthless footsteps.

"I'm unsure of the particulars, but Anne brought her sisters to Beetham five years ago with nothing but the clothes on their backs," Lady Danford said. "God knows what would have happened if I'd turned them away. They lease the old gamekeeper's cottage on the estate."

His jaw tightened and hatred chewed at his stomach. "I only hope that it's not too late to stop the engagement."

"Had she a dowry, it would be a good match." Lady Danford sipped her tea thoughtfully.

"Not to that family." Nathaniel stood and paced the room. He flexed his hands, itching to punch something.

Lady Danford carefully set her teacup down. "I thought you let that go, Son." She watched him closely, her face soft with understanding.

"Justice must be served." His voice was hard.

"What justice? Your father took the cowardly way out. He killed himself." Lady Danford's tone was cold, emotionless.

"Townsend forced him to when he lost everything. For that there must be justice."

"Oh, Nathaniel, what have you done?"

Nathaniel winced at the disappointment in her tone. The past ate at him like acid on skin. "I've given Sir John a taste of his own medicine. He is determined to repeat his father's mistakes" He stared out through the window at the garden. Devoid of leaves, it was as desolate as he.

A wrinkled hand tugged at his arm. "This is beneath you, Son."

"I had to stop Sir John before he ruined another man." Before he caused a good friend to shoot himself to escape his problems and left his family destitute. Nathaniel's hands tightened into fists. "I'll take Tony back to Town with me. Distance will cure any emotion he feels for this young lady."

Lady Danford sighed. "You can't stay longer?"

He winced. "I only came because you implied an emergency. Besides, you'll be in Town in a few months for the Season."

"I've not decided yet." Lady Danford shot him a meaningful look.

He looked back at her, startled by this sudden revelation. The London Season was Lady Danford's favorite time. He always looked forward to having his grandmother at the town house in London. "You won't miss a Season in London. You thrive on the gossip."

"I'm getting too old and stiff for the long carriage ride, dear."

Nathaniel watched his grandmother. She moved slowly. Her face was etched with deepening lines. Her shoulders had a slight stoop. He'd never thought of his grandmother as old until today. Panic clogged his throat and he had to clear it before he could speak. "Are you sick?"

Lady Danford laughed. "I'm just old, not sick."

At that moment, Tony burst into the room. "Nathaniel! You're here? Why?"

"Good to see you, as well. I'd say you look a bit worse for wear." Nathaniel took in his brother's wrinkled linen and lack of a coat. His hair was a mop of uncombed curls. At least he had shaved. "Didn't bring your valet?"

"Still the stick, I see. I'm sorry I'm not up to your usual standards." Tony slumped into a nearby chair and grinned. "Still, I make this look good."

"I was hoping university was going to make you realize your place in the world," he said dryly. "What have you been doing here at Beetham?"

"He didn't get in until almost dawn," Lady Danford grumbled. "Woke the staff trying to get into the house."

"What is there to do at that hour in Beetham?" Nathaniel said.

"Shared a pint with the locals." Tony ran his fingers through the tangle of his hair. "I repeat, what brings you here, dear brother? I know you didn't come all this way just to see me."

There was a bitterness in his tone that Nathaniel didn't understand. "I'm not allowed to visit our grandmother?" Nathaniel raised an eyebrow.

"You never leave London." Tony glared at his grandmother. "I suspect you told him about Sophia."

"Yes, she did."

Tony slouched lower in the chair. "I think I may have found my future wife. I've a mind to paint a picture of her."

"Paint? You?"

"It has to be better than the poetry," said Lady Danford.

Tony frowned. "It's not that bad."

Nathaniel laughed. "Why did you stop writing?" Tony had a tendency to flit from interest to interest, never staying too long. Currently he was supposed to be studying law.

"I couldn't get anyone to publish it. But Sophia inspires me. Such a beauty."

"Let's be honest here. Tony, your poetry is awful." Lady Danford waved the maid over with the tea tray. "You need a focus for your life."

Tony raised his chin defiantly. "I have a focus. Sophia and my art."

Nathaniel sighed. Once again it was up to him to be the responsible one, the voice of reason. "And do you propose to support this woman with your art? Have you given any thought to her connections or fortune?"

"I don't care what her connections are, nor that she lacks a fortune," Tony said. "It's not as if we need the money."

"The lack of fortune is a material issue," Nathaniel pointed out. "With your spending habits, we'll be in the workhouse in no time."

"I take it back. You're a bigger snob than you are a stick," Tony said. "You'll have to increase my allowance after we marry. And provide the younger sister with a Season. I suppose the eldest is firmly on the shelf. You'll probably have to provide for her as well."

Nathaniel cocked an eyebrow at his brother. The man had it all planned. Except it was the vision of a boy, not a man. "Why would I do that?"

Tony looked puzzled that he should ask. "It would only be right given they have no other protection."

"While it's honorable that you wish to take care of these young women, do you think it wise to marry someone of such reduced circumstances?" Nathaniel fought to keep the edge of impatience out of his voice. His brother was acting like a child. "We were left nothing by our father. He had no entailed property. You must consider what income a bride will bring to the marriage."

"You speak of dynastic marriage," Tony said. "I would rather marry for love than live such a cold existence."

"Poverty is a cold existence. Your young lady may not be suited for it. Unless you marry a fortune, there are few choices."

"We aren't poor."

"Nor are we wealthy, though your brother's investments and careful management have improved our circumstances," Lady Danford said. "It's time you did your part as well."

"And doing my part is marrying someone for her fortune? Someone I don't love?" Tony slammed his fist into the side of his chair. "That never made anyone in this family very happy."

"Enough!" Lady Danford pulled herself up slowly from her chair with the aid of her cane. "Don't assume that my marriage or that of your parents was less than it was. I loved my husband."

Nathaniel studied the stubborn look on his brother's face. "Tony, if you are serious about marrying this girl, then you have some decisions of your own to make. As of your birthday, your allowance will cease. Find a way to support your new family. Take your place with me in London. Practice law as you were trained to do."

"Gentlemen do not work." Tony jumped to his feet. "Nathaniel, be reasonable. Four months' notice is not enough time."

"All of us must attain adulthood at some point, Brother. Even you." Nathaniel sipped his tea, ignoring the growing color in his brother's face. "I suggest you think long and hard as to whether you can afford this young woman."

"Grandmother—" Tony whined.

Lady Danford paused at the door. "Tony, I must agree with Nathaniel on this. The next move is yours." The door closed behind her with a sharp bang.

Tony stared at the closed door. "She's in a fine temper."

Nathaniel shrugged. "With good reason, I think." He had to know where they stood. "Have you proposed to Miss Sophia?"

"Not yet," Tony mumbled.

Good. It would be a bit easier to extricate Tony if he hadn't proposed. "But her family is expecting you to?"

"Of course." Tony looked up. "This is madness. Why can't I marry for love?"

"You can—just make sure she brings money to the marriage."

Tony groaned and collapsed back in his chair. "I hate this."

Anger bloomed as Nathaniel witnessed his brother's petulant behavior. "You do realize who her father was, don't you?"

Tony raised his head, his eyes cold. "I'm not an idiot. I don't hold the children accountable for their parents' mistakes."

"Unlike me?" Nathaniel held his brother's gaze for a long time, waiting for confirmation. While Nathaniel had borne the brunt of the stigma and cleanup after his father's suicide, Tony had been protected from it all. He'd only been nine at the time, too young to remember the worst of it.

"I didn't mean that." Tony stood and started pacing in front of the fireplace. "I thought you'd be more supportive, especially given the nightmare that was our parents' marriage."

Nathaniel sighed. "If her relations were anyone else, I might consider, but not this family."

"It was a long time ago, Nathaniel." Tony sat across from him. "Do you really blame Sophia and her sisters for their father's sins?"

Nathaniel studied his brother for a moment. How much should he tell him? He fought the urge to protect him, but decided against it. It was time for Tony to deal with the consequences of his choices. "Have you met Sir John, the brother?"

Tony shook his head.

At least he wasn't moving in those circles—yet. "I caught him cheating at cards at White's."

"Does Grandmother know?"

"No one does." Nor would they, if he had anything to do with it. "You certainly can pick them, Tony."

"I had no idea!" Tony plopped back into his chair and draped one leg over the arm. "I still think you should meet the family. It will at least prove that the sins of the father have nothing to do with the children."

Nathaniel sighed. "If you insist." He had no doubt that the girls would be charming. He already liked Anne Townsend. Hell, even Sir John was charming when he wanted to be, but good manners did not imply scrupulous behavior. In his experience, good manners served more as a veneer for the unscrupulous to hide behind.

Anne walked briskly toward home as the wind picked up. She pulled her shawl around her and quickened her pace. The old lady she'd spotted at the steps must be from Beetham. Or perhaps the Gypsies were back in the village, though they usually went south before now. It'd be easy enough to find out. Beetham was a thriving community of gossips. Someone would know who the old lady was.

She should be focusing on Nathaniel Matthews. Not because he was handsome as sin, but because of why he was here.

To keep his brother from marrying Sophia.

Instead, she was worrying about some old lady and fairies. But there were no fairies.

The air came alive with sound, causing Anne to jump. She looked around her to see Cecil Worth, the vicar, leaning against a tree, watching the path back to the cottage. She quickly stepped back out of his line of sight. Maybe he wouldn't see her. Please God, don't let him see her.

"Miss Townsend!"

Lovely. Could this day get any worse? "Mr. Worth." She dipped a curtsy. "What brings you out this far?"

"I was hoping to find you, Miss Townsend. Miss Sophia said you walk this way most days." He doffed his hat and bowed prettily. He was dressed in a blue coat that stretched across his girth.

"You came to see me? For what reason?" In the three years he had been the vicar of St. Michael's, he'd never even noticed her before.

"Do I need a reason to visit a young lady?" He chuckled as he replaced his hat with a flourish. "My dear Miss Townsend, I have shocked you."

"Sir, I—uh." Shock was an understatement. While the man never missed a chance to speak with the lovely Sophia, he wasted no time on plain Anne Townsend. Being plain and poor had a dampening effect on most men's ardor.

He moved closer to her and smiled. "I imagine you have come to expect only sermons from me."

She took a step back, not liking the strange heat in his pale gray eyes or his scent. The man had apparently bathed in perfume. "You are the vicar, sir. Why would I expect anything else?"

He clutched dramatically at his chest. "Ah, you wound me, Miss Townsend."

Anne forced a laugh at his comical expression. "Then I offer my apologies."

"Apology accepted." He offered her his arm.

Anne took it and fell into step beside him. "How is your mother, Mr. Worth?"

"She is quite well. I will tell her you asked after her."

Mrs. Worth would probably give him a severe tongue-lashing for walking with Anne. Anne and her sisters were not rich enough for her precious son, despite having a baronet as a father.

"I wanted to speak with you privately before I spoke to my mother." He paused, looking down at her hand on his arm. "Such a small hand for the burdens you carry."

"Burdens?" Anne desperately needed him to get to the point. She had the beginning of a headache brought on by his cologne.

"You've taken care of your sisters for years, all on your own. Such a strength of character." He stroked his hand over hers, caressing her skin.

Anne snatched her hand away and put some distance between them. She suddenly didn't like that she was in these woods alone with Cecil Worth. She glanced around, hoping that perhaps someone else would also be walking in the woods this afternoon. But they were quite alone. Too alone. A frisson of fear coursed down her spine.

A twitter sounded in the trees around her. Was it the old lady? Please let it be the old lady. Anyone to keep her from being alone with the creepy vicar.

Mr. Worth shot her a pitying look that caused her temper to heat. "Have you heard from your brother?"

"My brother? No. I suppose he is still in London."

"Being so connected to a baronet, I can't imagine why you would abandon the position it offers you and your sisters. I imagine he worries about you all. Three young women quite unprotected."

John, worry about them? As if that would happen. Anger bubbled up and out of Anne's mouth before she could stop it. "Thank you for your concern, but this is none of your business."

"I only meant that it would be better for you if you had stayed with your brother."

"You've no idea what you're talking about." Anne started down the path toward the cottage.

"And to settle for being the companion of an elderly lady." Cecil Worth's voice echoed through the empty woods.

Anne turned and glared at him. "Lady Danford has been very generous. I feel privileged to be of assistance to her."

"Still, your brother . . ." He let the thought trail off.

Enough was enough. "Mr. Worth, my half brother's title doesn't put food on the table or provide heat for winter, and, for that matter, neither does he."

"I can see you still harbor anger toward him. As the vicar, I must urge you to forgive. He is your brother. Perhaps you may yet reconcile."

"I harbor no hope of our brother seeking reconciliation." It would be a cold day before she let John enter their lives again. She glared at Mr. Worth and noted the odd expression on his face. He looked like a fish. She stepped farther away from him as he beamed at her, his gray eyes half-lidded and a crooked smile on his over-full lips.

She fought the urge to grimace. "I beg you to not discuss the matter further. Thank you for accompanying me. It looks to rain soon. I'd best hurry home. Good day, sir."

"But Miss Townsend—"

She ignored his cry and kept moving. Presumptuous man. How dare he cast judgment upon her and her sisters? They had no say in the decision. Leaning against a tree, she closed her eyes and still she could see his cloying, besotted face. "Fairy wishes indeed. Absurd."

Anne entered the cottage from the back. She hung up her pelisse and removed her bonnet. If, by some bizarre chance, she had been granted the wish she hadn't spoken, she needed to find a way to undo it before something even more horrid and humiliating happened. Lady Danford's grandson and Mr. Worth were quite enough.

"Anne, you will never guess!" Sophia rushed into the kitchen, but stopped short at the sight of her sister. "What's wrong with you? You're as pale as a corpse! An unkempt corpse."

"You've never seen a corpse, Sophia, unkempt or otherwise. Why do you ask?" She closed her eyes and tried to relax the scowl from her face.

"Your hair is tumbled, you are out of breath, and your expression is twisted more than usual." Sophia glided farther into the room, looking perfect, as usual.

"Thank you, Sophia, for reminding me." The comment flew out of her mouth before she could stop it. "If you have something to tell me, please do so."

"We are invited to Lady Danford's for supper and cards. But that isn't the best news. The best news is that Tony's brother is here!"

Anne bustled to the cabinet and placed cups out for tea. Just what she needed—another evening of men fawning over her sister. "Must we go?" She scooped tea into the pot.

"Of course we must go." Sophia plopped down into one of the kitchen chairs. "I will need a new gown."

Juliet huffed as she walked into the kitchen. "You had the last two new gowns, Sophia. I think it's Anne's turn." Seeing Anne laboring alone to set the table for tea, while Sophia sat like a princess, Juliet tsked and plated the cake.

"Anne doesn't need anything new. It's not like she'll attract notice." Sophia toyed with one of her dark, glossy curls.

Anne paused, the lid of the teapot suspended in her hand, and tossed aloft a prayer for patience. On the best days, Sophia was trying. Having Mr. Matthews in the village would only make her even more intolerable.

"Really, Sophia. You don't need to be cruel." Juliet plunked the cake on the table and glared at her sister.

"Thank you, Juliet." Anne poured hot water over the tea leaves and then returned the kettle to the stove. Sophia was working herself up into a fine temper.

"Well, I hope there will be some new people at the party." Sophia waved her hand dismissively. "I want to consider my options before accepting Tony. Did you see the invitations, Anne?"

"I thought you already had an understanding with Mr. Matthews," Anne said carefully. Her plans depended on Mr. Matthews coming up to scratch. If he didn't, she was going to have to come up with another way to buy the fuel they needed for winter. That meant borrowing money from Lady Danford. There was no other way.

"Not yet," Sophia said. "I do wish we could go to London for a Season. Then I could have the chance to marry a titled gentleman."

"Don't reach beyond your grasp. We have little to offer such a man," Anne said sharply.

"We? You do not, but I have had no end of offers, even without a fortune. Why wouldn't a titled gentleman want a pure, beautiful bride? Besides, the further I reach, the better I shall be able to take care of my sisters," Sophia said confidently.

Too confidently, in Anne's opinion. She rolled her eyes. This plan to marry off Sophia was getting more complex as the day went on.

"You have had no end of offers from the local gentry, Sophia," Juliet snapped. "I thought you liked Tony."

"I *do* like Tony," Sophia said. "I just want to make sure he's the right one. Anne, if you would only contact our brother, I'm sure he would invite us to London. I don't know why you hate him so. What has he ever done to you?"

Anne clenched her teeth to keep the bitter truth behind them. Her sisters would never know the extent of their half brother's perfidy, if she had anything to do with it. "We've not heard from him in five years," she reminded them. She took a seat at the table across from Juliet and poured the tea. "We must go on without him."

"But we can't be seen by Lady Danford's guests in these old rags," Sophia whined.

"Since we will be meeting some of them for the first time, they won't know these are our old dresses." Anne passed a cup of tea to Juliet.

Sophia huffed. "Why must we be so poor? Our father was a baronet!"

"Be thankful that our mother left us a little to live on," said Anne. That was something John couldn't take from them no matter how he tried.

"Sophia, some things we must accept," Juliet said, and pushed her old spectacles back on her face. "Besides, no one notices your dress."

"Well, it isn't fair." Sophia pushed away her cup. "I think I'll go see if I can make over a dress. I'll take the lace off of your dress, Anne. And the flounce."

"As you wish." Anne waited until she heard Sophia's steps on the wooden stairs. "You don't have to defend me, Juliet."

"She can be so hateful," Juliet said. "As if her beauty entitles her to act like that."

"Sophia will save this family if she marries well. She can be a bit overbearing, but she knows her duty."

Juliet crossed her arms. "I don't have to like it."

Anne laughed. "Perhaps marriage will soften her up a bit."

"That's doubtful, isn't it? I don't want her to marry Tony. She's not good enough for him."

"I see." Anne laughed at the blush that rose on her sister's cheeks. "I'd wondered if you admired him."

"Don't be ridiculous."

So that was how it was. Juliet was suffering through her first infatuation. Better that she learn now that Sophia would capture everyone's attention. No matter what.

"Take care, Juliet. He has eyes for Sophia." Anne patted Juliet's hand.

"It doesn't matter. He sees me as a child, not a grown woman of eighteen," Juliet complained as she stood to clear the dishes.

"There will be other men like Mr. Matthews. I'm sure you'll have your pick of gentlemen in the coming years. You're every bit as pretty as Sophia, though I doubt she agrees."

www.ingramcontent.com/pod-product-compliance
Lightning Source LLC
Chambersburg PA
CBHW020741250626
47155CB00003B/859